From Across the Sea

Annie Seaton

Daughters of The Darling:1

This is a work of fiction. Characters, institutions and organisations mentioned in this novel are either the product of the author's imagination or, if real, used fictitiously without any intent to describe actual conduct.

Annie Seaton lives near the beach on the mid-north coast of New South Wales. Her career and studies spanned the education sector including working as an academic research librarian, a high-school principal and a university tutor until she took early retirement and fulfilled her lifelong dream of a full-time writing career.

Larapinta, the fifth book in the Porter Sisters series, won the Romance Writers' Association of Australia Ruby Award for long contemporary novel in 2023.

Kakadu Dawn, the sixth and final book in the Porter Sisters series, was a finalist in the Australian Romance Readers Awards for 2023.

Whitsunday Dawn, her first book with Harper Collins Australia, was a finalist in the 2018 ARRA Awards and was voted Book of the Year in the AUSROM Readers' Choice awards.

Kakadu Sunset, Annie's first traditionally published book with Pan Macmillan Australia was shortlisted by the Romance Writers' Association of Australia Ruby Award, in the long book category in 2015.

Each winter, Annie and her husband leave the beach to roam the remote areas of Australia for story ideas and research. She is passionate about preserving the beauty of the Australian landscape and respecting the traditional ownership of the land. For those readers who cannot experience this journey personally, Annie seeks to portray the natural beauty of the Australian environment—its spiritual locations, stunning landscapes and unique wildlife.

Readers can contact Annie through her website, annieseaton.net, or find her on Facebook and Instagram.

Also by Annie Seaton

Standalone Books
Whitsunday Dawn
Undara
Osprey Reef
East of Alice
Bowen River

Daughters of the Darling
From Across the Sea
Over the River
By the Billabong
Books 4-5 to follow

Pentecost Island Series
Pippa
Eliza
Nell
Tamsin
Evie
Cherry
Odessa
Sienna
Tess
Isla

Others
Four Seasons Short and Sweet
Deadly Secrets
Adventures in Time
Silver Valley Witch
The Emerald Necklace
An Aussie Christmas Duo

Richards Brothers Series
The Trouble with Paradise
Marry in Haste
Outback Sunrise

Bindarra Creek
Worth the Wait
Full Circle
Secrets of River Cottage
Bindarra Creek Duo
A Place to Belong

The House on the Hill series
Beach House
Beach Music
Beach Walk
Beach Dreams

Sunshine Coast Series
Waiting for Ana
The Trouble with Jack
Healing His Heart

Second Chance Bay Series
Her Outback Playboy
Her Outback Protector
Her Outback Haven
Her Outback Paradise
The McDougalls of Second Chance Bay

Love Across Time Series
Come Back to Me
Follow Me
Finding Home
The Threads that Bind
Love Across Time 1-4 Boxed Set

The Augathella Books
Outback Roads
Outback Sky
Outback Escape
Outback Wind
Outback Dawn
Outback Moonlight
Outback Dust
Outback Hope
An Augathella Surprise
An Augathella Baby
An Augathella Spring
An Augathella Christmas
An Augathella Wedding
An Augathella Easter
An Augathella Masquerade Ball

As always, to Ian, my ever-patient and loving husband.
You are always there for me.

'The green pastoral plains, the fruitful valleys, as well as the wild hillsides and the dreary bogs, has equally ceased to be animate with human life. The "land of song" was no longer tuneful; or if a human sound met the traveller's ear, it was only that of the feeble and despairing wail for the dead.'
George Petrie (1855)

Chapter 1

***Ceann Mara Station - Darling River - Tuesday, late
September.***

Caitríona O'Byrne woke suddenly.

Her eyes flew open, her heart pounding as she stared at the
high ceiling above. It was still early; the soft, pink light of dawn
stole into the darkness through a narrow sliver between the
curtains. She lay rigid, wondering what had disturbed her sleep.
If indeed, it could be called sleep—those restless hours where
dark dreams tormented her each night. The nightmare had been
different last night; it had woken her just after midnight. She
could hear a voice this time and waited for him to stop talking as
her bedroom door opened and closed. That was a first. She'd
turned the light on to check that no one was there and then went
to the bathroom to refill her water bottle.

Now, as she tried to straighten her legs, her eyes moved
swiftly from left to right as she checked she was alone in the
room. The first-floor window was locked shut, and she had key-
locked the bedroom door before she went to bed last night. The

top sheet was wrapped around her ankles, and she pushed it away with her toes.

No. Not again, please God, not again. Her breath caught, and her mouth dried as the door handle turned with a soft clicking sound.

'Cat,' a soft voice whispered. 'Are you awake, sweetie?'

The doorknob clicked again. Cat closed her eyes, and her body loosened with relief.

'Yes, Mum, I'm awake. What's wrong?' She forced saliva into her mouth, swallowed, and ran her tongue around dry lips.

'I think your door's locked.'

'Just give me a moment.' She sat up, untangled the sheet from around her foot and then slid both legs over the side of the bed. Her heartbeat was gradually returning to a normal pace, but her mouth was still dry, and her head ached. Pulling her long-sleeved robe over her cotton pyjamas, Cat turned the bedside lamp on and waited for her eyes to adjust to the light before she walked over and unlocked the door. She fluffed her hair and pulled her curls around the front of her neck.

When she opened the door slowly, Mum was standing in the hall, her brow creased by the worry that had been there for the last three weeks since Cat had arrived home unexpectedly at the family cattle station.

'I really wish you wouldn't lock the door, sweetie. What if there was a fire?'

'I guess if there was a fire, my smoke alarm would go off,' Cat replied, her voice husky.

'There's no need to lock your bedroom door, Cat. Dad locks the front and back doors last thing every night.'

'I know. I remember.' Cat forced a smile.

Her mother reached out to touch her shoulder, and she took

a quick step back.

'I've only got a minute.' Mum folded her arms, but Cat saw the fleeting hurt on her face. 'Dad's gone to the shed already. I just wanted to let you know that we're leaving for Broken Hill earlier than Dad said we would last night. Will you be all right by yourself?'

Cat tensed. 'You're leaving now?'

'Yes, there's a strong westerly forecast to hit mid-morning, and Dad wants to be on the ground in Broken Hill before it arrives. It'll be too early for the appointment with Craig, but we can have breakfast when we get to town.'

'Who's Craig?' Cat asked.

'The new accountant. Reg Green retired last year. Craig's his nephew and Dad's happy with him. Anyway, knowing your father, he'll have booked the local history room at the library for after the appointment, so he can change that around, and hopefully, we'll get home earlier.' She shook her head and sighed. 'That family history. He's getting more obsessed with it every year.'

'He loves it. And it's good for him to have something apart from the station.'

'At least I can do some shopping while he's at the library. Is there anything you need?'

Maybe some courage.

Cat shook her head. 'No, thank you.'

'Okay, we should be back mid-afternoon if we get everything done before lunch. Or at least I hope we will; it depends on the wind. Are you sure you'll be all right if we have to stay overnight?'

No, being alone at night might just about do my head in.

'Yes, I'll survive.' Cat's response was clipped. She pulled

her robe sleeves down over her hands, looking away as her mother stared at her intently. It was good being home safe, but it was hard dealing with her parents' constant surveillance and concern.

'Why don't you come with us? You and I could have coffee while Dad sees the accountant. And we could shop together. We've got time to wait for you to have a shower.'

Cat bit her lip and shook her head. Her fingers gripped the sleeves of her robe as a tremor ran through her limbs. 'I'll be fine here.'

'Are you sure?' Mum's face crumpled, and tears shone in her eyes. 'I wish you'd tell us what's wrong, sweetheart. Dad's awfully worried about you, but he said you'll talk to us when you're ready.'

She stepped back as her mother reached out to touch her.

'For God's sake, Mum. Leave me alone.'

Her mother pulled her hand back, her eyes widening in shock.

'How many times have I stayed at the station by myself? I think the first time you and Dad went away for a couple of days I was only fourteen. We were home from boarding school for the holidays and you had to go and see Grandma Daph.'

'I don't remember that.'

'She was in hospital in Dubbo. You took Shea and Bridget with you and left Roisin in charge. She would have been sixteen, and Erin was fifteen.'

'Well, there were three of you, and Elise and Gary were still across the river then. Cat, I don't like the idea of you being home alone considering…'

Cat pulled herself up to her full height, her hands still clutching the silk, making sure it covered her forearms.

'Considering what, Mum? Considering I'm a mental wreck? Considering I've got no confidence? Considering you don't think it's safe to leave me here by myself?' She couldn't hold back the raw anger lacing her words. 'Don't worry, I'm not that inconsiderate. I'm not going to overdose or anything.'

Her mother lifted her hands, palms facing forward, and took a step back. 'No, Caitríona, that's not what I meant. I just want to make sure that you're okay to stay by yourself because there is a chance that we may not get back tonight.'

Cat tried to move forward, but her feet wouldn't budge. She would have loved to hug her mother and reassure her, but since Sydney, she couldn't bear to touch anyone. 'I'm sorry for snapping, Mum.' She was angry at herself for not being able to get herself out of the state she was in. An emotional state that spiralled down more every day. She'd come home to heal, but it wasn't working.

Maybe I need help.

As they stood there staring at each other, the sound of the shed door rolling open drifted through the open window at the end of the hall.

'Did you open that window, Mum?'

Her mother frowned and nodded. 'Yes, I did on my way past. It's very stuffy up here. I usually leave it open, seeing this floor is rarely used now that you're all away.'

'Do you mind if I keep it shut?'

Another frown, but her mother nodded. 'Yes, probably a good idea today. I think we're in for a dust storm.'

The sound of an engine starting drifted in as Mum went over to shut the window. It puttered to a stop after a few seconds.

'Go, Mum. You know what Dad's like—if he wants to go, he wants to go *now*. I'll be fine. Honestly.' She forced herself to take a step forward, reach out her hand and briefly touch her mother's arm before she retreated into her room. 'I'll be fine. I've got a lot to do today.' The lie came easily to her lips.

'Okay, I'll call you this afternoon and let you know what time we're flying home, okay?'

'Maybe give me a call when you get there safely?' Cat said softly.

Her mother's eyes glinted with moisture. Guilt trickled through Cat; it was the first kindness she'd shown to Mum since she'd arrived home. She'd spent most of that time in her room, occasionally surfacing for dinner, but making civil conversation had been too hard. She'd eaten, taken her plate to the dishwasher, and returned to the sanctuary of her childhood bedroom.

'Thank you. I will. What—'

'Is anyone coming here today?' she interrupted her mother. Even though she'd opened the emotional door a crack, she wasn't ready for any in-depth conversation.

'No, the water truck came yesterday, and the wool buyer from Brewarrina is coming later in the week. I don't think Dad's expecting anyone else today. He would have said.'

'What about the tourist thing?'

'The volunteers left last week now that the season's over; bookings closed at the end of August. There's no one around. Why don't you go outside and get some fresh air before the change comes through? It's mail day; the mail truck only comes once a week now. So, if you feel like riding out to the front gate later, grab one of the ag bikes and take the dogs for a run.' Her mother's eyes met hers. 'But watch the weather. If the wind gets up too much, stay in. Dad thinks it will hit hard and then blow itself out pretty fast.'

'Okay, I'll check the mail for you. Don't want it blowing

away, do we?' Cat forced lightness into her voice even as fear crawled through her at the thought of going outside.

'Thanks, love. I'll call you when we land at Broken Hill. If you're not in, I'll leave a message.'

'Okay.'

'Do you want to come down and lock the back door behind me, or are you okay with me locking it from outside with the key?'

'I'll do it. That way, I know it's locked.'

'Okay.'

Cat turned away, unable to cope with the concern that had been in her mother's eyes ever since she'd arrived home. She'd given them no notice she was coming and barely remembered the sixteen-hour drive; she'd driven it in one leg, from Sydney to *Ceann Mara*, stopping only three times for fuel and water.

Mum and Dad's surprise when she had driven in at dawn three Sundays ago had quickly turned to shock.

Dad held his arms open for a hug when she got out of her car in the shed, but Cat ignored him. She lifted out the small bag she'd thrown some clothes and toiletries in and left her laptop on the back seat.

Dad followed her to the house, and Mum came to the door with a wide smile. She took one look at Cat's face and held her arms open.

'Are you sick, sweetheart?'

'No.'

'What's happened, Cat?' Dad said. 'On Friday night, you said you had to work and wouldn't be home for a few more weeks. But I'm not complaining at all; this is a great surprise.'

Cat had shaken her head and refused to tell them why she was home. 'I just need to go to bed. And please don't tell anyone

I'm here. Okay?'

'Why not?' Dad asked, his bushy brows lowered in a frown. 'What's wrong?'

'Not even the girls,' she'd replied, her voice cold. 'If you tell anyone, I'll leave and go somewhere else. I don't want to see or talk to anyone.'

Despite her parents' worried expressions, they reluctantly agreed, and she went upstairs to her room. She knew she'd break if she had to face any questions. She needed time to process—and try to remember—what had happened.

Cat locked herself in her bedroom upstairs and slept for two days straight. She'd heard Mum outside and had answered her a couple of times when she'd tapped on the door before she eventually came out on the third day. She'd eaten no food, filling herself with water from the bathroom tap. Her eyes filled with tears when she noticed the tray of food Mum had left on the floor outside her door. She'd had to grip the banister on the way down to the kitchen; she was as weak as a kitten.

'Thank goodness.' Mum put a hand on her chest. 'Your father was going to break the door down if you didn't surface today. I'll put the jug on. How are you, sweetheart?'

'Hungry.'

'There's some leftover spaghetti here. Would you like that?'

'Just toast. Vegemite.' It was hard to form words after barely speaking for almost three days.

Now, almost three weeks had passed, and Caitríona had no intention of returning to Sydney.

Or telling her parents why she was home.

Mum's soft voice drew her back to the present. 'I just have to get my handbag from the kitchen and grab a cardigan. Dad threw some things in an overnight bag in case we do have to stay, and he's taken it to the plane.'

'Go, Mum.'

With one final glance, her mother hurried down the hall to the staircase that led downstairs to the back of the house. A couple of minutes later, the back door closed.

The homestead, built in the 1850s, had undergone several refurbishments, as well as extensions over various generations. Dad was proud that his family still owned the station purchased by his great-great-great grandfather and his wife, the original Caitríona, when they had emigrated from Ireland during the Great Famine. Dad's love of history had passed onto Cat, and he was always nagging her to help him with his research.

'One day, Dad. After I finish my degree,' she'd often said when he'd phone to tell her about the latest information he'd unearthed.

Well, now she'd left university and moved home. Maybe once she got her head together, she could help him.

Maybe. *If* she got her head together.

Cat walked slowly along the hall to the staircase, the polished timber cool beneath her bare feet. She stopped at the small window at the head of the staircase and flipped the lock over.

She gripped the polished banister as she made her way downstairs. Out of habit, she avoided the step third from the top, which always creaked no matter how many times Dad had replaced it. Roisin had always called it the haunted step, and she, Erin and Caitríona had terrified their younger sisters, Shea and Bridget, with ghost stories until Mum had intervened.

The main downstairs hall ran down the centre of the house joining another hall that turned right at the kitchen end and ran along the back of the building to the west wing.

Cat checked the back door opposite the kitchen; Mum *had* locked it; the key was hanging on the hook beside the door.

The shorter hall ran to the western side of the house, where it met the staircase leading up to the five bedrooms on the first floor where Cat and her sisters shared the two bathrooms when they were growing up.

Roisin always said that Mum and Dad had been trying for a son, but they'd given up after five daughters. It had always been the triumvirate of the three big sisters who had led the two younger girls as they'd grown up. Taught them how to ride, how to swing from the rope into the river, and showed them all the hiding places when they were in trouble.

And there had been a lot of that as the five girls ran wild.

According to Dad's research on the homestead and the family, the first floor that now held the sisters' bedrooms had originally been the nursery, schoolroom and guest accommodation in the late 1800s. There had been fireplaces in each room, and despite the fireplaces being sealed up long ago, the chimneys still graced the roof of that wing.

From the sweeping circular drive at the front, the house looked like a single-storey dwelling, but when approached from the western side, the two-storey wing on that side of the house came into view. Behind that was a small stone building that had once been a chapel and a small graveyard; its proximity to the homestead had provided content for Roisin's ghost stories. Even though Caitríona knew they were fiction, she was still hesitant to go into the graveyard after dark. Even in the daytime, it made her sad to see the grave of her namesake, the first Cat who passed away in 1900. According to Dad, she had outlived her husband by twenty-five years and continued running the station with her son, James' help. Their three daughters had married and left the station, and Dad was still waiting for the records that would tell him where they had moved to. There were no graves for them.

As Cat walked along the downstairs hall, her thoughts flitted around; maybe she would work with Dad now that she was home. They had such a wonderful heritage; it would be good to have the family history researched and documented.

Mum and Dad's bedroom on the eastern side of the ground floor had been the drawing room in the original homestead, but a couple of generations back, it had been turned into the master bedroom. She walked past the dining room, Dad's study, the master bedroom, the guest bedrooms, and the bathroom. After sharing the small unit with Scarlet for three years at Newtown, the homestead seemed bigger than she remembered.

A light puff of wind met Cat as she reached the front door, and she pulled a face. Mum might have locked the back door, but the front door was wide open—and possibly had been all night, knowing Dad. Stepping out onto the screened veranda, she bit her lip and sat on the top step.

Wrapping her bathrobe around her, Cat sat down and lifted her head to the sky. Above the eastern horizon in the direction of the river, the sky held a soft, pinkish hue, heralding the imminent rising of the sun. Delicate filaments of cirrus clouds shot with gold sat high in the pink expanse, foreshadowing the arrival of the wind forecast to arrive later in the morning. Dad wouldn't have gone to the weather channels for the forecast; he would've simply looked at the sky and known what was coming. Her father was a true bushie; he understood the landscape; it was as much a part of him as he was a part of the bush. He knew more about the seasons and the weather from observing the sky, the birds, and the behaviour of the sheep and cattle than any forecast of *El*

Niño or *La Niña* on the excitable weather stations.

Cat held the same love and interest in the elements; she could read the clouds as well as Dad. This morning, the air held an expectant quality, and she took a deep breath. The smell of red dirt was already puffing in on the slight breeze from the west, and by the look of the sky and the electric feel of the air, a westerly wind was on the way. A loose feeling of reconnecting with herself touched Cat briefly, and she fought to keep it, but it fled when the side gate creaked open.

Chapter 2

Ceann Mara Station - Tuesday, late September.

Cat calmed as she looked across the yard and let out the breath she held. It was only Mum shutting the gate on her way to the big shed.

She didn't notice Cat sitting on the step as she came around from the back of the house and then disappeared behind the conservatory. A few moments later, she appeared on the other side of the building and headed across the dirt road towards the modern shed that housed various vehicles. As she passed the dog pens between the house yard and the big shed, the working dogs set up a ruckus.

A lifetime of habit had Cat standing to go over to the dog pen, and then she stopped herself and sat down again. She was in her robe, and the dogs would settle without her going over. It had been so long since she'd last been home, she wasn't even sure which dogs were still there; she hadn't had a conversation with Dad about the station for ages. During the last two uni breaks, she'd waitressed full-time to get some money behind her to do her next and final year of study.

What a waste of time that had been. The familiar tightness gripped her chest, and she closed her eyes, willing it to go away.

I will never go back.

The erratic gurgle of the Cessna's engine and the metallic clattering of the propellor broke the silence as her father started the engine again. Cat drew in deep breaths until her heart rate returned to normal, and she waited for the gurgle to develop into a roar. Soon, she caught a glimpse of the red wing as the aircraft moved from the shed to the dirt road leading to the short dirt airstrip adjacent to the river.

Gradually, the whole machine came into view as her father taxied across the road towards the airstrip. Without thinking, Cat pushed herself to her feet, walked down the steps and crossed the lush green lawn that was her mother's pride and joy. The garden and conservatory had always been Mum's main interest as they were growing up, and she wondered if it still was, now that she had moved her focus to tourism, although the garden edging the lawn was colourful with spring annuals.

Moving along to the corner of the fence where she and her four sisters had always lined up to watch Dad's plane take off when they were children, she climbed onto the bottom rail. The familiarity of the action and the feel of the smooth timber beneath her bare feet soothed her. That feeling of reconnection with herself flickered again.

From her vantage point, she would be able to see the Cessna when it reached the end of the airstrip and lifted into the air. Watching Dad take off and then, later in the day, waiting there for him to come home had formed a regular part of their childhood. Cat missed her sisters. Maybe if they were all home, she would be able to cope better and be immersed in chat and arguments.

The motor deepened to the roar she'd waited for, and Cat climbed up to the next rail of the fence. The fresh breeze whipped her red curls into disarray as she rested her arms on the top and watched as the aircraft soared into the air, then banked to the south. She stood there until the Cessna holding her parents became a tiny red speck in the sky as the plane followed the river six hundred kilometres south to Broken Hill.

The high-pitched screech of a galah broke the silence, and her fingers tightened on the rail as she gradually became aware that she was outside.

And alone.

Alone and away from safety.

On half a million acres.

Swiftly turning her head from side to side, she drew in a sharp breath as a loose curl caught on the scab that was coming away on the side of her neck. She reached up and untangled her hair and pushed it back over her shoulders. Holding her breath, she scanned her surroundings, but all was quiet; even the dogs had settled.

Familiar and safe.

She jumped off the fence rail and hurried across to the front of the house before running lightly up the concrete steps to the veranda and into the safety of the homestead.

She secured the front door behind her, both the lock and the deadlock, before systematically going through each of the twenty rooms of the sprawling house. She checked every window and door that led out to the veranda surrounding three sides of the building that had been home to the O'Byrne family for more than one hundred and fifty years.

The five girls had grown up knowing they were seventh-generation inhabitants of a homestead built in the 1850s. As kids, that had meant very little to them, no matter how much Dad tried to get them interested in the family history. They'd been too busy horseriding, fishing in the Darling River, and doing their school-of-the-air lessons before they each left home for boarding school at twelve to be interested in old photos and even older stories.

With a sigh, Cat headed down the hall that ran the length of the house. When she'd checked all the doors and windows and found another window open in her parents' room—she still felt guilty going in there because Mum and Dad's room had always been their private place—she hurried back upstairs. Her robe slipped open as she grabbed the banister and looked down to secure the tie.

Bile rose in her throat, and she averted her eyes from the scabs healing on her thighs as she stood on the bottom step.

Chapter 3

Gutana Station - East side Darling River - Tuesday afternoon, late September.

'Bourke Seed and Feed.'

Logan Wainwright turned away from the window as the rural store he'd been trying to contact for most of the morning finally picked up their phone. Phone service was shit out here, but he'd set up a Star Link connection so he could browse the internet and keep in touch with the world when he wanted to, and he could use his mobile on the Wi-Fi connection.

He held back a curse. By the sound of the voice, it was the old bloke who'd had little idea about the fencing materials he'd wanted when he'd driven to Bourke last week.

'G'day, mate, Logan Wainwright here. I was up there last week, getting some materials for my property. *Gutana* on the east side of the Darling, south of Louth.'

'Yeah, mate, I was the bloke who served you.' Logan rolled his eyes. The old bloke who hadn't had a clue about fencing.

'What can I do for you?'

'I'm having a bit of trouble with the one-way trap gates. I seem to be missing some hinges.'

'Ah, that's not good.' The old fellow cleared his throat. 'Did you get a jump-down gate or a spear gate?'

'No. You told me the swinging one-way gate was the best.'

'Probably did. Did you get the diagram that came with bits and pieces from Blue Gig?'

'What's Blue Gig?'

'The manufacturer.'

'No, mate, there was no paperwork in the stuff I bought. Just the wire, the three posts and one hinge lock.'

'Have you got an um . . . one of them fax machines? I can maybe dig one out and fax you a copy.'

Jesus. Logan wrinkled up his nose and shook his head. 'No, mate, I don't have a fax machine. Could you email it to me?'

He was sure he hadn't been sold the right number of hinges. He'd queried it with the old guy when he was at the store last Saturday morning; the store had been about to close at noon, and he'd been hurried along. The roller door was pulled down, and the guy drove off while Logan was still loading his ute.

'Don't know about that, I don't know how I'd do that. I can't use the computer here.'

'Okay, just take a photo of it with your phone and send me an email.'

'It's a bit in the too-hard basket for me,' the fellow said. 'I haven't got one of them phones.'

'Is there someone else there I can talk to?' Logan tried to stay patient.

'Nup. Just me today. Where did you say you were? *Gutana*?'

'Yes. About sixty ks south of Louth.'

'East or west side of the river?'

'East.'

'You'll be right then.' The old guy sounded satisfied.

'How would that be?'

'You'll be pretty close to Tom O'Byrne. Do ya know him?'

'No, I don't.'

'He's got a big spread around there on the west side of the river. Same setup with the goats. He'll be able to give you what you need. Or give you a hand to put together what you've got. Why don't you go across there and have a yarn with him?'

Because I bought the gear from you and it should be right.

'Okay, I'll give it some thought,' Logan said, trying to calm down. His counsellor had told him not to lose his cool with things he had no control over. That was before he had decided the counsellor was a waste of time and money even if the Queensland Police Service was paying for her. 'Thanks for your time.'

He hung up the phone. What sort of business couldn't send an email with a diagram these days? Or sell him the right bloody hinges and posts in the first place. He was tempted to go to the fridge and grab a beer, but Logan always made himself wait until sundown; he didn't want to end up like his old man.

Logan had grown up on a small farm in the hinterland of the Sunny Coast. When he was fourteen, Mum had pissed off with the guy from the farm next door and his old man had sent him to boarding school in Toowoomba. When he was expelled from boarding school and came back to the farm, he had no interest in the place. He'd been too busy getting himself into trouble with his mates in the small town up the road.

His old man had given him an ultimatum. 'Clean your act

up, son. Show some interest in the place or get a job.'

Logan could still hear the gruff chuckle two and a half years later when he got accepted by the police force on his eighteenth birthday.

'Jaysus,' Dad said, shaking his head. 'Just what the state needs. Another bloody crooked cop.' Dad had spent those years after he moved away drinking and smoking. He'd sold the farm and moved to the coast two years after Logan left for Brisbane. Lung cancer had got him a couple of years after that.

His mother? Well, he didn't know where she was these days. She'd tried to make contact with him over the years, but he'd ignored every email and phone call. She'd eventually given up.

His old man would roll in his grave if he knew Logan was now a landowner on the Darling River. He'd bought the place with his inheritance and taken leave from the force. Now, here he was, with another failure under his belt.

He couldn't even figure out how to build a friggin' fence. The challenge of putting together this bloody fandangled gate for the goats was doing his head in. The last thing he wanted to do was go across the river and make the acquaintance of a neighbour who would probably look at him like his old man used to.

Logan had built a kit home a couple of kilometres back from the riverbank over the past few months, camping in his swag until he got the kit to the lockup stage. According to the stock and station agent from Brewarrina, who'd shown him the place last year, the power had still been connected to the property after the original homestead had burned to the ground about six years ago.

He'd built his house, so why the hell couldn't he put a gate together? After some thought, he decided to visit his neighbour; going across river would be quicker than driving to Bourke and back. He could be civil and sociable if he made the effort. He would have to wait though; he'd heard the plane fly over this morning, so he assumed that Tom, the owner of *Ceann Mara*, wasn't home anyway.

Damn it, he'd wanted to get this gate set up today; seeing the number of goats roaming around his property and hearing how lucrative the market could be had made him determined to make goat mustering his priority before he put any sheep on the place.

What he should have done was get Tom's phone number off the old bloke. He'd watched the small plane come and go often over the past months, but his neighbours had made no effort to meet him, which suited him just fine. According to the agent, the property had been owned by the same family since it was settled back in the nineteenth century.

Probably thought they were landed gentry.

He grabbed his hat from the hook in the laundry, unlocked the gun cupboard, and lifted his rifle out. He'd never seen so many snakes since he took possession of the five hundred acres on the eastern side of the Darling River. He wasn't going to risk having a run-in with one today. He knew he wasn't supposed to shoot them, but if it was a choice between his life and a snake's life, he knew what he'd be doing.

Logan clomped down the back steps and put the bullets into his pocket. He sniffed the air. He might not be a bushie yet, but he could smell the dust in the air, and that wind was picking up a lot.

Chapter 4

Newtown, Sydney - Friday night, August.

'Come on, Scart, please. It's been months since I've been out. I'm hanging for a dance and a drink.' Cat put her hands together and knelt next to the kitchen table where her roommate and best friend, Scarlet Donaldson, was working.

'Cat, I'd love to, but I have to finish this submission tonight. Absolutely must do. I've got an appointment with my potential supervisor first thing in the morning. Seven-thirty, before he starts his first lecture.'

'On a Saturday?'

'Yes, he comes in for an extra class for the honours students.'

'That's great about the interview, who did you get?'

Scarlet's smile was a bit self-conscious as she hesitated. 'Well . . .'

'Who?'

'You know that hunky associate professor I told you about?'

'Not Paul Hepplewhite with the gorgeous blue eyes? The guy you've been lusting over all year?'

Scarlet nodded. 'That's the one.'

'You go, girl!'

'Who did you get?' Scarlet asked.

'Don't ask. Don't deflate my fabulous mood.'

'Not Hairy Harry?'

Cat nodded glumly. 'You got it.'

'He'll be fine. He might look like Hagrid from Harry Potter, but he's got a great academic reputation. Anyway, go celebrate. *You've* got your submission for your thesis in. And we'll hit the dance floor tomorrow night. How does that sound?'

'Sounds good. I need to get out tonight. I've got cabin fever after being at my desk for two weeks. And being finished feels freaking amazing.'

'I can imagine. You'll hear me screech when I finish this tonight. Why don't you give Jilly a call? She's always up for a night out. And . . .' The look Scarlet shot her way spoke volumes.

'And if I sit home, I'll be in your way while you try and focus,' Cat finished for her. 'Good thinking, Jilly will be up for a night out.'

'She's a party animal, that's for sure. She's taken your crown.'

'I did play up a bit our first year, didn't I?' Cat gave a rueful grin.

'You did. Sometimes I think Jilly's got the right idea,' Scarlet said. 'She's got a job she enjoys, no uni, no deadlines and submissions and —'

'No exams and studying. You could be right.'

'Plus, plenty of cash to go out, money for decent clothes, and she doesn't have to frequent the op shops.'

Their friend, Jilly Burton, worked at one of the many coffee shops on King Street, and they'd been friends since Cat and Scarlet had picked up their coffee there the first month they'd been at Sydney Uni. They'd seen Jilly work her way up from waitress to manager in those three years.

Cat pushed herself up from the table and reached for her phone. 'Want me to make you a coffee while I text her?'

'Yes, please. I could do with a caffeine shot. Have we got any biscuits left?'

'Sorry, Mother Hubbard, the cupboard is bare. I haven't been shopping. I promise I'll go tomorrow.'

'If you have a big night, and you have a sore head tomorrow, there'll be nothing for breakfast either. I'll do an online shop in a while.'

'That'd be great. Tell me how much it comes to, and I'll leave you half.' Cat walked across the small kitchenette and opened the fridge, pulling a face at the bunch of celery, two carrots, and the bottle of mayonnaise sitting on the middle shelf. 'Will you get Tim Tams, Scart?'

'Bloody oath I will. And frozen pizza. Hopefully, they can deliver tonight, and I'll have something to eat while I work.'

Cat stopped before she picked up the kettle. 'Instead of texting Jilly, I'll go down to the cafe and pick you up a real coffee. Two birds with the one stone.'

'Would you really? You are a gem; they'll still be open, seeing it's Friday.'

'How about a cappuccino and a Danish?'

'Good thinking.'

Cat grinned as she watched Scarlet pick up her pencil and stare at the paper on the table. 'How about *two* Danish and a skinny cap? The skinny'll make up for the second Danish. You need the energy to get those words down. I know what it's like. I haven't eaten properly for a week or more.'

'Make sure *you* eat something before you drink tonight.'

'Yes, Mum.'

Scarlet pulled a face at her. 'So, do you think your proposal will be accepted by Hairy Harry?'

Cat held up two sets of crossed fingers. 'I'm pretty confident, and if it is accepted, things are probably going to change.'

Scarlet frowned. 'Change? In what way?'

'You might have to find someone else to share with.'

'Oh no. Why, Cat?'

'With my honour's year being thesis-based, I might move home and work from there. I'd come to Sydney when I had to— a few times during the year. I'm only thinking about it at this stage, and I'd have to get approval. So, it's only a possibility now, but I'll give you plenty of notice.'

'I'll miss you, but I get where you're coming from. It's so exxie to live in the city. Your parents would be pleased to have you home.'

Cat nodded. 'Another pair of hands on the station would be appreciated, plus my thesis is very relevant to our station. Dad's on several committees keeping tabs on the management of the Murray Darling. It takes up a lot of his time.'

'As well as writing your family history,' Scarlet said, aware of the number of phone calls where the research had been discussed with Cat.

'That's Dad's hobby. The Murray Darling is his other passion. Roisin and I always argued with him; she's passionate about the river too. He's always looked at it from a regulatory point of view.'

'And your thesis doesn't? Is environment-based different to that?' Scarlet shook her head. 'I don't understand all the government control and the controversy that's always in the news. I mean, how can you sell water? Isn't it simply in the river and it flows down to the Murray? It's water, and it's there. Water in the river that's *always* been there.'

'So speaks the chemist.' Cat chuckled. 'Don't get me started about the Murray-Darling, or you'll get no work done tonight. If I sat down to explain it, you'd be bored shitless within five minutes. Roisin is the one who can make it sound interesting.'

'Is she the one who studied law?' Scarlet said

'Yep, she's working for a well-known firm in Newcastle. She was headhunted at graduation.'

'I'm still going to come out and visit your station one day. I'll see this land and your precious Darling River you're always talking about. And maybe meet your sisters.'

'I do miss *Ceann Mara*. It's part of me. I'm not a city girl.' Cat slipped her phone into her jeans pocket and looked around for her shoes. 'I'm looking forward to getting home for a visit soon. I'd say we won't hear back about our proposals for a month or more. And I can't apply to work from home until I get accepted. I might have to re-jig my proposal if Harry knocks it back.'

'*If* we get accepted,' Scarlet rolled her eyes.

'I'm sure we will. We might just have to tweak our proposals a little. You know the academics; they like to have a say.'

'Makes them feel like they're earning their money,' Scarlet said with a laugh.

'Anyway, whatever happens, I'll be here until the end of

the year, but I'm going to have to find some more part-time work. I'm fast running out of cash since I left that waitressing gig,' Cat said.

'I thought you had millions of hectares. Doesn't your father pay your uni fees?'

'We're certainly not the wealthy gentry that our forebears were. The station was a million acres when the first O'Byrne settled there in the early 1850s. It's half that these days. Dad does help me a bit with the fees and the rent, but he's always had the philosophy that when we move out and make our life choices, we're independent. Roisin and I are the only two to go to uni so far.'

'And the next one close to you is married?' Scarlet had always been fascinated by Caitríona having four sisters.

'Yes, Erin married Joe when she was nineteen, and they're still travelling around Australia, much to Dad's disgust. He said that's what you do when you retire.'

'Generation X. We're changing the rules. Who did she marry?'

'We are.' She nodded. 'Joe's dad owns the pub at Tilpa, and he's got a bit of land but nothing on the scale Dad expects his daughters to marry into.'

'So, he expects you to marry a wealthy landowner?'

'Yes, but what he expects and what he gets will be two very different things,' Cat said with a laugh. 'From me, anyway.'

'And the others?'

'Shea left school last year, and she's working as a vet nurse at Wilcannia, and Bridget's still at boarding school. She's in year ten.'

'You're so lucky to have a big family,' Scarlet said wistfully. 'My brother was in his teens when I was born, and we're not close at all.'

'You wouldn't have thought that growing up out there. We all fought when we were home from school.' Cat laced up her Doc Martins. 'Okay, Scart, put your head down and get that finished, and I'll go and see Jilly. Won't be long.'

The back door of their unit block opened onto a dingy lane in Newtown. She wrinkled her nose, passing overflowing garbage bins and inhaling the smell of stale urine. In the mornings, the laneway was often littered with broken glass—and worse—after a night of underage drinking. The frequency of assaults and robberies had increased since they'd lived there. She and Scart knew not to come home via the laneway after dark.

As always, the city environment brought the call of home tugging at Cat. Home, where the air was fresh, and even the dust-laden air held a purity that was never evident in the city. The odours out on the Darling were natural, even if the smell of sheep and cattle and now goats pervaded the landscape more often than not.

She pinched her nose with two fingers as she walked to the end of the laneway. She could cope with the strong, mucky stink of a virile buck over the smell of the laneway any day.

The sound of traffic on the main road reached her, and she felt like covering her ears too. Horns blared, car motors revved, and tyres squealed as everyone raced home from work and school, ready for the weekend.

She turned right into King Street, forcing her way through the crowd and heading for the coffee shop. Growing up on the station, and attending a regional city boarding school had meant that when she moved to Sydney for university, the city had been a total culture shock for her. It had taken a few months for her to settle in, but after three years of living in Newtown, she'd adjusted. Days like this, when she longed for the open spaces of home, were becoming more frequent.

Maybe doing an honours year was a mistake. When it came down to job opportunities, it probably wouldn't make that much difference anyway.

But Cat loved learning, and the research side of her degree had been fascinating. She'd learned so much, and she wanted to keep learning and make a difference, not only on their station but for the whole Murray-Darling basin.

If she left this year and graduated without doing her honours year, what would have been the point of going to uni in the first place? She might as well have stayed at home.

Cat frowned as she walked through the bustling crowds on King Street. Workers were heading home for the day; drinkers were heading to the bars, and tourists were getting in everyone's way as they meandered along. Was an extra year at uni really going to make a difference? Professor McMinn—known more commonly as Hairy Harry—had even hinted at her continuing to a doctorate and that had really stroked her ego.

Maybe she *should* just go home and work with Dad.

Cat shook her head as she approached the corner.

Stupid idea. She just needed a break. She still had a lot to learn and a lot to give.

The *Crazy Goat Café*—goodness knows why anyone would give a cafe in the bustling heart of Newtown a name like that—was still open, and all the tables out front were full. There was a queue at the counter.

Jilly was working at the coffee machine, and Deb, the part-time barista, was at the counter. It took a couple of minutes before Cat reached the cash register and placed her order.

'Hi, Deb, how are you going? Busy afternoon by the looks

of things.'

'Don't talk about it,' Deb said. 'We're both looking forward to getting out of here. It's been crazy busy all day. How are you, Cat?'

'I'm great. I'm looking for someone to come partying with me tonight.'

Deb grinned. 'We were just talking about going out. We've earned it today.'

'Would you mind if I tagged along too?'

'The more the merrier,' Deb said.

'Where are you planning on going?' Cat grinned at Jilly as she walked across and put two coffees in front of Deb.

'Hi, Cat. Take these out to the two guys sitting just to the left of the door, please, Deb,' she said.

'Will do, boss.' Deb turned to Caitríona. '*The Singapore Sing Song.*'

'That new bar? I've heard of it but haven't been there,' Cat said.

Jilly picked up the order Deb had written. 'How are you, Cat? Did you get your work finished?'

'I sure did. And I'm looking for company on a night out.'

'Deb and I were talking about trying a new bar out tonight.'

'Yeah, she told me. The *Singapore Sing Song*. Great name.'

'It's been getting fab reviews too. Come with us.'

'What time are you going?'

'About nine?'

'Sounds good. Is it dressy?'

Jilly shrugged. 'Just the usual. *Our* usual, not yours, country girl.' She rolled her eyes. Jilly's "usual" was very different from what Cat would wear. No matter how long she'd lived in Sydney and how long she'd seen what was acceptable, she was still a jeans and T-shirt girl.

Jilly picked up the order and walked back to the coffee machine, and Cat moved along the counter.

'The skinny cap's for Scarlet, plus the two Danish. She's still working.'

'She's in luck. There's two left, but they're both cherry.' Jilly peered into the cabinet.

'Cherry's her favourite. Put them in a bag for me, please.'

'Do you want them warmed up now?'

'No thanks, I'll pop them in the microwave when I get home.' Cat stood back and looked around the café. The hissing of the coffee machine and the hum of conversation surrounded her as she waited for Jilly to make Scarlet's coffee. Deb came back with some empty cups and then went back to the till as another queue began to form.

'Here you go.' Jilly put the takeaway coffee cup on the counter and handed over the bag with the two Danish. 'Tell Scarlet not to work too hard.'

'I will. See you later.'

'And Cat?' Jilly called out as she turned towards the door. 'Get dressed up. Wear something spangly.'

Cat grinned at her. 'We'll see.' As she walked back to the unit, the noise of the traffic and the crowds pushing along the footpath hurried her along. It would be good when Scart finished her proposal. Maybe she could take her out to *Ceann Marra* for a visit before the end of the year. They'd been talking about it for ages.

Chapter 5

Newtown, Sydney - August.

Caitríona had no trouble filling in the evening until nine o'clock. With no more pressure to work on her proposal, she stripped the sheets from her bed and made it up with clean linen, put three towels in the wash with the sheets, and piled up a heap of clothes ready to wash tomorrow; she was fast running out of clean clothes. While the sheets and towels dried in the clothes drier, she got the vacuum from under the stairs and vacuumed her room. When she offered to do Scarlet's room, her friend raised her eyebrows.

'My God, if this is what it's like when you finish, I can't wait,' she said. 'Washing and cleaning. Clean sheets and fresh towels. Wow.' She chuckled and shook her head before she stretched her arms above her head. 'I'm so close, Cat. I took a quick break while you were out and did the online shopping. I have to go and collect it though at ten.'

'That's a bugger. But at least you'll have something to keep you going while I'm out.'

'I ordered bacon and eggs too, so you've got something for your hangover in the morning.'

'You're a good friend.'

'And Tim Tams.'

'You're an amazing friend. Now get back to work!'

When Cat finished cleaning her room, folded the washing and put it away, she pulled out her phone. She closed the door so she didn't disturb Scarlet. She pulled up Roisin's number and hit speed dial. Even though her older sister was in Newcastle and Cat a couple of hundred kilometres away in Sydney, they didn't see each other very often. When they were kids, they'd drive that far to visit a friend without thinking twice.

She missed her sisters. Even though they hadn't gotten on all the time growing up—there had been the usual teenage fights and the occasional accusation of Cat being Dad's favourite—they were still a tight unit.

Roisin didn't pick up. She tried Erin, but it went straight to voicemail.

'Only me, Cat, ringing to say hello and see what spectacular place you're staying at now. Call me when you're back in range.'

She glanced at her watch. There was still an hour and a half before she left, so she decided to call home.

If they answered.

Her family were all leading busy lives, and Mum and Dad had a huge concern going at the station these days with little help. Cat knew she left it too long between calls because she'd been so busy with that damn proposal.

With Bridget still at boarding school, and Shea staying in Wilcannia, Mum and Dad were the only ones living on the station most of the time. The stockmen and station hands they employed were all on a casual basis these days, and Dad was forever lamenting how hard it was to get workers.

'The days of station hands spending three of four years on one property are long gone. Bloody social media. It's going to be the end of the land for us.'

Cat had grinned as Roisin caught her eyes the day Dad dropped that one. They'd all been home for Christmas at the end of her first year at uni.

'How can social media do that, Dad?' she'd asked.

'Everyone we've employed this year has come via a Facebook group.'

'And?'

'And those groups, and the employment agencies all paint life on properties as "the grass is always greener on the other side". They come here with expectations, and when they arrive, it's not what they expected. The last young bloke who turned up lasted one day. One day! Said it was too far to town! And then he complained there was no Wi-Fi out in the paddocks. I tell you what, I was glad to see the back of that one.'

But Dad soldiered on, and with casual local contractors, he managed to stay afloat with the merino sheep and his growing goat enterprise.

The year before Cat left for boarding school, Dad had started goat farming. When she'd come back in the winter holidays, *Ceann Mara* had been a different place, and Dad had been full of excitement. 'No grazier would still be viable here on the Darling these days without the income provided by feral goats.'

Cat had smiled at his enthusiasm. Goats were the last thing she would ever have imagined co-existing with the merino sheep that had been grazing on *Ceann Mara* for almost two hundred years. Once upon a time, they'd been considered a nuisance.

'Next year, we're going to put in goatproof fencing around three of the back paddocks, and we'll keep the nannies and kids and just sell off the billies. The paddocks will have one-way trap gates, so goats can get in, but not out.'

'Sounds really effective, Dad.' Caitríona was the only one of the sisters who loved working out on the station with Dad. Shea loved the animals but not the work that went with them.

'And they're bloody great breeders too, love. The nannies start breeding around seven months, and they deliver twice a year, and they often have triplets and quadruplets. Breed better than rabbits!'

Ceann Mara had been one of the first properties on the Darling River to take up goat farming, and it turned out to be a lucrative endeavour. She wondered if the tourist side of things would be the same. While Dad was immersed in his goats and family history, Mum had supervised the creation of the campsites and guest cabins on two hectares half a kilometre from the homestead. Construction had been full-on when she'd come home last year for a quick visit; concrete trucks and electricians seemed to be there every day.

She hadn't been out in the winter since the volunteers had started and the tourists arrived; she'd guessed she'd see it operating next year because the longer she stayed in Sydney, the more certain Cat was that she would head back home for good after she graduated.

From all accounts, the camping side of things was going well, and despite the volunteers running the physical side of it, Mum still handled the bookings. Volunteer couples spent a month there cleaning the amenities and camp kitchen, emptying the bins, cutting firewood, and keeping the small caravan and camping area clean. The last time she'd called home, Dad had told her, as well as the eight powered sites in the campground, they'd set up unpowered campsites along the river and around the huge billabong that began at the western end of the airstrip.

She pressed speed dial and was just about to hang up when Dad answered.

'Cat, how are you going, love? I was just thinking about you this afternoon.'

'Why, do you need some cattle drenched?'

Dad's hearty laugh sounded down the phone. 'Actually, yes. You want to come home and give your dear old Dad a hand?'

Cat grinned; that slight sibling jealousy might have held a grain of truth. She and Dad had a close relationship; they could always pick up without any awkwardness, even if it was weeks between conversations. She'd been the only daughter who was interested in the history, as well as in her element out there with Dad, fencing, moving stock, and drenching cattle and sheep.

'Busy there?' She settled back against the bedhead, ready for a yarn. As she moved, the clean pillowcases filled the room with a floral fragrance.

'Really busy. The last lot of volunteers left a week ago—we finish up the season before the heat, and your mother's been down there every day. She's cleaning out the fire pit and scrubbing the camp kitchen today, but she won't let me help. I had a load of goats picked up this afternoon and the downside was I had to make my own smoko when I got back to the homestead.'

'Poor you. Do you still send the goats to Bourke?'

'No, we sell to the local Louth goat depot now. They pick up from our yards and take them to Albury Wodonga, on the border. They're slaughtered Halal style for the Muslim market. The price per kilo has dropped this year, but the upside is that it's seen the reopening of some old export markets and some new ones.'

'Sounds like it's still going well.' Cat closed her eyes and imagined the paddocks with the sheep and goats. She could almost smell the red dust.

'Too right it has. The feral goat market is going great guns. When are you coming for a visit, love? Or better still, when are you coming back for good?'

'I was just thinking about that after I talked to Scarlet about our thesis proposals today.'

'And?'

'You'll be the first to know.'

'I want to show you the museum I've set up.'

'Where did you do that? You're not going to have tourists traipsing through the house, are you?''

'No. In the room between the amenities block and the dining room near the cabins. I've done a lot of scanning from the diaries and printed some photos of the O'Byrnes and their children not long after they built the homestead. I've found some great stuff, and it's been really popular with the tourists. I've typed up some documents with the station's history and added some old photos. You'd be proud of my computer skills these days, Cat, but I do wish you were closer.'

'Won't be long, Dad. You're addicted to that family research.'

'It's important; it shows us where we come from, although I think that's half the reason your mother started this accommodation setup. She said I was driving her crazy, me talking about the past all the time. We've had some interesting volunteers this year, and she's always down there having a yarn. It's been good for her socially, and she's getting lots of return visitors. Anyway, when you have your uni break, you can come home and help me find some really interesting things. Over the past few weeks, I found some documents in the NLI. They sent me some digital copies of—'

Cat interrupted before Dad could go off on another tangent. 'What's the NLI?'

'The National Library of Ireland. They have a whole section for family history, plus an online service.'

'That's great. Keep me up to date.'

'When are you coming home?'

'Well, I finished my submission. I want to work for a couple of weeks to get some money, and then I'll take some time off.'

'That'd be great. How about you forget about the work and come home sooner, and I can help you out?'

'Thanks, but no. I've committed to some waitressing. And when I come out, I was going to ask if it's okay if Scarlet comes for a visit. Is that okay?'

'Sounds great,' he said. 'And, of course Scarlet is welcome. She's the one doing chemistry, isn't she?'

'She is, and my flatmate. Thanks, Dad. I'll let you know what's happening.'

'Can't wait to see you, love.'

Cat smiled. 'Not too long now. Gotta go, Dad. Give my love to Mum.'

'I will. You should see the barbeque area and gardens she's set up for the tourists. She's a clever woman, *yer ma*,' he said in his best Irish accent.

'She is. I must take after her.' Cat chuckled, but as usual,

Dad tried to have the last word.

'Get away with ye.'

'Love you, Dad. Even though you think you're Irish.' Cat smiled as she disconnected the call.

Chapter 6

Ceann Mara Station - Tuesday, late September.

After checking all the doors and windows, Cat went back to her room; it was the first time she had been alone at the homestead since she came home three weeks ago. Even though she hadn't been forthcoming about the reasons that had seen her fleeing home at the end of August, her parents had eventually—and begrudgingly—respected her need for privacy. On her third night at home, she'd had a brief and vague conversation about needing to come earlier than she'd planned and then retreated to the safety of her room. Later that night as she made her way down the hall to get her water bottle out of the fridge, her parents' voices drifted through the open door of their room.

'She'll tell us when she's ready,' her father's voice rumbled down the hall. 'Be patient, Laura.'

'I need to know now.' Mum's voice shook, and Cat tensed. 'I honestly don't know how to deal with her. Do you realise, Tom, she hasn't smiled once since she's been home? She hasn't initiated any conversation, and she sleeps all day. Something is very wrong. It's just not our Cat.'

'Leave the girl be,' Dad had said. 'She's working through some issues. I can't understand why she didn't tell me she was coming home when she rang the Friday night before she turned up. Something must have happened that weekend. Did she have a boyfriend we don't know about, do you think? Maybe they broke up. Or have all these submissions and study just got too much for her?'

'If it is something like that, that's what we're here for,' Mum said. 'We're here to help our girls.'

'Caitríona is twenty-three years old, and if she wants help, she'll ask. You know her, she's always been our independent one, solved her own problems, fought her own battles. She'll come good. We just need to give her some time and space. And not hassle her.'

'And make her eat. She's lost weight.' Her mother's voice hitched with a sob.

Cat had walked silently upstairs without retrieving her water bottle. She avoided the creaky step; she didn't want Mum and Dad to know she'd overheard their conversation. If she got thirsty through the night, she'd go into the bathroom and drink from the tap again.

If only it was as simple as breaking up with a guy.

That wouldn't have created these crazy thoughts going around in her head every minute she was awake. Maybe she was losing her mind.

Since overhearing them worrying, she'd retreated even further into herself. She knew they were worried about her, but she was unable to reach out; it was as if there was a physical barrier enclosing her. It felt like she was surrounded by glass and separated from everything.

Maybe it was a nightmare she was going to wake up from soon. Maybe none of it happened. She didn't want to talk about it, but she knew she was going to have to do something. She couldn't hide in her room for the rest of her life. The worst part was how she felt inside and how she was treating her parents. The Caitríona O'Byrne of the last twenty-three years—up until that Friday night three weeks ago—wouldn't have reacted like this; she knew she had to dig for courage and get herself out of this state of mind because she could feel herself spiralling further down every day.

Cat pulled her robe tightly around her, noticing how much looser it was. Mum was right; she had lost weight. She straightened her shoulders and tried to put some energy into her steps as she closed and locked her bedroom door. She forced herself to go into the bathroom between hers and Roisin's room. Breathing deeply, she gripped the edge of the stone vanity top in the bathroom. The girls' bedrooms and shared bathrooms had been renovated when each of them left home. Erin and Shea shared a bathroom, and Bridget used the small guest bathroom at the end of the hall downstairs. Bridget was still waiting for her room to be done; it was still decorated as a little girl's room. She complained long and hard to anyone who would listen about pink everything and Barbie dolls. Her turn would come when she finished high school.

Cat didn't pay any attention to the new patterned tiles and fancy vanity as she stared at the pale face looking back at her from the large round mirror. Her fair skin was almost translucent, and the spray of freckles that had plagued her all her life was more visible than ever beneath the LED lights that circled the mirror. Usually, her cheeks held a rosy flush, but there was no sign of any colour now. She lifted a shaking hand to her hair; the matted, greasy curls stuck to her forehead. No wonder Mum had looked at her the way she had.

Today, she would take control and do something about the way she looked. She stripped off her robe and pyjamas and turned the shower taps on full. When the first bathroom was renovated, Dad had installed a pressure pump between the shed and the house, and the water flow was strong, stinging her still tender skin as she stepped into the shower cubicle.

Cat grabbed the soap and the scrubbing brush, and as she had done the morning she left Sydney, she scrubbed her skin until it was pink. That morning, the water gurgling into the drain had been red from her blood mixing with it.

She tipped her head back and let the water run over her thick curls until her hair was soaking wet and then reached for the shampoo Mum ensured was in the bathrooms. The soothing smell of lemongrass and coconut surrounded her as she massaged her hair, then rinsed and soaked again before reaching for the conditioner. She dragged her fingers through her hair before letting the warm water strip the conditioner out.

Tipping her head back again, the hot water ran down her face. Her face stinging as though tears were running from her eyes, but tears were one thing she'd avoided; maybe if she let go and had a good cry, the healing would start.

Stepping out of the shower, Cat reached for the fluffy burgundy towel that matched the heritage feature tiles at the top of the walls. The shower had invigorated her and she began to take notice of her surroundings for the first time. She patted her neck dry and forced herself to look at the nick on the left side of her neck; the scab had almost lifted and it had left a small pink scar below her ear.

She'd be able to hide it with her hair while she thought up

an explanation for the scar. She pressed the thick, soft towel against her skin and focused on drying herself.

It didn't matter to Mum that they lived over a hundred kilometres from the nearest town and that they rarely had visitors stay in the homestead these days; the interior of the whole homestead was beautiful. It was Mum's pride and joy and she took pleasure in their home.

Cat reached for another towel and rubbed her hair hard before wrapping it in a turban style. As she dried her body, she forced herself to stand in front of the mirror again, unable to believe how much weight had fallen off her in such a short time. She pulled out the scales from underneath the vanity cabinet and was shocked to see that she was down five kilograms, which, for her height, made her look almost anorexic.

Mum had tried to feed her up when she'd joined them in the dining room for dinner a few nights since she'd come home, but the effort of eating and making conversation had been too hard. She'd picked at the meals, not interested in food. Nothing tempted her appetite; nothing interested her. If she didn't think, she didn't feel, and the fear stayed away.

Her laptop was still in her car in the shed and she hadn't had to deal with phone calls because, in her hurry to get away from their unit before Scarlet returned from her meeting that day, Cat had left without her phone. She'd left a brief note for Scarlet and put her share of the next fortnight's rent in an envelope on the table. She was going to have to contact her and send some more money and tell her to find another tenant.

She walked into the bedroom, opened the small bag she'd thrown a few things into before she left, and pulled out clean underwear. The soft cotton knickers slid over her legs; her skin felt so much better since she'd showered, but she still avoided looking at her arms and legs. The bag of washing she'd thrown in the car was still in the boot.

The heat had already been building when she'd been outside before; today was going to be a scorcher. Despite that, Cat was determined to go to the mailbox; she would leave the house and achieve that this morning.

Small steps.

The spring sunshine would burn her fair skin, so she needed to cover up. Crossing to the wardrobe where her work clothes for the station were kept, Cat put on a pair of light, khaki cotton pants and then pulled a long-sleeved green T-shirt over her wet hair. For a moment, she thought about getting the hairdryer out but then figured her curls would dry quickly as she rode to the mailbox.

Showering and dressing had exhausted her, and for a moment, she looked longingly at the soft white pillows on her bed. The sheets were still in a tangle, and she noticed there were some light blood stains where her legs had been bleeding. Over the past few weeks, much to Mum's dismay, she had refused to let her in to change the bed linen and had also refused to put it out to wash. The blood would probably stain the sheets permanently; if Mum and Dad stayed away overnight, she'd have a go at bleaching them tomorrow.

She walked around each side of the bed and slowly made it up. After plumping the pillows, she took a deep breath and forced herself to unlock the bedroom door and step into the hallway.

On her way to the kitchen, Cat checked all the doors and the windows were still locked. The original drawing room halfway up the hall had been turned into a dining room about ten years ago when Dad's obsession with the O'Byrne family history had taken hold. Papers, diaries and books spread all over the formal dining room table had become too much for Mum, so she'd cleared out the dining room and got Cat—who shared Dad's interest—and her sisters to help her move the dining room table and chairs down to the drawing room. Unbeknownst to Dad, she had bought a huge desk at a sale at Broken Hill and had it delivered in time for his fortieth birthday. His passion for their family history had never left him and he was determined to document as much as he could.

To Dad's credit, he'd always kept the new workspace fairly tidy, and now as Cat walked in, she was still taken aback by the neat piles of documents, the new computer and printer sitting on the corner of the desk. She walked across the room looking at the photos on the wall. There was one in particular she was looking for this morning, to try to give her the motivation to get back in her own skin. She'd started with her physical appearance today and now she would start on the emotional healing.

At last count, there were fifty-six framed photos going back as far as her great-great-great-great grandparents' photograph taken when they'd left Ireland for the colony of New South Wales. Cat's interest flared as she walked around; she found the family history fascinating. Dad had now labelled many of the photos with names and dates; he'd discovered a lot since she'd last been in here.

She scanned the photos as she wandered along the far wall; he'd also rearranged them into chronological order since she'd been home earlier in the year. She moved to the wall adjacent to the door and immediately found the one she was looking for.

A professional photographer had taken the family photo when the family went down to the City Art Gallery in Broken Hill, three weeks before Cat left for university. One of Shea's paintings had been on display at a school exhibition. Erin hadn't moved out at that stage, and Roisin had been home for a visit, so Mum had decided to organise a professional family photo,

'Goodness knows how long it'll be before we're all together again,' she said.

The photographer had taken them out to the Living Desert west of Broken Hill, much to Dad's disgust. His only interest in Broken Hill was the library, but even he admitted it had been worth it.

'A cracker of a shot,' he agreed when the proof had arrived.

Mum and Dad stood at the back and the five sisters sat on a wide, flat rock backlit by the setting sun as they looked out over the plains below.

Cat scanned the photo as she tried to retrieve the sense of joy she had carried inside those days. Shea and Erin were laughing up at Dad; their hair was as dark as his. Bridget and Roisin were looking serious, their fair hair—the same colour as Mum's—picking up the golden rays of the afternoon sun. She was the only one who'd inherited the red curls from several generations back on the O'Byrne side.

Cat stared at the photo for a long time, absorbing the happiness of her family, and then walked to the opposite wall. It was uncanny how much she looked like the first Caitríona in the family. The Caitríona who had married an O'Byrne and emigrated to New South Wales.

As she stared at the photo, she noticed for the first time the sadness on her four-times-great-grandmother's face.

Chapter 7
Country Kerry, Ireland - 1843.

Caitríona Lowe scrubbed the dirt from the potatoes she had peeled into the stone sink and then placed the peelings into the tin that young Jimmy O'Sullivan would take out to the compost heap at sunset. Mrs Baker, cook at the big house, had loaded her up with extra tasks today, and Miss Ellis, the housekeeper, had appeared in the scullery several times with various chores for Caitríona to complete upstairs.

Caitríona had worked at *Ceann Mara* estate ever since she left the local school before her fourteenth birthday. If it wasn't for Miss Ellis, she would have been happy to spend her life working here. Until recently she had expected she would marry a local farmer, settle in another cottage and start a family. But there was no way she was going to have as many children as Mam and Da. Caitríona was wise to the ways of nature and she knew what caused babies to be born.

Over the past few months, there had been many impromptu

visits by the Carroll brothers. They would sit around the copper still over the open turf fires with Da, drinking the *poitín* he distilled from the potato crop last winter. The cottage would be full of farm talk, raucous jokes and laughter as the brothers' eyes followed Caitríona as she'd helped Mam.

The year and a bit she had spent at the big house had been hard, but she enjoyed the work and the feeling that she was contributing to the running of the estate. She had learned much about the running of a household. Her tasks were many—Caitríona loathed scrubbing out the chamber pots each morning—but her life working at the manor was a happy one, and the few silver pence she took home each month made a difference to her family.

But that wasn't the best thing about spending her days there.

She huffed a sigh of relief as she washed her hands and wiped them on her apron. Now, she could finally leave; even with all the tasks that had increased as the day went on, time had dragged as excitement churned in her stomach. Caitríona had even refused the edges of the cake that Mrs Baker had offered her as she had prepared for afternoon tea.

The anticipation of her afternoon had fuelled Caitríona's daydreams as she scrubbed and dusted, and even the wrath of Miss Ellis when a vase had slipped from Caitríona's grip in the master bedroom had not dampened her happy mood. Luckily it hadn't broken as she knew that would have been taken out of her pay.

Mr O'Byrne was in Dublin attending to business and would be gone for the first month of spring. Mrs O'Byrne, the mistress of *Ceann Mara,* was away visiting her sister for two days and nights, and her absence was taken as an opportunity to beat the carpets in the bedrooms upstairs as well as clean the entire top floor of the manor house. It seemed that the ash from the winter fires had found its way into every nook and cranny of the manor, and Caitríona was responsible for the spring cleaning. She had muttered under her breath as she cleaned the mantlepiece in the master bedroom; she was a housemaid and Mrs Baker's assistant. Surely the housekeeper could help? But no, Miss Ellis was above these menial tasks and watched Caitríona like one of the hawks that soared above the wood where she was going this afternoon.

A rush of warmth suffused her body as she thought of the cool glade where she was meeting her Sean and of course, as she paused and waved her hands in front of her hot face, the old crow had been watching her.

'Caitríona, you still have two rooms to dust before lunch. Master Thomas will come in from the fields shortly. Stop wasting time.'

'Yes, Miss Ellis.'

'I want these rooms finished before you go down to Mrs Baker to peel the vegetables.'

'Yes, Miss Ellis.'

Please, don't make me serve his meal.

Thomas had been showing way too much interest in her lately, and she avoided him.

'I will serve Masters Thomas and Samuel while you help Mrs Baker.'

'What about Master Sean?' Caitríona asked innocently, knowing full well the third son would not be at the table today. Sean had told her he was going to the river early to read. 'Will he be eating a midday meal?'

'Why do you ask?' Miss Ellis narrowed her eyes.

'I am making sure I leave enough time to help Mrs Baker with the lunch preparation.'

'If you focused on your dusting and spent less time chattering, there would be ample time for everything.'

'Yes, Miss Ellis.'

Silly old crow.

At first, Caitríona had been excited to hear that her eagle-eyed mistress and the master were going away, but her joy had soon palled as she had carried the first of the heavy carpets downstairs to the cobblestones at the back of the scullery.

She had helped Mrs Baker serve lunch on the fine china plates; finally, the hands of the grandfather clock in the drawing room reached three o'clock.

'Don't think you're going to run off home now, missy,' Mrs Baker called out as Caitríona went to collect her shawl. 'I've got a few more jobs for you yet. There are still potatoes to peel for dinner.'

Caitríona shook her head. 'I'm sorry, Mrs Baker. Mam is expecting me at home; she needs me to help with the children. Mrs O'Byrne agreed that I could leave at three before she left this morning.' She crossed her fingers behind her back as the lie tripped easily off her lips.

'You should not have spoken to Mrs O'Byrne!'

Caitríona jumped as Miss Ellis' voice came from the doorway behind her. She turned slowly to look at the sour face of the housekeeper.

'You seek permission from me. The mistress said nothing of that. You will finish the chores Mrs Baker has for you before you leave for the day.' The woman's lips thinned further, if that was at all possible. She was the ugliest woman Caitríona had ever seen, and she found it hard to believe the downstairs gossip.

Mr Samuel might be a rake, but surely, he would not put his hand on such an ugly woman. Jimmy swore black and blue he had seen them kissing in the garden last week.

Caitríona fought the mutinous gaze that was building and quickly bowed her head. 'My mam was not well this morning, Mrs Ellis, and I'm to see to the boys' dinner.'

Sometimes having six brothers was a blessing.

'I suppose your mother is in the family way again.' Miss Ellis rasped, disgust lacing her tone. Her voice matched the rest of her, shrivelled and nasty.

'I wouldn't know that, Miss Ellis.' Caitríona kept her head down; there was no way she was going to stay a minute longer.

Mrs Baker walked over and touched her shoulder. 'I'm sorry to hear your mam is unwell. Off you go now. You can start earlier in the morning. Mr Thomas is having guests tomorrow afternoon. Miss Ellis may require you to serve the afternoon tea.' The older woman shot a triumphant look at the housekeeper.

'And we both know that won't happen,' Caitríona thought uncharitably, but her response was polite. 'Why would that be, Mrs Baker?' she said.

'Amelia has accompanied Mrs O'Byrne to Killarney.'

Ah, perhaps I will if the other housemaid has accompanied the mistress.

'I will be here at first light.' Caitríona nodded, grabbed her shawl and hurried to the door that led to the back garden.

'And make sure you wear a white blouse and that it is clean.' Miss Ellis had the last word.

Caitríona's boots clattered on the cobblestones as she hurried across to the back gate. She would follow the towpath that ran along the western side of the River Finnihy, and that way she could avoid going anywhere near home. The Lowes lived in a cottage not far from the big house, as the manor had always been known, and she knew Da would be out in the fields digging the earlies; she'd heard him tell Mam that last night. She'd also heard those noises that came from their bed and had put her hands over her ears.

As ucht Dé. For God's sake, her mother had not long given birth to baby Finn, and her father still had to . . .

Caitríona shook her head in disbelief. She didn't want to think about it.

As her fingers touched the latch, Master Thomas walked around from the back of the stables. His face changed when he saw her, and the grin that spread across his face gave her pause.

Thomas had caught her in the library one day last month as she was wiping down the leather on the large desk underneath the bay window. He'd walked in silently and closed the door behind him, and a trickle of uneasiness ran down her back.

'Caitríona, how are you enjoying working at *Ceann Mara?*' he asked.

'Why on earth would you ask me that now, when I've been here for more than a year, Thomas?'

His eyes narrowed. 'That would be Master Thomas to you.'

'Yes, Master Thomas.' She picked up her cleaning rag and turned towards the door.

'No, Caitríona, wait. I've only to be here for a minute or two, and then you can finish your chores.'

She waited near the window, staring out over the lush green fields as he took some papers from beneath the glass paperweight and flicked through them. Thomas pulled out a single letter, folded it in half and put it in his jacket pocket before closing the drawer.

Caitríona froze as he moved closer to her.

Too close.

'You've grown up into quite the pretty little thing, haven't you, Miss Cat?' he said, his voice holding something unfamiliar as he used the nickname she had at the local school.

She had grown up with the three O'Byrne brothers and attended the village school with them. Thomas and Samuel had always been tormentors, but Sean had been kind to her when they had played together as children. He was different to his two older brothers; Mr Haydn had often told him he would be a gentleman and a scholar, and he'd taken some ribbing in the playground.

Heat stole into her cheeks. As she thought of Sean, she lowered her eyes. 'Perhaps.'

'Perhaps, sir,' Thomas said.

She lifted her head and scowled at him. 'Perhaps, sir.'

'Come, come, Caitríona. You've known me since I was in britches running around the schoolyard with you, throwing stones and playing marbles.'

He reached out, and both his hands touched her shoulders. Before she could step away, Thomas ran his hands from her shoulders down her sides to settle on her hips. He pulled her close to him, and she stiffened.

His laugh covered Caitríona's soft cry as his fingers moved around to her buttocks, and he squeezed the soft flesh between his fingers. Thomas lowered his head as he held her, and cold lips pressed on hers so hard that her teeth ground against his, and she tasted blood.

He leaned back and looked at her, a predatory smile on his face. 'Looks like someone needs to teach you how to kiss properly, madam, and I am just the man to do it.'

'Over my dead body.' She lifted her arm and wiped the back of her hand across her lips. Her cheeks burned as she stared back at him. 'Don't you ever lay a hand on me again, Thomas O'Byrne.'

'Or you'll tiddle-tat?' His voice was cold. 'You need to learn your place, Miss Cat. I can do what I like and there's not a damn thing you can do about it.'

'Do not touch me. Ever. Again.' She stepped back and held his dark gaze.

Finally, Thomas chuckled. 'Oh, a challenge. Just what I love. We'll see.' He turned away, closing the door behind him.

Caitríona's hands were still shaking an hour later when Mrs Baker called her to the scullery.

She hadn't told Sean what had happened, because she knew he would probably thump his brother with little thought of the consequences, and she couldn't allow that to happen. If anyone knew that she and Sean were spending time together in their glade, she would lose her position at the big house, and her family couldn't afford that.

She would be extra careful; Thomas and Samuel favoured their father, and Sean was the gentle dreamer.

Now, this afternoon as Thomas approached when she opened the gate, her heart pounded.

'Caitríona, where are you going?'

She quickly opened the gate and latched it behind her. 'I have permission to leave early today,' she said as she began to walk away. Her mind ran in circles. Had Miss Ellis spoken to Thomas? In the absence of his father, he was the master of the estate and the big house.

Had Thomas seen her with Sean one day? Had he watched Sean open this gate a short time ago?

She had watched from the window while she was wiping the china before the midday meal was served. Sean had unlatched the gate and entered the fields, and she had hurried to finish her work so she could follow him to their secret place.

Thomas didn't speak again, but she was aware of his gaze on her as she hurried across the open field before she reached the edge of the woods. Knowing he was watching, she turned to the right, away from the river, as though she was heading home towards their cottage.

Once she was in the cover of the woods, she stepped behind a broad tree trunk and peered around it. To her relief, there was no sign of him. For a moment, she'd been worried that he would follow her into the woods. She didn't trust Thomas O'Byrne one bit.

Caitríona backtracked along the path, listening for footsteps and keeping an eye out as she stepped onto the path that led to their glade beside the stream.

Chapter 8
Country Kerry, Ireland - 1845.

A strong friendship was forged between Sean and Caitríona in their years at the village school. Girls attended the school to learn to read and write, sew, cook, and pray. But along with Sean, Caitríona held a love of learning, and Mr Haydn, the teacher from Dublin who had been at the village school for most of his life, appreciated and nurtured their willingness to learn. Sean had no interest in the playground fights his brothers relished, and were more often than not responsible for. Of course, being from the big house, a blind eye was turned to their behaviour. The big house subsidised the meagre teaching allowance paid to Mr Haydn by the National Board.

Caitríona had learned to trust Sean over the years. They sat next to each other at the double wooden desk at the front of the single classroom near the fire. The high ceilings of the brick schoolhouse adjacent to the church meant that the heat was lost quickly. Sean's task was to bring the dried peat in for the fire each morning and to "smother" the fire without extinguishing it each afternoon, so it would gently smoulder overnight.

She knew he didn't belong in the O'Byrne family; he was a kind and gentle soul in a family known in the district for their tempers and hardness.

One afternoon, in the year she would turn fourteen, Mr Haydn asked her to stay back so he could speak to her. Sean scowled and waited in the schoolyard; they'd planned to go fishing at their favourite spot on Finnihy Stream that afternoon, and now they might not have enough time before dark.

When she came out, Caitríona's smile was wide, and she skipped over to the churchyard, bursting with her news. Sean was wandering through the cemetery reading the headstones.

'What was that about?' he asked as they walked towards the woods.

'Mr Haydn told me that the Model School in Dublin is now accepting girls for teaching. He says it would be a waste if I left school and that he will write a letter to my parents and suggest that I stay, and then go to Dublin to study.'

Sean stared at her. 'When?'

She shrugged. 'I don't know. But it won't happen. I can't see Da saying yes anyway. It would cost too much, and we can't afford it.'

'I could ask Father to help. It's his duty, to look after his tenants.'

She shrugged again.

'You'd make a good teacher,' Sean continued as they entered the forest between the school and the stream. Spring had carpeted the woods with bluebells, and the buzz of bees feeding on the nectar filled the air. Butterflies swarmed around the wood anemones growing in the dappled shade beneath the broad oak trunks.

'I don't know if I want to go away to Dublin. Da said it was dirty and noisy when he went there. I'd miss home.' It would be easy to leave the cramped cottage with the constant smell of wet washing, the stink of the peat, and the noise of her siblings. What she would miss would be the beauty of the country . . . and Sean.

The burbling of the stream over the rocks grew louder as they stepped out of the woods.

'You get the worms,' Sean said. Caitríona looked at his back as he headed over to the two rocks where he left the willow fishing poles. He was a year older than she was, and this year he'd grown tall, and his shoulders had broadened. His voice had broken, and a strange feeling would curl in her stomach as she looked at him. Sometimes she felt shy when he looked back at her.

'Come on, Cat! Stop dillydallying.'

All shyness disappeared at his teasing.

As Sean strode to the bank with the two rods in hand, she pulled a face at him and then crouched beneath the tree where the mealworms were plentiful in the moist, dark earth.

##

Four months later, Catriona started work as a kitchen maid in the big house; as she had expected there had been no money to send her to teacher training, and she accepted that. Time passed quickly as she learned the skills of working in a big manor. It was very different to the small cottage where she lived with her family.

She missed school, but not as much as she missed the hours with Sean. She rarely saw him these days, and she knew it wasn't proper for him to speak to her on the rare occasion that she saw him in the house. She spent most of her time in the scullery and cleaning the rooms when the master and the boys were out. By the time Sean came home from the school each afternoon, she would be on her way home to help Mam with the meal. Sometimes she dreamed of leaving and being somewhere else with Sean, but Caitríona was smart enough to know that would never happen.

'I don't know why that woman won't let you serve in the dining room,' Mrs Baker often complained. 'You would be much better than Amelia. She dropped another serving dish yesterday.'

'Why does she dislike me so much, Mrs Baker? I try my best.'

'You are a good worker. It is your pretty face that causes the problem.'

Caitríona came home exhausted most evenings and then had to prepare the children's supper and help Mam get them into bed. Sundays, her one day off, were taken up with going to church and then helping with the children. Her mother had given birth to another boy, Finn, the week after Caitríona's sixteenth birthday. She did as much as she could to help; Mam was thin and always looked tired. Once everything was done, Caitríona could escape the cottage and go walking. Poor Mam was stuck in the cottage day and night.

Sunday was her one precious day and Da would always have a job for her and the boys, but, if she was quick enough to get away, the afternoon was hers.

One Saturday afternoon, she took tea up to the master bedroom; Mrs O'Byrne had a heavy cold and was feeling poorly. Miss Ellis, who would usually look after the mistress, had gone to Kilgarvan to visit her ailing mother.

Caitríona smiled and smoothed the counterpane at the end

of the bed. 'I hope you feel better soon, madam.' She waited until the teacup was empty and removed the tea tray from the bed.

'Thank you, Caitríona. You're a good girl.'

Sean took after Mrs O'Byrne, both in appearance, with his fair hair and skin, and his kind, gentle manner.

Mr O'Byrne, Thomas, and Samuel had gone to a sheep sale according to Mrs Baker; being Saturday, Caitríona had hoped she might see Sean, but there had been no sign of him in the house, and she didn't like to ask Mrs Baker where he was.

As she walked along the carpet runner to the top of the staircase, a door opened ahead of her and he stepped out of the room.

His face lit up in a wide smile. 'Cat, I was listening for you,' he whispered.

She smiled back, reaching up to smooth the loose, springy curls away from her face. 'There's no need to whisper. Everybody is out.'

'What about the Ellis?' he asked, looking around furtively.

'Don't tell me you're scared of her too?' she asked with a chuckle.

'The woman is a witch. I think even Father is intimidated by her.'

'She's gone to the village. There's only me and Mrs Baker in the scullery.'

He reached out for her hand, and warmth ran up her arm as he held her fingers. 'I miss you, Cat. It's not the same without seeing you.'

'I miss you too, Sean. Life is so busy now. The days just run together and the weeks hurry by.'

'Are you happy?' he asked.

She shrugged. 'I do what I have to. Happiness doesn't

come into it. Mam had another baby, and I'm looking after the others at night so she can get some sleep.'

His eyes widened. 'That makes eight of you?'

'No, only seven.'

Sean shook his head. 'Only seven!'

'Yes, me, John, Michael, Patrick, Joseph, Tommy, and now baby Finn. With Da and Mam, and now my grandad, it is very cramped in the cottage. And Da is angry because when he dug the potatoes, all he found was a black sticky mess. He is working with your father some of the time, as you probably know.'

'Others are too. Several tenants have experienced that this year. They say it is the blight and the wet summer washed the spores into the soil. It doesn't bode well for next year's crop; I heard Father tell Thomas at dinner last night.'

'It is not pleasant at home. I try to escape on Sundays, and Mam is happy for me to go walking. I know she is grateful for my help.'

'Where do you go?'

She held his gaze steadily. 'I go to our glade and I sit by the stream with my back against the rock. I tip my face to the sun and then I dream.'

'I wish I'd known that. I don't go there anymore because it's not the same without you.'

'I'm there Sunday afternoons when the weather is clear. And sometimes in the winter if it is not snowing. The glade is my favourite place.'

'Then I will see you there tomorrow and I'll bring our fishing poles.'

She laughed. 'You still have them?'

'Of course I do. Can you still dig mealy worms?'

She stared at the two dimples in his cheeks. Even though Sean's face was now manly, the dimples had stayed. 'Of course I can.'

Very little had changed when she met Sean the following afternoon. He carried the rods, she dug the worms, and they chatted as they caught several fish each.

'Will you take them to Mrs Baker?' she asked.

'No. You take them to your family. I suspect you have more need of them than we do at the big house.'

Mam was very grateful for the fish and looked carefully at Caitríona. 'That was clever of you. Perhaps you could take the boys with you next time and catch more. Those will barely feed us all, but thank you, *mo stór*.'

My treasure. She nodded at the endearment, knowing that Mam appreciated what she did, but had no intention of taking her brothers to the glade.

Caitríona didn't mention Sean; her family would not accept her spending time with him. No one had cared about them running wild when they were children. But they were no longer innocent children, and she had begun to suspect that Sean had feelings for her too.

They were seeing each other most Sundays, and when they weren't fishing, they would lie on the grass on the banks of the stream and Sean would read poetry to her, and tell her myths and legends from the books she dusted in the library at the big house. He was enamoured with the classics; something she had never learned at the school.

Sean would seek her out in the big house when no one else was around. Opportunities became less frequent after Miss Ellis caught them talking one morning. A sharp click of her tongue and a frigid stare had Caitríona hurrying back to the scullery. The housekeeper was always around where Caitríona was working in the house, but Miss Ellis stayed out of Mrs Baker's scullery most of the time. The spring and summer passed quickly, and her love for Sean grew with each Sunday afternoon they spent together, as did her knowledge that nothing would ever come of it.

Chapter 9

Ceann Mara Station - Tuesday afternoon.

Cat's stomach rumbled as she stood staring at the photo of the first Caitríona. The resemblance was strong; genes were an incredible thing. It was uncanny how she could look at a photo from over one hundred and fifty years ago and see so much of herself. Perhaps she'd inherited her forebear's strength; from all anecdotal accounts passed down, the first Caitríona had been a strong woman.

Her stomach gurgled again; if she was going to go out to the mailbox, she should eat. With a determined step, she walked down the hall to the kitchen and opened the fridge. A glimmer of a smile pulled at her lips as she saw the breakfast tray Mum had set for her—a bowl of freshly made Bircher muesli, a plate of sliced fruit, a small jug of milk, and a smaller bowl filled with Mum's homemade preserves. She looked over at the counter beneath the window, and sure enough, there were two slices of wholemeal bread under a sheer cloth next to the toaster. The coffeemaker was turned on, and a selection of pods sat in a container beside it.

Mum knew how much Cat loved her coffee. She selected a pod, turned the machine on, and soon the fragrant aroma of coffee filled the room. Even though her stomach was rumbling, food still didn't appeal but she forced herself to take the tray out of the fridge, and sat down and attempted to eat some of it.

She managed to eat half the muesli and fruit before walking over and putting a toast slice into the toaster. As she sipped her coffee, she nibbled at the piece of toast and felt quite proud that not only had she managed to have a shower, wash her hair, and eat breakfast; it was still before nine o'clock in the morning.

As Cat stood to take her plate over to the dishwasher, the shrill bell of the phone rang loudly in the hall and startled her.

It would be Mum letting her know they'd landed. She walked to the hall and picked up the old-fashioned receiver that had been deliberately kept in keeping with the turn-of-the-century style on the lower floor of the homestead.

'Hello?' she said hesitantly, not willing to identify herself. *Just in case.*

'We're here safely.'

Her shoulders relaxed as her mother's voice came down the phone line.

'You got there quickly.' The flight usually took a good three hours.

'We had a strong tailwind.'

'That's good, Mum. I hope the flight wasn't too rough?' It was easier to speak kindly when she was alone, without someone staring at her, looking worried.

'Dreadful. It got worse after we passed over Wilcannia, and it's blowing a gale here at Broken Hill already. We won't be home today. Is that all right?'

'Yes, I'll be fine. You'll be pleased to know I've had a shower and eaten breakfast—thank you—and I'm about to go to the mailbox.'

She could imagine the expression on Mum's face; her voice held so much relief. 'Oh, that's good. I have to go. Dad's got the hire car already. I'll talk to you later. Bye, Cat . . . and sweetheart?'

'Yes, Mum?' Her voice was guarded.

'We love you.'

Before she could answer, the call disconnected.

After she tidied up the kitchen, Cat went to the laundry and opened the shoe cupboard. Sure enough, her work boots were there, lined up where they always had been, with several pairs of socks in a bag attached to the inside of the door. She pulled out a pair, sat on the stool, and pulled them on before checking her boots for spiders—or worse. She'd never forget the day Erin had gone to get her boots and found a brown snake curled up inside one. She could still hear the scream that had reverberated through the homestead.

After her boots were laced up and her cargo pants tucked into the socks, Cat reached for her battered Akubra, still hanging on the hat board beside the boot cupboard.

It was as though the last three years hadn't happened. Just another normal day at the *Ceann Mara Station*. If she kept that at the forefront of her thoughts, the darkness would stay away.

With a deep breath, she unlocked the back door and stepped outside for the second time today. The mail came into Louth by air, and the contractor always tried to beat the livestock trucks on the red dirt road, so she was sure their mail would have been delivered by now.

It would be good to go out and look around the property and look at the new tourist facilities that were running as a sideline on the station. A couple of months ago, Cat had encountered the *Riverbeds* site on Instagram and had been surprised by the photos a tourist had posted. *Riverbeds* was quite well-known and being recommended in Facebook groups and on travel sites. She'd clicked through and been surprised to see not only a Facebook page but also a website. She wondered who'd set it up. As far as she knew, neither of her parents had those technology skills.

With no one around today, she'd have a good look at the buildings, but she'd keep an eye out for any sign of dust on the road that looked like a vehicle coming to the station. She let the dogs out of the pen and smiled when old Jonty, the Kelpie Huntaway, raced out, yapping excitedly and jumping all over her.

'Hey, beautiful boy. You're still as energetic as ever.' He settled when she spoke but leaned over and quietly licked her hand, strangely bringing tears to her eyes.

'Ah, sweet.' It was as though Jonty knew she needed comfort. The other two dogs were new and wary but settled as Jonty welcomed her.

The wind was getting up, and dust swirled on the road to the front gate. Cat briefly considered Mum's ag bike suggestion. She headed to the big shed, the dogs following as they sensed an outing. In typical Outback station form, the keys to the various vehicles were hanging on the board inside the door above the two ag bikes and the quad bike.

Across the shed, which housed various vehicles and equipment, and the Cessna in the left-hand bay, she spotted her and her sisters' pushbikes still sitting on the bike rack on the far wall. It looked like Dad had been taking care of them—dust-free, shiny frames, and clean, pumped-up tyres showing evidence of his maintenance.

Memories flooded through Cat.

Peddling furiously along the levee wall edging the homestead side of the billabong to see who got to their picnic area first. Coming a cropper and ending up in the green slime the day she decided she was going to beat Erin—who always won—and took a shortcut to the grassy area near the end of the airstrip.

She reached up and lifted down her bike, the first glimmer of a smile in three weeks tipping her lips as she put the bike on the ground. All their bikes had names—Gertie, Elsie, Beryl, Joanie, and her own Barbie—each carrying memories of happy times from her childhood.

Cat's smile widened as she wheeled her pushbike across the concrete floor of the shed and onto the dusty track. She pushed it to the fence gate surrounding the homestead, the house paddock, and the shed. When she and the dogs were through the gate, she jumped on and pedalled leisurely past the campground, flicking a glance at the new buildings and the concrete pads set up for caravans as she headed for the front gate and the dirt road that led from Louth to Tilpa.

No sisters to race today. In their teenage years, Roisin and Erin had pen pals and were always desperate to get the mail.

Ten minutes later, Cat squinted as a great gust of wind, full of red dust, hit her face when she lifted the lid of the milk can that served as the mailbox at the front of the property. A small parcel addressed to Dad and some letters were weighted down by the painted rock that had protected their mail from the wind for as long as she could remember. She tucked the parcel into the basket first, put the letters on top, then pulled the elastic-edged cover over to stop the mail from blowing out.

She whistled for the dogs sniffing along the fence line and turned her bike towards the homestead. A lot of tension had left her as she'd pedalled to the road; she should have done this before. Being out in the fresh air made her feel a lot better, but the sudden plume of dust rising a couple of kilometres down Louth Road had her hurrying to the front gate. She swung it closed and reached for the padlock, clicking it over.

It wouldn't matter if the front gate was locked until Dad was home again. Mum said no one was coming today, and if anyone turned up, it would be someone who wasn't expected, so they could keep going.

Cat wasn't ready for people yet. It was hard enough being here with Mum and Dad. She didn't want to see anyone else.

Yet.

At the edge of the next paddock, she jumped off the bike. As she suspected, the cattle gate was open. There'd been no stock in the front paddocks when she arrived, and she knew it wasn't the time of the year for sheep or cattle to graze in the dry front paddocks. She rested her bike against the fence post beside the gate that led to the southern paddocks and swung the gate shut. The metal was already hot enough to burn her hands, but she lifted the gate out of the soft dirt, pushed it shut, looped the chain around it, and found the padlock hanging up at the end. She secured it, and a small measure of confidence surged through her. She knew that she would be free from visitors for the day; that was the only other entrance to the property that neighbours, contractors, or meandering tourists would use. Since the Darling River Run had been promoted as a destination, it hadn't been unusual to have the occasional tourist or grey nomie in a motorhome turn up in the back blocks of the property looking for a free campsite.

Resolve filled her as she called to the dogs and quickly rode back towards the homestead. After a hundred metres, the road curved, and she would be out of sight of the main road. The paddocks between the road and the second gate near the tourist accommodation were bare of trees to impede the view from the road. Once she'd rounded the curve and was out of sight of the public road, her pedalling slowed, and Cat began to relax again.

This morning had been a turning point for her. She was going to deal with the crap she'd been through. She would get out in the fresh air every day, and she was going to get better.

I am.

A little voice niggled at her.

How are you ever going to get over that, Caitríona? You don't even know who it was.

She knew she'd been careless and too trusting and put herself in a stupid position. What had happened was entirely her fault. She couldn't blame anyone else.

No brains.

It didn't matter. No one should ever have to go through what had happened. She probably wouldn't go back even if Harry accepted her proposal.

Cat rolled her eyes. She didn't have her phone and hadn't even got the laptop out to check her email yet. She didn't want to know; not when she didn't know what she wanted to do. If her proposal was accepted, she'd have to return to Sydney and have a couple of interviews before her honours program began.

And there was no way she could do that; the way she felt now, she would never go back to Sydney. Until she knew who it was—and she doubted if she ever would—she didn't want to have anything to do with any of those people again. She couldn't blame them; the situation she got herself into had been all her fault.

Nausea churned in her stomach as the events of the night—those she could remember—jerked through her mind like a movie in slow motion. She gagged, stopped the bike and jumped off, bending double at the side of the track as her breakfast moistened the red dust.

Cat groaned, and as her heart thundered in her chest, she lifted her arm and wiped her mouth clean with the back of one hand. It simply reinforced for her that she was home to stay; if she reacted this way to thoughts of the pleasant and happy beginning of the night at the *Singapore Sing Song bar*, what would happen to her if she remembered the rest of the night?

Chapter 10
Singapore Sing Song Bar - Newtown – August.

Caitríona hadn't been to the *Singapore Sing Song* Bar yet, even though it was within walking distance of their unit. It had been a few months since she'd been down this end of King Street. She decided to walk down but went out through the main entrance of the apartment block and avoided the back lane. She knew that as the night passed, the tone of Newtown would change, with drunken patrons spilling out of bars, drug deals being done, and frequent fights in the street, and it would be much safer to get an Uber home.

She could share a ride with Jilly and Deb although she wasn't sure where Deb lived; the barista hadn't been out with her before. As well as working at the coffee shop, Deb worked a couple of other part-time jobs, as well as doing her degree at night.

Cat strode along through the crowds milling around King Street in search of a pub, cocktail den, dance club or brewery; there was a place to fill every need. Maccas was packed with young people, some of whom would no doubt end up partying in the laneway at the back of their unit later in the night.

Nothing could dampen her mood. She was ready to have a big night and put the stressful and busy past weeks behind her with a few cocktails and a lot of dancing. Her limbs were loose, and she smiled as she made her way to the new bar. Relaxation filled her in anticipation of the night ahead. As much as she disliked living in the city, the nightlife was great. The closest pub to *Ceann Mara* station was a hundred kilometres away. The occasional B&S ball had provided entertainment when she was in her late teens, but they were few and far between these days due to liquor licensing and insurance. COVID had also put a cap on the number of people who could attend. The local ball along the Darling had been an institution for many years. Community-funded, the committee had raised money for rural charities, but Mum had said that they could no longer afford to run it.

Jilly had texted when they closed the coffee shop and arranged for them to meet her at the bar at nine-thirty. There was a queue at the entry of the bar for ID checking, and Cat joined the end of it, rubbing the goosebumps that rose on her bare arms as the cold southerly buster swirled around the street.

Her ID was cleared by the security guy with a wink as he looked down at the front of her skintight T-shirt.

'You'd win, gorgeous,' he said.

'Win what?'

She frowned.

'A wet T-shirt contest. Shame there isn't one.' His appreciative chuckle followed her into the cool interior of the bar. Maybe the tight-cropped T-shirt hadn't been a wise move. Not when it was cold, and every bit of her was responding to the chill wind. Cat folded her arms over the white crop top until she warmed up.

Jilly had said, 'Go spangly', so she'd worn her tight red jeans and found the cropped T-shirt with sparkles around the neck. It did leave a bit too much bare skin above her jeans.

Scarlet whistled when she came out of her room. 'Woo hoo, look at you. You look good, Cat.'

'Not too much?'

'No, you look great. I would kill for your hair and skin.'

'What? These bloody freckles? You can have them!'

'Your skin is beautiful. Your hair looks great too. I like it out like that.'

Cat grinned. 'I found some gunk in the bathroom, and it fluffed up nicely.' Her hair was the bane of her life. Tight red curls that looked like an eighties perm from all the music videos she'd seen. 'This top's not too tight? Or short?'

'It's perfect. I wish I was coming out too. I'll probably still be up working when you get home.'

'I doubt it. We'll be late.' Cat picked up the small plastic bag that held the front door key, her license, credit card and a fifty-dollar note. She slipped the plastic bag into the tight flat pocket near the zip on the front of her jeans, easy for her to get at, and impossible for anyone to access without her knowledge. Her phone went into the other front pocket.

Scarlet stood up and hugged her. 'Have a great night. You deserve it.'

'You do too. I'll see if Jilly's up for tomorrow night too. I'll let you know in the morning. If she's busy, you and I can go out.'

'I've got an early meeting in the morning, remember.'

'Okay, good luck with it. I'll see you when you get back.'

As she walked into the bar, Cat wrinkled her nose as a

sweet, almost sickly, smell surrounded her. It was white lotus pumping through the air conditioning. Soft music was playing in the front bar, but she could hear the music pumping from the back of the establishment. She walked past a bar that ran the whole side of the long, narrow room; all the stools were taken already. Her eyes widened as she took in the array of spirit bottles that went from the back of the bar at counter level almost to the ceiling. Bottles of every colour and shape provided a bright kaleidoscope reflecting the light from the lights above that swept the bar like spotlights every few seconds. That'd be hard to take if you had too much to drink.

She wondered if the selection of bottles was just for show, but as she walked past, one of the girls behind the bar reached up a third of the way and pulled down a bottle of something bright green.

She grinned, remembering the last time she and Scarlet had gone out for a big night about six months ago. Scarlet—being the chemist she was—had the bright idea of a "colours night", trying different coloured cocktails and they'd both overindulged. The colours had been vivid, and she could still recall the thumping headache she had after trying a variety of cocktails and spirits. Tonight, she'd be more sensible and stick to the one spirit.

Cat stepped into the back bar, and as she headed towards a vacant booth in the far right-hand corner, she heard her name called.

'Cat! Cat, we're over here.' She turned with a frown and then smiled as she realised it was her uni friends; it was too early for Jilly and Deb to have arrived yet. A group of students from uni sat around a circular table in the centre of the room. Some from her year she knew well, Rod Barnes, Gavin Symons and

Esther Griggs, were in her tutorial group, and she also recognised a couple of first- and second-year students, but there were three of four unfamiliar faces around the table tonight.

'Hey, guys! What's happening?' she said.

'We're having a last big one before the final exams start. You've finished, haven't you?' Gavin asked.

'Hi, Gav. No exams for me. The units I took this year are all assessment-based, thank goodness. The last two years were bad enough.'

'Lucky us, hey, Cat.' Rod lifted his glass. 'We picked the right subjects.'

She and Rod had worked together closely over the past three years, as they both had a Western Downs station background and a strong interest in the Murray Darling. He was doing an honours year too.

'We did, and it sure feels good,' she said. 'Finished your proposal?'

'Yep.' He nodded. 'A big night tonight.'

'Have you heard from the dreaded Harry?' She knew Rod was worried about his proposal. She'd offered to have a look at it with him, but he'd declined her offer.

'No, not yet, have you?'

'No. We'll just have to be patient, I guess.'

'What do you want to drink, Cat?' Gavin interrupted. 'You're looking hot tonight. Come and sit next to me.'

She pulled a face at him; Gav was always trying it on; they'd been good mates for a while, but when he'd got a bit too handsy one night at the uni bar a few months back, she'd pulled back. 'Thanks, but I'm meeting a couple of friends; they're on their way now. I'm going to grab that vacant booth before it gets nabbed. But I'll come and have a drink with you *all* later, for sure. End-of-semester celebration drink,' she said, tilting her head to the side as Ariana Grande's *Focus* came through the speakers. 'Great music.'

'Make sure you do,' Gavin said. 'All work and no play make Cat a dull girl.' He never handled his drink well, and his words were already slurring. Maybe she wouldn't come back over. Gavin held her eyes for too long, and she looked away. 'How about a dance later?' She caught a glimpse of his suggestive hand gesture from the corner of her eye.

A couple of other guys she didn't know grinned, but a firm voice interrupted their chuckles.

'Settle down, Symons.' The guy sitting back in his chair caught her eye as he spoke. He was one she didn't know. He nodded and lifted his glass to her.

'Hi, Cat. I'm Rohan. I don't think we've met before.'

'Hi, Rohan. What course are you in?'

'Ag and Environmental Science. I'm a latecomer. I switched over from Canberra Uni a couple of months back.'

'Third year too?'

'Yes. I've just applied for an honours year here.'

Cat nodded. 'Me too. And hey, welcome to Sydney,' she said. He locked eyes with her, and a tug of attraction hit as their gazes met and held. 'Is that a slight trace of an Irish accent I hear?'

'To be sure, it is. You have a good ear.'

She smiled and walked around the table to stand behind his chair. 'I've got an Irish background too. Our station is called *Ceann Mara.*'

'The head of the sea,' he said.

'Yes, the furthest point where the sea reaches up in the bay, my dad tells me.'

Nice. And a good looker in great shape too.

'So, Cat would be short for Caitríona, not Catherine.'

'Spot on,' she said with a smile. 'Anyway, good to meet you, Rohan. Have a great night. Don't let these guys lead you astray.'

'I wasn't going to stay long with these fellas, they're on the tear tonight. But now something tells me to stay.' He smiled and the fair skin around his blue eyes crinkled into laughter lines. 'Love the club, love the music, and love that white lotus.' He held her gaze, and when he smiled, that tug of attraction moved lower.

Hmm. Maybe the night would get interesting. It had been a while since she'd had a casual relationship. A night spent in the company of a good-looking guy with similar interests was tempting.

'Maybe we could have a chat later?' she said.

'For sure,' Rohan said. 'And a dance?'

Rohan was altogether too good-looking for her comfort. Thick dark lashes fanned around those piercing eyes. The pleasant tingle spread through her body. 'I'll look forward to it.'

The music vibrated in Cat's chest as she headed over to the bar and ordered a cocktail. She was aware of Gavin's scowl and Rohan's eyes on her when she turned and carried her cocktail, sliding into the padded seat of the vacant booth. Rohan raised his glass with a wide grin, and when she sat down, she raised hers and smiled back.

The first sip went down like a dream, and she knew she'd have to pace herself, especially if she was going to go out tomorrow night too. The lime and mango cocktail tasted like a Splice ice block. It would be easy to drink it too quickly.

Cat sipped slowly as she waited for Jilly and Deb. She

avoided looking over at Rohan, but when she finally did, he was engrossed in conversation with one of the other guys she didn't know. Despite the thumping music, there weren't many on the dance floor yet. But as she watched, Gavin moved across to the table next to his and tapped Esther on the shoulder. She smiled up at him. He held out his hand, and they went to the dance floor. Cat wondered idly if Gav had put the hard word on Esther yet.

Her three years in Sydney had educated her. Growing up on the station and going to boarding school ensured that she had led a sheltered life in an environment where she knew strangers were few. She had gone to a couple of B&S balls in her late teens and had seen what went on in the paddocks, with people hooking up and disappearing into swags, and in the back of utes, but as she'd usually travelled in a group, she'd tended to stay with people she knew and had always gone home. Her first year at university had brought out her wild side. After six months of fairly continuous drinking and quite a few episodes of casual sex, she woke up to herself and realised that she didn't really enjoy it. It was more of a novelty, and it was about that time that she started to focus on her university studies. There had been a couple of relationships in the years since then, and some strong friendships formed, but Cat had been totally focused on her studies for the past twelve months.

She took another sip of her cocktail, wondering where Jilly and Deb were. She looked up and noticed those dark eyes on her again, and a shiver of anticipation ran down her back. She would make sure she had a dance with him later. He was a very attractive guy. She wondered why she hadn't noticed him around on campus.

Fifteen minutes later, she finished her cocktail and glanced at her phone a few times. Tempted to text Jill, she resisted knowing they probably had a late finish at the coffee shop, but not late enough since they still hadn't arrived at the bar by nine-thirty. Her fingers hovered over the screen ready to text, but her phone buzzed in her hand before she could type. It was a text from Jilly, and disappointment flooded through Cat.

Not going to be able to make it, babe. Got sideswiped on the way home. Only just back from the police station. Both okay. Fair bit of damage, got breathalysed. Luckily no drinks had. Don't feel like a night out. Hope you find someone to hang with. Tomorrow night. Jilly.

She quickly typed a reply.

Sorry. Hope you're okay. Some friends here. Will have an early one. Cat.

Well, that was a bummer. Cat looked at her empty glass and over at the table of her uni friends. There was a lot of hilarity and laughter coming from the table, and a couple of girls had taken two of the spare seats, but there was still one left. She went across to the bar and ordered a second cocktail; she'd make this her last drink, have a chat for a while, have a dance with the luscious Rohan, and head home.

The room was crowded, and she was jostled as she tried to make her way across to the table. She looked up as she got closer; Rohan's eyes were on her, and a slight smile tilted his lips. Magically, the chair beside him was now empty, and she bit back a grin.

Looked like the attraction was mutual. Wouldn't hurt to relax for tonight.

'Hey, guys, do you mind if I join you? My friends, Jilly and Deb, had a car accident on the way home from work.'

'Are they okay?' Gavin asked.

'Apparently, but they didn't feel like coming out.'

'Well, pull up a pew. Cat, good to have you join us,' a voice said beside her.

She turned to her left and moved back slightly; Rohan's cheek was almost touching hers. An enticing smell of an expensive cologne tickled her nose.

'Sorry,' he said. 'I didn't think you were turning this way. I was about to tell you I'm pleased you joined us.'

'Me too,' she said. 'How about that dance?'

His eyes crinkled in a smile; he pushed his beer away, got to his feet, and took her hand. 'Have you got a bag?'

She shook her head. 'No. Phone, money, and unit key get tucked into my jeans. I've had too many friends who've lost bags at bars and nightclubs.'

'Sounds like you have a very social life,' Gavin interrupted.

Cat chuckled as they made their way through the crowd. She had to speak loudly to make herself heard. 'Would you believe this is the first night I've been out in over six months?'

'Well, we'd better make it a good one, hey?'

Rohan's smile sent a pleasant shiver down her back.

Chapter 11
Ceann Mara Station - Tuesday morning.

Cat got back on the bike and whistled for the dogs. The two new kelpies kept their distance but followed Jonty. They were well-trained and didn't run off, keeping slightly ahead of her bike for the kilometre back towards the homestead. On her way out to the mailbox, she'd followed the road past the campground straight to the main gate on the public road, but this time, she stopped, deciding to take the left turn onto the back track that approached the homestead from the direction of the airstrip. It would be a bit more exercise, and when the dirt got soft at the river end of the airstrip, she could walk her bike the short distance back to the shed. Her leg muscles were pulling as she pedalled; the lack of activity over the past three weeks had certainly taken its toll. Even when she was working and going to lectures, Cat exercised regularly, a morning jog when the weather was kind, and a Pilates class in the union building at the university a couple of times a week.

Once the dogs were through, she closed the gate and rode along the levee towards the airstrip. The wind was picking up even more now, and she checked that the mail was secure in the basket. She rode along the levee bank and then pushed herself hard along the two kilometres of the flat, hard surface of the airstrip. Her calves were burning, and she was out of breath when she reached the end near the river.

But her heart was pumping, and her mind was clear; she felt alive for the first time in three weeks. She didn't want to go back into the house yet, and that was a small emotional victory. Reaching the fork in the track that led to the house and back to the main road, she decided to look around the new campground. Dad had sounded proud of Mum when he was talking about it that night before she left for home, so she'd check it out. She'd only given it a cursory glance on the way to the mailbox.

She wheeled the bike to the side of the first building and put it against the wall out of the wind. It sounded like Dad's forecast was right. The wind was getting worse; there was already brown dust on the plastic cover over the mail.

Cat widened her eyes as she walked through the area that had previously been a paddock full of weeds. She hadn't realised how much work they had done this year. There were eight powered sites with concrete pads beside power poles and a privacy screen of trees between each site. The trees were a good size, obviously thanks to the good winter rain this year. As she walked through the sites, two parrots hung upside down from the branches and squawked at her cheekily as if to say, this is our space. Fairy lights adorned the right-hand side of the first four sites, which were arranged in a T-shape. The other three faced a bar with the words **"Sunset Bar"** burned into a piece of old timber, a bit of Dad's handiwork. The bar was decked out like a tropical bar with coconut palm fringing along the top, although there was nothing in it except a couple of empty shelves. She guessed when the season was on, there would be coasters and glasses, and knowing Mum, the inevitable vase of flowers.

She walked along the flagstones between the bar and the camp kitchen, which had been there the last time she visited. Back then, there the structure had simply been four posts and a roof with an old, rusted gas fridge inside. Now, it was closed in on three sides, with new cane furniture, a couple of prints on the wall, and a brand-new electric refrigerator, microwave, sink, and hotplate on the new black Laminex benchtops.

Wow. Pretty classy.

Cat picked up one of the brochures from a coffee table that sat between the two cane sofas. It was a shame that the area was partially open to the weather as the brown dust was going to get into everything. Maybe when the wind had gone, she could come up and help wipe it out.

She flicked through the brochure, *Outback Beds on the River Run*, and was surprised to see how many properties along the Darling were offering the same sort of facility. There was also a brochure for their campground, *Riverbeds*, slick and glossy with great photography. As well as the eight powered sites and the upmarket amenities, camp kitchen, and fire pit, she knew there was unpowered camping around the billabong and a couple of kilometres along the river, too. Something else that the volunteers apparently looked after was emptying the bins, providing firewood, and keeping an eye on the campers who booked the sites a few kilometres away from the homestead.

It was an inviting area, and Cat could imagine tourists sitting here, watching the sun set over the billabong and having a few drinks. Mum had mentioned in one of her emails a few months back that she and Dad often wandered down for an evening drink and that they'd met people from all walks of life. Apparently, the powered sites had been in great demand all winter.

Mum had tried to run the new business the first year herself but had soon realised it was impossible; she'd heard about another station where they offered a volunteer program. With so many grey nomads on the road looking for somewhere to stay and something to fill their time, they'd implemented a scheme where volunteers would come and stay for a month at a time, doing tasks like checking people in, cleaning the toilets, keeping the camp kitchen going, cutting firewood for the fire pit, and lighting the fire every night.

It looked like it was really well underway. There was a new amenities block built out of corrugated iron, and out of curiosity, Cat walked over and opened the door. It was neatly tiled, and on the wall a rustic benchtop was formed out of old timber with a vanity in the middle and the bronze taps above likely retrieved from somewhere on the property, perhaps in one of the woolsheds.

One property up the river ran tours to a historical part of their property where there was an old store where the paddle steamers used to call in during the late 1800s. Cat had chuckled when Dad complained about it.

'Not as big as the store that our Samuel built in the 1860s or thereabouts,' he said. 'We'll clean it up and open ours up one day. Maybe a job we could do together when you're home in a uni break.'

Maybe I could start on that now. She needed something to focus on. Cleaning up the store half a kilometre upriver from the homestead would be something she could focus on; it would be good therapy.

If she wasn't going back to Sydney, she needed a purpose, and seeing what Mum and Dad had already done gave her some ideas for expanding the historical side to the tourist development.

As Cat pedalled back to the house, the wind picked up, and her curls tangled together and flew across her eyes. She brushed a hand across her eyes and slowed down, paying attention to where she was riding.

Cat was thoughtful as she headed back to the house.

All things happen for a reason. That had been a favourite saying of Dad's mother, Grandma Daph.

Maybe she should look at what had happened in Sydney as a catalyst for change.

Ceann Mara was a very different station from the one she'd grown up on where it was just the girls running wild and Dad and the station hands working on the property. Maybe when Mum and Dad came home tomorrow, she would sit down with them and see if they'd be interested in her helping out.

No more city, but she wasn't going to tell them that she wasn't going back. That would mean too much explaining, and Cat wasn't ready to go there. Her hands started to shake as she thought about what had happened, and she closed her eyes, pushing the fear away.

Thinking about it isn't going to help me get better.

Maybe some more days like this, out in the fresh air focusing on external things and not on the darkness inside her, would help her heal.

She put the dogs back in the pen and looked up at the sky. The sun was high, and she realised it was after lunchtime, and she was actually hungry. She'd surprised herself by eating most of the breakfast Mum left out for her, and knowing Mum, she was sure there would be more food in the fridge waiting for her.

Cat had enjoyed being out in the fresh air, and it had made a difference being there by herself, making her push her boundaries. She put the bike back in the shed and carried the mail over to the house, took the key out of her pocket, and unlocked the back door.

As she stepped into the coolness of the dim hallway, the house was silent. She put the mail on the table beside the door before closing and locking it again. She'd make a sandwich, get a drink, and take a late picnic lunch to the river.

When she was a teenager, Dad had built a seat not far from the water tanks and the shed that housed the farm vehicles and the Cessna. It was close enough to the house that if she got panicky, she could cut across the backyard and be inside in a couple of minutes.

Cat went via the kitchen and grabbed a bottle of water out of the fridge. Sure enough, there was a packet of sandwiches on the bottom shelf that she hadn't noticed this morning. She took the packet out and smiled. Egg and lettuce; Mum knew her well. She unlocked the door and decided to leave it closed but unlocked; a smile crossed her face when she realised that that was a small step forward.

A small brown snake lay at the bottom of the back steps sunning itself. Cat picked up the stick that was always by the door, lifted it and flicked the small snake across the yard. It slithered into the long grass and headed towards the river.

Another smile tilted her lips as she thought of her sister, Shea, who had a pathological fear of snakes. Maybe she'd call her sisters tonight and have a chat. Tell them she'd come home.

Another step forward.

She scanned the back garden for any other reptiles, but the lawn was clear as she walked across to the gate that opened onto the river path. Mum's garden was looking dry; she'd put the sprinklers on for her when she got back. Even if the wind was strong, some moisture would be retained.

The wind carried heat now, holding the promise of the summer heat to come. It had picked up even more, and Cat gazed up at the sky. Her eyes widened as she saw the brown dust building in the sky to the west. It would be here in a couple of hours; at least, she knew all the windows were shut. She bit her lip as she walked past the shed and looked into the hangar where Dad kept the Cessna. They weren't coming home today.

Fear gripped her throat. The ease that had blanketed her in the last hour shrivelled up and died. She didn't know how she'd cope with being alone in the house in the dark.

Trying desperately to push the black fear away that clawed at her throat, Cat forced her feet to take her to the gate.

Chapter 12

Ceann Mara Station - Tuesday afternoon.

Opening the gate, Cat walked slowly along the short track that led to the western bank of the Darling River. The seat Dad had built years ago was still there beneath two large gum trees, even though it had been underwater in the flood two years ago. She took a deep breath and composed herself.

Leaning down, she checked beneath the timber seat for cobwebs and spiders and surveyed the ground between the seat and the river.

All was clear.

She sat down, leaned forward and put her head in her hands.

No one knew she was here. Mum and Dad would be back tomorrow, and then she wouldn't be alone in the house; that would ease her sleep, hopefully.

Three black cockatoos flew over the river, and she focused on the languorous flapping of their wings until they disappeared around the bend. Her hands had stopped shaking; being out in the fresh air had done her a world of good, and she began to hope that she might be making her way out of this black hole.

She was traumatised by the events after the night at the *Singapore Sing Song Bar*, but it was more from the thought of how foolish she had been, and a lot of it came down to the fact that she couldn't forgive herself for putting herself in that situation. She should have gone straight home when Jilly texted her. Hindsight is a fine thing.

When Cat had had problems in her teens, or when she'd been worried about anything, and there had been a few times she'd had some issues to deal with, she'd been strong and able to deal with them.

Like the time she'd had unprotected sex with one of the Carruthers boys at a B& S ball and missed a period.

She'd managed to get through that, and when her period finally arrived late, she'd learned a good lesson.

She'd had a few relationships since then, but nothing more than casual friendships. Focusing on her uni studies had put Cat's social—and sex—life on hold for a couple of years.

Now here she was at almost twenty-four years old and as useless as a baby kitten because of one night gone wrong.

What a waste of time going to uni had been. She should have stayed at the station and worked with Dad; he would have loved that. She could still see his face when she'd headed off to uni three years ago. He'd been sad, but he had encouraged all the girls to follow their dreams.

What was her dream? Did she want to do an honours year?

Maybe, but she certainly wasn't going to if it meant living in Sydney.

But then, if her thesis proposal was accepted, maybe she could go back for the interview—or do it online—and then complete her research externally. Possibilities began to flourish in her mind, and she welcomed them.

Maybe she'd missed the opportunity of an interview; later today, she'd boot up her laptop and finally check her emails.

Maybe.

If she had, that would decide for her, and she'd get Scarlet to pack up her stuff and send it home. Or maybe she could drive via Newcastle and pick up Roisin, and they could do it together. Cat leaned forward and put her hands over her eyes.

She had many decisions to make.

She had to decide where her future was going to be.

***

After lunch Logan followed the track from his house to the west until he spotted the river ahead; he'd only been down there once when he first looked at the land, and he vaguely remembered where the house and sheds were on the property on the other side.

He stood under the shade of a large gum tree and looked across the narrow strip of green water. The waterway was narrow compared to the Queensland rivers and estuaries where he'd grown up and worked. But no matter how narrow it was, there was no way he'd swim across; he'd seen too many snakes in rivers in his lifetime.

There was an old shed on his place that had survived when the original house had been burned down a few years back; when Logan had taken possession, he had been surprised to find the many tools and fencing wire the previous owners had left behind.

One thing he had been pleased to see was a small wooden punt that he could use to get across the river if he ever needed to.

The alternative was a hundred-and-twenty-kilometre round drive to Tilpa and cross the bridge to the western side of the river. Or he could go back north to Louth and cross it there.

Thinking about the shed gave him the idea of checking out

the fencing materials in there. Maybe he wouldn't need help after all; there could be something useful in the fencing stuff left behind.

He'd go back and take a look, and then his next move would be to try to get the neighbour's phone number from the rural store.

Before he went back to his house, he'd check out the property across the river. The sun glinted off a roof not far from the edge of the river, and in the distance, a stand that looked like it held water tanks rose above the tree line. By the look of things, the house mightn't be too far from the river.

Logan lifted his rifle and peered through the telescopic sight. Yes, there was a large shed behind the water tank stand, with another small shed beside it. He swivelled the rifle to the left, and a stone house with about eight chimneys came into view.

Yep, landed gentry with a place like that. He moved the rifle further and nodded. A lush green lawn and a colourful garden ran along the side of the huge house.

As he peered through the scope, the screech of a cockatoo and a movement near the riverbank caught his attention. He moved the rifle to the left and jumped, not expecting to see a person in his sights.

The sun glinted on the bright red hair of a woman sitting on a seat at the top of the bank on the other side of the river. Logan hadn't noticed the seat before; he'd been too busy looking for the house. As he watched, she leaned forward and put her head in her hands, and he felt a bit like a voyeur. He went to lower the rifle, but the woman must have sensed his movement. She jumped to her feet, staring at him, one hand to her mouth, the other holding a hat. She was close enough that he could see her eyes widen and that she looked terrified.

Bloody hell. Of course she would be; he was holding a rifle, and it probably looked like he was going to shoot.

He dropped the gun to his side and lifted his hand to wave in reassurance, but she'd already turned and fled. She was running away from the river and was too far away for him to call out.

Good one, Wainwright. A great first impression for the neighbours.

Logan shrugged and turned to go back to his house.

He'd have to head to the O'Byrne's sooner than later now and make an apology. He'd ask about the fencing hinges at the same time.

***

The screech of a cockatoo broke into Cat's thoughts as she sat there with her hands over her eyes. She sat up and blinked; the afternoon light was bright, and she squinted as her vision cleared. The wind had eased slightly, and the surface of the river ruffled only occasionally as a strong gust blew down the high banks. She watched the cockatoo as it soared up into the sky, along the tops of the trees and then disappeared into a thick stand of bush on the property where Gary, her uncle, and his wife Elise used to live.

There was movement in the bush directly across from the old tree where the rope swing used to hang over the water. They'd had a small punt in those carefree days, and Cat and her sisters had pulled themselves across to the other side to *Guntana* in *Ding-a-Ling*. She had forgotten about those days; it had been a long time ago, and so much had happened since then.

Her gaze came down the tree trunk and ran along the branch. She remembered where the rope had been attached, and sure enough, the last remnants of a frayed knot were just visible.

A shadow filled her vision, and her mouth dried as her gaze settled on a tall, dark-haired man standing beside the tree.

There shouldn't be anyone over there. Fire had destroyed her uncle's house a few years back. They'd moved to the coast, and as far as Cat knew, Gary and Elise still owned the land.

She kept still, knowing that she'd be standing out so obviously in the clearing where she was sitting on the seat at the edge of the property. The man looked over and seemed to be looking over her head. As she stared back, she could see he was holding a rifle, looking across the river through the telescopic sight at where she was sitting—a target on the seat.

Cat gasped and jumped up. She ran away from the river, adrenaline churning through her blood.

Chapter 13

Newtown - August.

'Cat did what?' Jilly stared at Scarlet over the coffee machine.

'She left. She's gone.'

'What do you mean gone? Gone where?'

'Home. Home to their cattle station.'

'She can't be gone. I was texting her at the bar last night.'

'Weren't you with her?'

'No, we had a car accident on the way home and I texted her to say we were a no-show. She said there were some friends from uni there and she'd stay for a while and have an early night because she was going out with you tonight.'

'We were.'

'And I said I'd come too. Deb has something else on. So, what happened? When I saw you walk in, I thought you were here to get her the hangover-cure-coffee and a bacon and egg roll.'

Scarlet shook her head. 'I bought bacon and eggs last night ready for her today. But I had an early meeting with my supervisor, and I didn't get home until about eleven, but when I got home, I noticed her car wasn't in the carport. It was there when I went out, so I assumed she'd gone shopping or something.'

'So how do you know she's gone home?'

'When I went upstairs, I found a note from her on the table. I came to see if you knew anything. Did she call in to see you on her way?'

'No, I haven't seen her since yesterday afternoon. I wonder what's happened.' Jilly frowned as she finished frothing the milk.

'She didn't text you this morning?' Scarlet asked.

'No. I haven't talked to her since about nine last night. It's strange that she left you a note and didn't call you.'

'She left me an envelope with some cash for her rent. I texted her straight away to see what was wrong. I didn't ring because I knew she'd be driving. I thought it must be pretty bad for her to just take off like that. Like her parents are sick or something. So, I sat down straightaway and sent her a text, telling her to drive safe and call when she got there, and as soon as I pressed send, I heard her phone ding in her room. I opened the door, and her phone was on the floor next to the bed. I can't believe she forgot to take it. It's just not her.'

'Cat is absolutely addicted to her phone. She makes me laugh.'

'She is. There's no way she would've left it; even if she got in her car without it, she would've realised that she didn't have it. She still uses Google Maps on her phone to get out of the city. She doesn't get home that much. As far as I know, she hasn't been home for over a year. We were talking about me going home with her in a couple of weeks. If she'd just waited until I got home, I could've gone with her this weekend.'

'It's really strange that she just took off like that. I think something must have happened with her family and she just took off by the sound of things.'

Scarlet hesitated and then put her hands together in front of her chest. 'And the craziest thing? She's stripped her bed and I had a look in the laundry. The sheets weren't there. And she had a big housekeeping blitz last night. We were laughing about it. Before she went out, she stripped the bed and washed and dried her sheets and towels, and then remade her bed.'

'Did you hear her come home last night?'

'No. I ended up going out late to pick up the groceries and then went to Maccas on the way home. I was out until about midnight, and I knew she wouldn't be home, so I went straight to bed. I think I heard her come home not long after that, but I didn't get up. I set the alarm because I had to get up early and went out like a light.' Scarlet shrugged. 'I guess I assumed she got lucky and went home with someone, and that's why she was so late. I wasn't worried until I came home and read the note.'

'What did her note say exactly?'

Jilly waited while Scarlet pulled a crumpled envelope from her pocket. She read it aloud after Scarlet handed it to her.

'Going home. Will call you. Cat.'

She shook her head. 'That's so out of character. So abrupt. You'd think she'd say more about what had happened.'

'And her writing is really messy. It's hers, but it looks like she was in a real hurry when she wrote the note. I can't think of what she'd be doing. She ended up walking down to the bar to meet you guys.'

'And like I said, we didn't end up going.'

'I'm worried.'

'It's bizarre.'

'I just want to know that she's okay. That she hasn't been abducted or something.'

'Can you ring her at their station?' Jilly put the spoon on the side of the jug and poured the frothed milk.

'I've tried to Google the name. I've tried Kenmare and Kenmore and all the variations I can think of, but nothing comes up.'

'Wait there for a second, Scart. I'll just take these out to the table. Deb's not in yet; she had to go to the police station and do an accident report for her insurance.'

'What a day,' Scarlet muttered as Jilly took the coffee out to the table on the footpath.

'Can I make you a coffee?' Jilly said when she came back.

'Thanks.'

'How long would it take her to drive home?' Jilly poured milk into the jug and then frowned. 'Skinny cap for you?'

'Yes, please. And that's just it. I have no idea where the cattle station is, apart from in some isolated spot on the Darling River. I guess it might take a day or two.' Scarlet's voice held frustration. 'You'd never think we'd been sharing an apartment for three years.'

'I don't know either. She talks about the place, but I've never asked for exactly where it is. I just know it's on the Darling River too, and that's a huge river that goes from Queensland to the Murray.'

'And do you know how long the Darling River is? It covers about half of the state, I think!' Jilly poured the frothed milk into two coffee cups.

'I wonder if we could get her home details from the uni?'

'It's Saturday; there'll be nobody in admin.'

'I'll just have to wait and see if she calls to tell us to say she's got there safely. I can post her phone out to her. But you know, if she's forgotten her phone, will she know our phone numbers?' Scarlet asked.

Jilly looked around; there was no one waiting at the counter. 'Come and sit down, and we'll brainstorm.' She picked up the coffees she'd made and led Scarlet to the table closest to the register. 'But that sheets thing is really strange. Why would she take her sheets home if that's what she's done? Unless she's packed up and she's not coming back. Was anything else missing?'

Scarlet shook her head. 'No, apart from the stripped bed, her room looked the same as ever. Her clothes and stuff are still on the shelves.'

'It's just so unlike Cat.'

'Do you think we should report it or something?' Scarlet bit her lip, and Jilly reached out and touched her arm.

'Who to? And report what? We know she's gone because she left this note telling you she did. I guess we have to wait for her to contact us.'

'She'll know my uni email address, so that's one thing. She can email me. And I'll email hers. I'm probably overreacting, but I just have this strange feeling that something's not right.'

Jilly nodded. 'Look, the coffee shop's closed tomorrow, so I'll come round in the morning and see if you've heard anything.'

'Thanks, Jilly, appreciate it. I'll head home now. I'll do some Googling of her family name, and property names. See if I can find a phone number.'

'Okay, Scart, take care. I'll see you in the morning.'

'Bye.'

Jilly stared after her, worry niggling at her as Scarlet left.

Chapter 14

Ceann Mara Station - Darling River - dawn, Wednesday.

Caitríona woke with a jerk. She lay still and silent, not even brave enough to turn her head to see what time it was. She listened hard; her eyes squeezed shut. She'd been here before; please, God, not again.

She lay in the pitch darkness, enveloped by an uneasy stillness in her room that seemed to magnify the lowing of a beast in a distant paddock. The absence of her parents from the homestead left her vulnerable, increasing her growing panic. Unsure if she was awake or having another nightmare, she strained to identify the source of the unsettling feeling that was like a weight on her chest.

Maybe it had been one of the dogs barking?

Maybe it had been a branch falling on the roof?

Maybe it had been someone stepping on the creaking stair outside her room as they came to kill her.

A chill ran down her spine, but she refused to give in to the shiver. Fear gripped her entire body; she needed to use the bathroom, but she wasn't game to move a muscle.

As she lay there in the darkness holding her breath,

listening for a presence in the room, it was impossible to hear anything because of the blood pounding in her ears. An eerie stillness filled her room as if an intruder waited in the darkness beside the bed. Gradually the thumping in her ears stopped and all she could hear was the haunting howl of the wind outside.

Not again. Please God, not again.

How had he found her?

Was it the man from across the river?

Uncertainty gnawed at her, even though logically she knew there could be no one there in the dark. But she was unable to dismiss the sense of a presence in the room. Or in her mind.

Locked doors and windows offered no reassurance.

Cat lay motionless, but as dawn began to break, the faint pink light only accentuated the shadows. Squeezing her eyes shut, she waited for the slash of a knife or a shot ringing out as the image of a rifle pointing at her in the darkness was imprinted on her vision.

But there was nothing.

Each creak of the old homestead and gust of wind heightened her fear. Exhaustion eventually claimed her, and Cat drifted back into an uneasy sleep, haunted by the certainty that someone lingered in the shadows of her room.

Again.

Chapter 15
Ceann Mara Station - Wednesday morning.

Caitríona went for an early walk to the billabong and took the three dogs with her. She had finally talked herself into believing she had been dreaming last night. It had been the unexpected shock of seeing that guy on the other side of the river that had triggered it.

So, I overreacted, and my nightmares slammed in, she told herself as she walked along the levee bank near the airstrip. There was no way she was going near the riverbank today.

This time of the year, with snakes starting to appear, it was quite normal for someone on a station to carry a gun. She'd done it; Dad always had a rifle in the quad runner, so there was no need to get stressed by it. You never knew when you were going to come across an animal in distress, and often, on a property this size you could be a long way from the homestead.

What had thrown her was the way that the guy had stared at her. That had obviously brought back everything from last month and caused her nightmare. Goosebumps rose on her arms despite the warmth of the morning sun as the dream came back to her.

She had felt so helpless. Just like she'd been feeling the past few weeks.

Yesterday's howling wind was gone when she'd woke at eight to bright sunlight shining through the gap in the blinds. As she'd lain there terrified in the early hours, the westerly had increased again, and the creaks and groans of the old homestead, the tin roof rattling, and the guttering scraping against the stone had eventually broken the silence she had been enshrouded in.

Cat knew she'd got up three times to make sure that her doors and windows were locked, and the blinds were down completely, so those early morning horrors must have been a dream, triggered by the sight of that man.

There was no way anyone could've got into the house, and if they had, they would have had an ulterior motive, and she wouldn't be here to dwell on it this morning.

Cat knew she was going to have to do something to get rid of this fear that consumed her twenty-four hours a day. She would get online later today and look for some psychological articles, maybe some cognitive behaviour tricks she could focus on.

She was starting to miss her phone—perhaps that was a sign of her normal state of mind returning. In a way, not having it was a blessing. It meant no one from uni or any of her Sydney friends could call her. She was pretty sure none of them knew exactly where she lived, and even if they did, they certainly wouldn't have been able to find the number; the station wasn't in the white pages or any of the directories.

Only the name of the campground, *Riverbeds*, was in the public domain and no one would associate that with *Ceann Mara* unless they'd stayed here.

She picked up a stick and threw it into the billabong, and

the three dogs scrambled after it. The branches of half-submerged trees draped gracefully into the water. Even though the water was still brown from the floods earlier in the year, the slight morning breeze ruffling the surface was a pretty sight. Contentment settled in Cat's bones as she absorbed the peace; *Ceann Mara* was her place.

When the dogs tired of chasing sticks, she walked the loop around the billabong, past all the free campsites Mum had set up. She was surprised at what had been created. Each campsite was named after local fauna and fish; she walked past *Quoll, Echidna, Wallaby, Wombat* and *Possum*, smiling as she read *Lamprey, Cat Fish* and *Perch*. Dad must have had a say. He'd taught Cat and her sisters how to fish in the river.

She'd had no idea of the work that had been put in here while she was studying in Sydney. Flat areas were neatly mowed with long-drop toilets situated between every third campsite, garbage bins at the edge of each site near the track, plus a fire pit at each campsite with a pile of wood and kindling in a boxed area beside it. Mum had certainly gone all out to make decent campsites.

Cat wasn't sure how she felt about tourists staying at their station.

Ceann Mara was theirs. When she was growing up here, she'd found it hard when the contractors and the shearers came in. When there were contractors on-site, Mum wouldn't let them go down unsupervised to swim in the river. Now, she guessed, in the winter tourist season from about March to August, with the powered sites around the house and the dozen or so free campsites along the billabong and the river, she imagined the station traffic would be quite busy, and there would be a lot of people around. Times had certainly changed.

Cat took a deep breath as the low hum of a plane approaching signalled Mum and Dad's return. They were back way earlier than she'd expected; they must have left Broken Hill at daybreak. She was too far from the house to get back and change her clothes before they landed. She'd been out longer than she'd intended and didn't want them to see her in the sleeveless T-shirt and shorts she was wearing in an attempt to get some sun on her skin to heal the abrasions.

She looked down at her arms and closed her eyes as a memory of that morning slammed in.

Blood.

Blood everywhere.

By the time Cat got back to the road at the end of the airstrip, they had landed, and the plane had taxied to the shed. She hesitated and stood behind a big, spreading tree at the campsite closest to the house.

Damn. She bit her lip. Should she make a run for it and try to get in the back door before Mum got to the house? Or was there too much risk of encountering Mum on her way across the yard?

She decided to wait until Mum and Dad were in the house, and then she would sneak in the back way, and go up to her room and put on jeans and a long-sleeved shirt.

Calling the dogs to follow her, Cat walked through the *Quoll* campsite down to the river and sat on the high bank, taking a careful look across to the other side. Thankfully, there was no one there today.

Hopefully, Mum and Dad would guess she was out for a walk when they noticed the dogs were missing. She sat on the riverbank watching as a flock of birds skimmed along the top of the water, then created a flurry on the surface as they settled and started diving for fish. All three dogs slumped in the shade, panting from the heat, even though it was spring. It was going to be hot; the westerly wind yesterday had covered everything in dust and had brought the high temperatures of the centre in earlier than usual.

Cat waited for a quarter of an hour, giving her parents time to get inside. Knowing Dad, he would have gone to check the pumps and then see if the dogs had been fed. Mum would probably have a shower, and then it would be around time for smoko.

There was nothing for it; she'd suss out the homestead and try to sneak upstairs. Cat smiled as she remembered the time Erin had tried to climb up the big tree that had been near her bedroom window. That hadn't ended well, and Dad had chopped the tree down soon after.

Pushing herself to her feet, she brushed the leaves from the back of her shorts. 'Come on, Jonty, and you pair,' she said. 'Keep quiet and stay with me.' She must ask Dad what the new dogs' names were.

Things didn't go as planned. Cat walked along the edge of the tree line near the river until she was almost to the homestead. The dogs padded beside her. She stood next to the tree with the flood levels marked on it over the years and looked across to the yard at the back of the house.

All was quiet.

She set off quickly, keeping her head down, but as she got closer to the house, the three dogs took off barking loudly. Dad was obviously out and about somewhere.

The dogs ran past the pens and into the shed, so Dad must be over there. Now, all she had to do was avoid Mum at the house. She continued along the side fence, through the gate and headed for the open back door.

There was no sign of Mum. Taking a deep breath and folding her arms just in case she came face to face with Mum, she hurried up the back steps. Just as she reached the top step, her mother's voice came from behind her.

'Caitríona Mary O'Byrne, stop right there.' Her mother's voice held shock.

Cat hesitated and then took off down the hallway and up the stairs, raced into her bedroom, and slammed the door shut. She pulled off her clothes, went into the bathroom, and ran the shower, locking the bathroom door as soon as she turned the taps on.

Shit, shit, shit. She should've tried to cover up, but maybe Mum hadn't seen anything, but from the way she'd spoken to her, she must have.

Cat's whole body shook as she dried herself. She couldn't keep it a secret any longer; she had to tell someone what had happened.

Chapter 16

Ceann Mara Station - late Wednesday morning.

Cat's hands were shaking so much that she had to squeeze them in front of her chest to keep them from moving as she sat on the sofa in Dad's study. A weight descended on her shoulders, and she looked down; she was right on the edge and realised the pressure on her shoulders was Mum's arm.

'It's all right, sweetheart. Take a deep breath and calm down. We're here.'

Dad crossed to the bar that was in the corner of the room. He came back and handed her a small glass of brandy. Cat saw the worried glance he shared with Mum.

She tried to say, 'I hate brandy,' but her teeth were chattering so much she couldn't get the words out. When Mum saw the scabs on the back of her legs, Cat knew that she would have to tell her parents what had happened. The problem was being able to speak.

'Drink this, Cat.' Dad crouched in front of her and wrapped her fingers around the glass. 'I know you don't like brandy, but it'll help settle your nerves.' Dad's familiar aroma surrounded her, his fresh, soapy smell mixed with the leather of his good boots and belt, which he still wore from their visit to Broken Hill.

She leaned her forehead against his as she held the glass.

When Cat had taken off upstairs, Mum had yelled for Dad to come from the shed, and they had both been waiting in her room when she finally came out of the bathroom wrapped in a towel. Mum had taken some clothes from the chest and taken her back into the bathroom. Mum dressed her, sat her on the stool, and gently dried her hair with the towel.

Mum and Dad held her arms as they helped her downstairs to the study. Cat didn't say a word.

'Thank you,' she finally managed when Dad handed her the brandy. Cat leaned back, looked up at him, and lifted the glass to her lips. The spirit burned her throat as she gulped it down.

Anything to help.

Even her chin was shaking as reaction rolled through her in waves. Since her nightmare last night, she had been feeling better, but now she had gone back to the state she'd been in three weeks ago.

Now that she would have to explain what had happened, her whole body went into shock.

Dad stood by the desk that Mum had bought for his fortieth. It was the heaviest piece of furniture that Cat had ever helped carry. Mum and her four sisters had carried it in, so it was in pride of place here when Dad got up on the morning of his birthday. She'd never forget the look on his face. She had to focus on good memories like that now: Dad sitting there doing the accounts, his emails, and his family history research. Reading in front of the fire with her sisters. To the left of the desk was a double sofa that he had put in there for Mum to sit and keep him company. Cat remembered her mother sitting there knitting in the evenings.

Dad stood, pulled over a stool from the bar, and sat in front of the sofa. Mum's arm was tight around her shoulder.

'Caitríona, sweetheart, calm down. Take a deep breath. You're fine, you're home, we're here. We're not going to ask you to do anything or tell us anything that you don't want to, but you need to give us a clue at least.'

Cat nodded mutely and tried to drink again, but her hand shook too much to get the glass to her mouth. Mum took it from her and held it to her lips, and she tipped her head back and drank as much as she could. The liquid ran down her chin.

'Let that do its work,' Dad said quietly. He reached over and gently dabbed her chin with his handkerchief.

Mum turned to him. 'I've still got some of that herbal sedative that the doctor gave me when I had that episode a few years back. They're probably out of date, but Caitríona, it might help if you take something.'

'What episode, Mum?' Worry flashed through Cat, and the fear that held her in its grip lessened.

'Nothing that you need to worry about. I got through it, and I didn't need to take the sedative, but they're still there if we need to calm you down.'

'I'm all right,' she said.

'You're not all right.' Mum's arm was still around her shoulders.

Dad leaned forward, and she looked back at him. 'How long have you been doing it, Cat?'

'Doing what?' Cat's eyes widened with confusion.

'Cutting yourself.' Mum's voice trembled. 'We feel so bad that we didn't pick up that you were depressed. We should have come to Sydney to visit you. We let life get in the way.'

Cat gave a bitter laugh. '*I* didn't do it, Mum.'

'Sweetheart, you need to tell us the truth.' Dad reached out and took her hand. 'We won't judge you. We're here to help you. We're going to ring up Dr Morris in Broken Hill and fly you down as soon as you're up to it.'

'I don't need a doctor.' Cat shook her head, weariness making her limbs feel heavy. 'I'm not depressed, and I'm not having an episode.' She flicked a glance at Mum. 'I didn't do it, Mum. Have I ever lied to you? If I had been cutting myself, I would tell you. I've never understood why people do that.'

'Then you need to tell us what happened. Why you came home in such a state? You need to tell us why you've shut down.'

'I can't. I'm too embarrassed.' Cat tried to stand as the memory of that night slammed back. Mum gently pushed her back to the sofa. Dad jumped up and crouched beside her.

'It's all right, sweetie. We're here for you.'

Cat tried to speak. Goosebumps prickled her skin, and her vision was full of flashing silver lights. She felt like she was going to vomit. 'Mum, I feel faint, and I think I'm going to be sick,' she choked out.

Dad put her head between her knees. Mum hurried out of the room and returned quickly with a bucket she put on the floor between Cat's knees, but the nausea passed as quickly as it had come.

'It's okay, I'm sorry. I think I can sit up now without being sick.'

'Just take it slow. We don't want you passing out, sweetheart,' Dad said.

Again, her parents exchanged a look. Mum sat, and with her parents by her side, Cat felt slightly calmer.

'It was just such a shock. Never in a million years did I think it would happen to me.'

'What would happen, sweetheart?' Dad asked gently.

'I'm not going back to Sydney ever. I'm not going to do my honours year. A bachelor's degree will do.'

'Whatever you decide is best. It's up to you, but maybe it's not a good time to make a decision until you confront what's bothering you.' Dad stood, brought the decanter of brandy with him and topped up her glass again. The warmth from the previous drink had started to make its way through her body. This time, Cat managed to pick it up and slug it down herself.

'Okay,' he said when she put the glass down. 'So, can you tell us a little to start with? We knew there was something, but we were going to let you make your way through it. We probably made the wrong call.'

'I'll try to tell you, and you can maybe make sense of it.' She shook her head. 'But I doubt it. I can't.'

Dad sat down and took both her hands in his. 'So just tell us what you can.'

'Start at the beginning.' Mum squeezed her hand.

Cat sat back on the soft sofa as the brandy calmed her. 'Don't judge me, please. I don't think I did anything wrong. If I did, I didn't mean to. I had no idea what was going to happen.'

'Just take it slow.' Mum still held her hand. 'Tell us at your own pace. If you feel sick again, take a break.'

'Well, the night before I came home here, I went out.' Cat took a deep, shuddering breath and closed her eyes. 'I got ready at home. We were going out to celebrate the end of our work, but Scart wasn't finished, so I organised to go out with my friend, Jilly, who manages the coffee shop. We were going to a new bar in Newtown. I got there first. Her friend, Deb, was coming too. In the end, they didn't turn up because they had a car accident on the way home from work.'

'Were they hurt? Is that what's wrong?'

'No, Dad. They weren't hurt, and now that I've started, just listen.' A glimmer of frustration at being interrupted put Cat slightly more in control. 'I was all dressed up, and some other friends were there from uni. So, I decided to stay at the bar and have a couple of drinks. It was the first time I'd been out in months.'

'What were you drinking?' Dad asked.

'I had a couple of cocktails, that was all. No more. I had two drinks, Dad. *Two*. I didn't want to drink too much because Scarlet was home working, and we'd planned to go out the next night. When Deb and Jilly didn't arrive, I decided to go home early.' Cat's voice shook, and she swallowed a sob as the memory of the next morning came back to her. 'The last thing I remember is having my second drink at the table with my friends, and then nothing. I don't remember much after that. I have a vague memory of looking for the ladies' room.' Her voice shook, and she blinked as her eyes filled with tears. 'Then I was in bed and woke up once in the middle of the night. At least, I think I did, but my head was fuzzy, and the room was spinning, and then I went back to sleep. The sun was on my face when I woke up the next time.'

Dad's lips were set together as he stared at her. 'Where did you wake up?'

'I woke up in my bed. I don't know how I got there, and I don't know why I can't remember. I don't know whether I had some sort of episode and someone took me home. There were a couple of guys at the table who knew where I lived that could've taken me home, and my key was in my pocket. And when I managed to get up, the key was sitting on the table inside the front door. So, maybe someone took me home and'—she put her hands over her face and leaned forward— 'and put me in bed.'

Mum's voice shook, and her face was as white as Dad's. 'Do you know who—'

'No, I don't know who it was, but whoever it was, they, I think—' Her throat closed as she remembered lying there. 'I was hurting. Everywhere, and there was blood.'

'Oh, God, Cat. Why didn't you tell us when you came home instead of locking yourself in your room?' Mum's voice rose, and she started to cry.

Dad put his arm around Cat. 'You're doing well, sweetheart. Keep going.'

'I was assaulted, Mum, and I couldn't deal with it.'

Dad's hand gripped her shoulder so hard it hurt. 'What sort of assault, Cat?'

'The worst,' she finally said. 'I'm pretty sure, anyway.'

'How do you know if you can't remember anything?' Dad said quietly.

God, it was so embarrassing telling her parents what happened. She took a deep breath and looked down at her hand safely enfolded in Dad's strong hands.

'Because of how I felt the next morning, because of how I was hurting, and because of the blood.'

'What blood?' Mum choked out.

'Not only was I violated—for want of a better term—but I was bleeding. My arms and my legs were bleeding too. That's what you saw, Mum. And other places.' She hitched a sob. 'So bad that I still don't know how I managed to drive home the next afternoon.'

'Show me your arms,' Dad said.

Cat let go of his hand and pulled up her sleeves. She held out her arms so they could see the six cuts on each arm that went in vertical lines from the crook of her elbow to her wrist.

'Fucking hell,' Dad said. 'Are you telling me someone did that to you?'

Cat nodded. 'Yes, and there's more. Mum saw the cuts on the back of my legs.'

'You have no idea? No memory of it.'

'No.'

'What sort of person would do that to a woman?' Dad ran his hands over his face.

'Dad, I'm so sorry I had to tell you this. Don't be upset, please. Now that I've told you, I can start to put it behind me. But I'm not going back to Sydney.'

'Don't be upset? How do you think I feel knowing our daughter has gone through such a dreadful experience? How *we* feel,' Dad corrected, looking at Mum. 'For God's sake, Cat. Those cuts are so close to your arteries, he could have killed you.'

Mum's distressed cry filled Cat with guilt.

What grief had she brought home to her parents?

'Now I want you to tell me exactly who was there that night. And where you were. I'm going to get some paper and a pen and write it down.' Dad stood and looked down at her.

'What for, Dad? I don't want anyone else to know, not the girls either. It's between you, Mum, and me. Okay?'

Her chest tightened when he shook his head. 'No. We're going to call the police.'

'No. No!' Cat's voice rose to a scream. 'You can't do that. We're not.'

'Calm down, sweetheart. Look at this rationally. Someone has assaulted you. It's a crime that has to be reported and investigated,' Dad said quietly.

'No one I know would do that.'

'And what about Scarlet? Wasn't she in the flat?'

Cat shrugged. 'I don't know if she was, but she must have been. She wasn't there when I woke up; she had an early meeting with her supervisor.'

'Did you see her before you left?'

'No. I managed to get up, and I had a hot shower. It hurt; my arms and legs were still bleeding. I left her a note.'

'You didn't think about going straight to the police station?' Mum said.

'No. I just wanted to come home and forget it had happened.'

'Or a doctor? Or to Emergency?' Dad said. He kept rubbing his hands over his face.

'Dad, I didn't know what had happened. I was scared, Mum. I just needed to get out of there. I didn't call anyone. I ripped the sheets off the bed after I was dressed. I packed my bag, wrote a note for Scarlet, and left her some cash for the rent, and I got in the car and drove here.'

'What did you do with the sheets?'

Cat hung her head, feeling stupid. 'Once I was out of Newtown—that was the hardest part, walking from the apartment down to my car—I was terrified that he was still there, waiting for me to come out. But I got to the car safely, and I drove out. It wasn't until I reached Penrith that I stopped. I got lost because I forgot to get my phone and missed a turn onto the Great Western Highway. I was on a back street trying to find my way back to the motorway and saw a bin on the footpath. I stopped, took the sheets out of the car and put them in someone's garbage bin.'

'And no police?'

She shook her head. 'No. I was too embarrassed.'

'You didn't consider ringing us to come and get you?' Dad asked.

'I didn't know what to do, so I came home.'

'And then you couldn't tell us,' Mum said softly.

'No. I'm mortified now telling you. I don't want to worry you. We need to forget it and move on. No police, Dad, please,' she begged. 'It could have been my fault. Did I cause it? Did I invite someone home with me? I don't know because I can't remember.' Cat leaned forward and sobbed as her parents looked at each other.

Before they could answer, there was a loud knock on the front door.

'Who the hell's that?' Dad jumped up.

'I'm not expecting anyone,' Mum said.

Dad strode down the hall, his heavy footsteps pounding on the timber floor.

Mum's arms went around Caitríona again. She tried to stop crying, but her sobs got louder.

'Mum, I can't stop crying. I want to feel better.'

Her mother's lips pressed against her forehead. 'It's all right, sweetheart. You're here and safe, and we won't let anyone hurt you.'

Chapter 17

Guntana Station - early Wednesday afternoon.

The image of the expression on that woman's face stayed with Logan all afternoon. He considered getting out the punt and going across to the homestead, but he hesitated, thinking that if she was home alone, she could bail him up with a shotgun.

That night, he still couldn't get the woman's face out of his mind, so he decided to wait until he heard the plane come back. He'd go over and apologise because he knew he must have frightened the living daylights out of her.

The next morning, he was in the shed sifting through the old tools and fencing stuff that had been left behind, thinking it was almost time for a cuppa when he heard the plane fly over. The tone of the motor changed as it landed on an airstrip somewhere on the property across the river.

Yesterday afternoon, he'd pulled out the punt and checked it. It was certainly seaworthy—or river-worthy. Beneath where it hung from ropes on the wall of the shed was a small wheeled trailer for moving the punt down to the riverbank. It seemed the previous residents had thought of everything, and he was surprised they hadn't taken it with them when they left. With his limited boating knowledge, Logan could tell the vessel had been made by a craftsman; the lines were smooth, the joins perfect, and the timber had been oiled. The boat had even been given a cute name; the *Ding-a-Ling* was a nifty little tub. He'd also been taken aback this morning at the wealth of equipment that had been left behind in the shed, but he still hadn't found any fencing hinges.

He finished in the shed, but he knew there was no point calling the old goat at Bourke Feed and Seed. He couldn't help the grin at his pun—sad what living alone did to you. Instead, he decided to go over and meet his neighbours and make his apology.

Giving his neighbour a couple of hours after he arrived home, Logan made himself a sandwich and a mug of tea. He sat out in the shade on his back porch and browsed through the online news on his tablet.

He went straight for the crime pages. Once a cop, always a cop. Even though it had done his head in. At times, he kidded himself he missed it, and then he'd read some of the news reports, and get stressed by the political correctness of the world today. How the hell policing could be done effectively these days was beyond him, and he was glad he was out of it.

But he missed the analytical stuff, and he missed the company of like-minded detectives. The good ones, anyway. He'd seen too much corruption on both sides of the fence to have any faith in justice and integrity. Criminals, the police force, and the courts.

The way he'd gone on leave, under a cloud that had been the result of a malicious lie, had done his head in for a year or two. Technically, he was still employed—on "special leave", but Logan wasn't sure if he'd go back. It had taken six months for him to turn to consulting work; his mate in the force had enticed him back, and it was good to have something to focus on and work from afar.

Nothing major, just investigative work, looking for links, and then handing the file back.

Forcing himself to forget about it, Logan took a deep breath, looked out at *his* land for a while, breathed in the serenity, and then went back to the news reports.

So much gangland stuff in Sydney and Melbourne, and another murder in Newtown. He'd read a few reports in the Sydney media already.

Several women had reported assaults after going to a new club in King Street. Each of them had had the same experience: no memory of getting home, no memory of anyone being there with them, and each waking up the next morning with lacerations on their limbs.

The next report was much worse.

It appeared that the perpetrator may have escalated when a woman's body had been found at the back of the club the other victims had been at. The same club had been mentioned a few times in reports of gang warfare in the eastern suburbs of Sydney. Logan rarely forgot anything he read, and he'd thought what a stupid name it was the first time he'd read it. Who'd go to a bar called *Singapore Sing Song*?

A couple of hours later, he took his mug and tablet back inside and grabbed his hat. After he'd laced his boots up, he grabbed the stick he left near the door and headed back to the shed. When he was there, he pulled out his phone and took a photo of how he'd tried to put that damn gate together. He'd suss out Tom O'Byrne before he asked any questions. If the bloke was up himself, he'd make his apology to his wife, say his goodbye, come home, and keep to himself.

He lifted the punt off the wall, slid it on the small wheeled trailer, and headed to the riverbank, reluctantly leaving the rifle in the house.

The trailer was a little beauty. The punt was light and it was easy enough to pull the rope behind him with one hand, leaving his other hand free for the stick that would deal with any reptiles he might encounter on the way.

Managing to reach the riverbank without a snake or even a lizard crossing his path, he pulled the punt off the trailer and left the trailer tucked behind the tree he'd stood under yesterday. Remembering the embarrassing incident from yesterday, he looked up and down the riverbank. There was no sign of life across the river as he scanned the bank.

A tree he hadn't noticed yesterday about twenty-five metres upstream caught his eye. Beneath it, steps were cut into the steep bank, indicating a well-used access point to the river. A frayed rope hung from the tree; that section of the river must be used as a swimming hole, though it didn't entice him. Snakes swam too.

With a grimace, Logan shook his head. He had to get over this fear of snakes. If it was hot enough, he'd brave the river to cool down when the heat arrived. He gripped the edge of the punt and slid it down the steep bank ahead of him. It was hard to imagine how much water must come down this river in a flood. He knew that his property had been inundated last year by the big flood. That's why he'd built his house well away from the water and on the top of a small hill. Time would tell whether he'd chosen the site wisely.

Dragging the punt down the sloping bank, he put the boat in the water and stepped in. He crossed the narrow neck of the river with barely three strokes of the oars and was soon across to the other side without incident. He turned the punt and rowed down to where he'd seen the steps. Climbing out carefully, he tied off the rope to a small tree.

It was a beautiful day; yesterday's blow had gone. The air was clean again with none of that cloying brown dust swirling around.

Brushing himself off, Logan made his way up the steps and, when he reached the top, headed along a track that he assumed led onto the property.

As he walked through the low scrub, he spotted a clearing that led to a large shed that housed the red and white plane he'd seen flying over a few times. The homestead, with several chimneys, was visible a short distance from the shed. Passing a pen with three dogs that set up a racket as he walked past, he reached the road and turned left toward the magnificent homestead.

When he opened the front gate and walked towards a set of wide front steps, the barking stopped and he could hear voices inside. He frowned as he thought he heard a woman crying.

Reaching a wide veranda, he stood at the front door, took his Akubra off, raised his hand and knocked on the wood at the side of the front door.

The talking stopped, and all was quiet until approaching footsteps sounded on a timber floor.

A tall broad-shouldered guy with a lined, rugged face opened the screen door and came out to the veranda.

'Yes?' he said gruffly.

'Are you Tom O'Byrne?' Logan asked.

'I am. And who may you be?' His voice held suspicion.

'Sorry, Tom. If may call you that. I'm Logan Wainwright. I own the property across the river and I came over to apologise.

I think I may have upset your wife yesterday.'

Tom stared at him. 'How? We were in Broken Hill yesterday.'

'Ah, perhaps it wasn't your wife then. I was at the river yesterday afternoon—on my side—and I was looking through the scope of my rifle to see if I could locate your house from across the river because the guy at the Bourke rural store suggested I see you. When I swung it around, there was a frightened face in the sights. A woman with fair skin and red hair.'

Tom ran his hand through his hair. 'Shit, you're lucky she didn't get a gun and shoot you. Cat's the best shot on the station.'

'Cat?'

'Our middle daughter, Caitríona.'

'May I apologise to her?'

Tom shook his head and looked away. 'Look, mate. I'm sorry to be inhospitable; we're in the middle of a bit of a crisis at the moment. It's not a good time.'

'I'm sorry to hear that.' Logan stepped back and put his hat on. 'I'll leave you in peace.'

'Thanks. I appreciate that. We'll have you over and welcome you properly in a few days or so. I knew there was a new place being built over there, but I didn't know anyone had moved in.'

'I'll look forward to it. Good to meet you, Tom. Hope things improve for you.'

'Thanks. And listen, why did the rural store tell you to come and see me?'

'Nothing important.' Logan waved a dismissive hand. 'I'm having a problem with some gates on my goat paddock, but look, don't worry. I'll go for a drive and see them one day next week.'

'Have you got a phone over there?'

Logan nodded. 'Yes, I've got a Star Link service that my mobile runs off.'

'Did you drive around?' He looked past Logan for a vehicle.

'I rowed over. A punt came with the place.'

'Not the *Ding-a-Ling*?'

'Yes, that's it.'

A shadow briefly clouded Tom's expression. 'My brother built her. Anyway, Logan, give me your number and I'll give you a call in a day or two. Like I said, I'm sorry about today, but it's been a tough morning.'

Logan reached into his back pocket and pulled out a card. He'd had some printed off with his name, property name, and mobile number. It always gave him a buzz to see his name above *Guntana*.

After he'd handed over the card, Tom held out his hand, and Logan shook it.

'Good to meet you. Welcome to the Darling. We'll catch up soon.' Tom O'Byrne had a steady gaze and a firm grip. He wasn't the stuck-up property owner that Logan had dreaded meeting.

'I'll look forward to it.' As Logan walked away, he couldn't help wonder what family crisis was unfolding at the O'Byrne station. He was thoughtful as he headed back to the river and hoped it didn't have anything to do with the rifle episode yesterday.

Chapter 18
Country Kerry, Ireland -1846.

Winter set in, and Caitríona missed those summer hours by the stream so much. Many local people moved away as crop after crop failed for the second year. As the famine spread, Da began to talk of them leaving too.

'If you lose your position at the big house, Cat, we will have no choice.'

'But where would we go?' Mam looked stricken.

'I don't know, *a mhuirnín,* I've heard a lot of people are moving to America.'

'But we won't have to, will we, Da?' Panic shot through Caitríona. The thought of being so far away from Sean filled her with horror.

'I hope not. It will depend on this year's crop. It's only a couple of weeks until St Patrick's Day. Our problem this year is the lack of seed potatoes to plant; it will be a small yield at best in the autumn.'

Caitríona knew the significance of St Patrick's Day. It was the traditional day of planting. Before she worked at the big house, she had helped in the small fields they tenanted on the O'Byrne estate. Now her two middle brothers were of an age to help mark out the plot for Da while she was at the big house.

Long parallel lines about three feet apart would be dug in the soil with a piece of wood, ready to make the raised bed for the potatoes in the middle. In between the furrows, they would place a mix of manure, rotten seaweed and crushed seashells, and then the grass sod would be turned upside down, and the seed potatoes were inserted between the grass and the manure mix.

'Don't worry, Da. I will keep my position. I have proven to be a good worker.'

'That ye may have, *a leanbh*.' Her father shrugged and lifted the mug of *poitín* to his mouth. 'Depends on the master at the big house. I've heard a few fellas say O'Byrne is short of money. With so much land, he's got so many of us tenant farmers paying under the four-pound rent he has a huge rate bill. I can see that he will be moving us off the smaller lots. You might keep your place there, but he won't be able to pay you if that is true.'

'But he gets the rents from all the tenants,' Caitríona said.

'It doesn't work like that. Most of the rents nowadays, that is those of us who can still afford to pay rent, go to the middlemen. O'Byrne was greedy a few years back and sold half of his estate off to the Englishmen, and now he'll rue that day.' His laugh was bitter. 'And so will they. That black mush we dug last year meant no rent for anyone.'

'But why are they evicting tenants? Surely, they know that this will not last.'

'Because they will use the land for something else.' Da stared down into his mug. 'Bigger holdings, and run sheep. It all bodes ill for us.'

Caitríona knew she had to keep getting paid. She'd always been a worker, but now she worked even harder at the big house, and when she was at home, she spent every waking minute helping Mam. The threat of starvation loomed over them, but spirits lifted as the weather lightened, and the pigs and the chickens went back outside. There was more room in the cottage when John and Michael, the two oldest boys, moved forty miles away to West Cork to work on the ropes for the *Diúilicín*. When they came home to visit in the winter, they had bought a bagful of the blue mussels home. They had been received gratefully, and this week, the shells would go on the compost between the potato rows.

After weeks of heavy weather and no Sunday visits to the glade, spring finally announced its presence with a clear day and a warm breeze after St Patrick's Day. Spirits lightened and even Miss Ellis was seen to smile briefly.

Sean slipped a note into her hand in the scullery one afternoon when Mrs Baker's back was turned. Cook adored Sean, and he frequented the scullery for small treats that she baked especially for him. Not that she would say she had a favourite of the three boys, but Sean was the only one Mrs Baker called into her domain.

Meet me in the glade on Sunday afternoon.

That night, after she had helped Mam put the little ones to sleep, Caitríona sat on the warm floor by the fire and pulled out the note. Her mother had gone straight to bed, and the children were quiet. Tommy, the second youngest of her brothers, was asleep on Caitríona's hessian stretcher; she would sleep in the straw in front of the fire tonight with the two brothers who slept there each night. The mud cottage became more cramped each year, and as more babies arrived, there was little room. In the winter, when the chickens and the two pigs were inside, it was almost unbearable, but it also made her realise that even though she could dream, there would be no future with Sean. He was part of the Anglo-Irish ascendancy, and she was the daughter of a tenant farmer.

She ran her fingers over his beautiful script and vowed even if it was snowing, she would meet Sean on Sunday.

She gently pushed the note into the pocket of her apron and stared into the flames; the silence interrupted only by Da's snoring from the curtained alcove at the back of the cottage. Being grown up was awful; if it wasn't for Sean, there would be nothing good about her life. The threat of no food loomed over them, the thought of having to move away filled her with fear, and the work at the big house had become arduous, and apart from Mrs Baker's occasional sweetness to her and the snatched moments with Sean, Caitríona was beginning to hate every moment she spent there.

Wary of Thomas, she watched her back every moment of the day. He left her in peace now, but she was still aware of his eyes on her when she encountered him in the house.

##

On Sunday afternoon, Caitríona crept out while Mam was feeding Finn, and the boys were sitting outside with Da. She went quietly around the side of the cottage, expecting to be called back with every step she took. But luck was with her, and she was soon over the small rise that led into the woods. She pulled her shawl around her shoulders, and she hurried through the trees at the edge of the wood. Despite bringing spring, the wind blowing off the Ceann Mara inlet came through the hills and valleys and always took away the warmth of the spring sunshine. But it wasn't the spring wind causing the goosebumps to rise on her arms; her excited anticipation had her heart a-flutter, and a warm feeling ran down into her lower belly.

Her feet flew over the soft new grass in the woods, and she barely noticed the bluebells pushing their way towards the light. All she could think of was Sean waiting for her by the river. She had taken great care with her appearance and was careful not to let him see that she had done so. She'd worn a clean dress and apron and left her boots at home; they were so old and muddy she preferred to be barefoot.

She had stopped about a hundred yards away from the glade, leaving the woods at the bend in the stream. She washed her feet, face, and hands and ran her fingers through the wiry, tight curls that were the bane of her life. Pulling her ribbon from her pocket, she tied her hair back. Miss Ellis had always insisted that her hair was not loose as she worked, and Caitríona had replied, saying, 'But Miss, I have no ribbons.'

Mrs Baker had overheard and brought some ribbons from her cottage the next day. They were among Caitríona's most valued possessions. Today, she had pulled out a bright yellow ribbon that would be cheery against her red hair.

She walked the last yards to the meeting place slowly so she wouldn't be too out of breath or her cheeks too rosy. As she reached the line of trees that edged the glade, she stopped and looked across the green grass. Sean was sitting by the water, his back against their rock. The further away he was from the big house, the happier he always appeared.

This was their favourite place by the stream, a mile away from the estate beneath a natural avenue of oak trees. Caitríona had roamed these fields alone since she was a young child. The noise of the children in the small cottage and Da's yelling got too much for her at times, and Mam turned a blind eye to her escape as long as she was back to help with feeding the little ones at teatime. There was barely enough time to do all she had to now, with home and the big house, and it was rare for her to venture to the stream.

A wave of love trickled through her chest and warmed her as she stood there watching Sean, but it was soon replaced by a cold sadness as she realised this might be the last spring she would be in Kerry. Caitríona hated change and couldn't believe that the failure of the potato crop could threaten so much of their lives.

Sean turned his head as if he knew she was there, and she smoothed down the front of her apron with shaking hands and stepped into the clearing.

'My Caitríona, you're here! I was hoping you wouldn't be late.'

She walked slowly across to where he was sitting by the small stream that came off the River Finnihy. She positioned herself beside him—not too close, but not too far—on the soft spring grass, tucking her bare feet beneath her skirts.

'Nothing would have kept me away, Sean. I have missed seeing you so much through the winter.'

'As I have missed you too.'

She looked up at him. He sounded slightly different, and she wondered if his tone held a little bit of distance. Perhaps he realised he had made a mistake asking her to meet him. Perhaps riding the estate with his father while Thomas was learning the estate accounts with Samuel, he had seen more of how those in the tenant cottages lived and realised how unworthy she was.

There was an awkward silence for a while, and finally, Caitríona found the courage to look up at Sean. He was staring at her, his lips slightly parted, his eyes full of something that made her heart leap; her worries were for nothing. This was the Sean she knew and loved.

'I heard you have been out on the estate with your father,' she said. 'I worried . . .'

Sean nodded and pulled out a tuft of grass, running it through his fingers. 'Where did you hear of that? It appears our business gets around.'

'Oh, I didn't mean to pry,' she said. 'My father was talking about how things are changing.' She didn't want to go into detail. Or mention that Da had talked about moving away. She couldn't bear to think about that, let alone put it into words. That would make it seem more real.

'Caitríona, I don't mind talking to you about anything. It's not prying. I simply don't like to hear of your worry, and it hurts me to see how the tenants live. Things *are* changing.' He shook his head, but his eyes held hers. 'I just don't know anymore.'

She moved a little bit closer. 'You just don't know what, Sean?'

'I don't know where my place is, Cat.'

'What do you mean?' She rolled over onto her stomach, picked a stalk of grass and tickled his nose. 'What place? You live at *Ceann Mara*, one of the grandest estates in County Kerry.'

'For now.'

Caitríona's heart sank. She couldn't imagine her life without Sean as her friend. She threw the piece of grass away into the stream and watched it float away.

But only a friend; she well knew there could be no more than friendship. She'd held her dreams close in her heart, and now she avoided holding his eyes for too long and not touching him as she had been wont to do as they grew up together. Teasing, tickling, shoulder-to-shoulder as they fished in the stream; theirs was a deep and abiding friendship, and she knew no matter how much she dreamed of a future, there was no hope of her ever being anything more than Sean's friend, no matter how much she longed for it.

'Samuel is already assisting Father with the estate accounts.' Sean glanced at her. 'Show me some sympathy, Cat. I'm unhappy. Let me wallow in my unhappiness.'

'And why would a fine-looking fellow like you, with a rich family and a beautiful manor house and farm, be unhappy?' Even though she teased him, doubts crept into her heart. How could Sean say he was unhappy? Had he not just said he had seen the state of the cottages and the potatoes as he had ridden the fields with his father?

'We're not a rich family, Cat. Since Samuel has been doing the accounts, I have learned that is not so. Father has excessive rates to pay, and that's why he won't fund the journey I want to take. I doubt if I'll even be able to go to Trinity College next year.'

Caitríona sat up straight and stared down at Sean. 'What journey? And Trinity College? You've never mentioned that.'

'I want to go to Greece and Egypt and Italy. I want to see Herculaneum and Pompeii, the Coliseum and the Pantheon, and then I want to study classics at Trinity.'

'I would miss you, Sean,' she said softly. Sean had continued at the school after she had gone into service. Caitríona hadn't heard of some of those places and was reminded once more of *her* place.

She rolled over and jumped to her feet, brushing the loose

grass off her skirts. 'I'm going to go home now. Mam will need my help.'

Before she could take a step away, Sean reached up and grabbed her hand.

'Don't leave me. I'm sorry, but I'm not good company today. I'm being selfish. We haven't had time together for months and now I'm sharing my maudlin thoughts with you. It is so good to have someone to talk to who understands me, Caitríona. You know me better than anyone else.'

She stared down at him.

'Please stay?'

She sat down again, and a thrill ran through her as Sean's arm went around her shoulders, and he pulled her close. Her head rested on his shoulder.

'Thomas will take over the running of the farm for a short while and will look after the tenants and the rents until—' He looked at her sideways, but Caitríona looked away. He couldn't have put her in her place any more clearly, could he? She moved away and leaned back on the rock beside his.

'Until what?'

He shook his head. 'No matter. We have our problems. Change is everywhere. My father is barely speaking. My mother has taken to her bed this week.'

'I thought they were away.'

'They both arrived back at the estate late last night.' Sean dropped his gaze. 'Thomas has got himself into a bit of trouble.'

'What sort of trouble?'

'I can't say. There is talk of them going to the colonies.'

'Them?'

'Thomas and Samuel. Mother is distraught.'

'America?' she asked, her eyes wide.

'No. To New South Wales. My father's cousin has come home to visit his mother, and has asked Thomas and Samuel to join him there.'

'As long as it is not you,' she whispered.

Before she knew what was happening, Sean reached over and took her cold hands in his, gently rubbing her fingers as he looked at her with concern.

'Forget that I told you that. It was not to be shared outside the house. It is not to get around the tenants or the middlemen.'

Hurt flooded through Caitríona. 'I would not tell anyone that we have spoken. I never have, and I never would. I know *my* place.'

'I didn't mean to hurt you,' he said.

He had, but she wasn't going to say that.

'Why do things have to change, Sean? Why can't we keep going on as we were?'

'I don't know, *macushla*.' A shiver ran down her back at the endearment. 'But things are changing, and we have to cope with it.' His hand moved slowly, sliding up from her hand, along her arm, until it rested on the side of her neck. 'We have to make the most of each moment.'

He leaned forward, his hand moving to cup her cheek. Her eyes stared into his, and she felt like she was drowning, and he stopped, his blue eyes searching hers.

'My da is talking about going to America.' She finally looked away, not wanting to see his reaction. She didn't have to look up; his hand reached out and took hers, curling around her icy-cold fingers.

'Why?'

'Because of the black potatoes. If it wasn't for me working at the big house, we wouldn't be able to eat,' she said. 'Poor

Mam is getting more haggard every day. She's so worried about the little ones. If it wasn't for me bringing home the money from your dad, we would have to go.'

She looked up, surprised to see Sean leaning forward. Slowly, his other hand left her shoulder, reached up, and caressed her cheek. 'I don't know what I'd do without you in my life, Cat.' Sean rested his forehead on hers. 'You can't leave me.'

'As I don't want you to leave me either, Sean.' Her courage grew as warmth ran through her body. He gazed at her, a pink flush on his cheeks. His eyes held hers when she sat up and sighed.

As she spoke, their fingers intertwined in a silent acknowledgement of the connection they shared. Anticipation hung in the air, and she tensed as Sean pulled her closer.

'May I ask you something?' he said softly.

'What do you wish to ask me?'

'That's one thing I would like to know, but I was wondering if you think I would be too untoward if I asked if I may kiss you.'

'I've never been kissed by a boy before,' she said, looking down as excitement rushed through her.

'I'm not a boy anymore, Cat. It would be a great honour if you would allow me to be the first man to kiss you.'

'Then you may kiss me, *young* man,' she said. 'What do I need to do? I don't want to do the wrong thing.'

'Put your hands on my shoulders, and then you lift your chin so that your lips meet mine.'

She did as he asked. His breath was warm on her lips, and goosebumps ran down her arms. The shyness she had felt long ago as they chatted disappeared. Sean's lips were soft and gentle as they pressed against hers, and her eyes closed of their own volition.

All sorts of feelings ran through her body—feelings she had never experienced before, tugging at her belly and causing her nipples to pebble beneath her chemise. She wondered what was happening to her.

Sean pulled back a little. 'I'm sorry if you didn't like that.'

She met his eyes and worried that she might have liked it a little too much. 'I liked it.' Her voice was shy.

'You are so beautiful. May I keep kissing you?'

'You may,' she replied, but before his lips came back to hers, he moved away and spread her shawl on the ground next to them.

'It would be easier if you lay down,' he said.

'I don't know. I'm sorry.' She knew what Da and Mam did as they lay down at night.

'Don't be sorry.'

Caitríona's apprehension crept in. The fear of being seen, the dread of jeopardising her position at the big house, and the ever-present scrutiny of Miss Ellis hung over her like a shadow. Reluctantly, she pulled away, her eyes filled with a mixture of longing and trepidation.

'Sean,' she whispered, her voice tinged with a mix of desire and fear. 'We cannot do this. If we were caught, it would cost me everything. Miss Ellis despises me, and I can't risk losing my position. My family would starve if I lost my position.'

Sean's breath was warm on her lips. 'No one will know. And I would never let that happen.' He leaned forward and gently pressed her shoulders until she was lying back on her woollen shawl, her head cushioned by the soft moss at the base of the tree trunk.

This time, when his lips met hers, there was more pressure,

and a strange feeling went through Caitríona as her mouth opened beneath his, and his tongue made a tentative foray between her lips.

Sean stopped, pulled back, then kissed her again, and every time his lips met hers, warmth pooled between her thighs.

Breathing raggedly, his lips moved down her neck, and she was so taken with the sensation that it was a moment before she realised his hands were moving down her side. His fingers were warm as they reached up beneath her chemise and touched her bare skin. A shiver ran through her, and she sat up and pressed her lips against his.

'Don't stop, Sean. Please don't stop,' she begged as he lifted her blouse and fondled her bare breasts. Somehow, her blouse had come undone, and Caitríona couldn't think any more when his hands moved lower beneath her skirts.

Her moan broke the silence. Caitríona was lost.

Chapter 19

Ceann Mara Station - Wednesday afternoon.

Cat blinked as she lifted her aching head when Dad walked back into the room. She'd managed to stop crying as Mum held her gently, stroking her hair. Her eyes were red and raw, but she felt much lighter.

'Who was that, Tom?' Mum asked.

'Our new neighbour,' Dad said.

'What new neighbour?' Cat asked curiously.

'Gary and Elise have sold the block across the river,' Dad said, looking across the room, his face set.

'So, they finally sold,' Mum said. 'He didn't call to let you know?'

Dad was quiet for a few moments. Cat had often wondered if there was a problem between Dad and his brother, but she'd never asked, and he never talked about it. There hadn't been much contact from them since they'd left after the fire. The house had burned down, and her uncle and aunt had moved to the coast. Now, being away at uni most of the year, she didn't know if they'd reconnected or not.

Suddenly, yesterday afternoon made sense. 'Aha! So,

there's someone new across the river.'

'Yeah,' Dad said. 'He's bought Gary's place. He's built a kit home on that hill near the second gully. I should have gone over to say gidday.'

'We've been busy, Tom,' Mum said.

'We have.' Cat frowned. Dad's voice sounded strange; maybe it was because Uncle Gary had sold without telling him.

Mum nudged him with her shoulder. 'And besides, when you're not out on our property, you spend most of your time in the study working on the family stuff.'

'I'm surprised I haven't heard about him on the local grapevine.'

'What local grapevine do you access these days, Tom O'Byrne?' Mum said, shaking her head. 'How long since you've been to the Tilpa pub? How long since we've been to play tennis at Louth?'

'A few months, I suppose.'

'More like a year since you have,' she said. 'Now, don't be grumpy. I know you offered to buy it off Gary, but he's sold it, so move on. Nothing you can do.' Mum took Cat's hands in hers. 'And how are you feeling, sweetheart? We're getting back to a bit of normality here.'

'Sounds like your normality is pretty busy, Mum, and I'm really impressed with what you've done. After you left yesterday, I did what you said. You probably saw the mail on the front table when you came in. I went for a ride on the pushbike with the dogs out to the mailbox, and then when I came back, I went out again and rode down to the new campground. Then we went for a big walk again around the billabong. I couldn't believe how much you've done. An absolute credit to you.'

Tom nodded. 'Yeah, your Mum's done pretty damn good.'

'I'm pleased to know we've got a new neighbour, but he gave me a huge fright yesterday.' Despite the thought of that and the crying jag she'd just had, Cat was feeling much better.

Dad frowned. 'Yes, he said he wanted to apologise.'

'What happened?' Mum asked looking from one to the other.

'Scared the living daylights out of me. Any I have left anyway,' Cat said ruefully. 'I was sitting on the seat near the river, and when I looked up, a strange guy had a rifle pointing at me.'

'What sort of person does that!' Mum snapped.

'Calm down, Laura. Logan—his name is Logan Wainwright—had a perfectly reasonable explanation. One of the reasons he came over was to apologise. He thought you were my wife, Cat. He gave me his phone number, and I said we'd give him a call and have him over one afternoon.'

'What was his other reason for coming over?' Mum was slow to trust.

'He needed some advice with his goat fencing. Once we get sorted here and things settle down a bit, I'll give him a call. Now, where were we when he knocked on the door?'

'We were talking about calling the police,' Mum said firmly.

Cat sat up straight and folded her arms. Dad was standing by the window looking across at her, and she held his gaze steadily.

'No police, Dad,' she said. 'This is my problem, and I make the decisions.' He opened his mouth to speak, but she interrupted before he could say anything. 'And no calls behind my back. Can I trust you not to do that? Okay?'

'All right,' he agreed begrudgingly. 'But only on the

condition that you give it some thought. We'll talk about it again tomorrow. It'll give you some time to calm down. And think it through rationally. That's my deal.'

'Right, we'll talk tomorrow.' Cat kept her arms folded, feeling as though she'd just been chastised.

***

Logan was surprised when his mobile rang the following morning, and it was Tom O'Byrne. He recognised the number because Tom had texted him back last night to say that he'd be in touch and to apologise for not being able to spend time with him yesterday afternoon.

'Hi, Tom, I didn't expect to hear from you so soon.'

'Getting back to normal today, mate. I was wondering whether you were busy this morning. If you're free, I can come over and have a look at those hinges for you. I've found a few spares in the shed here, so I'll bring some across.'

'That'd be great. If you're sure,' Logan said.

'Yep. Happy to.'

'Can you get across the river?' Logan asked.

'No, that's why I was ringing.'

'Yeah, but I'm happy to wheel down the punt and bring you across.'

'*Ding-a-Ling* sounds good,' Tom said. 'You give me a time, and I'll meet you down at the river.'

'How about I come now?' Logan said. 'I was just having a cuppa and reading the news.'

'Yeah, that'll be great. I'll bring some tools too. Look forward to having a chinwag.'

A short while later, Logan wheeled the trailer out of the bush and stood on the riverbank. He might have to think about leaving the boat down at the river, maybe tied to a tree, or he could set up some sort of steel shackle in the ground.

Tom was waiting on the top of the bank on the other side of the river with a hessian bag in his left hand. He stepped nimbly down the track Logan had noticed near the seat yesterday and waited for him to row across.

'Room for both of us in here, if you're happy to take me across. My brother and I used to go across the river together, although you're a bit bigger than him,' Tom said.

'Not a problem, mate. So, your brother used to own the place?'

'Yeah, Gary and his wife lived there for about five years. Unfortunately, their homestead burnt down.'

'I heard that when I was looking at buying the place. What happened?' Logan asked curiously as he picked up the oars.

'Lithium battery. Buggers of things.'

'They are. I wouldn't have one in my place,' Logan said. 'What was it in?'

'A laptop. Left on to charge overnight. Luckily, they hadn't gone to bed, but the fire took hold so fast they only grabbed the cat and the car keys and got out just in time.'

'It would have been hard.'

'Yeah, they moved back to the coast. Didn't want to stay out here.'

'A question for you, Tom,' Logan said once they reached the eastern side of the river. 'If you don't mind—and let me know if it would interfere with your privacy—I was thinking about leaving the boat down here at the river. What do you think about that?'

'Not a problem at all. We used to do it,' Tom said. 'We had a shackle on both sides of the river, and in those days, when Gary first moved here, we had it set up as a proper punt. They were probably washed away in the last flood. We also had a rope going from a tree on each side of the river, and we just took the boat to the rope and pulled ourselves across without the oars. That way, it didn't matter which side of the river it was on. You could always get the boat back to the other side with the rope.'

'Sounds good to me. Saves me dragging it down every time I need to come across.'

'Yeah, mate, I'm happy with that. It's good to have a close neighbour. I'm sure I'll be coming over to give you a hand more than today if you need one. Also, I can often use a spare pair of hands if you're happy to reciprocate.'

'Sounds good to me. It can get lonely out here at times.'

'How long have you been here?'

'About six months. I camped out while I was building.'

'Fair dinkum. I feel bloody slack.'

'No problem at all. That was one of my reasons for coming out here. The space and the privacy.'

'Are you here by yourself?'

'Yeah, mate, it's just me,' Logan said as he looped the rope around a small tree trunk and tied it off. 'No partner. I was working long hours and I got away fast. I had a live-in girlfriend for a few months in Brisbane when I was'—he hesitated—'when I was working, but that didn't last long. Shift work tends to do that to a relationship.'

'You're on permanent shift work when you're on a property,' Tom said.

Logan checked the rope was secure. 'Don't want it to float away. You'd be stuck here or you'd have to swim back.'

'Done that many times,' Tom said.

'You've always lived here?' Logan nodded.

'I was born on the place, mate, back in 1971. Gary and I

were the only two kids in our family. He didn't have a real interest in the land, and I was the oldest, too. So, when Dad passed away, primogeniture kicked in. Gary didn't mind. Dad left him that bit of land across there, and I've been looking after the place since then. Almost thirty years now.'

'Married, obviously,' Logan said as they walked up the slope into the bush.

'Yeah, Laura is my wife. You'll meet her. I talked to Laura and Cat, our third daughter, who's home from uni at the moment, and we discussed inviting you over for a barbeque tomorrow night.'

'Are you sure?' Logan said. 'You said you were having a few issues.'

'Yeah, I was hoping to convince my daughter to take some action, but she's stubborn. I guess she takes after her old man. Having you over would give us a different focus. I've given her today to mull it over. I'm pretty sure she'll come to her senses. Having five daughters can do a man's head in sometimes.'

'Five?' Logan whistled. He was curious about what had happened, but it was none of his business. Might be easier not to go over until the daughter went back to uni. 'I can imagine. You deserve a medal. And no rush to have me over.'

'Mate, it's a difficult situation.' Leaf mulch crunched under their feet as they stepped off the track. 'But our Cat's a strong one, and she'll get through this.'

Logan could have sworn he heard Tom mutter, 'I hope' under his breath.

'Come this way, Tom,' he said. 'It's a bit of a shortcut back to the house rather than following the main track. Or I guess you know the place anyway.'

'Depends where you built the house.'

'Quite a way back, on a bit of a rise. I've read about the floods here over the years. Just watch out for snakes. Speaking of which, it must be your daughter who I have to apologise to. I think I frightened the life out of her the other day.'

'Yeah, she's not in a real good space at the moment,' Tom said.

'I'm sorry to hear that. Would it upset her if I apologised? Or should I just let it go?'

'I told her what happened, and she was fine with it. To be honest, it took her head away from her problem for a short while. Cat's reactions to anything at the moment are an unknown. I want her to contact the police about something that happened in Sydney, but she's adamant she won't.'

Logan swallowed. He didn't often share his past. 'I worked with the Queensland Police Force, and I did a lot of mediation and worked with counsellors, so I'm pretty good at talking to people.'

'That could be useful, mate. I might tell you a little bit about it after we sort out your hinges because I could sure do with some advice.'

***

Logan shook his head as the last hinge slotted into the side of the gate, and the enclosure was finished.

'I'm so pleased that worked out. Thanks so much for your help, Tom. I can't believe that old—'

'That old bastard at Bourke Feed and Seed,' Tom said with a grin. 'Would you believe he's been there for as long as I can remember, and he still doesn't have a clue about most of the stuff they sell down there? He's a local, and the new owners kept him on when the last bloke sold, but I think they get so many complaints that he won't last there too much longer.'

'Takes all kinds,' Logan said. 'Can I offer you a cuppa?'

Tom reached up and wiped the sweat off his brow. 'I could go a beer.'

Chapter 20

Ceann Mara Station - Thursday morning.

Cat was sitting on the porch in shorts and a T-shirt, soaking up some sun when Dad came home from across the river. Now that Mum and Dad had seen her scars, she wasn't as self-conscious. Last night she'd slept well and had not been troubled by dreams, the subconscious was a strange thing. With a bit of luck, she'd dealt with it and could move on now.

Dad had asked her to do some family history work in the study while he was across the river, and even though Cat had at first been reluctant—because she knew he was trying to stop her from going back to her room and sleeping—she'd ended up being sucked in and thoroughly enjoyed looking for information about the boats that had brought Irish settlers to New South Wales. She'd found it satisfying, and it was good to focus on something else.

But now Dad looked grim.

'Not a successful visit, by the look of things,' she said as she followed him through the front door into the hall. 'I guess the new neighbour's a bit of a—'

'Laura, where are you?' Dad called down the hall without

answering Cat.

Mum came down the hall from the kitchen, wiping her hands on her apron. 'I've made some scones, and I just put the kettle on. Who wants one?'

'In a while, thanks, love. I need to talk to you both. And then we're calling the police in Sydney.'

'What!' Cat came to a sudden stop in the middle of the hall. 'You said you'd let me think about it for the day, Dad.'

'Well, things have changed. Come and sit down. I need to talk to you both.'

Mum raised her eyebrows, and they both followed Dad into his study. He stood in front of the computer and turned the power on.

'What's happened, Tom?' Mum asked quietly as Cat stood just inside the door. Her heart was beating hard, and she tried to stay calm. She didn't know what had set Dad off, but he'd promised, and there was no way he was going to break it.

'I'll tell you both now.' He pulled out the chair from the computer desk, turned it around and straddled the seat, his hands gripping the backrest. 'Sit down, Laura. Cat, sit beside your mother.'

Mum frowned and did as he asked before her father turned to Cat, who had ignored his request.

'How are you feeling this afternoon, Cat?' he asked.

'I was good until you bowled in and told me what *we* are going to do.' Dad stared at her without speaking. 'I got into the study and sorted out all of those papers that you asked me to put into date order. And I got onto the National Library site for you in Ireland and had a good look around. I've learned how to navigate my way from family to family. And'—she left her success until last— 'I found—'

Dad cut her off before she could tell him she was pretty sure she'd found the name of the ship that Thomas and Caitríona had come across on.

'I asked how you are feeling in yourself. Any better? You've got some colour back today,' he said.

Cat glanced at her mother. Her brow was wrinkled, and she was staring at Dad, looking worried. 'What's going on, Dad? And yes, I feel a lot better. Almost back to my normal self. I've managed to concentrate and not get myself worked up, even the times I thought about Sydney. Between Mum asking me how I am every half hour and if I wanted a cup of tea or something to eat, or could she make me another sandwich, I'm feeling fairly "cared" for, I suppose is the word.'

'Good.'

Cat frowned as Dad ran his hand through his short-cropped hair.

'I need to talk to you seriously, sweetheart. Have you given any more thought to calling the police?'

'Yes, and I don't want to change my mind on that one.'

'Sit down, please, Cat.' Dad put the shed keys on the desk, leaned against it, and crossed his legs at the ankles.

She could tell he was trying to look relaxed, but the expression on his face, the set of his mouth and his hooded eyes belied any relaxation he was trying to convey.

Cat sat on the sofa next to Mum and folded her arms. 'So, do we need Mum here for "this talk" too? I thought we did enough talking yesterday.'

'Cat, please don't be like that. You have to hear what I have to say, and I know it's going to be hard for you. I just want to make sure you're okay, and you know Mum and I are here to support you.'

'I'm good. Dad, since I shared what happened with you both yesterday, I *have* been feeling a lot stronger. I'm not putting on an act.'

'She's right. Our Cat's back, Tom,' Mum said softly, but her eyes were worried as she stared at Dad.

'Okay, I am good, but I'm never going to go back. I'm never going to step into that bar again. If I have to go back to the unit to get my stuff, I'll take Roisin, or maybe Mum, with me, but I'm not going back to university, and I'm not going back there to live. So, tell me what you have to say.'

'Are you quite sure about that? What if we can get this sorted with the police?' Dad said.

'Dad, I told you I don't want the police.'

'Cat, our new neighbour, Logan, is waiting in the shed. He wouldn't come in until I talked to you. I want him to talk to you. You need to.'

'What the hell? You promised you wouldn't tell a soul, Dad.'

'I didn't tell him much, Cat. I respected your privacy. I want you to tell him everything and see what he has to say. Logan told me something that he'd read on the news.'

'Who the hell is this guy?'

'He was a detective, Cat.'

'Dad, I trusted you.' Disappointment flooded through Cat. 'I told you that I didn't want anyone to know.'

'What you need to know came up in conversation without me saying anything apart from mentioning that you were home from university and that you lived in Newtown, and Logan said something that absolutely blew me away.'

'And then you told him everything that happened, I guess.'

'No, give me some credit for keeping your trust, please.

Logan told me about a murder in Sydney a couple of weeks ago.'

Mum gasped, and Cat's heart started pounding slowly and heavily, and she could feel the blood trying to pump to her brain.

Dad came over and sat on her other side. 'Cat, it could have been you.' His voice caught, and he took her hands in his. 'When you talk to Logan, you'll see why we have to talk to the police. You were not an isolated incident. We have to help them catch this guy.'

'So, a woman was murdered in Sydney. There are murders in Sydney all the time, Dad. Every day. What's that got to do with me?'

'Her body was found at the back of the *Singapore Sing Song* Bar. And her arms and legs were mutilated.'

For a moment, Cat couldn't breathe. Her throat choked, and her head started to spin. Dad grasped her shoulders. 'Take it easy. Breathe in, breathe out.' Eventually, her head cleared, and her breathing returned to normal.

'Do you know who it was, Dad? Her name?'

'No. I didn't want to ask too much. I respected your wish for privacy, but I would really like you to talk to Logan and get his advice.'

'What do you mean? Why is a detective living over the back here?' For one crazy moment, Cat thought it might have something to do with her and Newtown.

'He's on some sort of leave. From the Queensland Police. He didn't say much, but I think Logan might've been through a bit of a tough time too. He's come out here for privacy and quiet. He's a good guy, Cat, and I would like you to talk to him. Are you okay if I bring him inside to talk to you?'

She shrugged. 'Yes, I want to know what happened. Although I suppose I could Google it or look at the news online.'

'No, I don't want you to do that. I don't want you getting yourself all worked up. How about you talk to Logan and then if you feel okay, we could ask him to stay for a barbeque? I imagine he'll have more answers than you'll find online. We might even get away from the house and go down to the campground to the barbeque area. Make it more casual.'

Cat nodded slowly. Maybe this would be another step to her getting over what had happened. 'I'm sorry I've been so hard to get on with, Dad. Of course, you're worried. Thank you for helping me, and yes, I'll talk to Logan.'

Chapter 21
Ceann Mara Station - Thursday.

Logan looked up as one of the dogs lying in the shade at the front of Tom's shed lifted his head and gave a short bark. Tom was walking across the road towards where Logan was waiting at the shed. He'd wanted to check that Cat was ready to talk to Logan and had asked him to wait here after they'd come back across the river together in the punt.

Tom's shed was almost a work of art; Logan had never seen such so much gear and kept so clean and tidy. Shadow boards lined the walls with many tools Logan didn't recognise. He had a lot to learn out here in the west. He shook his head as he thought back to his father's shed at Kilkivan: full of junk and always in a mess. Their house had been much the same, and as he'd made his way in life, Logan almost had a fetish for tidiness and things in their place.

Not only were the workbenches clean and neat, Tom had an array of equipment: hinges, bolts, screws, and tools to rival the aisles at the Seed and Feed store. Not to mention the vehicles parked neatly side by side along the eastern wall: a couple of four-wheel drives, a cattle truck, three ag bikes, a quad runner, and the Cessna in the middle.

Logan knew that he'd never have such a well-equipped property. The most he had so far was his old Nissan and the good ship *Ding-a-ling*.

'Good setup, mate,' he commented as Tom walked in.

'Years of collecting, Logan.'

'How did you go? Do you want me to stay or head back?'

'Stay. When I told Cat what you'd read online, she was shocked, but after a while, when she calmed down, she said she'd talk to you. I think she'll agree to talk to the police later too. It threw her for a while, but she's a lot better than she has been since she turned up three weeks ago. I told her about the murder because, without that, I don't think she would've talked to you or the police in Sydney.'

'I guess she knows now she has to.'

'She does. I told her that I didn't tell you too much about what happened.'

'Fair enough,' Logan said. 'I'll get her to tell me.'

'I want this bastard caught and jailed, Logan. When you told me about the murder in Newton, all I could think of was how it could have been Cat.'

'It makes me wonder, knowing how you said she hadn't told anyone, how many other victims there are that haven't come forward. You know, over sixty percent of sexual assaults are never reported.'

'I can imagine.' Tom shook his head.

Logan followed him around the side of the shed, along a paved area past a conservatory full of plants, and then around to the back of the house. It was an impressive property; the house was huge, the gardens beautiful, and the green lawn lush and inviting.

'Beautiful place, mate,' he said. 'Lot of work to keep it looking like this. You must have a lot of staff.'

'Laura, my wife, looks after it all. I'm not even allowed to mow because she says I cut it too short.'

Logan whistled. 'Wow, it's a credit to her.'

'We run a tourist facility up the road a bit, and she looks after that, too, but we do have volunteers to help out in the winter. The only staff we employ on the property are casual contractors who help with shearing and fencing. Anyway, come on in.'

Logan bent down, pulled his Blundstones off and put them next to the door.

'No need to do that, mate; we've got timber floors.' Tom left his on and held the screen door open for Logan to follow him in.

'Just habit,' Logan said.

'Okay, come on.'

He followed Tom down a wide hall that seemed to run from the back to the front of the large homestead. The ceilings were high, and light poured in from a couple of skylights above. Like the shed, the house was in a pristine condition; the old furniture looked to have been lovingly polished, and vases of flowers sat on several of the cupboards and small tables along the hall. The air smelled of blossoms and polish.

'Laura and Cat are in the study.' Tom paused outside the fourth door on the right.

Logan nodded, a little nervous about meeting them. He hadn't been anywhere for the last few weeks and had gotten quite used to not being with people.

A tall woman with blonde hair sat on a double sofa next to the young woman he'd seen yesterday. As he followed Tom in, they both looked at him. The older woman stood, but the one with the red curls stayed seated. He noticed her clenched hands resting on a cushion on her thighs.

'Logan, this is my wife, Laura.'

The woman with blonde hair stared at him. 'Hello, Logan. It's good to meet you.' She held out her hand, and Logan took it. For a woman, she had a firm grip.

'And this is Cat.' Tom moved over to stand by the sofa, and the young woman nodded at him and waved a hand but didn't speak.

For a moment, the silence was awkward, and then Cat broke it. 'Can we please get this over and done with?'

'Logan?' Tom gestured to a chair, but before he could sit, Cat interrupted.

'I'd rather speak to him alone, please, Dad.'

Tom looked surprised, and his wife looked uncomfortable.

'Dad? Mum?' she said again. 'You want me to talk about what happened, but I don't want you here. Okay?'

Tom nodded and went to go to the door, but his wife put a hand on his arm. 'Just wait, please.'

Cat, the daughter, raised her already-arched eyebrows. 'What's wrong now, Mum?'

Laura came over to Logan. 'Please humour me, Logan, but do you have any proof that you are who you say?'

'Laura!' Tom took his wife's arm. 'That's a bit rude.'

Logan held up one hand. 'It's all right, Tom. I've got my wallet and police ID on me, and you can log into the Queensland Police website and confirm my identity there, too, if you want more.'

Laura nodded and held out her hand for the ID card that he pulled out of his wallet.

She looked at it closely, and then looked at his face and nodded. 'Thank you, Logan. Just making sure.'

'Not a problem. You're a wise woman. Never take anyone at face value. It's a lesson I've learned quite a few times in my life.'

Laura's face softened as she smiled for the first time. 'We learn these things as we get older. I'll go and make some tea and coffee. When you've finished here, Cat, can you please bring Logan down to the kitchen? We'll have a cuppa on the back porch. Come on, Tom.'

Cat waited until her parents were out of the study, and their voices receded down the hall. She'd been sitting ramrod straight, but when they left, it was as though her body crumpled a little.

'So, Cat. Do you mind if I call you that? Or is it, Catherine?'

'It's Caitríona, but Cat, please.'

Logan was aware of her gaze on him as he sat on the single chair opposite the sofa. He watched her fingers nervously plucking at the cushion on her thighs.

'First thing, I want to apologise for yesterday. I had no idea you—or anyone else—was on the riverbank.'

'It's okay. Dad passed your apology on yesterday after you left. I'm just relieved that it was our new neighbour and not some random psycho.'

'I certainly have my quirks, but I can guarantee that's not one of them.' He was pleased to see her lips lift in a slight smile. 'I'm on leave at the moment, and also, I'm not part of the New South Wales police, so this is a private conversation, and I suppose you could say a neighbourly chat, but from someone who knows how these things work. You can be assured, though, that anything you tell me won't leave this room. Not even to your parents. Unless you want it to.'

'How what things work?' The smile had gone, and she raised one hand to her face and rubbed her forehead. He sensed that she was putting on a tough front so she didn't crack in front of him. From what he'd heard from the door yesterday, she'd been having a meltdown with her parents.

'Interviews, investigations into assaults. How old are you, Cat? Are you over eighteen?'

Her chuckle was husky. 'Well and truly. I'm almost twenty-four. Why?'

'I just needed to check you weren't underage. I didn't think you were, but these days, you never know.'

'Right. Fire away,' she said. 'What exactly did Dad tell you?'

'Tom told me you'd come home from uni and that you live in Newtown. I was telling him that I've heard there's been a few incidents in Newtown. He told me that you had been involved in an incident and that they were worried about you and would like you to go to the police, but you're reluctant.'

She nodded slowly, seemingly happy with what he knew.

'How about you tell me as much as you can? What you're comfortable sharing, and then I can ask you anything that I want you to elaborate on. That would be the best thing to do, and then I can give you some advice if I think it's necessary.' It had been a few months since he'd interviewed anyone, and Logan tried to keep his tone professional.

'Okay, let's cut to the chase. I'd been to a new bar. The *Singapore Sing Song Bar*. I was sexually assaulted. I suspect that I was drugged; my arms and legs were cut when I came to— woke up—the next morning.' She lifted the cushion and lifted her arms, palms facing him, so he could see faint pinkish lines running vertically towards her wrists. 'I woke up alone in my room, covered in blood, and so I got in the car and drove home here. End of story.'

'Fair enough, and you have no idea who did this to you?'

'None whatsoever.'

'Can you remember who you were with at the bar that night?'

'I can remember the people I know, and I would trust that none of them would do that. There were a couple of new people there that I didn't know, but I certainly wouldn't have gone home with anyone. Anyone I didn't know anyway.' Her face was set, and she held his gaze steadily.

Logan was struck by what a beautiful woman she was. Her face was vibrant, and her fair-skinned complexion held a flush high on her cheeks. Her hair was a tumble of glorious red curls that reached down past her shoulders, and her green eyes were clear and direct.

'So, what now?' she asked.

'Do you want me to tell you what I know about what's happening in Newtown? Are you up to it?'

'I guess I am,' she said.

'Okay, being on the force, I always read news reports from far and wide, and I've read about several assaults around the Newtown area in the past few months.'

'That's nothing new,' she said. 'It's been like that ever since I moved there three years ago. Before then even.'

'Yes, but when I search for those reports in the national database, I find there are common factors in the reports that aren't reported in the media. What you've told me of your experience is identical to the police reports I've seen. I also know that bar has been of interest because of gang-related drug issues.'

'Well, I certainly don't have anything to do with gangs or drugs. It was the first night I'd been out for six months, for fuck's sake.' Her voice trembled. 'Sorry.'

'No, I'm not suggesting that nor am I saying the other assaults are related to that either. It's just that there's been a lot of intel gathered on what's been going on there, and I've seen that bar's name pop up in the notifications quite frequently.'

'If you work with Queensland Police, what are you doing looking at New South Wales reports? And what are you doing living here?' When she put the cushion back on her legs, he wondered why she was covering them up. Maybe she was self-conscious about wearing shorts.

'I'm on leave, but I'm keeping abreast of what goes on. I would strongly advise you, in light of what you've told me, that you make a report to the Newtown police.' He looked across the room and noticed the wind was picking up again outside. 'And what am I doing living here? It's a long story, and I'm not sure of the outcome yet.'

'Sorry, that's none of my business.' Cat sighed and then nodded. 'I've pretty much come to that conclusion. As much as it terrifies me, it's the right thing to do. Do you know the name of the girl whose body they found?'

'I did read it, but I don't recall it. She was a uni student who worked part-time in one of the bars in Newtown. I can look it up and tell you if you're sure you want to know.'

'I do. I wonder if I knew her?' Cat's eyes filled with tears. 'I was very lucky, wasn't I?'

'I would say so. But you know, the more information the local detectives have, the more chance they have of catching him before he escalates.'

'I'd say he's escalated now. And are we assuming it's a he?

Couldn't it be a woman?'

Logan nodded. 'It could, but it would be unusual. I'm sure the police will cover all the possibilities. When do you want to talk to them? Do you want your parents with you?'

She shook her head vigorously, and when her curls fell over her face, she brushed them back impatiently. 'I'm not a child, Logan.'

'Would you like me to make the call and explain the background and see what they say?'

She nodded. 'Thank you, that would be good because if it was me or Dad, we would get too emotional, I think.'

'How about we have that coffee your mum mentioned and then come back here, and I'll make the call?'

'Thank you, I appreciate it. I'm sorry if I've been rude.'

'You've been through an extremely traumatic experience, Cat, and hearing what I told Tom today would have brought it all back.' He wasn't surprised to see tears in her eyes. 'I believe you only told them about it yesterday. How long have you been home?'

'Three weeks.'

'It's a long time to carry something like that and not share it.' Logan stood ready to rejoin her parents. 'One more thing. Did you live alone in Newtown? I meant to ask that before.'

'I share the apartment with another student. Scarlet Donaldson.'

'Did you tell her what happened?'

'No.'

'Okay. Let's go and have that coffee, and then we'll make that call.'

Cat jumped up from the sofa and the cushion fell to the floor unnoticed. 'Can you find your way back to the kitchen? I'm going to go upstairs for a while.'

Before he could reply, she turned and walked across to the door. She was gone quickly, but not before he'd seen the marks on the backs of her leg.

Bastard, he thought. He knew that Caitríona O'Byrne wouldn't start to heal properly until her assailant had been caught. And Logan vowed he would do everything he could to help make that happen, even if he was a long way away and not working in the police force at the moment.

Chapter 22
Country Kerry, Ireland - Spring, 1846.

Caitríona's happiness had increased tenfold, and as she walked to the manor each day, her heart was full of joy with the anticipation of seeing Sean.

She was a woman now, but she had to make do with the occasional glimpse of Sean throughout the day. He always made sure he sought her out when there was nobody else around, stealing kisses behind the drawing-room door or a quick cuddle in the scullery.

This morning, he passed her outside the scullery as she carried the cane basket of wet linen out to the garden. She held his gaze and mouthed a quick 'No.'

She tilted her head to the side, and his eyes lifted to the window. Sean must have seen Mrs Baker watching them because he touched his hat and walked past Caitríona without speaking.

She had planned to tell him last Sunday that he must be more circumspect; she couldn't afford to lose her position at the big house.

At their cottage, food was scarce. Last month, Da's brother, Uncle Seamus, who had not been impacted by the blight as much as they were in the west, had turned up unexpectedly with a bag of oats. Since then, they had lived on porridge. Caitríona had been worried because during that visit, Uncle Seamus and Da had talked long into the night, and she was worried that he was going to assist them with a passage to America. If only Da would be patient, the crop had to be better this year.

It *had* to be. She couldn't bear the thought of change, or her family leaving. Until Sean declared himself, and she had a certain future. Perhaps then she would be able to cope with her family leaving her.

Caitríona's patience was being sorely tested as her monthly bleed was late, but she refused to let it worry her. It had been late before, and she had to put it out of her mind. It could be because she was always hungry, and lately, that hunger had made her feel ill. Her main worry was helping to get food on the table at home and making sure that her family didn't starve.

It was all right for the O'Byrnes; they had plenty of money and sufficient food, no matter what gossip circulated around the county. The potato blight wasn't taking the food from the table at the big house. Sometimes, Caitríona looked at the loaded trays of fine food that Amelia carried to the dining room for the midday meal, and her heart bled for her family and the others in the county who were suffering. She found it hard at times to keep her emotions in check. Sometimes, she wondered if Sean understood what was happening to the tenants; he seemed oblivious to the suffering and focused on his needs. He hadn't matured as much as his older brothers had.

As they had grown into men, Thomas and Samuel had seemed to leave their bullying ways behind. Thomas, the older son, was not loved in the county as much as his father, and despite her wariness of him, from what she'd seen so far, he was fair in his dealings with the tenant farmers. He didn't have the charm and good demeanour of his father or, if the truth be told, of his youngest brother, Sean, who took more after their mother.

Samuel was an enigma to Caitríona, always coldly polite and preoccupied with whatever it was that he did with the estate. Sean was very different to his two older brothers.

Her knees shook as she thought back to that wonderful Sunday afternoon in the glade. She'd thought of nothing else for the three weeks—day and night, and the exquisite sensations that had arisen in her as she became a woman.

Sean's hands had cupped her cheeks, and he looked down at her, his eyes holding hers as he had shown her his love in the age-old way. Since that afternoon, she had begun to let her hope build that there was a future for them.

Sean O'Byrne loved her; she knew it. She had been in love with him since she was old enough to know what love was. For as long as she could remember, and before that wonderful afternoon, their relationship had always had a strong foundation. Roaming the woods together, collecting eggs, swimming in the river, and sharing their dreams.

That friendship had now developed into an adult relationship, and Caitríona was sure that Sean would soon declare his love for her.

She dreamed of it each night as her stomach gurgled with hunger, and she listened to Mam sobbing in the bed she shared with Da.

##

Country Kerry, Ireland - Summer, 1846.

Caitríona carried the jug over to the fire and smiled at Da. James Lowe had always been a fine style of a man, tall and rangy but as strong as an ox, his red hair making him stand out in a crowd. Along with his height, she had always been proud of her dad's strength and honest character. She knew she had a special place in his heart, being the only girl, even though there were six boys after her.

When times had been better, Da had always been generous with little gifts for her from the market, a ribbon here, a posy of flowers there - one for Mam and one for her every time he went to market.

How times had changed.

The worry etched on his fine features and the weight he had lost over the past year had turned him into a shadow of the man he had once been. Da's smile wasn't as ready these days, but he still reached out and squeezed her arm as she walked past him with the jug.

As she topped up his glass, Caitríona frowned as he glanced at one of the men who was about to speak. He nodded towards her and then shook his head.

She knew there were things that she was not privy to, and she despaired. Patrick and Joseph were old enough to understand that change was coming, but they didn't seem to care. They would eat their bowl of gruel and run out to play. She did miss John and Michael, even though since they had gone away to work on the mussels, more of the work at home had fallen on her shoulders. By the time she worked at the big house all day and then came home to help Mam with the little ones, her bones would ache with tiredness, and her stomach would rumble with hunger.

Mrs Baker would always make sure that Caitríona had

something to eat after the midday meal was served. 'We can't have you fainting from hunger,' she would say, her eyes full of kindness.

Caitríona often thought that Mrs Baker knew everything that was happening, and in her way, she was trying to protect Caitríona. In the early days of the blight, there was enough food at the big house that the kind cook would sometimes send home with her some remainders from the dinner of the night before.

Caitríona's greatest fear was that she would lose her position. At least her wages at the big house provided a few silver pence for Da to buy some vegetables at the market. Those that he could find anyway.

Now she listened to the conversation of Da and the other tenants as they sat around the fire, their voices getting louder as they drank more and more of the *poitin*.

'It's the only way,' the man Da had silenced said, glancing over at Caitríona.

'If it comes to that, it will be,' Da said.

Caitríona, wondering what "it" was and what it would come to, whatever it was. But the conversation turned to a farm not far away where the bailiff had come in and removed the tenants from the land.

'No compassion, no sympathy. No care. They sit up there. They get their money; their bellies are full. Don't they realise what we're going through?' Parick O'Sullivan said, shaking his head.

'This country has changed, all because of some bleedin' black potatoes,' Ronan Duff chimed in. 'Not to forget those fecking English bastards.'

'Next year will be better; the blight will be gone. It was all that rain we had in May that caused it,' Father McIlveen, the local priest, said. 'God's ways are known to him, but have faith, and we will endure.'

'We shall see, Father,' Da said, staring into the fire. 'Faith doesn't fill my children's bellies.'

Once the men had gone home and Da was snoring on the floor in front of the fire, Caitríona crept onto her pallet at the back of the cottage. Since the older boys had gone, there were more beds, and she wasn't sleeping on the floor in front of the fire anymore. The cottage was warm, and she could hear the baby snuffling as he fed.

'Mam, are you awake?' she said softly.

'I am, *macushla*. What's wrong? Can't you sleep? You should be tired. I worry about how hard you have to work.'

'I was just worrying about what Dad and the men were talking about. What is this "it" they keep talking about?'

'You're old enough to know, sweetheart. The O'Connors are going to America.'

Caitríona sat up so suddenly that her head knocked on the shelf above her pallet. 'America? Why are they going to America?'

'Apparently, it's almost as though the roads are paved with gold over there.'

'Surely it can't be that good, Mam.'

'I don't know, but nothing can be worse than it is here at the moment.'

'Is it really that bad? We have food to eat. We are not starving.'

'Not enough,' her mother said. 'It is just as well that John and Michael have gone away to work and that you have the position at the big house. A lot of people are much worse off than us. Many are starving, and many are going to *Teach na mBocht*.'

Caitríona frowned. 'The house of the poor? Why?'

'Because they can get fed there in return for working. There is one in Dingle, and talk of one at Ceann Mara soon.'

'Mam?' Horror filled Caitríona. 'Will we have to go there?'

'No, I would not let that happen, and neither would Da. They are crowded and filthy, and if you don't starve to death, it is just as likely that you will die from infection. You heard your da talking a little bit tonight, and I was listening. I know that he changed the conversation, but I do think you need to know.'

'Need to know what?'

'The ship the O'Connors are taking leaves next week, and there will be a wake for them on Sunday night.'

'A wake, but they are—'

'An American wake,' Mam said. 'Here on our land.'

'But we can't feed all these people; we can only just feed ourselves.'

'Everyone will bring something.'

Mam sat up and put the baby on her shoulder, and a burp erupted from little Finn's lips. Mam laid him down carefully on the other side of her. 'Come up here, my sweet,' she said to Caitríona and patted the straw beside her.

Caitríona crawled up and lay next to her. 'Mam, doesn't look like Da is going to come in tonight.'

'No, he's got a lot on his mind, sweetheart, and I want to prepare you for it.'

'Prepare me for what?' There was a long silence, and Caitríona, tense, waited for the news that she knew wasn't going to be good.

'We can't afford to pay our rent anymore.'

'All will be well. The master at the big house will

understand. He knows that Da will pay it as soon as we have some more potatoes.'

'He doesn't own our land anymore.' Mam's voice was bleak.

'What do you mean? We are tenants on his estate.'

'No, only a small part of the estate is left. A few acres around the big house. They are doing it as hard as we are, perhaps even harder because they have staff to pay and a huge house to keep warm, plus the stables and the animals.'

'While we're in the summer, things will be all right because it's not as hard as when the winter comes. And then we will have the new crop of potatoes in the autumn. We will be all right, won't we, Mam? We have to be.'

'We will be gone before the autumn, Caitríona.'

'But why, Mam? What will we do? Where will we go? Not to America like the O'Connors?'

'We still don't know. But as we are not able to pay our rent, the bailiffs will come.' Mam's hand reached out and held Caitríona tightly. 'Your da has been writing to his uncle in America, and I would say we will be leaving before the autumn.'

'But we can't, Mam. I have my job, and what about the boys down at Lough Mahon?'

Caitríona jumped as a wet splotch landed on her arm. She sat up. Tears were rolling down her mother's face.

'If we go, we can't afford to take you, Caitríona. Or John and Michael.'

'What can you mean?'

'Well, you have a position at the big house, no matter what happens. I'm sure that the master will be keeping you. At least you and Mrs Baker. I heard that Miss Ellis is moving away to Dublin.'

'Every cloud has to have a silver lining,' Caitríona muttered. 'But what about the boys?'

'They're working hard, and they're old enough now to make their way in life, as you are too, my sweet girl.'

'But when will I see you if you go?'

'We'll ensure that you join us when we are settled and when we can afford it. But don't fret. It is only talk at the moment, but I wanted to prepare you. I didn't want it to come as a huge shock to you.'

Country Kerry, Ireland - Summer, 1846.

Caitríona looked at Da in shock and disbelief; she dropped to her knees, her hands covering her face. 'No, Da. I don't want you to, you cannot leave, you can't go.'

He had taken her aside after the meagre porridge they had shared for dinner and told her that their passage had been booked for two weeks hence.

'I have spoken to Mr O'Byrne,' Da said, 'and there is a room at the back of the stables that you will be able to live in. He has also agreed that he will increase your pence slightly, as you will be taking over a lot of Miss Ellis' duties when she is gone. If you save what you earn now, you'll be able to join us sooner. I have enquired about the cost of a single passage, and it will take you four months to save enough money to book your passage.'

'But I don't want to go to America,' she said. 'I want to stay here, and I want you to stay here.'

'I'm sorry, Caitríona. We can't go on like this. The alternative is we all starve to death or, worse, the bailiff comes. They shot two farmers over in Lissyclearig last week.'

'Why?'

'Because they refused to leave the land.'

'But they can't do that. It's against the law.'

'Scarce a week goes by without some sort of atrocity in our country, and our communities facing the possibility of imminent eviction are rising against the landlords, their agents, and the bailiffs.'

'The famine is leading to the unthinkable.' Caitríona lifted her apron over her face and sobbed.

'And that is why we are leaving. Your Uncle Seamus has secured us a passage to Liverpool and thence to New York.'

'I'm not coming to the wake,' she said, jutting her chin out.

'Ah, *macushla*, you look just like my mam, your grandmother. I know you have a lot of her strength and that you will be fine. It will be easier for you once we have gone.'

'It won't. I will miss you all. I will not be at the wake.'

'You must. It's your way of saying farewell to us.'

'No, I will come to the port when the ship leaves, and I will say farewell to you there.'

'No, you cannot take time away from the big house. You will say your farewell to us at the wake.'

'When do I have to go and live in the stables?' she said, finally accepting her fate.

'Not until we leave. We'll be packing up and travelling to Galway, where the boat leaves from.'

Caitríona drew in her breath to stop the deep gulping sobs that threatened.

'It will only be for a few short months, and then you'll be with us in a new country—a country full of opportunities, a country that will be delighted to have a young woman with so many skills.'

Something deep inside Caitríona told her that she would never be going to America, whether it was because she didn't want to or because she had some sort of premonition. It would mean leaving Sean.

Chapter 23
Country Kerry, Ireland - Summer, 1846.

The moon was full, and the wind blew warm on the night of the American wake for her family. However, Caitríona picked up her shawl before she went outside; the wind could still be chill at night. Ever since Da had told her they were leaving, she had been cold and scared and wondering what was going to happen.

And sick.

All she wanted to do was talk to Sean and see if it was true that the big house was struggling too. She also needed to talk to him about what she suspected, but there had been no sign of him at the house this week, and Caitríona didn't want to ask where he was or give any hint that she and Sean had a special friendship. Thomas had been nice to her for a change and had even given her a small bag of carrots and turnips to take home.

'I've got a feeling these may help your family,' he said roughly. 'I'm sorry to hear that they are leaving. Your da is a good man.'

Her eyes widened, and she looked up at him. 'Thank you,

Thomas. I'm sure Da will be very grateful.'

He grunted and walked out of the kitchen. Mrs Baker raised her eyebrows. 'I think that young man is finally growing up,' she said.

'Perhaps,' Caitríona said. It was the first time she had seen Thomas being nice.

'I can't see it lasting, though,' Mrs Baker said, shaking her head. 'Times are changing, girl. But you know that more than most.'

Caitríona put her head down and focused on the pastry that Mrs Baker had her rolling with a huge rolling pin. She worked up her courage and swallowed, 'Mrs Baker, my mam told me that Miss Ellis is moving to Dublin. Is it true?'

Mrs Baker's face was turned away, and Caitríona wondered what her expression was as the portly woman nodded. 'Yes, that's right, dear, at the end of next week. You'll be doing some of her duties.' Mrs Baker turned and looked over the top of her spectacles.

Caitríona nodded. 'Oh.'

'Don't worry; we both will be doing some of her work. And there will be a few fewer mouths to feed shortly.'

'Are the master and mistress going to England again?'

'No. 'Tis the boys.'

Caitríona's head flew up. Did she mean Sean?

'What boys?'

'Thomas and Samuel.'

She didn't let on that Sean had already told her they were leaving.

'No, I wasn't earwigging, but I heard a conversation that's best left private. You'll see in good time, girl.'

Now, as Caitríona made her way out of the cottage, she

pulled the shawl around her shoulders. The wind wasn't as cold as she expected, but still, she kept her shawl around her.

Da had a huge fire burning about a hundred yards from the back of the cottage, near Finnihy Stream, where a large crowd had gathered. Patrick O'Flaherty was singing a maudlin song, and as she walked towards the group, she could see that many of the women were crying. Loud cries came from small children as they played happily on the bank of the stream, not realising what a sad occasion this was. Mam and Da and two of her brothers were standing to one side, and Caitríona watched as women and some men went up to say goodbye. Her eyes filled as Mam lifted her apron and buried her face at one stage, and when she lowered the fabric from her face, Caitríona could see the desperation and sadness in her mother's eyes.

She walked over and put her arms around her mother, pushing her own fears aside.

'We shall send the remittance to have you join us as soon as we can.' Her mother's voice broke.

'It will all be good, Mam, and I will be there with you before you know it.'

Mam nodded and hugged her back, and Caitríona stepped aside as two more women stood beside her mother to say farewell.

'Caitríona.'

She jumped as a warm hand reached beneath her shawl and touched her elbow.

She spun around, the firelight putting macabre shadows beneath Sean's eyes. It didn't look like her Sean, for a moment.

'I have come to pay my respects to your parents. Father asked me to tell your da what a good tenant he has been, and he will be sorely missed.'

'Thank you.'

'I cannot stand it any longer. It is so unfair.'

'Stand what? What's happening? Sean, I've been looking for you all week.'

'Perhaps walk down to the stream with me? Would that be acceptable?'

'In these topsy-turvy times, Sean, I don't care what is acceptable. Come, take me walking.'

Sean led the way and she followed him in the shadows until they reached a place where the noise and the crying and the sad music receded into the background.

'What can't you stand, Sean?' Caitríona was cold inside and out. The wind was warm, but her fear was growing. Something was very wrong.

'We'll walk a little bit further, and then I'll tell you.'

A few moments later, they reached the edge of the forest, where slivers of moonlight seeped through the thick canopy above. Sean took his jacket off and spread it on some soft moss beneath the trunk of a huge oak tree, then took her hand as she sat down. He sat beside her, and she could feel the warmth of his body, but he didn't hold her. She needed to be held, but he seemed distant.

'I'm sad, Sean, and I'm so confused. Why do things have to change so much? Just because some stupid potatoes rotted in the ground.'

'It's got a lot more to do with the way that the situation is being handled,' he said. 'Did you know that Father has sold most of our estate?'

'I had heard that,' she said. 'What does that mean?'

He rested his head back against the trunk and closed his eyes.

Caitríona reached out and touched his hand lightly. 'Sean, talk to me. What's happening? I'm scared.'

'Why are *you* scared?'

She hesitated. 'Because I am being left behind. And I will have no one.'

She waited for his reassurance or his kiss, but Sean was quiet and turned his head away.

Sickness roiled in her stomach, but she kept trying. 'And the same for my brothers, John and Michael. They are not going to America either.'

'Then they will be here to look after you.'

'Can't you look after me?' She couldn't help begging, and that made her feel even sicker.

'No. Thomas and Samuel are leaving in six weeks, and Mother and Father are going to England to live on the estate that Father owns there.'

'But he has an estate here; why can't they stay here and look after his tenants? By God, they need support.'

'They are no longer Father's tenants, and because of the situation, it is dangerous to be in Ireland at the moment. There is much aggression towards the landowners.' Sean's voice was bitter. 'It is all right for me to be at risk, though. I will be looking after the estate. I am the one who most wants to leave this godforsaken country, and yet I am the only one who will stay.'

Perhaps it was the time to tell him that she thought she was having their child. Perhaps that would make him happy. But Sean's distant and whining tone held her back.

'Well, at least we'll get to see each other more often,' she finally ventured.

His jaw tensed in the faint moonlight, and he looked away from her.

'I'll be in the stables,' she said. 'We won't have to meet in the glade. You can come to me.'

'I know you will be there. I couldn't have you in the same house, Caitríona; it would not be the right thing to do. And I cannot come to the stables. Someone would see, and then where would I be?'

Where would *he* be?

Confusion filled Caitríona, and she tried one more time to make him listen to her, to how she felt, and then perhaps she would tell him what she suspected. 'Oh Sean, you do know how I feel about you, don't you? You have never told me if you feel the same.'

'If I told Father that I had been with women from the cottages, he would cut me off without a penny, and I too would be homeless,' he said.

Women? What did he mean?

'We could be homeless together, Sean.'

'No.' His head lowered towards hers. 'But I need comforting tonight, Caitríona. Perhaps you can show me some comfort?' She tensed as his lips ran down her cheek towards her mouth, and his hand groped beneath her shawl.

Disgust raced through her, and her stomach roiled so much she thought she was going to vomit.

A foolish, gullible woman. That's all I am.

'No.'

'Come on, my sweet. I am unhappy.' His fingers touched her bare skin, and Caitríona shoved him away.

'Unhappy? You are a selfish, thoughtless man, Sean O'Byrne. Do you not realise that tomorrow is the last time I may ever see my parents and my brothers? Do you even care?'

'Please, Caitríona?'

'No,' she spat. 'Go and seek your comfort elsewhere. I'm sure there will be a *woman* who is willing.'

Sean jumped to his feet and strode away. Any hope that Caitríona had harboured dissolved into dust.

***

Saying farewell to her family was the hardest thing that Caitríona had ever done. Last night, she went to Da and begged him to let her go with them. He was in his cups but still sober enough to shake his head.

'Not yet, Caitríona. But soon.'

This morning, Uncle Seamus had helped pack their few belongings onto the cart that would take them to Galway before their passage to Liverpool, where they would wait for two weeks before they boarded the ship to America.

Her brothers were full of excitement, the smallest three too young to realise what leaving would mean, but Patrick clung to her when she kissed him goodbye. Mam's eyes were bright with unshed tears, but she had vowed last night when Caitríona had crawled into bed with her that they would not cry this morning.

Caitríona had shed all the tears she held last night, and Mam had held her close, thinking she was crying about them leaving this morning. That was a big part of it, but she cried because of the uncertainty of her situation. She didn't want to go back to the big house, but she had no choice. She never wanted to see Sean again, and most of all, she was terrified of going to the workhouse and having her baby there.

Da held her close and rubbed his rough cheek against hers. Mam held her so close it hurt, but as promised, they shed no tears.

Soon, they were on the cart, and Uncle Seamus flicked the

whip, and the donkeys pulled it away. No one looked back; Mam and Da's backs were stiff as they stared ahead.

Caitríona's steps dragged as she walked to the big house, carrying her small bag with her ribbons, her shawl and her handful of possessions. She had taken Da's mug last night and slipped it under her shawl, so she could look at it and think of her father.

'Ah, my darling girl.' Mrs Baker met her as she walked into the scullery. 'Come and we will set you up.' The kindly woman clucked around her as Caitríona walked into the house and put her small bag on the floor beside the door. She went to the linen press down the main hall and brought out a soft feather pillow and a blanket. 'This will ease your pain if you have a comfortable bed,' she said.

The old tack room at the back of the stables was a much more pleasant space than their mud cottage. It may not have had the woollen rugs and the fine ornaments of the big house, but it was large and clean, and Caitríona closed her eyes as Mrs Baker helped her make up the bed.

A real bed. She didn't tell her she had never slept in one before. A place of her own to sleep that she didn't have to share with anyone.

The tears that had ached behind Caitríona's eyes all morning finally burst free, and Mrs Baker cradled her against her bosom. 'Come, girl; it will be all right. When I said goodbye to your mam, she told me you will join them shortly anyway.'

'I don't want to go there,' she said. If she did, her parents would know about the baby.

'Why would you want to stay here?' Mrs Baker shook her head. 'I've watched Master Sean and you sneak off together. You have to realise there is no future there for you.'

'Oh, I well know that. We are a different class, and we can never be together. He will not be coming to me; I assure you of that. I have already told him.'

'Good. Come to the scullery when you are set, and you can roll the pastry for an apple pie. Perhaps that will cheer the household up.'

When Mrs Baker left her, Caitríona ran from the tack room. She hurried through the gate, clattering over the cobblestones and went to the grass behind the stables. Crouching, she leaned forward and rocked backwards and forwards before she started to retch.

The following Sunday morning, Caitríona did not go to Mass as she normally would before helping Mam with the boys. She sat in the glade, her back against the rock, her head bowed. The rolling hills, the quiet stream and the familiar oak tree, did not ease her as it always had. As she lifted her head and stared at the water, a black cloud descended as she grappled with the certainty that she was carrying Sean's child.

She sat, her fingers curling in the soft grass, her back against his rock, in the place where she had become a woman.

Tears rolled down her cheeks as she wondered what her future would be. How long could she work for? Could she hide the fact that she was carrying a child? Or would she end up in one of the workhouses when her condition became obvious?

She covered her face as her tears began to fall.

'Caitríona.'

For a moment, she thought Sean had come to her, and then, as she sat up, she knew it wasn't his voice.

Her eyes clouded as her gaze lit upon Thomas. Her fear of him had long gone. He could do nothing to hurt her anymore.

'Thomas. Why are you here?' She had never seen him in the glade before.

'I thought I might find you here. I've seen you come to the glade on other Sundays.'

Her eyes widened, hoping that Thomas hadn't seen her here with Sean.

'I needed some fresh air,' he said. 'And I was hoping you would be here. You too have heard of what has happened at the house today?' he asked quietly.

Caitríona scrubbed at her eyes with her apron, and when she looked at him, she could see the sadness in his expression. If she didn't know better, she would think that his eyes were red too.

'No, it is my one day off. What has happened?' For a moment, she thought perhaps Sean had had an accident.

Thomas was pale, and his eyes were sad. 'It is my father.'

She jumped to her feet and took his arm before she could think. 'The master? What is wrong?'

'The physician is with him and says my father will not live to see another sunrise.' Thomas blinked.

'I am very sorry to hear that. Why are you not with him?'

'I was, but I needed to clear my head while Mother sits with him.'

'Where are Samuel . . . and Sean?' she asked hesitantly. 'I will come back to the house. I am sure Mrs Baker will need me, even if it is Sunday.'

Thomas looked at her long and hard. 'Samuel is with the bailiff, and Sean is still in Berkshire.'

'Berkshire? Does he not know of your father's illness?'

'He does, but he has chosen to await Father's passing at the estate of his betrothed.'

His words struck Caitríona like a thunderbolt, the weight of her mistake pressing down on her.

'His betrothed?' Her mouth was dry, and stars spun at the edge of her vision.

'You did not know?' His voice was bitter. 'None of us are what we appear to be, dear Caitríona. I'm afraid my brother led you astray. I hope you didn't think your future was there.'

'I know that.'

'Father has arranged a marriage with a young woman from England. Lydia will bring enough dowry with her to keep this household running, so that will be paying your wages. I'm sorry that my brother cannot fulfil your dreams, but it appears, Caitríona, you already knew they were merely dreams.'

'I cannot stay here,' she whispered.

'That's why I wanted to speak to you,' Thomas said. 'You know I have always admired you. You're a strong woman, and you are a hard worker.'

She looked up at him. His hands were twisting his hat around and his cheeks held a flush. Thomas and Samuel didn't have the fine looks of Sean, but they were both handsome men.

'What did you wish to speak to me about?'

He held her gaze steadily. 'I am seeking a wife to accompany me to New South Wales. I believe you will be most suitable.'

Her head flew up, and she stared at him. 'What . . . what are you saying, Thomas? Suitable?' Her thoughts were in chaos as she tried to understand what he was saying.

'It may come as a shock to you, Caitríona, but I'm asking you to be my wife. There is nothing for you here. Your parents have gone, Sean is getting married and will take over the estate, and Samuel and I have been banished to the colonies. It will remove you from Sean's temptation.' His eyes remained steady on hers.

'Why are you going to the colonies?'

'There is no need to know the details of the why, but be assured that Samuel and I are not able to stay in Ireland due to an event that took place recently.'

'I know nothing of that, and I know nothing of the colonies.'

'Life will be very different there. I would say it will be hard, but I think nothing can compare to the hardship we are encountering in our country at the moment.'

'What will you be doing there?' Her curiosity was growing at the prospect of a solution to the situation she was in.

'My father's cousin has had much luck in the goldfields in Victoria, and he has purchased a large amount of land. Samuel and I are going to help him stock the property with sheep. It may be different from our estate here in Ireland, but our knowledge will help him. My uncle has no agricultural knowledge; he is an engineer which assisted him greatly in the goldfields, so he has requested that Samuel and I return to the colonies with him.'

'What would I be doing?'

'You would be my wife. You would take care of my household, and I would hope we have children. In return, I give you my promise that I will look after you and give you a satisfactory home, as best I can afford and a pleasant life.'

Thomas reached out and took her shoulders, and Caitríona tried not to flinch; she was still uncertain of his motives and had yet to be convinced he was serious. Surely, he would not jest, on the day that his father was dying?

Her experience with his younger brother had destroyed her trust.

'So, I am asking, Caitríona, whether you would consider accompanying me across the sea and starting a new life as my wife.'

'You are not speaking in jest?'

'No, I am not.'

Her emotions were in turmoil. She didn't know what to say or what to do; logically, her mind told her it was a solution to her problem. Whether she would consider it or not was something she would have to give much thought to.

Even though Sean had used her, Caitríona knew she still loved him; they had been friends for many years, but the thought of working in the house he would bring his new wife to was one she could not abide.

Her heart told her she wanted to be with Sean, but her head told her that would never happen. He had taken advantage of her friendship, of her love for him, and now he was marrying an Englishwoman.

She took a deep breath and looked up. 'How long will you give me to think on this, Master Thomas?'

'Thomas will suffice,' he said. 'I will need your answer by tomorrow.'

'Very well, I shall consider your unexpected proposal.'

Thomas looked down. 'I apologise for . . . for laying hands on you in the house months ago. It was unseemly behaviour, and I apologise for forcing my unwanted attention on you,' he said.

'Thank you, Mas—I mean, thank you, Thomas. I accept your apology.'

'Very well. May we meet here at sunset tomorrow?' he asked.

'Yes, we may. I will consider your request, and I will have an answer for you tomorrow.'

##

The marriage of Caitríona Lowe and Thomas O'Byrne was celebrated in the Catholic Church in Kenmare town three days after Thomas' father was buried. There was no need for banns or consent of either's parents, as they were both of legal age, and Thomas was keen for Caitríona to accompany him when he and Samuel left in three days.

Guilt consumed Caitríona, and she forced it away as best she could. It had not been hard to decide to accept Thomas, as he had presented her with the only solution she was likely to have. However, she well knew if she told him she was carrying Sean's child, he would be certain to retract his proposal and she would end up in the workhouse. She would cope with that, but she was not prepared to risk the life of her child. Already, she was thinking of the child she carried as hers; Sean had been wiped from her heart.

So, when she met Thomas in the glade at sunset the day after he had proposed, Caitríona agreed to become his wife and to travel from Ireland far across the sea with him.

Their wedding day was fair, and Caitríona wore the dress she wore to mass each Sunday. She was surprised when Thomas presented her with a posy of fresh flowers before they climbed into the carriage to travel to the church.

Sean was still in Berkshire; Mrs O'Byrne was still prostrate with grief after the death of the master; Samuel and Mrs Baker witnessed the ceremony. Thomas' lips were cool on hers as the priest instructed him to kiss his bride, and Caitríona closed her eyes, desperately trying not to think of Sean and his kisses.

Their marriage was consummated in a lodging house in Galway as they awaited their passage to Liverpool. She had been on tenterhooks, wondering if it would be obvious to Thomas that she was not pure, but he said nothing and showed no regret as he held her close afterwards.

Their journey to Port Melbourne was to take seventeen weeks on a sailing ship, and Caitríona hoped that by the time it was obvious that she was with child, Thomas would have no doubt the child was his. She would be a good wife and make it up to him for the rest of her life. But he must never know.

As they made their way down to the dining room in the lodging house at Liverpool a few days later, Thomas' hand was warm on her elbow.

'I hope you have no regrets, Caitríona.' His lips were close to her ear. Since they had spent five nights in the same bed, an easiness had developed between them.

'No, I have no regrets, thank you, Thomas.' Her eyes were still wide from the new sights she had seen sailing on the ship to Liverpool from Galway and the new clothes and shoes that had been purchased for her.

She was grateful that she had worked in the dining room at the big house on occasion because the dinner table in the lodging house was very different to that in their mud cottage.

'When you write to your parents, I would like to enclose a letter for your father. You have an address in America?'

'Yes, Da told me, and I wrote it down before they left.'

They were sailing to Australia on the *Avoca* and their departure was three months hence. As Thomas and Samuel discussed their plans for breeding sheep in New South Wales, Caitríona couldn't stop herself from comparing Thomas to Sean. It wasn't a favourable comparison for Sean. Thomas had a strong face, and he spoke with confidence and certainty.

Perhaps she had judged him too harshly.

Chapter 24

Ceann Mara Station - Thursday.

Cat stood in the bathroom, gripping the counter of the vanity and trying to compose herself. All she could think of was the girl who'd been murdered, wondering if it was someone she knew or someone she'd seen around campus. It was horrendous, whoever it was.

Her thoughts went back to the night that she was assaulted, and she knew how lucky she'd been; it could have been her in that skip bin. Her family could have been burying her.

As she stared in the mirror, her shoulders sagged as a wave of exhaustion rolled over her. Last night, she'd woken up and not been able to get back to sleep when a door had closed quietly downstairs, and a flashback had slammed in.

That night in their apartment she'd heard a door shut. She was aware of someone in her room when she'd heard it, but everything was fuzzy and she had lain there motionless, holding her breath. Her head had been spinning and she'd felt nauseous, but she'd known she wasn't dreaming.

Now she realised it must have been Scarlet coming home.

But from where? She hadn't gone out. As Cat lay there, after the front door had shut, someone had quietly opened and then closed her bedroom door. After that, she'd heard the front door close quietly. It must have been when she remembered waking up briefly with a fuzzy head and going back to sleep. This was the first time she'd remembered the sound of the door. Maybe more would start coming back to her now.

Turning the tap on, she sluiced her face with cold water. Hoping desperately that the fragment of memory would return and bring more with it. More she could tell Logan, and more she would have when she spoke to the police.

Strangely, she had trusted Logan instinctively. Maybe it was the detached skills he had developed as a detective, but she felt comfortable talking to him. He was a good-looking man, calm and in control. He'd been so apologetic about frightening her with the rifle yesterday. Even though she sensed that there was more to him than Dad knew, she had felt strangely comfortable in his presence.

When she told Mum and Dad everything yesterday, she was worried that they would judge her and find her wanting.

She hadn't gone into the details of all her injuries with them; it was too embarrassing.

She picked up the soft hand towel and pressed it against her face, absorbing the cool water. Once her face was dry, she rubbed her hair with the towel and fluffed it up. Walking into her bedroom, she slipped her shorts off and pulled on a pair of jeans and a long-sleeved shirt. She certainly wasn't going to show her scars over a computer connection. If they needed more information from her, they could come out here because there was one thing she was sure of: she wasn't going back to Sydney.

Not yet, anyway.

***

The afternoon sun cast long shadows across the O'Byrne

back porch as Logan sat with Tom and Laura for a late afternoon tea. Cat hadn't reappeared since she'd gone upstairs. The atmosphere was heavy with tension as they sat quietly on the porch.

'Is Cat all right?' Tom finally asked.

'Yes, she was good. And after we have coffee, she's agreed for me to ring the Newtown police and she'll talk to them.'

Laura put her hand on her chest. 'Thank God for that. Thank you, Logan. I didn't think we were going to be able to convince her. And she's an adult, so we couldn't interfere and —'

'No, you couldn't, Mum.'

Logan looked to the door where Cat had appeared. She'd changed her clothes and tied her hair back, but he could still sense the tension in the way she held herself.

'I'll get you a fresh coffee, love. This one has gone cold.' Laura jumped up.

Cat shook her head. 'It's fine. I can drink this one quickly and we can get this over and done with. And then I'd like something a bit stronger. Is there any wine in the fridge?' She walked over and sat on the chair beside Tom. Logan noticed that her father reached out and squeezed her hand, and she smiled. The more time he spent in their company, the more he could see how close the O'Byrne family were. She shook her head as Laura gestured to the plate of scones.

'There is,' Tom said. 'Logan, we've taken some steak out and were hoping you'll stay for a barbeque afterwards.'

Logan blinked at the unexpected invitation. 'Well, that would be good. If you're sure.' He glanced at Cat.

'I'm not an invalid, and it would be good to have some normal conversation after this interview is over,' she said.

'Okay then, thanks, Tom.' Logan spread his hands. 'I've come empty-handed.'

'I'm sure we'll manage,' Laura said. 'Tom has one of the biggest wine cellars known to man. Are you a wine drinker?'

'I'm known to be partial to a fine red,' he replied with a smile.

'I'll show you my cellar later,' Tom said.

Logan was pleased to hear Cat chuckle. 'You'll be sorry, Logan. You'll be down there for hours. It's Dad's pride and joy.'

Laura laughed too. 'Between Tom's cellar and his family history research, it's a wonder he gets out onto the station at all.'

'I'll look forward to hearing about both.' Logan put his coffee mug on the table; he noticed that Cat had drained hers. 'Are you right for that phone call now?'

She nodded and stood. 'Let's go.'

He paused and looked back at Tom and Laura as Cat headed to the hall. 'This could take a while,' he said quietly. 'Don't worry, I'll keep an eye on her.'

'Thank you, Logan. We certainly owe you.'

He shook his head as he followed Cat. 'No, you don't.'

Chapter 25

Ceann Mara Station - Thursday.

'So, what are you studying at uni?' Logan asked, turning to face her as she sat on the sofa in the study.

Cat knew he was trying to get her mind off the interview and calm her nerves.

'Environmental science. I've finished my degree now, and I can start putting some plans in place here with Dad.'

'What sort of plans? Agricultural type things?'

'No, river management.'

'I don't know much about that, apart from what I've seen online. I'd be interested to learn more now that I'm starting up out here.'

'You spend a lot of time online?' she asked curiously.

'A bit. Keeps me from becoming too much of a hermit.'

'You'll have to tell me what made you move out here, Logan.'

'I will. One day,' he said, taking his phone out of his shirt pocket. 'Are you able to log onto the computer there, or is it Tom's?

'I can log on. Why?'

'I'd say once we have the phone conversation, the

detectives may want to have a conversation face to face. It's easier for both sides to see the body language, and to get more of an understanding of the questions and answers. Would you be okay with that?'

She nodded.

'So, you're right to go?'

'Yes.'

Logan must have put the number into his phone while she was upstairs, as he pressed a speed dial, and she could hear the phone ringing as he put it on speakerphone.

Cat closed her eyes as it picked up and Logan introduced himself as Detective Logan Wainwright from Brisbane C.I.D and then explained why he was calling. It took several minutes, but eventually, another man came onto the line and introduced himself as Senior Detective Jack Nichols.

'Detective Wainwright?' he asked.

'Yes, this is Logan Wainwright. Thank you for taking my call,' Logan said. 'Before I start, I'll advise that I am not calling in an official capacity. I'm currently on leave and at my farm in New South Wales, out near Bourke. Also, the phone is on speaker.'

'What can I do for you, Logan?'

'I've met a young woman by the name Caitríona O'Byrne who until recently resided in Newtown and is a university student. I believe that you are heading an investigation into a series of assaults in the local area and, more recently, a murder investigation.'

'That's correct.'

'Caitríona was recently the victim of an assault in Newtown, and she would like to speak to you about it.'

Cat opened her eyes to see Logan watching her carefully.

His eyes were a deep olive green, and he was close enough that she could see gold flecks around the irises.

'Okay?' he mouthed silently.

She nodded.

'Where is she now?' Nichols asked.

'Sitting in the study beside me. We're at her family station that is across the river from my property.'

'Is she able to speak to me now so I can take a few details to begin with?'

Logan looked at Cat again and she nodded, breathing in and out evenly, forcing herself to remain calm. This interview was going to make a difference to her and she didn't want to hold it up or come across as a cot case by getting upset. She glanced across at the small bar in the corner and wished that she'd thought to pour a glass of brandy to fortify her.

'I'll hand the phone over to her. Also, Jack, we have access to a computer if you wish to make this a virtual face-to-face interview.'

'Thank you.'

Logan's fingers brushed hers as he handed her the phone, and she got a whiff of a citrus aftershave or deodorant. She focused on speaking clearly and firmly as she introduced herself.

The phone was still on speakerphone so she placed it on the desk while she spoke so Logan could hear too.

'This is Caitríona O'Byrne.'

'Hello, Caitríona, thank you for speaking to me. I just have to ask some questions, and then we'll decide whether we'll come out and see you.'

'Come out and see me way out here?' she said.

'It may be necessary, plus we need to get the names and addresses of everyone that you were with that night as well.'

'I don't know all of them,' Cat said.

'Okay, can you please tell me your full name and date of birth, the date of the incident, your address in Sydney, and the name and address of the property you are calling from?'

Cat gave the information as requested, spelling her Christian name and their surname. Her voice strengthened the more she spoke.

'Thank you. Now I want you to tell me very slowly and in clear language exactly what happened.'

##

By the time she finished talking to the detective, Cat's whole body was shaking. She hadn't noticed that Logan had moved closer and was holding one of her hands. She gripped a glass of water in the other and vaguely remembered Dad bringing it in after she'd been talking for a while. She lifted the glass to her lips, finished the last mouthful, and handed the glass to Logan. He let go of her hand as she slumped back into the sofa.

'You did well, Cat,' he said quietly.

'Strangely, even though I'm shaking like a leaf, I do feel better,' she said. 'Talking to Detective Nichols has made it feel like something can be done. I'm so pleased that a little bit came back to me last night. Remembering that I'd heard the door shut.'

'A huge investigation is underway, and your information will add a lot to it. You were very clear, and your answers were great,' he said. 'And something will be done.'

'I was shocked when he said they'd fly out here. We'd better go and tell Mum and Dad. I forgot to tell him there's an airstrip here.'

'Are you all right? Your legs aren't going to give way or anything?' Logan's voice held concern.

'I'm fine. A little shaky. Nothing that a big glass of red can't fix.'

Logan stood and crooked his elbow. 'Another red drinker?'

'We didn't get much choice growing up in a house with Dad's wine cellar.' Cat stood and slipped her hand through Logan's proffered arm. 'Take me to the inquisition, Logan.'

Mum and Dad were still out on the back porch, but a bottle of red wine sat open and breathing on the table with four wine glasses, replacing the coffee and scones.

Mum jumped up; Cat smothered a smile as Mum looked at their linked arms as she came across to them and held out her arms to Cat. Logan went over to Dad, and Mum wrapped her arms around Cat. A wave of emotion rolled through her, and she held Mum tightly.

'All good, love?' Dad asked.

Cat cleared her throat and blinked away the tears that threatened as reaction set in. 'I'm fine, but I'd love a glass of that.' She pointed to the wine.

'Dad and I were talking while you were in there. We don't think you should go back to Sydney for a while. Until they arrest this person,' Mum said as they walked across to the two sofas. Logan waited until she sat, and then he sat beside her. Cat shot him a smile; he had been awesome while she was on the phone.

She lifted her head and stuck her chin out in her stubborn pose, one that her parents were familiar with. 'You've got no reason to worry. I'm not going back to Sydney.'

'At all?' Dad frowned.

'Well, maybe someday. I had thought about working towards a PhD, but I've got my degree, and I'll graduate in absentia. I've given it a lot of thought, Dad. I don't need to do honours or my doctorate. I don't plan on being an academic or working for a government agency, so I don't need it,' she said.

Mum frowned, but Dad looked happy. 'So, what are you going to do with your life?' Mum asked.

'Do you know the biggest priority for me at the moment?' Cat said, taking the glass of shiraz that Dad passed to her.

'No, what's that?' Mum asked.

'Staying alive and doing what I love, where I love to be.'

Mum's face crumpled, and she reached into her pocket for a tissue.

'You should know out of all of us, it's me and Shea who love being on the land the most.' She smiled as Dad put his arm around Mum as she dabbed at her eyes. 'I'm okay, Mum. Please don't cry. I'll let Logan give you a quick rundown of what's going to happen. I need to make a couple of phone calls,' she said. 'I gave some names to the detective, and I need to let them know. I need to speak to Scart and Jilly, my friend from the coffee shop. I need to tell everyone that I've come home and that I won't be back. Especially Scart. I'm sure she'll be wondering when I'm coming back. She'll need the rent.'

'I'll fix that up, love,' Dad said. 'Do you have her bank details?'

'Yes, in my banking app on my laptop. It's still in my car.'

'Don't make any hasty decisions,' Mum said. 'Not until you're feeling a bit better.'

'No, I'm not going back. I've made up my mind. Scarlet's going to have to get a new roommate for next year, and they both need to know that the detectives will be contacting them. I gave both their names and a couple more.'

'Okay, do you have their numbers?' Mum asked.

'No, my phone is still in Sydney. I don't know their numbers off the top of my head, but I know the name of Jilly's coffee shop, and she's got a landline in the shop. I'll talk to her, and that way, I can get Scarlet's number too.' She turned to Logan. 'I left Sydney so quickly I left my mobile phone there. I'd better do it now because she closes about four-thirty. Unless it's Friday? I've lost track of the days over the past few weeks.'

'It's Thursday,' Logan said. 'What about the others you mentioned? The two guys. Will you ring them?'

'No,' Cat said slowly.

Dad sat up straight. 'Are you saying you know who it was? Have you remembered?'

'No, Dad. The detective asked me not to—yet—but he said I could speak to Jilly and Scart. I'll need to tell Rod sooner rather than later that I'm not doing my honours year. We were thinking of collaborating. So, he'll need to change his proposal.' Cat put her nose up to the wine glass and sniffed, savouring the rich aroma of the shiraz. She took a good sip and stood.

'Dad, can I use your computer while Logan fills you in?'

'Of course, and when he's done, we might go down and have a look at the cellar and pick a decent bottle to go with the steak.'

'I'll get some salads sorted and then make a potato bake while you're in the cellar,' Mum said.

'I'll help you when I get off the phone.'

'Thanks, love, that would be nice. You just call out if you need me, all right?'

'I will, and thank you both. I have the best parents in the world.' She picked up her wine glass, and as she walked past Logan, Cat put her free hand on his shoulder. 'And thank you for supporting me through that phone call, Logan. You made it a lot easier.'

'You were great.' He lifted his hand and touched hers, and

she smiled down at him.

'I'll see you at dinner. Don't let Dad bore you to tears in the cellar, will you?'

'Our Cat's back.' Cat heard Mum's whisper as she strode down the hall. And she *was* feeling more like herself with every hour that passed. Speaking to Logan and then Detective Nichols had been cathartic. Her head was clear now, and there was no more fuzziness.

Chapter 26
Ceann Mara Station - Thursday.

Cat pulled Dad's swivel chair out and settled onto it, putting her feet on the footrest beneath the ornate timber desk. She clicked the mouse, and the browser came up to the Google home page. Her hand shook slightly as she looked at the screen; it had been more than three weeks since she had been online. Her laptop was still in the car in the shed. She swallowed her nerves and typed in *Crazy Goat Café*.

As she'd expected, like many businesses these days, there wasn't a website for the coffee shop but a link to Facebook and Instagram pages. The café number was listed in the Google search results, too, and she took a screenshot of it and sent it to the printer, suspecting Dad wouldn't have Facebook on this computer.

Much to her surprise, when she clicked on the blue Facebook icon on the desktop, the program opened to a profile called *Riverbeds*. A few *Crazy Goat Cafés* were listed on the left in the search results. She clicked on the one with King Street, Newtown, beside the name. Sure enough, there was a landline and a mobile listed on the Facebook profile, plus a note that said Messenger was live for coffee orders.

Cat smiled; she'd love a Jilly coffee, but it was just a little bit too far to go. The closest coffee shop to the property was in Bourke, more than a hundred kilometres north. A strange feeling took hold as she scrolled through the photographs and the posts, recognising some of Jilly's signature cakes and interior and exterior views of the cafe; it was as though she was looking at an unfamiliar world, not one that had been a part of her life for the past three years.

Before she let her stress build again, Cat closed down the browser and picked up the handset on the desk. She took a deep breath and punched in the number of the coffee shop.

'Crazy Goat.' She recognised Deb's voice.

Suddenly, Cat's mouth dried, and her tongue almost stuck to the roof of her mouth. She picked up the wine glass, took a hefty slug, and then cleared her throat.

'Hello, Deb, It's Cat. Cat O'Byrne.'

'Cat? Shit, Cat, where are you? We've missed you,' Deb's voice rose in pitch. 'We've been worried.'

Cat could hear voices in the background, and then Deb said, 'Here's Jilly. She wants to talk to you.'

'Thanks, Deb, good to talk to you.'

Jilly's voice was so loud Cat had to move the phone away from her ear. She hadn't thought to put the handset on speakerphone. It was so long since she'd used a landline, she couldn't remember how to do it anyway.

'Cat, where are you? Are you back? We've been worried about you. We couldn't ring you because you left your phone in the flat, and Scart and I had no idea where your family property was. We've emailed and had no reply, and we Googled everything we could think of but had no luck. I'm so relieved you've called. Have you seen Scart yet? Are you okay? Is your family okay? What happened?'

'Too long a story for a phone call, Jilly, but everything's okay. I'm not in Sydney; I'm still at home. I need to talk to you about something. Hang on, don't go away.' Cat put the handset down and reached for a tissue from the box on the side of the desk. Annoyingly, tears were leaking from her eyes and that made her angry. When she'd blown her nose and wiped her eyes, she picked up the phone again. 'Are you still there?'

'Yes, are you sure you're okay?'

'Yes, I am now. Look, something happened in Sydney, and I had to get away. Everything is okay at home, and I couldn't ring you because I forgot my phone and I didn't have anyone's numbers, but I had a brainwave today. I realised I could contact you by looking up the cafe and getting yours and Scart's numbers.'

'It took you a while to think of that, but hey, it's good to know you're okay. What happened?'

There were loud voices in the background, and she heard Jilly yell, 'Sorry, no more orders. We're closing now.' Her voice lowered. 'Sorry, Cat. I want to concentrate on your call.'

'Before I talk to you, can you give me Scart's number too, please? I'll give her a call when we finish. Just in case we get interrupted.' Cat picked up a pen and took a piece of blank paper out of the printer drawer.

'Sure, I've got it in my phone. Hang on a minute. Can I text it to you?'

'No, I'm on a landline. Can you read it out, and I'll write it down?'

'Hang on a sec. I'll pull my contacts up on my mobile. Right. Got a pen?'

'Yes.'

Jilly read out the number. 'I'll give you my mobile too. It's not on the Facebook page; that's the shop one.'

'Thanks,' Cat said after she'd taken down the two numbers. 'Listen, I'm okay now, but I've had a few bad weeks. There was a bit of an incident the night before I left, and I've been talking to the police today.'

'The police? What the hell happened?'

'I was assaulted. I feel bad because I should have called Scart before because I think it happened in the flat.'

'What! You think?'

'I've been a bit vague and haven't been able to talk about it until the last couple of days, but I'm on the mend now.'

'Oh, sweetie, are you sure you're okay? What happened? What sort of assault?'

'The worst kind. But I'm okay. I've got a lot of support here.' She didn't mention the cuts.

'Oh, Cat. I'm so sorry to hear that. When are you coming back?'

'I don't know. I have to talk to Scart first. But listen, Jilly, the police will probably contact you and Scart because they took a few names from me today. Plus, they have the address of the flat and the name of the coffee shop.'

'Why us?'

'Because you were going to come out with me that night. And because Scart might have heard something too or found something in the flat. They'll probably turn up and have a look at my room. So, I'll call Scarlet now in case they arrive this afternoon. I've not long hung up from talking to them. Maybe they'll talk to you, maybe not.'

'Shit, Cat. Did you know there have been other assaults? And some of them have been connected to the *Singapore Sing*

Song Bar.'

'I do, but I've only just found that out. If I'd known there were more, I might have pulled myself together faster and got in touch. But I've been totally off social media and the news. I've been a bit of a mess.'

'I am so sorry to hear that. Are you sure you're okay now?'

'I'm getting better every day.'

'I don't know whether I should tell you this, but'—Jilly lowered her voice— 'did you know there was a murder? They found her body at the back of that bar.'

'Yes, I know that now. I only found out today. That's why I finally contacted the police. Do you know who it was?'

'I don't know her name, but Scart will be able to tell you. She was in your year.'

'Oh, shit.' Dread gripped Cat's chest, and her voice choked. 'Okay, I've . . . got to go. I'll stay in touch. I'll call Scart now.'

'Okay, sweetie. But give me your number first. And where the heck are you now? What's your address?'

'I'm at my family's station. *Ceann Mara* near Bourke.'

'We looked that up. Do you spell Kenmare, K E N—?'

'That's how it's pronounced but it is spelt with a C.' Cat spelled out the name of the station.

'Jeez, no wonder we couldn't find it. You've got no idea how hard we tried. We tried uni admin, but they wouldn't give out personal details. Scarlet thought your friend, Rod, might have known because he lives out that way.'

Cat shook her head. 'He's from down at Pooncarie. A long way from here. I'm really sorry I didn't call earlier.'

'As long as you're okay now. You look after yourself and get better. We'll see you soon, I hope.'

'Thanks, Jilly, and thanks for being my friend.' Cat disconnected, and exhaustion overtook her as her emotions took hold of her body. She picked up her wine glass, took a big sip, and sat back, letting the alcohol warm her on the way down. But she knew she couldn't afford to give in to the lethargy that was gripping her limbs; she had to talk to Scarlet.

Cat glanced at the time on the computer; it was just after four. She still hadn't booted up her laptop to check her emails; that was a job for tomorrow. So, she had no idea what Scarlet's schedule was now. Lectures had finished for the semester, thesis proposals would have been sorted, and who knew where Scarlet would be? She might even have gone home from uni already.

Cat put in the number that Jilly had sent through, and it only rang twice before the call was picked up. Scarlet didn't identify herself. Cat knew they were all wary of unknown numbers these days; there were so many scams—and worse— around.

Scarlet answered hesitantly. 'Who's calling please?'

Cat spoke quickly and stayed calm. 'It's okay, Scart. It's me, Cat.'

'Oh my God, Cat, where are you? I've been so worried.'

'I know. I just got your number off Jilly.'

'Why haven't you answered my emails? Haven't you got internet at the station? Are you still there?'

'Yes, I'm still home at *Ceann Mara,* but I haven't had my laptop on yet.'

Scarlet's voice dropped to a whisper. 'I'm sorry, Cat. Did someone die?'

'No, Scart. It's all right. I'm okay. Now. Where are you?'

'I'm at the flat. I've been working in the library at the uni for the past three weeks. Shelving books. I just got home about ten minutes ago. When are you coming back to Sydney?'

'I don't know if I am yet. I'm thinking twice about doing my honours.'

'Why? Did they want to change your proposal that much?'

'I don't know. I haven't checked my email.'

'People have been trying to get in touch with you,' she said. 'A couple of the guys asked me where you were too.'

Cat froze. 'Which guys?'

'Gavin and Rod and another new student who was with you one night when we went out, Royden, I think, his name was,' Scarlet said.

'I don't know any Roydens.'

'Oh, I'm sorry, Cat; I shouldn't be rabbiting on. Please tell me why you went home. And what do you mean you're okay now?'

Going through the whole story again wore Cat out, but Scarlet didn't say anything as she listened. Cat finished up. 'I finally spoke to the police today, and they'll be calling you. I'm sure they'll want to come to the flat.'

'Cat, I am so, so sorry. If only you'd told us, I would have taken you home. And Jilly too. She's been worried.'

Weariness took hold of Cat. She reached for her glass, but it was empty. 'I'm sorry, Scart; I'm going to have to go. If you want to talk to me, call me on this number, but not for a day or two. If you need to get in touch with me to ask anything, I can talk to you in a couple of days, or send me an email. I'll boot up my laptop tomorrow. This is my dad's landline number, and the station is about sixty kilometres south of a place called Louth. I don't think I ever told you exactly where our station was.'

Scarlet's voice was still quiet. 'I knew it was on the Darling River. It's so good to talk to you, Cat. I can't wait to see you.

Are you sure you're okay, hun? It's been a tough few weeks here. I didn't even think of the same thing happening to you.'

'Do you mean the murder?' Cat asked quietly.

'Yes, and more assaults. We've all been very careful. We haven't gone to that bar. We've pretty much stopped going out at night. We're always home before dark. It's been lonely here without you. I've watched a hell of a lot of Netflix series on my iPad.'

'Who was it, Scart?' Cat whispered.

There was a long silence before Scarlet answered. 'Esther Griggs. I think she was in your lectures.'

Cat's throat closed. 'Yes, she was,' she finally managed to say. 'She was in my tutorial group too. She was another station girl from up near Moree.'

'I thought so. Gav and Rod are really upset. She was part of their group that always went out on Friday nights after squash.'

'Oh, shit, Scart. That's awful.' Cat took a deep breath. 'How did she die?'

Another long silence.

'I can't talk about it.' Scarlet sounded as though she was crying.

'Tell me, Scart. I can look it up. I'd rather know from you than read all about it.'

'He cut her throat.'

'Oh, fuck.' Cat grabbed for the desk as the room spun around her. Gradually, everything righted itself, and she was aware of Scarlet talking.

'Sorry, I missed that. What did you say?'

'I need to see you in person, Cat. To make sure you're okay.'

'I'm okay.'

'How about we FaceTime?'

Cat knew she couldn't do it now. After going through what had happened so many times this afternoon and hearing how Esther died, Cat was exhausted.

'That would be great, but not for a couple of days, okay? I'll call you when I'm ready. Scart, can you do me a favour?'

'Anything, hun.'

'Can you post my phone out to me here?'

'For sure. I'll grab it and should be able to make the post office now if I hurry.'

'Thank you.' Cat gave her the station address, spelling out *Ceann Mara*.

'Shit, no wonder we couldn't find it. I didn't even think of it starting with C.'

'That's what Jilly said. I'm sorry I didn't call.'

'It's okay. It shows me what a bad place you've been in. We'll talk in a couple of days. I'll run down to the post office now.'

'Scart? Be careful.'

'I will. Love ya, Cat.'

Chapter 27

Ceann Mara Station - Thursday afternoon.

After she hung up, Cat spent some time alone in the study. Her energy came back slowly, and she felt better. Stronger. Talking to Jilly and Scarlet was another hurdle crossed. However, knowing it was Esther Griggs and how she was murdered was something she set aside to process later. She refused to think about it now.

She couldn't.

The smell of garlic drifted down the hall, prompting her to switch off the computer. She stood, took a deep breath, and walked down to the kitchen.

'Cat. Are you all right, sweetheart? At least you've got some colour back in your cheeks.' Her mother was sliding a dish of potato bake in the oven.

Cat sniffed appreciatively and focused on normality, not murder. 'I'm good, and that smells wonderful, Mum. I must remember the way you cook the onion and the garlic with the potatoes before you layer it into the casserole dish.'

'How did you go?' her mother asked. 'Did you talk to Scarlet?'

'I did, and she was relieved to hear from me.'

'That's good. You've improved so much these last couple of days. I hated the thought of leaving you when we went to Broken Hill, but I think it was the best thing we could have done. We've got our Cat back,' Mum said, holding out her arms.

'It made me get outside. I'd probably still be locked in my room if you hadn't gone.' Cat put her arms around Mum's waist, resting her head on her shoulder. They stood there for a quiet moment, and Cat could feel her mother's love enveloping her, healing her. Eventually, she took a step back. 'I love you and Dad, you do know that, don't you?'

'You don't have to say it, sweetheart. We know,' Mum said. 'But you know what I want to do? I want all my girls to come home for a visit. I want to have all my family around me.'

'That would be good.' Cat stepped away and walked over to the window. 'I'm sure they all miss *Ceann Mara* as much as I did. It's been a long time since we were all together. Where are Erin and Joe now?'

'Not too far away. In New South Wales somewhere anyway. Maybe we could all be here for Christmas. It's not that far away. What happened to you has made me think, Cat. It's brought back a bit of my anxiety,' her mother admitted.

'Anxiety? Is that what you meant when you said you had some sedative stuff you took during some episode?' Cat asked, recalling their conversation. The last few hours of talking blurred together, and she couldn't remember exactly what Mum had said.

'It was nothing much, sweetie. Just when Bridget went off to boarding school for her second year, and you were all gone, it took me a while to come to terms with being alone here with Dad.'

'You should have said something,' Cat said.

'I mean, don't get me wrong, I love your father. Your dad and you and your sisters are the most important people in my life. But for a while, when you went off to uni, Bridget went back to boarding school, and then Shea moved to Wilcannia, I felt as though I wasn't needed. Dad was busy out in the paddocks because it was so hard to get workers, and we had a lot of contractors in. You girls were all busy with your lives. Bridget was only home in the school holidays. Shea was home the occasional weekend. I felt like I wasn't important to anyone. I mean, I know you love me, but there was no reason for me to be here. I'd cook your father's meals and keep the house clean, but that didn't matter. No one needed *me*. I needed to find myself.'

'I'm so sorry to hear that, Mum. I guess we all get so involved in our own lives; we don't think about what we leave behind as we find our way,' Cat said sympathetically.

'It's all right, I sorted it out. Dad flew down to Broken Hill to go to the library a few times, and I saw a clinical psychologist. She was a good help to me, but it took me a few weeks to tell him what I was doing.'

'Did Dad spending so much of his time on the family history bother you? Was that a part of it?'

'It did at that stage, but I'm fine now. He gets so much pleasure out of it, and I know he's looking forward to you being home to help him with it because he knows you love it just as much as he does.' Mum reached down and set the timer on the oven.

'So, how did the psychologist help you?' Cat asked, wondering if it would be worth getting a referral.

'I learned some cognitive behaviour exercises and went to a naturopath on her recommendation and got a herbal supplement to help me sleep at night. I got myself sorted in about two or three months.'

'You should've told us, Mum,' Cat said with concern.

'I was embarrassed, and I felt weak.'

'I know what you're saying. It was pretty embarrassing having to tell you and Dad what happened that night in the flat, but it's also hard to admit that you're not coping emotionally.'

'I could see the state you were in as soon as you walked in a month ago. I knew what you were feeling. I should have tried harder rather than listening to Dad and leaving you alone.'

'I was in a pretty bad way when I got home. I'm sorry I worried you and Dad for those few weeks.'

'It's fine, sweetheart. Everything's sorted now, and you're just going to get better and better every day,' her mother assured her. 'And I'm going to feed you up. I made your favourite lemon cake today.' Mum went over to the sink and started to wash the lettuce that was sitting on a tray.

'Thank you. Now, what can I do to help?' Cat asked.

'You don't want to rest before we eat? You've had a very emotional day.'

'No, I'm better if I'm doing something.' And if she was busy, she wouldn't be thinking about poor Esther. She deliberately hadn't told Mum because she knew she'd lose it if she talked about it. She'd face that later.

'You can slice up some of that cooked beetroot and put it in some apple cider vinegar for me,' her mother replied.

'Where is it?'

'In the fridge. I cooked it last week. We've had a good veggie crop this year. It's been hard to get tinned beetroot lately, so I've been growing my own, and it's much nicer.'

They worked together companionably for a while, chatting

and exchanging the occasional smile as they moved from one end of the kitchen to the other.

'I feel sorry for Logan. Dad's obviously taking him through every vintage and every bottle, telling him the value of each one and where he bought it and how long it's been cellared,' Cat remarked. The cellar was underground beneath the conservatory and part of the original nineteenth-century structure.

Mum chuckled. 'Probably. But I'm pleased Dad has his hobbies. I always remember how your grandfather was immersed in the station.'

'Grandad was. Dad will be in his element down there. Poor Logan.'

'He seems like a nice young man,' Mum said.

'Not that young, Mum. How lucky were we that he bought Uncle Gary's place?'

'I think he was pretty helpful with you today, wasn't he?' her mother observed.

'He was. He does seem like a really nice guy, but I wonder what he's doing out here,' Cat mused.

'He didn't say, but I don't think he's got any family out here. He's from Queensland.'

'People have a lot going on in their lives and in their heads, don't they?' Cat went to the pantry for the vinegar.

'They do. I might sound like an oldie, but I honestly think it's worse these days.'

'Maybe people talk about it more. Plus, it's always shared on social media too.'

'True. Now, when you finish that beetroot, I'll get you to grate the cheese for the top of the potato bake,' her mother instructed.

Cat smiled. Things were slowly getting back to normal.

##

When they finished in the kitchen, Mum took off her apron.

'I'm going to go and get changed, brush my hair, and put some lipstick on,' she said. 'Dad and I've decided we'll cook and eat in the campground. Is that okay with you?'

'I'll look forward to it. I can pretend I'm a tourist,' Cat said. 'I might go up and have a bit of a wash and put something warmer on.'

'It won't be cold there. We'll get the fire going as soon as we get there.'

'I'll just grab a light jacket then.'

By the time Cat came back downstairs, Dad and Logan were sitting out on the back porch. She smiled as she came through the door from the kitchen. There were two bottles of red and one of white wine lined up on the table, and Dad was extolling the virtues of one red over the other.

She walked in, stood behind her father and looked over the top of his head at Logan. He seemed to be interested in what Dad was saying. Maybe he was being polite.

'You survived the orientation of the O'Byrne cellar by the look of things, Logan,' she said when Dad paused to draw breath.

'I certainly did. What a great collection Tom's got down there.'

'Only problem is, we all drink it when we're home, and Dad doesn't like us doing that. And please explain, dear Father, why have you got three bottles out for tonight?' she teased.

'Don't stress; we're not going to drink them all. I was just showing Logan the different labels from the same vintage in the Hunter last year. I reckon that hand-drawn one will be worth a bit in a few years.'

'Well, we sure won't open that one, Tom,' Logan said with

a grin.

'That's your favourite vineyard, isn't it, Dad?'

'It is, but the ones from Mudgee are coming a close second this year. They'll be pretty good after they've been cellared for three or four years.' He glanced into the kitchen. 'Where's Mum?'

'She's getting changed, and then we're going to head down to the campground.'

'Okay, I better go scrub up a bit too.'

'Anything I can do to help. Take stuff down to the campground?' Logan asked.

'No, just sit here and keep Cat company, if you would.' Dad flicked a glance her way, and she knew he was still worried about her. She reached up and grabbed his hand as he walked past.

'Stop worrying, Dad. I'm good.'

'Did you make all your phone calls?'

'I did, and everything is fine.'

Sounded good, anyway.

'Okay, I'll be back quickly.'

Cat sat down and met Logan's eyes across the coffee table. 'Sort of fine,' she said.

'What do you mean?' Logan looked at her curiously. 'What's happened?'

'The girl they found at the back of that bar—she wasn't exactly a friend—but I knew Esther. She was in my tutorial group, and her thesis was going to be based on the water management of the rivers out here as well.'

'That's a bit close to home.' Logan frowned.

'There's one more thing that the police might be interested in too. Maybe you could call Detective Nichols back for me.'

'Yes?' He frowned.

'My friend said that a few of my friends have been asking after me, and they said a guy called Royden wanted to know where I was. I don't know any Roydens.'

'Certainly worth mentioning. I'll give him a call back.'

'I'd like to say thank you, Logan. It was good having you here today. Especially with the call to the police.'

'I'm glad to be of help, Cat. You really are feeling better?' She nodded.

'You've got a lot more colour in your cheeks.'

'Just as well,' she said. 'When I'm pale, all my freckles stand out.'

'I think they're pretty,' he said, holding her eyes with his. 'You are a standout woman, Cat.'

'You mean, I stand out in a crowd with my fire engine red hair.' She chuckled to hide her self-consciousness at his compliment. 'You can come over and visit anytime you want.'

'I'd like that,' he said. 'Now, what can I do to help you?' Logan asked.

'I'll grab Dad's keys off the hook at the back door, and if you could bring the twin cab around, we could load it up. I'll get the meat, salads, and stuff out of the fridge. Mum said there's crockery and cutlery at the campsite, so it's only the food and the wine we need to take.' She stood and walked over to the key hooks along the picture rail beside the back door and brought the ute keys back to Logan. 'It's the white ute parked at the end of the shed. Just bring it along the front road and park outside the front gate, and we can carry the stuff out through the front door.'

'I'll make a quick call to Nichols while I'm out there. You're quite sure you don't know a Royden?'

'Totally.'

Fifteen minutes later, Mum and Dad reappeared, and Cat and Logan loaded all the meat, salads, condiments, and potato bake into the back of the twin cab.

'Thank you, you've done well,' Mum said.

'I'll just get the wine,' Dad said. 'Jump in, and we'll drive up. I'll only be a minute.'

'I think I might walk up,' Cat said. 'It's a lovely night, and it's going to be a cracker of a sunset. Would you like to walk with me, Logan?'

'That sounds good. If I'm drinking that wine tonight, I'll need some fresh air and exercise.' He chuckled. 'I'll just have to be careful not to drink too much, or I might get lost on the river on the way back in the dark.'

Dad shook his head. 'I was going to suggest you stay the night. It could be dangerous navigating across in that punt in the dark; you wouldn't want to hit a submerged log or anything. The river's changed since the last flood. I wouldn't even be confident in the dark.'

'Yes, Logan,' Mum chipped in. 'We've got plenty of spare rooms, and the three downstairs are made up. You're most welcome to stay the night. That way, you can have as much wine as you want and not have to worry about getting home safely.'

'Well, I appreciate that. There's no chance of me going DUI, but I wouldn't be feeling very confident about navigating that river in the dark. Or facing snakes in the dark.'

'Snakes?' Cat asked with a frown.

Logan shook his head. 'You're sure to find out eventually, but a big tough detective has to have one weak spot. And snakes are mine,' he said. 'Thank you. I accept your kind offer, Tom and Laura.'

Chapter 28

Ceann Mara Station - Thursday night.

The evening down at the campground with her parents and Logan was very pleasant. They ate in the undercover area near the barbeque and then moved to the fire pit with the second bottle of red wine. Cat relaxed, her limbs light and fluid as she stared at the flames. The longer she sat there, the more her emotions settled. She'd only had one glass of wine, as she was feeling very tired and didn't want to fuel any nightmares tonight.

The night had been full of laughter, and that had been better than medicine for her. Dad's sense of humour had come to the fore, and then Mum had rolled her eyes as the conversation turned to their family history.

'My grandfather, Harry, was the second-born son. His older brother, Gilbert, didn't come home from the First World War. Their grandfather, James, was—'

'Tom, you're putting Logan to sleep,' Mum chided gently.

Cat smothered a grin as Logan sat up straight and shook his head. She'd noticed his eyelids drooping when Dad had moved from talking about the property to his favourite topic, their family tree.

'Not at all, Laura,' Logan reassured her. 'It's interesting, and it makes me wish I had more idea about my family and where they came from. You truly belong to this land, whereas I'm a blow-in.'

'What do you know about your family?' Dad asked.

'I haven't much idea at all. I was an only child. My dad passed away not long after I joined the police force, and I've got no idea where my grandparents came from . . .' he hesitated, and Cat waited, but he didn't finish.

'What about your mother?' Mum asked, forward as always.

'She left when I was young. I don't even know where she is these days. Or if she's still alive.'

'Oh, my God, Logan, that's so sad. I'm sorry I asked.' Her mother looked embarrassed.

'It's okay, Laura. I came to terms with it a long time ago.'

'And you don't know anything about any of your family heritage?' Dad persisted. Cat frowned; honestly, Dad never knew when to stop.

'No, I'd be interested to see how you do it, actually.'

'You'll be sorry, Logan. You'll be over here with Dad all the time,' she said.

One thing that hadn't been talked about tonight was how long Logan planned to stay across the river. Cat wondered if he was going back to Queensland to work. His reluctance to talk about his work past was obvious. All she knew was that he was a detective in Queensland, but he hadn't indicated whether he was going back or whether he'd moved here permanently. It was very much the elephant in the room, or rather, the elephant around the fire, and Mum and Dad must have sensed that because neither of them asked him about it either.

'I've got a lot to do on the station this week,' Dad said. 'I'm depending on you, Cat, to come in and find those dates and names I'm after at the moment. I printed out a lot at the library when we were in Broken Hill, but I haven't had a chance to look at it yet.'

'I just remembered something, Dad,' Cat said. She glanced at Logan. 'Sorry, this won't take long.'

'What, Cat?' Dad waited

'I started to tell you this afternoon; it seems like days ago, but this morning, I found the name of the boat that Thomas and Caitríona came out on.'

Dad sat up straight. 'And?'

'I think it was the *Avoca*,' she said. 'It sailed from Liverpool in 1847.'

'And James was born in 1846 or 1847, I can't remember,' he said. 'I'll have to have a look tomorrow.'

'And it's almost eleven. Time we were packing up. We'll never get going in the morning. Come on, Tom, you've got a lot to do tomorrow.'

'I have. What are you doing tomorrow, Logan?'

'Well, I want to check my new gate and see how many goats got in the paddock.'

'You'll be surprised.' Dad stood and picked up the now-empty wine bottle. 'Why don't you hang around for a while in the morning, and Cat can show you what she's doing? She might need some company, and I'd like her to stay in the study for most of the day. What do you think of that, dear daughter?'

Cat rolled her eyes and pretended to be unhappy. 'Oh, I don't know; surely there are other things I'd rather be doing than looking up the O'Byrne family history.'

'Don't be silly, girl. You're as bad as your father,' Mum laughed as she picked up the empty glasses and carried them across to the camp kitchen sink.

'Are you sure it's all right to stay the night?' Logan asked. 'I don't want to be a bother.'

'Of course it is, come on. We'll get packed up, and we'll show you to one of the guest rooms.'

'I'll walk back, Mum, once we get packed up. It's such a beautiful night,' Cat said.

Logan glanced at her. 'Would it be all right if I walked back with you?' he said.

'Of course.'

They'd washed up the dishes in the camp kitchen after dinner before they'd moved to the fire pit, so it was only a matter of putting the dishes, glasses and a couple of empty bottles into the back of the car, and they were soon packed up. Logan and Cat stood as the tail lights of the twin cab disappeared around the bend towards the house before she walked across and turned the lights off around the campground. It took a while for their eyes to adjust to the darkness. There was no moon, and the Milky Way had almost dropped below the horizon.

'It's certainly calming out here, isn't it?' Logan commented as they stepped onto the road.

'It is when you're outside. I regret to say that my last three weeks have been spent pretty much within the confines of my bedroom. The best thing I did was get out here and ride to the mailbox the other day. I realised how ridiculous I was being, shutting myself away in the room and dwelling on what happened.'

'I can see that you've even improved in the less than twelve hours I've known you.'

Cat chuckled. 'I take after Mum. I come from strong female country stock. I think being in the city has made me a bit weak.'

She stumbled as her boot stubbed a rock, and Logan took her arm. As they kept walking, he didn't let go, and Cat was quite comfortable with his touch; she wondered if he was doing it deliberately to desensitise her.

'So, what *are* your plans for tomorrow?' he asked as they walked along the road.

'Don't listen to Dad. You don't have to stay here with me. I think he's just a bit worried because he forgot Mum was going out. She knows I'm okay. Otherwise, she wouldn't be going.'

'I am interested in having a look at what you're doing with that family history.'

'Oh, if you want to stay, I'm happy to have the company.'

'I might go across the river early and have a shower, check the goats and come back later in the morning, if that suits you.'

'Whatever suits you best. One of the other things I want to do tomorrow—I haven't talked about it with Dad yet because he'll go off on a tangent— is have a look at the old store.'

'Store?' She could see Logan's frown in the faint starlight.

'About a kilometre upriver, there is a sandstone building. You might not have noticed it. Samuel, one of the first settlers, had a store there when the paddle steamers went up and down the river in the late 1800s. He was a bit of an entrepreneur, and there is a little more information available about him than his brother, Thomas.'

Logan looked at her with interest. 'Wow, that's pretty special. I didn't realise how early the river had been settled until Tom told me how old the conservatory and cellar were. It's been a bit of an eye-opener talking to you and your dad tonight. What's in the building?'

'A veritable treasure chest. I know that no one has ever been right through everything. There's a whole attic on one side, and I'm hoping that there might be some family documents stored there somewhere.'

'Would they have lasted that long if there were?' Logan's voice held genuine interest.

'That's what I want to look for. It's been a bit of a quiet quest of mine, and then uni interfered. Dad thinks I'm mad because the floor of the store is filled with metal.'

'Metal?'

'Buckets of nails, ancient shearing gear, horse stuff, ploughs and things we don't even recognise. I can see it being turned into a tourist attraction to complement what Mum's done once—*if* we get it sorted.'

'You guys are amazing. I had no idea what was across the river from my small place. I still can't believe that you're the fifth or sixth generation that's lived on this property. It must give you a real sense of place knowing where you've come from.'

'It's my home. And where I want to be,' she said simply.

'And you don't ever get bored here?'

'No, not at all. Coming back and being out and about the last couple of days made me realise and appreciate how much more I enjoy being here than in Sydney. I've got my degree now, and I'll stay home.'

'Tell me about your sisters. Will they come home too? Are they studying?'

Cat quickly filled him in on her four sisters, where they were and what they were doing. 'But as you'll see when you meet them. I'm the one who's keen to take over from Dad one day.'

They reached the house, and the light was on in the hall. Dad was still in the shed; she could hear him talking to the dogs. 'Come on in, and we'll see what room Mum set up for you,' she said as she opened the back door.

Mum met them in the hall. 'I've put you into the blue room, Logan, because there's a bathroom next to that one.'

'I don't expect that, Laura,' Logan said. 'I'll go home tomorrow and have a shower. I'll come back and have a look at what Cat's working on later in the morning.'

'Well, it's there if you want to use it, and I've put a clean towel out for you on the bed.'

'Thank you very much. I've had a great night,' he said. 'Nice to have company and such good company.'

Laura looked at him and said, 'No, thank *you*, Logan. You don't know what you did for us today.' She put her arm on Cat's shoulders. 'I've got my girl back.'

'Your new saying, Mum.' Cat smiled as she said goodnight before she made her weary way upstairs.

***

The next morning.

Despite having a late night, Cat woke not long after dawn, had a quick shower, and pulled on some work clothes for the day. She made her way downstairs quietly, avoiding the creaky step.

To her surprise, Logan was in the kitchen, filling the kettle. She stood in the doorway for a moment, looking at him; he was unaware of her presence. He was a tall man with well-defined muscles and broad shoulders. His skin was lightly tanned, although it looked like he hadn't spent a lot of time out on his property yet.

She could tell he was a new chum; he didn't have that weathered, rugged look that came with working in the outback heat. But as well as being a totally nice guy, he was very easy on the eye.

Relief flooded through her. It appeared that the assault hadn't had too much of an impact on her in being able to look at and appreciate a good-looking guy. When she first came home, the thought of anyone touching her, even Mum and Dad, had put her on edge.

'Good morning, Logan,' she said brightly. 'You're up early.'

Logan turned around, his smile lazy and wide. 'Good morning. I should say the same to you. I thought I'd get back across the river, but I was going to have a cuppa out on the porch and wait until you came down. I wanted to check whether it was still okay for me to come back over later.'

'As long as you're not in cahoots with Mum and Dad to babysit me.'

Logan put his hands up in front of his chest. 'Not guilty.' His grin was wide, and his eyes crinkled at the corners.

'Good, I would have been disappointed.'

'Not to be in my company for the day?'

'No, disappointed to putting the skids under you if you were only here because it was a setup.'

'Do you want me to be honest?' Logan held her eyes.

'Yes?' she said warily.

'I'm keen to come over to see what you're working on, but the main reason is I enjoy your company.'

A warm flush filtered through Cat as he held her gaze, and after a few long seconds, she looked away self-consciously.

'And I enjoy yours. Plus, I had a brainwave this morning.'

'A brainwave?' he said.

'If you really want to spend the day in the study, I'm happy to show you the photos and documents and stuff, but I think a much better way to get a feel for the place would be to go on an excursion.'

'Where to?' Logan pointed to the coffee jar, and she nodded.

'Yes, please. Well, I was thinking we'll have *Ding-a Ling* on our side of the river when you come back. I love that little punt. If you're feeling energetic, we could row up the river to the store, and I can throw in a thermos and some sandwiches, and we can have a picnic lunch up there. There's nothing to beat rowing on our river. If we have time—and you don't get sick of rowing—I can show you the old woolshed a bit further up too.'

'That sounds like fun, plus a history lesson too.' Logan added the hot water to the two mugs of coffee.

Cat opened the fridge and took the milk out. 'Milk and sugar for you?'

'White with one, please.' Logan waited until she added the milk and pushed the sugar jar over to him.

'I really had nothing much planned today. This goat-herding business should be pretty easy now that I've got the fence done. All I have to do is wait for them to go in there, Tom tells me. Then the work starts.'

They carried their coffee out to the back porch. Logan had indicated that he didn't want anything to eat, and Cat wasn't hungry after the big meal they'd eaten last night. They sat down and watched the early morning sun change the gum leaves from a soft pink to a lush green. The only sound for a while was the squawking of the galahs as they landed in the treetops.

'The place looks good after all the rain we've had. Dad said it's been a really good winter.'

'It's very different to what I was expecting. Can't imagine it brown and dry.'

'How long have you been here?' Cat asked.

'I bought a truck and drove down from Queensland about five months ago with all the gear I needed on the truck. The stuff that wouldn't fit—like the roof trusses—I had delivered. It's taken me about fourteen weeks to build a pretty basic little kit home.'

'You built it by yourself?'

'I did.'

'How did you get the roof trusses up?'

'I used a block and tackle to drag them up. Hard, but it was pretty satisfying when I did it.'

'Well, you're an innovator, aren't you?' she said.

'I do like building, and I enjoy spending a lot of time by myself. I'm a pretty boring bloke,' he said.

'Do you mind if I ask you something personal?' Cat asked. She tipped her head to the side and watched as his expression shuttered a little.

'Well, I know what happened to you over the past month, and you've been very open with me, so I can't say no, can I?'

'If you want to answer, you can, and if you don't want to answer, just tell me,' she said. 'What are your plans out here, Logan? Is it just a holiday place, or are you here to stay?'

He lifted his hand and rubbed his unshaven jaw. A ripple of something unfamiliar went through her as she looked at his strong jaw darkened with that attractive, early morning shadow. She pushed it away.

'Well, I'd like to be able to answer you,' he said, holding up a hand. 'But—'

'No, I'm sorry. It was too personal. Too soon.'

'Let me finish. I *would* like to be able to answer you, but I really don't know. I'm weighing up my options.

'Are you still employed? Do you still have a job back there?'

'Yes. I worked—or rather work—in the Financial and Cyber Crime Group, but I'm on leave at the moment.'

Cat nodded.

'That's one of the reasons that I've reacted to your trauma with a bit more sympathy than I would have once had to your situation. About a year ago, I went through something traumatic.'

Her eyes widened.

'Nowhere near as invasive as what happened to you, but something quite confronting emotionally. I learned very quickly that honesty and integrity don't count when somebody's got a hidden agenda.'

'Can I ask what happened?' she asked. 'Is it confidential?'

'Not really. It made the papers. Or rather one interpretation of what happened was in the media. The sanitised version that was fed to them by the police media unit. Naturally, I didn't come out looking good. But I'm tenacious, and in the end, justice was sort of served.'

'And you still have a job?'

'I do. I became aware of something quite corrupt happening in our unit. Rather ironic when we were investigating financial crime. I wasn't sure what to do. Naïvely, I went to the chief and told him of my suspicions.'

'And then?' she asked.

'And he showed me great interest and great concern about what was happening. It was only a couple of days later that he came to me and asked me to keep it to myself while he put some processes in place. That night, I had what was officially reported as an accident, and I was put on leave.' Logan's mouth was set and his voice firm.

'You don't have to talk about it if you don't want to,' she said.

'It helps, as you discovered yesterday, I think. But I've come to terms with it now. I've had a year to work through it. I was shot in the line of duty, and the investigation found that I had done the wrong thing. Amazing what a cooked-up investigation can do.

'I was walking over to my car, and I bent over to pick up a bolt that I noticed on the ground in the car park. I was thinking I didn't want to run it over on my way out. That bolt saved my life.'

'How?' she whispered.

'The shot that was meant for my head got me in the side as I bent.' He touched his side, just above his waist. 'I was lucky. It was a flesh wound. The guy who shot me took off because a couple stepped from the lift and saw him before he could shoot again. He took off, and they called the ambulance and the police. Otherwise, I wouldn't be here telling you what happened.'

'But how could it say you were shot in the line of duty?'

His smile was grim. 'If you could read the investigation report where I had allegedly shot at this guy first—that I had stalked him with the intent of finding out how much he knew— you would think you were reading a Lee Childs novel. I was put on leave and under investigation. My boss—the corrupt one— was the one behind the whole setup.'

'So, was the truth made public in the end?' she asked.

'Of course not. My boss suddenly retired, and a couple of other guys were put into protection until it was sorted out who the goodies and who the baddies were, as one could say. I went on leave, and I was told it would probably be wise if I disappeared for a while. So here I am. I've disappeared.'

'Oh my God, it's so hard to believe that there's corruption like that in the police force.'

'Sweetheart, there's corruption like that in every level of government.'

'So, you don't know whether to go back or not?'

'I don't know that I want to. I've lost my trust, and in the months that I've had out here, I feel happy. It's a bit lonely, but now I know I've got good neighbours across the river. I'm sure I'll be spending some time over here. I'll be happy to help your dad. He was telling me last night how hard he finds it to get contractors, and everything I can learn from him I can apply to my own place.'

Cat wrapped her hands around the mug and looked down. She was aware of Logan looking at her, and she turned her head and looked at him.

'I think I'd like you to stay too, Logan. I can do with a friend.'

Chapter 29

Newtown - Friday morning, late September.

The *Crazy Goat Café* hadn't been open for long on Friday morning when Scarlet strode through the front door.

'Good morning, Scart, you're out and about early.'

'I've had a brainwave, Jilly, and I have something to ask you.'

'Have the police called you yet?' Jilly asked as she turned the coffee machine on.

'Yes, I had a call yesterday afternoon. I'm actually on my way into Newtown police station now.'

Jilly nodded. 'So did I. They talked to me on the phone and asked me some questions, and they said they'd be in touch if they wanted to talk to me face to face.'

'I have to be interviewed, and then they'll come around to the flat.' Scarlet pulled a face. 'I'm a bit nervous.'

'Are you right to go to the station by yourself, or do you want me to come along with you?' It was easy to see how nervous Scarlet was. She'd been that way since Cat had taken off, and the news of the assaults had started to make the news.

Scarlet raised her eyebrows, hopefully. 'Are you able to get away from here? It would be good to have company. I've never been interviewed by the police before. It was hard enough just talking to them on the phone yesterday afternoon. Let alone being in the police station.'

'Sure, I can come with you. What time do you have to be there?'

'Not until ten. I came to see you and to have a few coffees for courage. It's too early to have a drink.'

'Works out well. Deb's coming in soon. About twenty minutes, and we've got another young girl waitressing for us. Bella comes in at nine. If you can wait until then, I'm happy to come with you.'

'That's fine. It's not far to walk.'

'I'll make your first coffee as soon as the water heats up.'

'Sounds good to me.'

'Have you had breakfast?'

'Not yet.'

'What would you like?'

'The usual.'

Jilly was pleased to see Scarlet smile. 'A cherry Danish or two?' she asked.

Scarlet nodded. 'One will be heaps, thanks. Even though I'm relieved we've finally heard from Cat, I've been sick in the stomach worrying about everything that's happened. Being home alone at night gives me too much time to think, and I can only watch so much Netflix.'

'No need to worry, Scart. We know Cat's fine, and the police are on the case.'

'To be honest, I was scared being in the flat last night. I wondered if there had been someone in her room with her and whether they might have taken her key.'

'That's a good point. Mention that to the police this

morning. Have you thought about getting the locks changed?'

'I don't know how hard it would be to do with it being a rental.'

'Wouldn't hurt to ask the property manager,' Jilly said. 'Listen, I've got a spare room in my apartment. Would you feel more comfortable staying with me for a few nights until you see if you can get the locks changed?'

'Really? That would be fantastic. Thank you so much. Anyway, I want to talk to you about something else.'

Jilly looked up as the door opened, and three customers came in.

'You've got to get the café going, so I'll tell you more about my idea when we walk down to the police station,' Scart said.

'Sounds intriguing,' Jilly said as she reached down and put the milk delivery in the small fridge under the coffee machine.

'It's just an idea I had, but I'm keen.' Scarlet headed for one of the small tables near the window, and Jilly made her first coffee.

Half an hour later, Deb had arrived, and Jilly had the café organised for the day. The glass display cabinets were now full of enticing baguettes, croissants and cakes, and the healthy options that she had made a speciality of in the café filled the bottom two shelves. Bella, the new waitress, who was proving to be an excellent worker, had arrived and was taking orders at the counter while Deb manned the coffee machine.

'I might be a couple of hours, girls,' Jilly said as she headed for the door behind Scarlet.

'Not a problem at all. We'll be fine. Just get everything sorted.' Deb lifted her free hand in a wave.

'Have you talked to any of the others?' Jilly asked Scarlet

as they stepped into King Street.

'Yes, Gavin and Rod, they both rang me last night after a call from the police and they wanted to know what the heck was going on. I didn't tell them much, but they've been asked to go down to the police station later today too.'

'Did you tell them Cat rang us?' Jilly frowned. She'd never liked Gavin; he was a bit of a sleaze. She vaguely remembered Rod from Cat's twenty-first at the Coogee pub.

'I just said that Cat was home and she would talk to us all later.'

'Probably wise. You can't be too careful. It could be anyone, even someone we know.'

'I don't think it would be. We're a pretty close group. I can't imagine any of our friends being deviates; they're all smart uni students.'

'That's a bit naïve, Scart.' They waited at the pedestrian crossing as the light turned to red. 'I was reading an article the other day about the IQ of some of the best-known serial killers.'

'God, Jilly. Why would you read something like that?'

Jilly shrugged. 'I'll read anything I pick up. I didn't go looking, if that's what you're thinking. I was at the dentist.'

The light beeped and turned back to green, and they set off across the road, horns beeping and buses roaring on the cross street. They passed Newtown Railway Station and turned into Eliza Street.

'I think it was just some random that she hooked up with that night,' Scarlet said.

'I still feel bad that we didn't get there. I blame myself in a way.'

'Don't be silly. You had a car accident. You didn't stand her up for no good reason.'

'I still feel bad. Anyway, you haven't told me what you wanted to talk to me about?'

'Well, I don't know how hard it would be, seeing as you've got the coffee shop, but I'm thinking about heading out to visit Cat once the police have talked to me. I was going to go home to Lismore next week, but I was thinking that a visit might do Cat good. Plus, I'll work on her to come back to Sydney next year.'

'That sounds like a good idea. And yes, I'd like to come. I'd feel less bad about letting her down that night if I went out to see her.'

'How would you go with getting time off?'

'I'm due for a month's annual leave. Louis, the owner, is hassling me to take it,' Jilly said. 'I was thinking about taking a holiday. How soon would you be going?'

Scarlet bit her lip. 'Well, I've got shifts at the library all next week. I was thinking about heading out the weekend after that.'

'If I didn't come, would you be all right driving out by yourself? How far is it?'

'A bit over eight hundred ks to that town she mentioned, and then about another sixty to their place. I Googled Louth on Google Maps,' Scarlet said. 'I'm used to driving long distances, but I'd break the trip overnight if I was travelling by myself. If you came with me, I'd try to do it quickly and get you to share the driving. With maybe one overnighter, depending on what time we got away.'

'I'm keen,' Jilly said. 'Leave it with me. I'll talk to Louis and see if Deb can step up and train Bella, and if he can hire another casual, I don't think it will be a problem. He'll agree because he doesn't want me off in the summer.'

Scarlet pulled a face. 'That's the best time to take a holiday!'

'Yeah. Anyway, business has dropped off a bit since the end of the uni year, and there are a couple of new cafes in town that have been slowing business, too. I've even wondered how much longer I'll stay there. Might be the time to move on. The more I think of it, the more I like the idea. I could get paid in lieu of taking leave. I've been thinking about moving up to North Queensland. Lots of jobs up there and a better climate.'

'Okay, sounds like it might work out. If you do come with me, that would be great.'

'Would you tell Cat we were coming or just turn up?'

'I think I'd like to surprise her.'

Jilly nodded. 'Shouldn't hurt and if we can't stay, we could find accommodation close by.'

They slowed their steps as the three-storey dirty cream brick police station loomed in front of them.

'Looks inviting. Not,' Scarlet said.

'I'll wait here in the sun for you. You okay?' Jilly leaned against the building as Scarlet nodded and went inside.

***

After walking back to the cafe with Scarlet after her interview, Jilly checked everything was running smoothly before she made two coffees and sat down with her. Scarlet was pale and had been very quiet on the way back.

'Now, tell me how it went.'

'Well, they kept saying how I should be careful, and that scared me a bit. They're coming into the unit this afternoon to have a good look around. I guess they might do some fingerprinting or something; I had to give my fingerprints. I felt like a criminal.'

'No need to feel like that, sweetie. They're only eliminating you from anything that they might find.'

'I guess they'll have to do that with Cat, too,' she said.

'I'd say so. What about changing the locks? Did they have any advice on that?'

'They agreed it was necessary, and they've given me the name of a locksmith in Newtown who should be able to do that pretty quickly. That scared me a bit too. I kept thinking I've been there nearly a month by myself, and he could have come back any night if he had a key.'

'But he didn't.'

'If it's still okay with you, I'll stay over at your place until I—or we—go.'

'Not a problem at all. Okay, you still want me to come with you?'

'Are you going to come?' Scarlet's face brightened a bit.

'I've been doing some thinking, you know me, I make decisions pretty fast.'

'You are impulsive. I'd like to be more that way. What have you decided?' Scarlet asked.

'I've decided not to take any leave.'

'Oh, it's okay. I'll be able to drive it by myself.' Disappointment crossed Scarlet's face, and Jilly hurried on.

'No need. I'm not taking leave because I've decided to put in my notice. I can get my leave paid out, and then I'm going to pack up the apartment and head north.'

'Oh wow. I'm so pleased you're going to come with me, but we'll all miss you if you move. Not just the café, but you.'

'I intend going somewhere nice up around the tropics. I hate the cold in Sydney. You and Cat can fly up and visit me when I get settled.'

'Wow, that's a big decision to make so quickly.'

'But one I'm feeling pretty good about. It's time for me to move on.'

'What will Louis say?'

'He'll be cool. I'm the third manager here in less than two years.'

The colour had come back into Scarlet's face, and she grinned at Jilly. 'Okay, I need to get organised. I'll head back to the unit now and pack a few things to come to your place.'

'Why don't you pack your bag to go away, and then you won't have to go back to the unit at the end of the week.'

'I suppose I can. I'll have to organise to get the new key from the locksmith too; it would be awful to get home and not be able to get in.'

'Do you like living in that apartment?'

'Not really, not after what happened there. And not without Cat.'

'How much longer is the lease?'

'We only go month to month now because we've done two years.'

'Would you be interested in subletting mine?'

'How do you mean subletting?'

'Well, I've got about three months left on my lease, and I'd rather sublet it than hang around now that I've decided to move north. Even though I'll have my payout, I'd rather not have to hang around here until the lease runs out.'

'I'll think about it. And I'll talk to Cat about your place. I want her to come back to Sydney. And I reckon if she wasn't coming back to the flat, it would help her make up her mind.'

'Have you been to my place? I can't remember.'

'No, I haven't. I know Cat's been there a couple of times

when you had drinks, but I was always working.'

'Okay, see what you think when you see it. It's a pretty nice place and close to Bronte Beach,' Jilly said. 'The rent's not too bad, and if you and Cat share, it'll be pretty affordable. There's a third bedroom too. You could get someone else and split the rent three ways.'

'You've got me interested now,' Scarlet said, putting her cup back on the saucer and picking up her purse. 'I'm going to head back home. I've got some calls to make.'

'Okay, be careful going back to that unit. Why don't you come back here about four, and you can follow me across to my place?'

'Sounds like a plan,' Scarlet said.

Chapter 30

Ceann Mara - October.

Day by day, Cat felt stronger and was feeling like herself again. Taking to her bed for those weeks now felt like a part of the nightmare. Telling Mum and Dad everything that had happened and talking to Logan and the detectives in Sydney had brought her confidence back. The realisation that she had been lucky and escaped a more serious outcome actually contributed to her healing.

Mum and Dad kept her busy each day. Mum had a project underway in the campground amenities block, and she insisted she needed advice every morning.

Cat went willingly.

Dad came in for lunch each day, and then he took the afternoon off and dragged her—although she wasn't terribly unwilling—into the study to work on some papers with him. Cat knew that Mum and Dad were in cahoots filling every minute of her day, and then Logan invariably turned up for smoko every afternoon. He was obviously on the "keep Cat busy" team, too. She enjoyed his company and began to see a keen sense of humour as they relaxed in each other's company. Their planned excursion to the store had been put off a few times as he'd been busy on his property.

'I had no idea there were so many goats on the place,' he'd told them yesterday afternoon when he'd come over for smoko. Cat looked forward to Logan's afternoon visits. They'd all sit over a cuppa, and then he'd row back home before dark.

'We really need to get to the bottom of those first few years here,' Dad said as they went to the kitchen.

Mum had called them into the kitchen, and Cat smiled as they walked in. Her favourite coconut cake with lemon icing was sitting in the middle of the table.

'I thought Logan might like to try this one today,' Mum said.

'Forget Logan,' Cat said. 'I love that cake. Trying to fatten me up, Mum?' Cat walked over to the sink and dropped a kiss on Mum's cheek. She was rewarded with a wide smile.

'I am.'

'You're spoiling me.'

'You deserve it, sweetheart. I've got some news too. I think the girls will be here for Christmas this year. First time in three years we'll all be together.'

'That's worked out well.'

'No, I pulled the "come home for Christmas" request. I wanted to have everybody home at the same time. I don't know what I'm going to do once you girls all get married and have children if you're not near.'

'I can guarantee that I'm going to be near you, but I can't guarantee that I'm going to be married and have kids,' Cat said, her mother's hand reaching out and touching her.

'I know you went through a dreadful experience, sweetheart, but please don't let it impact your decisions.'

'Leave the girl alone, Laura,' Dad said in his best Irish accent. 'Now, can I please have a slice of that cake, or is it just for looking at?'

Cat and Dad ate their first piece of cake standing at the sink so the crumbs didn't go on Mum's clean kitchen floor.

'So, Dad, what will we work on now?'

'Well, I've got all those documents in the National Library of Ireland, like I told you, and I picked up some records from the settlement back in the 1850s at Broken Hill. Thomas settled where we are now. We know that he built the homestead. We've seen the graveyards, and Samuel isn't in the graveyard there. Not that we can find anyway. What I want to know is which was Samuel's property. I always assumed it was the one across the river. But I can't find that in the records.'

'And if that's the case,' Cat interrupted. 'Why did he run the store on Thomas' property? We know that he did, don't we?'

'Yes, because his name is in the few account books that survived the 1880s, and remember, Thomas died in 1875. So, was Samuel working the river before then? Did he live here in the homestead after Thomas died? Did the first Caitríona move away? There's also a piece about him in the Walgett Spectator that I found on *Trove*. Come, and I'll show you.'

They brushed the crumbs into the sink, and Cat turned the tap on and wiped the sink down before she followed Dad to the study. He went across to the desk and lifted up a piece of paper.

'I printed this out a few days before you came home. I haven't had a chance to look any further. Been busy with the goats,' he said gruffly.

'And me,' she said, giving him a quick hug.

'This is an article written about the end of the paddle steamer era.' Dad began to read the paper he held. 'The greatest era of the paddle steamers was in the 1880s, when one hundred and ninety-three of them, consisting of approximately 30,000 tons, carried cargoes of wool, wood, dried fruit and livestock down the Darling and the Murray.'

'Wow, the river must have been busy in those days. It's hard to imagine those paddle steamers coming around some of those narrow bends these days the way the river is now.' Cat leaned over his shoulder.

'Yeah, read this bit.' Dad pointed to the middle paragraph.

'Skippers on the old paddle-boats were courageous men. Between 1853 and 1896—' Cat broke off. 'That's about the time of their arrival and the establishment of *Ceann Mara*. "The navigation of the river was fraught with danger; innumerable snags, erratic currents. Heroically, our river men battled on." I just wish we could find out more. Leave it with me, Dad; I'll get online and do some more digging. There might be more newspaper articles from the nineteenth century. I'll trawl online.'

'One more thing. Read the last paragraph.' Cat looked up. Dad's smile was wide, and she scanned to the bottom of the page. Cat's eyes widened as she read.

The biggest barge seen in Bourke was the Kerry, which was pulled by a paddle boat, named the Ellis. This barge carried 1200 bales of wool from the depot at Louth Bridge to Bourke, where the railroad operated. That was certainly the biggest load taken from the Louth district. Between Wilcannia and Bourke is a big station called Ceann Mara.

Her grin matched his. 'Oh wow. That's us! Right, I'm going to get to work. Where do you want me to start?'

'Samuel is our priority at the moment. There's a whole lot of stuff in that horrible tiny writing from the history documents at Broken Hill Library. It's been photocopied, and I've been finding it hard to transcribe. A hand to do that would be great. I don't know if it's relevant, but it needs to be read. You know what my eyes are like.'

'Have you seen about getting glasses yet?' Dad was always borrowing Mum's reading glasses.

'I'll get there one day.'

Mum poked her head through the door as she walked past with an armful of folded towels. 'When I put these away, I'm going up to the campground, but I'll be back in time for smoko.'

'Did you want me for anything this afternoon, Mum?'

Her mother shook her head. 'No, sweetheart, you stay and help your father. It's just good to see you looking so much better. Your rosy cheeks are back, and I think you've put a little bit of weight back on.'

'Thanks to the coconut cake. You keep cooking them, Mum, and I'll keep eating them.'

'I thought I'd make Melting Moments tomorrow,' Mum said. 'Logan needs feeding up too. He must be lonely over there by himself.'

'Maybe,' Cat said. 'His choice, though. What are you doing at the campground?'

'I've had more enquiries about accommodation. I want to go and check our brochures. I'm sure I put the dates the season ends on them.'

'It's on the website that we're closed for the summer.' Dad shook his head. 'You've got no idea what it's like, Cat. The phone runs hot. The email's always full, with people wanting to stay here at this end of the season, even though we close the last week in August.'

'I checked out your Facebook page too. It's fabulous,' Cat

said. 'Did you get someone in Broken Hill to do it?'

'No,' Dad said with a grin. 'You've got a very clever sister who created it.'

'Shea?' she said, raising her eyebrows.

'No, Bridget. She's been doing computing studies at her boarding school, and apparently, she's got a real flair for it. For her project this year, she did our website and Facebook page. We had to check that it was okay, being a real business, but her computer teacher said he couldn't see a problem with it.'

'Well, it's fantastic. She's very good,' Mum said. 'If people click on the website, I get an email in my email folder. And business has taken off, thanks to Bridget's work.'

Cat chuckled in contentment as she headed for the study. Christmas was still a while off, but it would be so good to see her sisters. She couldn't believe how much better she felt now.

The couple of times Scarlet and Jilly had called, it had been good to have normal conversations; Scarlet's thesis proposal had been accepted.

'What about yours?' Scarlet asked carefully. 'Have you heard anything yet?'

Cat had been quiet for a moment and then admitted that she still hadn't looked at the email.

'Am I sensing that you really don't want to come back?' Scarlet asked.

'I think so. It's not my place. I'm so much happier here. It's not because of what happened, Scart.'

'Cat? Can I just ask you one question, and then we won't talk about it.'

'Sure. Scart, I'm fine now.'

'What did you do with the sheets off your bed that morning?'

'I put them in a bin on my way home. I told the police that. Why? Did they look in my room?' she asked.

'They did your room from top to bottom. They had little ultraviolet lights and fingerprinting stuff and samples from the bathroom and goodness knows what else. Apparently, they're going to try and match whatever they found using a database.'

Scarlet's voice trembled before she tried to speak. 'I'm so sorry I wasn't there that night, Cat. If I hadn't been out picking up the groceries or gone to Maccas, none of this would've happened.'

'You could have been in danger too if you had been home.'

'Are you sure you don't remember anything?'

'Nope. Absolutely nothing. I remember going to the table and sitting with the guys and some of the girls from uni and heading for the loo, and that is my last memory until I woke up. The police reckon my drink was spiked with the date rape drug.'

'Did you know everybody at the table?'

Cat bit her lip. 'I'd rather not talk about it now, Scarlet. Maybe when you come out and visit. I'd still love you to come out one day.'

'I'll try my best,' Scarlet said.

Dad came into the study, and Cat turned her thoughts to the past. The happy past, a past she was determined to unravel.

'Right to keep going, love? We've got an hour before smoko.'

'Sure am.' Cat sat at the desk and was soon back in the nineteenth century.

Chapter 31
Liverpool - 1847.

The O'Byrne's departure from Liverpool had been delayed by eight weeks as the *Avoca* was late returning from its journey to America due to bad weather. Then, when the vessel docked, it needed some work on the rigging, and they were delayed by a further four weeks.

Samuel was impatient to get going and made several trips to London while they waited for their journey to begin. Each time he returned, the number of implements they were taking to the colonies increased.

Samuel was more talkative in her company since she had married his brother, and there was a degree of acceptance by him. Very occasionally he would direct a question to her, and each time he returned from London he enquired after her health.

The relationship between Caitríona and Thomas had settled into a comfortable state. He had been delighted when she told him that she was expecting a child two months after they arrived in Liverpool.

'Can you be sure?' he said.

'I think I am sure, but time will tell. I am missing my Mam,' she said, guilt plaguing her every moment of the day. She knew that if Thomas knew the child was not his, he wouldn't have married her, and she would have ended up in the Irish workhouse. Since their marriage, she had seen a different side to him; he was gentle and kind and always concerned about her well-being, even before he knew she was with child. At times, she was tempted to tell him, but she was reluctant, loath to damage the comfortable relationship they had stepped into.

The only way to deal with it was to tell herself that Thomas was the father of her baby. Some nights, she dreamed of Sean and wondered how he was. His name was never mentioned by Thomas and Samuel, and she sensed that there was a great deal that she did not know about them going to the colonies and Sean taking over the estate.

Caitríona relieved herself of her guilt by writing to her mother to tell her of her marriage. She had carried the address to where her family were going in the city of New York since Uncle Seamus had scrawled it on a piece of notepaper for her and knew that the chance of the letter ever reaching her family was very slim. Letters took months to cross the Atlantic.

'Dearest Mam,

I hope this reaches you and you are in good health and settled in America. Please give my love to Da, and Patrick and, Joseph and Tommy. I am sure Finn has grown, and I wouldn't recognise him now; he would be almost one.

I hope that you have found America to be all that you wished for and that you have settled well in the city. I am sure it is very different to home. You will not be able to write back to me for a long time, and any letters you may have sent to the big house will not reach me as I have news, Mam.

Mr. O'Byrne passed away suddenly three months ago. Samuel and Thomas decided to travel to Australia because much of the estate had been sold off. Sean is now in charge of the estate, and he is betrothed to a lady from Berkshire.

Her mother would not pick up from those words the sadness that gripped Caitríona as she wrote them.

Thomas came to see me the day that his father died, and you will be very shocked to hear that he asked me to be his wife. I believe he was concerned about me having no family to ensure my well-being.

I considered his proposal and accepted, and we married in the village a week after Mr. O'Byrne was buried. I told Mrs Baker if John and Michael came home to visit, to tell them that I have married and moved away.

The separation of our family breaks my heart. A tear fell onto the paper as Caitríona wrote. It was also the thought that Sean had taken advantage of her, and she had foolishly believed that he cared for her, which made her sad.

She sat straight and swallowed as she made sure the ink had not run.

We are now in Liverpool, awaiting our journey to New South Wales on a vessel called the Avoca.

I am full of nerves about travelling on the ocean, but Thomas assures me we will be safe. Since we have been in Liverpool, I have heard many stories of the sailing ships that have taken our people to countries across the sea, and I hope that you had a safe journey.

Oh, Mam, I am happy that we are all away from the difficult times in County Kerry, but I am sad. I will be even further away from you now, and I don't know if we'll ever see each other again.

But I will hope and pray that our lives are happy and that we will meet at some time in the future, even though it may be years before we see each other again. But I am grateful that I went to the village school, and that I can write, and I can read anything that you may write to me.

Please write back to me, Mam, and hold your letters until I write to you again in many months and tell you where we are. By the time I receive a communication from you, I, too, will be a mother.

I am with child. I love you, and I hope you are happy.
Your loving daughter,
Caitríona O'Byrne

##

Twelve years later.
Ceann Mara - Darling River, 1861.

Caitríona sat on the banks of the Darling River, carefully writing on the notepaper that Samuel always brought when he visited. Thomas had brought a plank of wood for her to rest on as she carefully formed her letters. She had no idea what they were waiting for, and when she asked, Thomas smiled and said, 'You will see.'

He had persuaded her that something momentous was about to happen, and she knew it involved Samuel, who had been away for almost a year.

'When?' Caitríona was not known for her patience after having four children. Every moment of the day was precious as she taught the older children their letters, baked bread, washed the clothes, and kept the large homestead clean. At times she thought she could have done with a Mrs Baker, and perhaps even a Miss Ellis, but that thought made her smile. She was the mistress of the new *Ceann Mara.*

'Soon,' Thomas said, placing his hand on her shoulder as he stood behind where she sat on the bank of the river.

'What will I look for?'

'Be patient, my dear. Write your letter. It could be an hour; it could be longer.'

'Until what?'

Thomas leaned over and kissed her cheek. 'Until you see what we are waiting for. Now write your letter as you will not have time later. I am going to walk downriver a way.'

It had taken several years of marriage for Caitríona to learn what a good man Thomas was and to accept she loved him dearly.

In 1856, when their fourth child was stillborn, Thomas had built a small family chapel, and baby Sinead was buried in the small graveyard close to the homestead. Caitríona had known it was God punishing her for the lie that she carried in her heart, and she almost confessed to Thomas that James was not his son. But sense had prevailed, and she knew that she would never tell him. It would ruin too many lives, and they had a good life here on the Darling River.

She dipped the nib in the ink and began to write as her children played happily at the edge of the water.

Dearest Mam

Until the day I leave this earth, I will never forget the day that your first letter arrived. I had given up any hope of hearing from you and often worried that you had perished on the way to New York.

Your news that little Finn had died on the journey broke my heart, and I pray that you and Da can seek solace with the boys.

A squeal had Caitríona looking up. 'Aisling, come away from there,' she said as her two-year-old daughter tripped over in the dirt. Her feet were bare, and Caitríona couldn't help but smile. Her youngest daughter reminded her so much of her own brothers as they were growing up, always wanting to be outside and playing in the dirt.

But the countryside her four children had grown up in was very different to the soft green hills of Ireland and the soft, gentle rain of her childhood. Once her little girl was sitting happily drawing in the mud with a stick, Caitríona continued writing.

James Thomas, our first-born son, was named for Da and is now eleven years old. He is a strong boy with a kind heart and a worker who reminds me of John and Michael. Have you ever heard from them, Mam?

James was born on the Avoca as we crossed the equator. He was an easy baby, and I remain thankful we all stayed well on the long journey to Port Melbourne.

Caitríona lifted her pen and thought back to their voyage. Luckily, the sailing ship they were on was not one of those they had heard horror stories about as they awaited their passage in Liverpool. The *Avoca* was a good sailing ship, and their voyage was pleasant as she and Thomas got to know each other. There was fresh food to eat that was replenished as they stopped at ports on their journey, and she discovered many different fruits and vegetables.

She had stayed healthy as she carried James until his birth during the long journey across the sea from their homeland to the new country beneath the equator. She had seen another side of Thomas in those seventeen weeks that they travelled on the sea. Kind and considerate to her well-being, he was impatient to arrive and had filled the long weeks by assisting on the ship.

Our beautiful Maeve was born two years after James as we travelled to the Darling River through the goldfields in Victoria, where Samuel had considerable luck. Erin was born the year we settled on the Darling.

She didn't write about Sinead. It broke her heart to even think of putting her grief into words.

Thomas and I, James and Maeve, lived in a small shanty on the bank of the river, and by the time Erin arrived, our homestead was almost complete. Oh, Mam, you should see it. Our house is as grand as Ceann Mara in County Kerry, with eight chimneys and our own chapel, conservatory and cellar and I sometimes pinch myself to believe that I, Caitríona Lowe am Thomas' wife, and the mistress of my own Ceann Mara.

Even though the weather in the western expanses of New South Wales is hot, harsh, and dry most of the time, the torrential rain arrives and reinvigorates the land when it is needed. It is as though nature knows when the rains should come.

Travelling through this country was a new experience for the three of us. Samuel and Thomas worked as we made our way north, not knowing what news was to greet us upon arrival. We stayed in small wattle and daub cottages, not very different to our cottage at Ceann Mara, as they worked, and we made our way, following the river north to their uncle's land. Samuel rode ahead on horseback and arrived three months before Thomas and James, and I.

By the time we arrived in the spring of 1853, Samuel had received the news that their uncle had passed away in Melbourne and had left his properties to Thomas and Samuel. His land holdings covered much of the country, and Samuel, being the astute businessman that he is, agreed to oversee many of them. Thomas was quite happy to be granted our land on the

Darling, and we have made a very comfortable life here. Thomas has employed stone masons to build a beautiful homestead for us.

I look forward to hearing all your news. I am pleased that Da has found a position on the railways, and I hope that your life is comfortable. Please give my love to my wonderful Da and my brothers. Tell them how much I miss all of you.

Your loving daughter

Caitríona

'Here it is, Ma.' James' excited voice broke into her thoughts.

Caitríona looked up, and her eyes widened as a huge timber boat came around the bend in the river. 'What is it, Thomas?

'It is Samuel's paddle steamer.'

Chapter 32

Ceann Mara Station - Friday morning.

By the time Cat heard Logan's boots on the back steps, Mum had left for tennis, and Dad had gone off to the sheep paddock with the wool buyer from Dalgety's. They'd organised for Logan to come over in the morning, and they were finally getting to the store upriver. As soon as she had the kitchen to herself, she boiled some eggs, made a thermos of tea, and quickly put together some sandwiches, wrapping them in cling wrap before putting them into a chiller bag. She put two mugs, some milk and sugar, and some slices of the lemon coconut cake Mum made yesterday into the esky.

'Leave your boots on,' she called out. 'I'm almost ready.'

'I'll wait out on the porch,' he said.

'Don't be silly. We all come in here with our work boots on. Just wipe them on the mat.'

A minute later, Logan strode into the kitchen. She turned around and smiled at him.

'This is becoming a bit of a habit,' he said.

'A nice habit. It's good to have company,' she replied. 'Makes those three weeks of self-isolation seem like a bad dream.'

'You've been busy.' He looked at the esky and the chiller bag. Lunch?'

'Yes. I hope you like egg and lettuce sandwiches because that's what I've made to take upriver.'

'Having any food prepared by someone else is good. I enjoyed dinner the other night too. I'm not much of a cook.'

'Dad loves firing up the barbeque. When we were growing up, there was always someone visiting. I think it's died off over the years as we've all grown up, and neighbours have moved away.'

'I think I've hit the jackpot with my neighbours.' He grinned at her.

'You'll get sick of us when my sisters come home, and we're all talking at once.'

'I can't imagine it,' he said. 'Anyway, how are you sleeping?'

'Surprisingly good. No nightmares.'

'Good. Right to go? Anything else to take?' He lifted the small esky up.

'Just the chiller bag. I'll bring that. I'll just grab my boots and hat. I'll meet you at the back of the shed,' she said.

'Okay.' Logan picked up the esky and headed outside.

When Cat met him at the shed, he pointed to the various buildings along the edge of their road. 'It's almost like a small village here. Is that building down there some sort of chapel?'

'It is. I think Mum's got a bit of a map drawn up that she's going to use for the tourists next season. You know, the conservatory with the cellar underneath. Behind the chapel is a small cemetery. It's really moving because you can actually see the gravestones of the last five generations of our family. The oldest grave is the little baby daughter of Thomas and Caitríona, who established *Ceann Mara*. My grandparents are buried there too.'

'Wow, it's almost English, isn't it?' he said.

'Irish,' she commented with a grin. 'Thomas and Caitríona, and Samuel, the first of the O'Byrnes, came here from County Kerry.'

As they walked around the buildings towards the river, they passed the seat where she had been sitting when she had first spotted Logan with the gun.

'Are you a fisherman, Logan?'

'Not a regular one. Back in the days when Dad and I used to get on before I went off the rails and turned into a sulky adolescent, we used to go out on a dam not far from our farm. Sometimes we went down to the coast and Dad's mate would take us out to sea. I really enjoyed that.'

'So, you haven't fished the Darling yet?'

'I didn't think there'd be any fish in there.'

'There is. We've got carp and Murray cod, yellow belly. But if you like sweet ocean fish, you might not be too impressed with the taste of the river fish.'

'I tell you what I do like. I found a bit of a dam down the back of my house, and I did some yabby fishing with a bit of meat and string. Got a great haul the other day; it was just like eating fresh prawns.'

'I know that dam well. Uncle Gary stocked that for a lot of years, and no one would've been fishing there for a while, so they've probably bred right up.'

'There were some big ones there.'

'Yum. I love yabbies.'

'I'll have to take you over there one day.'

They reached the bank, and Logan climbed into *Ding-a-Ling* first, holding out his hand to her. Cat didn't say that she'd been negotiating that steep bank down to the water since she could walk. She took his proffered hand and climbed into the small vessel with a quick 'Thank you.'

'Now direct me to this store,' he said as he picked up the small oars.

She pointed upriver. 'That way.'

'You really do enjoy your family history, don't you?' Logan said as he turned the boat around and started rowing. 'I sense your passion when you and Tom talk about it. Both of you.'

'I do. It grounds me, and in a way connects me to the land. Might sound silly, it's hard to explain.'

'I think it sounds great. I'd like to belong somewhere like that.' His voice sounded sad, and sympathy filled Cat.

'Maybe you can start your own place here?'

'It's a possibility.' Logan chuckled. 'I just have to learn my goats and sheep.'

'We can help you with that. I'm going to be hanging around here for a while. Being home and away from study and university, water management and government regulations, and all of that academic reading I've been doing have really put being back here into perspective. You know, I think I'd be quite happy if I didn't even have anything to do with the Murray Darling Basin issues anymore.'

'Don't be too hasty in making decisions. Even if you feel better, it's not the time to be making decisions.'

'And is that guy who speaks from experience?'

Logan looked sheepish. 'Probably. I made my decision to buy the land when I was at my worst, so don't take my experience as advice.'

'At your worst?'

'I bought my land about a fortnight after I'd been through all my shit. I was just out of hospital and browsing, as I do, flicking from YouTube to Gumtree to eBay to the news. It was an absolute spur-of-the-moment thing. I saw an ad come up on Facebook, and it just spoke to me. It might sound impulsive, but it was well within my means. I got a small inheritance from Dad, and I put quite a bit of money away when I was working for the police force. And . . . well, here I am. Made a decision in the middle of one of the worst periods of my life, and so far, it's turned out well.'

'Okay, so you can't criticise me for making any decisions in one the worst times of *my* life. The worst time,' Cat said. 'But I'm feeling fine today about where I think I'll go. Or won't go as the case may be.'

'I hope you won't regret it.'

'Do you regret coming here?'

His eyes held hers. She was getting to quite like that green-eyed gaze. 'No.'

'Dad talked to you about the rope across the river; I heard him last night.'

'He did, but I've chosen the oars today. Bit far to tie a rope to trees.'

The late morning on the river was pleasant. The sunshine was warm, but a gentle breeze blew from the south, keeping the day cool. Ripples ran on the river ahead of them from the slight wind, plus the ripples from the oars as Logan rowed. Cat couldn't help admiring the bunching of his muscles. He had shed his work shirt and wore a black T-shirt. She wondered if he knew how good he looked. A man, not the young uni students she'd spent the last three years with.

'One more personal question,' she said. 'Last one, I promise.'

He lifted his eyebrows but didn't speak.

'How old are you?'

'Thirty.'

Cat simply nodded. She looked up as a flash of white caught her eye and pointed above them. 'Look, the pelicans are heading for the lakes. They breed down there after floods.'

Logan looked up and whistled. 'Wow, there must be hundreds of them up there.'

'Yes, they're riding the thermals. Most of them go down to the Menindee Lakes, but we also see them in the billabongs up here, too. Shows how healthy our ecosystems are after the rains. That's a place you have to go and visit while they're full,' she said. 'The Menindee lakes are one of the most magnificent sights you'll see in the outback.'

'I'll have to take a trip down there. I've got a lot to see,' he said, 'but first of all, I have to get my property up and running and decide whether I can make a living out of it. I can't live off my savings forever.'

They were quiet as Logan rowed the last two hundred metres to the wharf near the stone building. Cat closed her eyes, put her head back and lifted her face to the sun as peace filtered through her. She could have stayed out on the river all day. The wind lifted her hair, and she sensed a shift in the atmosphere. She opened her eyes and sat up. Logan was staring at her neck.

'What's that mark?'

'What mark?' She put her hand up to her neck, cranky that she'd forgotten about it; she'd been feeling so good.

'The one on the side of your neck.'

'Just another little nick from that night.'

'A *little* nick,' he said, anger lacing his voice. 'And it's still healing a month later? Why didn't you mention that to the detective?'

'I didn't even think about it. It was only tiny.'

He frowned and kept staring at her neck.

'What are you thinking?' she said.

'Nothing. We'll talk about it later. Let's not ruin a lovely day.'

***

Logan tried to get his contented mood back, but seeing that cut right near Cat's jugular artery had thrown him. He had read the reports about the girl who had been murdered, and he was sure that it must be the same perpetrator. The uni student's throat had been cut, and she'd bled out. It would be interesting to see the injury patterns on the other victims. He shook his head. It wasn't his case, nor was it his business, but he could make sure that Cat remained safe.

Although he didn't think there'd be a problem way out here, hundreds of kilometres from where it happened, he did wonder if she was known to the perpetrator and whether he knew where to find her. Experience in the force had taught him that victims needed to be wary.

'Okay,' Cat said. 'See up here, just through the trees? You can see the brick building and the tin roof shining. There's a jetty about fifty metres ahead on the left. Some of it is the original one that the paddle steamers used to come to, but Dad's strengthened it over the years.'

The dinghy made a slight thud as the front of it hit the small wooden jetty that jutted out into the river. Before Logan could do anything, Cat was on her feet and had jumped nimbly onto the short wharf.

'Throw me the rope,' she said. He reached around and got the rope that was hanging in the water over the back of the punt and threw it to her. 'Like a pro,' she called, and tied it off to a piece of timber jutting out from the side of the jetty. 'Now, pass me the esky and the bag. Climb out and don't fall in,' she said.

As Logan lifted the esky, he looked up to where the branch of a gum tree hung over the punt, trailing some eucalyptus leaves into the water.

'Holy jumping Jesus,' he yelled. He threw the esky out of the boat and scrambled out onto the wharf. 'Cat, get away from it.'

She smiled and ignored his outstretched hand as he backed off the wharf to the cleared area on the riverbank. 'It's only a green tree snake.'

'I don't care what colour it is,' he called from the clearing. 'It's a snake. They're all the same.'

Chapter 33

Newtown - midday Friday.

Scarlet's hands shook as she put the key in the lock of the unit. Ever since she'd heard about Esther, she hadn't felt safe, and now she knew that Cat had been assaulted in their unit; she'd been really scared here.

It was crazy to worry because it was almost four weeks since Cat had left, and nothing had happened. But now that she knew how concerned the police were, she was thinking the worst. She was also a bit cross that Cat hadn't told her why she'd gone; surely, she would have known that the unit might have been unsafe. And then she thought of what Cat had been through and realised that maybe she hadn't been in the right headspace. Scarlet stepped inside and waited near the door, listening and looking around.

Had she left that book on the lounge? She didn't remember doing that. Was the fruit bowl in the centre of the table slightly off-centre? The flat was silent, and she gradually worked up the courage to look in each of the rooms. She felt silly as she opened each wardrobe and looked under the beds.

Gradually her heart stopped beating so fast as she checked

her bathroom and then Cat's small ensuite. It smelled strongly of bleach. There was no one there, and everything was where it should be.

The quicker she got out of here, the better. She'd pack a bag, put it in her car, and go back to the police station and give them her key. Then she'd go and park at the beach to make the calls she wanted to make.

It was a shame she'd posted Cat's phone yesterday; it would have got there sooner if she'd taken it out with them. As Scarlet quickly packed a bag of clothes and sorted her toiletries out, she wondered if they should let Cat know they were coming.

Now she knew the name of their property, she'd Google it and see what it looked like. Hopefully, she could get it on satellite view, and she'd be able to see how big the house was and whether there were any pubs or Air BnBs nearby.

Cat had never talked much about the house she'd grown up in. Just lots about her sisters and how much she loved living on the land. Scarlet knew that they'd been on the property a long time, so she imagined it would be an older, small house. But, having had five girls there, maybe there would be spare bedrooms, but she still felt bad about them just rocking up and expecting to be put up.

She picked up her laptop and small suitcase and headed for her car, grateful to be leaving the unit for a while. She drove to Coogee Beach and snagged a park near the surf lifesaving club.

She opened her laptop and looked at the time. She still had an hour and a half before Jilly would be ready to shut up shop. She logged in, opened Google and put in the spelling that Cat had given her.

Ceann Mara. As Scarlet read through the hits and scrolled down, she was quite taken aback to see the beautiful homestead that was pictured on the top of the Facebook page. Maybe that was a tourist site nearby because underneath, there was a subsection that said *Riverbeds* accommodation, so perhaps that wasn't the house they lived in. She couldn't imagine anyone living in such a huge old homestead. It looked more like a National Trust destination.

She read the spiel underneath.

We offer five cabins and powered sites, plus we're in the process of building two glamping tents for next season. The season is closed from September 1, but please feel free to call or email and make inquiries about future bookings.

Before she could think twice, Scarlet put in the mobile number; it was answered straight away.

'Laura speaking.'

'Hello. Is that Riverbeds Campground? It's Scarlet Donaldson here and I was just looking at your website. Am I speaking to an agent or am I speaking to the people that run the accommodation out there?'

'Hello, Scarlet, that's such an unusual name I must ask, you wouldn't be Cat's friend, Scarlet, would you?'

'I am. Is that Mrs O'Byrne?'

'Yes, sweetie, it is, but please call me Laura. It's lovely to hear from you. Cat said that she's spoken to you.'

'How is she?'

'She's actually quite good, considering. I won't say too much, but I believe she told you what happened.'

'Yes, I went down to the police station for an interview.'

'Did you want to speak to Cat?'

'No, not now. I was actually looking for accommodation out there.'

'Accommodation?'

'Yes, our friend Jilly and I would like to come out and visit and I wasn't sure about where we'd stay, I thought we might have to go into town and get an Air BnB or somewhere. Even a pub.'

Laura chuckled 'Scarlet, there's no Air BnBs within cooee of us. But I'd be happy to have you stay in our cabins if that suits you. They're quite close to the house, and now that the tourist season is over, they're all empty.'

'I did see that on your website, and I wondered whether we could stay there in the cabins.'

'How many of you are there?'

'Just the two of us.'

'That's fine, and if anyone else wants to come, we have a lot of room out here.'

'Thank you. We were thinking about early next week.'

'I'm so pleased you called,' Laura said. 'I think a visit will do Cat the world of good. Every little thing helps her get back to normality. Oh, Scarlet, I'm sorry, I have to go now. I'm playing tennis today, and my next game's about to start. When you're a little way out, maybe around Louth, just give me a call and let me know, and I'll meet you down at the accommodation, and we'll surprise Cat. How does that sound?'

'That sounds fabulous.'

Scarlet sat watching the waves for another hour, before she drove back to Newtown, arriving back at the *Crazy Goat* just before four, and when she walked in, Jilly was smiling from ear to ear.

'I guess you've talked to your boss,' she said.

'I sure have, and guess what? I finish up next Friday. He's already talked to Deb, and she's going to take over as manager. Bella is happy to stay, and he had another casual waitress lined up, so I'm as free as a bird at the end of the week.'

'That's fantastic! You didn't muck around. Are you sure about this?'

'Absolutely. Have you got your bags packed?' Jilly asked.

'Yes, they're in the car. I jagged a park outside. Things are looking up.'

'Okay, I'll be an hour or so yet. Deb's going to spend all next week with me, so I want to get the books up to date this afternoon. I'll give you my key, and you get settled. I'm at Unit 19, 27 Reid Street, Bronte. I'll send you a screenshot from Google Maps.' Jilly dug out a set of keys, took a door key off and handed it to Scarlet. 'Make yourself at home, and I'll bring Chinese home for us. The place down from the café is amazing.'

Scarlet reached for and hugged Jilly. 'Thanks so much. I'll pick up some wine to have with it.'

Chapter 34
Ceann Mara Station - Friday afternoon.

When Cat had stopped giggling at Logan's reaction to the snake, he followed her along the cleared path. As they stepped out of the trees, he whistled. The paddock ahead of them, as far as they could see, was cleared, with maybe three or four trees offering shade to the cattle and sheep in around ten acres. In the distance, he could see some dark cattle, and further along, at the edge of the paddock, was a building.

Cat pointed ahead. 'That's the wool shed from the 1880s. Do you know what happened here?' He shook his head. 'Actually, do you know much about shearing and the history of shearing out here?' she asked.

'Nothing,' he said. 'That's why I've started with goats; sheep are next.'

'Well, *Ceann Mara* was the second station to use mechanical shearing in the 1880s.'

'This place is full of history, isn't it?' he said.

'I'll show you the woolshed one day too.'

They walked about fifty metres towards the large sandstone building that sat close to the river.

'This is my great-great-great uncle's store,' she said.

'What on earth would they have done with the store out here?' Logan looked bewildered.

'Apparently, Uncle Samuel built the store. Dad and I haven't discovered much about Thomas and Caitríona yet. We know they had the land and built the homestead, but we want to know more. Da suspects they had another relative here, but we're still digging.'

Logan shook his head as they stepped off the wharf. 'I had no idea this was here.'

'Apparently, there were stores up and down the river from the Murray as far as Collarenebri on the Darling.'

'What did they do? I mean, I guess they sold goods.'

'They offered a transport service for the many people who lived out here. The Murray and the Darling were the "roads" of the time. The paddle steamers delivered the mail and fresh food.'

'It would have reduced their isolation in those days. I still feel it out here at times, even with all our modern technology and connection to the world.'

'I read that it greatly improved living standards at the time. Dad and I haven't discovered that from our family research. It's in the general history of the region that we've read. Apparently, there were many benefits. The price of food and goods fell for people living inland as they didn't depend on slow overland transport, and with the decrease in freight costs on wool, sheep production became more profitable. Because of that, more land was opened up for settlement. Industries such as sawmilling boomed, and inland port towns sprang up. Did you know that Bourke was at one time the largest inland port?'

Logan shook his head. 'I didn't know any of that.'

'Of course, much of that happened after our forebears

settled here, so they would have done it tough to begin with.'

Cat put down the chiller bag, and Logan put the esky beside it.

'Wait here.' She walked across to the river and, counted five trees from the edge of the building and then moved across to the big rock. She lifted it, watching out for scorpions and snakes, smiling as she thought of Logan and his reaction to the green tree snake. Poor guy. He certainly had a good case of snake phobia.

Cat pulled out the big brass key and carried it over to the door and put it in the lock.

'The original key?' Logan asked.

'Of course, everything in here is original. Wait till you see inside,' she said.

'So, what are we doing today? Just looking, or do you want to start your cleanup?'

They stepped inside the entrance of the old store's dim, shadowy recesses. Cat led him through the small foyer that still held the original shopkeeper's counter and then into the huge open space with the high, original roof.

Logan whistled.

'Yep,' Cat said. 'Buckets and buckets of rusty nails and shelves of crap. Still want to help?' She turned and grinned up at him, and Logan smiled back.

'I'm up for a challenge.'

Filtered sunlight came in from a gap between the roof and the top of the brick wall on the western side.

'Wouldn't the rain come in here?' he said.

'It does, but you'll notice there's nothing stored on that side,' Cat turned around and pointed to the side of the store that was on the river side. 'See up there? There's a whole floor up there, but the steps have long since rotted away, and Dad and I've never been up there. We've always talked about it, but Dad reckoned it wasn't worth having a look at because of what's down here. But I've just got a feeling that there might be something important up there. If there's not, I'll have satisfied my curiosity anyway.'

'How will we get up there?' Logan looked along the store and scratched his head.

'There's a ladder around the back of the woolshed. I was going to carry it down here one day and climb up and have a bit of a look.'

'Do you want to do that today? It wouldn't be safe to do it by yourself. You'll need someone to hold a ladder. If you fell when you were here, you'd be stuck for a while until you were missed at home,' he said.

'Yeah, that's the main reason I haven't gone up there when I've been home in the holidays. Plus, I've always been busy helping Dad with the sheep and the goats. It's quite a treat to have some spare time to come and have a look around.'

She looked past him over the river and spoke to herself, 'I could've been doing this instead of malingering,' she said.

'Well, no more malingering. You've got an offsider now, and I'll help you as much as you like.'

He reached out and took her hand. 'Let's get to work.'

***

Logan walked alongside Cat as they left the store and headed towards the woolshed. It was mid-afternoon, and the sky was a brilliant blue, the sunlight bathing the stone building in a warm golden glow.

'I never had any idea that there was history like this out here,' he said as they approached the old woolshed.

'Like I mentioned earlier, *Ceann Mara* was the site of the second mechanical shearing in the late 1880s,' Cat said. '*Dunlop Station*, just a way upriver, was the first woolshed to do mechanical shearing in 1888.'

'I suppose back in those days, they would've been well acquainted with their neighbours on the river.'

'I'd say so, but the only diaries that we found in the house were left from about the early 1900s by Dad's grandfather. His brother Gilbert was killed in World War I, and there's some really poignant diary entries from the family at the time about how they lived.'

'That sounds really interesting.'

'Yes, we just wish we had it for way back when because it would give us so much more of a picture about when the place was settled and what they did.'

'I suppose they would've cleared the land. It would've been natural bush all the way to the river back in the day,' Logan looked around. Beyond them, as far as he could see to the west, the paddocks were cleared, with the occasional tree standing sentinel in the middle of the paddock. Ahead was a sprawling timber building; the timber faded to a pale grey.

'So, this is the woolshed?'

'Yep, this is the original forty-five stand woolshed. Of course, when Dad was running a lot of sheep, it was very different to what it is now. But we've sort of turned it into more of a historical site; Dad's even put some photographs and things up around the walls inside.'

'Do we have time to look now?' Logan asked hopefully.

'Well, you can have a quick peek if you want, but I'm pretty keen to get this ladder and go back down to the store. If you stay for a while across the river, you've got plenty of time to suss out everything,' she said.

'You'll be sick of me,' he said, holding her eyes. He was pleased when Cat looked at him and smiled.

'Never. I'm enjoying your company very much, Logan, and I'm sure I'm going to appreciate your muscles very shortly when you hold that ladder and come up to the loft.'

'Is that an invitation?' He grinned at her and was pleased to see the slight flush on her cheekbones, but she smiled at him

'Are you flirting with me?' Cat said. 'That's what it sounded like.'

'I was merely offering to come up to the loft with you and help you find whatever is there,' he replied. Her flush deepened. 'Sorry, Cat, I'm teasing, and yes, I guess I was flirting with you.'

The smile stayed on her face.

The ladder was quite heavy, a timber construction that seemed as old as the woolshed itself. When he commented on that, Cat laughed.

'It probably is. They made things sturdy back in those days.'

'And I suppose if it was kept out of the weather, it wouldn't rot.'

'Yes, the woolshed's a pretty dry place, got a good roof on it,' she agreed.

They took one end each and trudged back to the store. They carried it inside and laid it on the ground, and Cat stood there with her hands on her hips. Logan looked at her closely. Since he'd spotted that mark on her neck, she'd made sure her hair covered it.

One thing he would do, was ring Detective Nichols again and tell him about it. When he'd called to let him know that Cat's friend had mentioned someone else was asking about her,

Nichols had thanked him.

'Thanks for the information, Logan, I appreciate it. And listen, I know that you're not at work at the moment, but I'll keep you informed if we find anything that relates to Cat. I'm just going to have a look at the availability of an aircraft, and I'll be flying out with my colleague, Detective Lisa Branson. I'll confirm it when the time is set.'

Logan hadn't mentioned that to Cat; he didn't want to spoil her happy mood. Her excitement about what might be up in the loft was contagious, and he found himself looking forward to helping her find something useful for their family history. He looked around the bottom floor of the shed and shook his head. 'It's certainly full of—'

'Junk,' she finished off for him. 'There's not much useful stuff here, but I suppose it gives us a picture of the property over the years. I really don't know how old some of those things are.'

'Why would there be so many buckets of nails and bolts?' he asked.

She shrugged. 'Who knows? That's why it would be so handy if we could find some sort of inventory of the store when the paddle steamers were running.'

'Okay, where would you like to put this ladder?' he said. Cat was still standing, hands on hips, her eyes running from left to right on the floor that ran along the southern end of the shed above the floor. The light at that end was coming through the four twelve-paned windows he'd noticed next to the door on the way in.

'Maybe on the left-hand side,' she said.

'What do you think? It looks like there's just timber mainly piled on the top, right there.' His eyes widened as he looked up there. 'What's the chance of there being snakes up in the timber?' he asked.

She laughed. 'Probably pretty good, I'd say.'

'Okay, let's start at the other end,' he said.

'How about you hold the ladder, and I go up first?'

'How about you be careful and keep an eye out for snakes while you're up there?'

'I haven't met a snake yet that I'm scared of,' Cat said.

'Well, you should; you know they can kill you.'

'I have a healthy respect for them, and I know how to treat them.'

Together, they carried the ladder across to the corner of the shed. A few buckets of nuts and bolts and a dozen bottles had to be moved before they could position the scaffold safely on the floor. That was one thing about the shed: it had a beautiful timber floor that looked like it had been polished at one stage. 'Once you get the dust off this floor, I'd say it's in pretty good nick.'

'It is, isn't it? So, I'm hoping that timber up there is just as good. It must be, because it looks like it's been bearing a lot of weight for a long time. I'd hate to have it crashing down on us.'

Once the ladder was in position, Cat climbed up, and Logan tried to play it cool, avoiding looking at her rearview as she quickly and nimbly ascended the ladder. She stood on the third rung from the top and peered over the top of the ladder to the shelf. 'Okay, I think I can clear a little bit of space and make some room so that I can sit up here and have a bit of a look around,' she said.

'Okay,' he said, 'well, you just be careful, and I'll keep an eye out for snakes.'

'The only snake you'd get up here would be a python; we wouldn't get browns or blacks up here,' she said.

'Should have brought my rifle,' Logan commented.

Cat chuckled after he said it. 'Our first meeting wasn't a good one.'

'I've apologised.' He smiled up at her.

'You have, but you still frightened the living daylights out of me.' Cat balanced on the ladder and reached over, and he could hear her dragging some sort of wood up there across the shelf. 'I've cleared the space. Don't go away with that ladder. Otherwise, I'll be stuck up here for the rest of my life,' she said.

'I wouldn't do that to you. What can you see up there?' he asked.

'Well, there's a whole lot of timber boxes, and they seem to be sealed.' Her voice held excitement.

'What sort of boxes?'

'You know, like the old apple crates that fruit used to come into the market in ages ago.'

'Vaguely, but I haven't ever taken much notice,' he said.

'Well, they're sort of like that, with slatted timber on the top, and that's been nailed on. I really need a hammer or something to prise them open.'

'How about you have a good look around first and figure out what's there before you start getting into it because as soon as you do, you're going to go down the research rabbit hole if you do find something,' he suggested.

'True. Okay, I'll just organise a bit up here and see what I think is around, and then we might put the ladder in the middle bit, and I'll see what's there. But we won't go over to the other corner where all the timber is stacked just yet, and then I'll come down and grab some tools.'

'Did you bring some?' he asked.

Cat turned around and peered at him from the top of the ladder. 'Have a look around.'

Logan grinned, feeling silly. There was a plethora of chisels and screwdrivers and others that he'd never seen before hanging on the wall; they might be rusty, but there were certainly plenty of tools there. 'Okay, well, I'll hold the ladder. You be careful climbing over the top there,' he said.

'I will.'

Small shards of wood and clouds of dust descended as Cat moved the boxes around. He could hear her talking to herself and muttering as the sound of timber sliding drifted down with the dust.

'Okay, I think we've got a veritable treasure chest up here. It's a shame you can't come up too.'

'Do you reckon it'll be safe if I climbed up the ladder and stayed on the ladder while you looked at the stuff?'

'It should be. I don't think it's going to move much on that floor down there, but we can prop it up. Rightio, I'm coming down,' she said.

'Okay,' he replied. Cat started to back down the ladder, and as Logan held it securely on the bottom, her boot slipped, and she slid down the rest of the way. He reached up and caught her before she could fall on the timber floor.

His arms were around her, and her back was against his chest. 'Oh, sorry about that,' she said. 'These blasted boots. I should be used to them, but it's been ages since I wore them.'

He hung onto her, and she turned in his arms. For the life of him, he didn't want to let her go. He felt as if she was safe when he was holding her.

Cat tipped her head back, and her curls fell over her shoulders as he held her gaze for a long time. He kept his eyes away from her neck.

***

'Probably time for a break,' Logan said as Cat stepped away from him, her cheeks burning. 'What do you think? Time to eat?'

As they collected the esky and chiller bag and walked to the river, Cat's legs were shaky and she knew it wasn't from climbing up and down the ladder. The shakiness was from being in Logan's arms when he had caught her at the bottom of the ladder.

For a moment, she'd thought he was going to kiss her, and as he held her, she looked up at him. Cat had been tempted to stand on her toes and brush her lips across his. It was a long time since she'd felt that so strongly.

But it was too soon.

She barely knew Logan, but what she did know she liked very much. As he looked up at the tree above the punt as they looked for a nice spot to have lunch, Cat grinned.

'We're going to have to desensitise you, I think, if you're going to be staying over there. You can't wander around with a gun and frighten people all the time.'

'Hey, do you see a gun now?' he said, lifting his hands with a grin but still looking warily up into the branches.

Cat walked along the bank ahead of Logan until they reached a clearing with short grass and no overhanging trees.

'No shade here. Is that okay?'

'That's fine and very thoughtful of you. And yes, I do need to get over this irrational fear of snakes. I guess it will take time.' He sat on the grass and stretched his legs out while Cat unpacked the food.

'Egg and lettuce sandwich first?' She glanced at him and held the sandwich bag out to him; he was staring out over the water, looking thoughtful.

'Thank you.' Their fingers brushed as he took the sandwich, and Cat couldn't believe the tingle that ran up her arm. It was like being a teenager again. She had it bad, but it was a nice way to feel.

They sat quietly as they ate the sandwiches, and then she pulled out the mugs and poured the hot water from the thermos onto the tea bags.

'Why does food taste so much better when you eat outdoors?' Logan commented as he put the sandwich bag into the esky, and then brushed egg off his jeans.

'Mum's food,' she replied. 'I hope I can cook as well as she does one day. I used her secret mayonnaise recipe when I mashed the egg.'

'It was good.'

'Wait until you taste this. Or maybe you have already.' She passed him the biggest slice of the lemon coconut cake and watched as he took a bite. Logan closed his eyes as he chewed.

'I hope you realise I'm going to be visiting your place a lot at morning tea time from now on, as well as smoko. Your mother's cakes are the best I've ever tasted.'

'I'll look forward to it.' Cat grinned, and when she'd finished her tea, she brushed the cake crumbs from her cargo pants and reached for his empty mug.

'What do you want to do now?' he asked. 'Back to the store or head home?'

'We probably should go home. I can't take up all your day.'

'Okay, if we do that, I'll do some work this afternoon, and then I can come back tomorrow to help you move those boxes and make a space for you to work.'

'Sounds good. If you're sure?'

'Yes, I was thinking when I was holding the ladder, we

could probably secure it to the timber floor temporarily so we can both go up and down safely without one of us having to hold it.'

'That would be great. Let's get packed up and hit the river.'

Cat put the lid on the esky as Logan pushed himself to his feet. As she turned, he offered his hand to pull her up, and something flickered in his eyes when her hand took his.

Their eyes met and held, and Logan's arms went around her, and he held her close. Her face rested on his shoulder, his head bent, her lips close to his neck. Cat smiled; she could feel Logan's heart thudding against her chest.

She lifted her head, and he lowered his lips to her, murmuring, 'God help me, Cat, I can't help it.'

'Go right ahead,' she whispered.

'Are you sure?'

In answer, Cat stood on her toes and brushed his mouth with her lips. His lips were warm and soft as he took his time kissing her, and soon, her heart was thudding in time with his. After a minute, he dropped his arms from around her, and their lips stayed together as he gently threaded his fingers through hers.

It was the most gentle and romantic kiss of her life. Eventually, he pulled back and his dark green gaze held hers. She smiled at his flushed cheeks; they were as pink as she was sure hers were.

'Home time?' he said huskily.

Cat smiled, and Logan's fingers held hers as they made their way back to the punt.

Chapter 35

Bronte - the first Saturday in October.

Jilly rang the buzzer downstairs rather than using her key to come up. She'd noticed last night how nervous Scarlet was, even when the lift dinged as the neighbours came up to their apartments on the same floor.

'Hello,' Scarlet said as she answered the buzzer. 'Jilly?'

'Hi, it's me, and I have pizza.'

'I bought wine on the way home from the library,' Scart said. 'I've unlocked the door.'

'We're set for the night. All food groups are covered. I'll be up in a minute.'

By the time Jilly stepped out of the lift on the floor for her apartment, Scarlet had the door unlocked. She reached out and took the pizza.

'I'll put it in the oven. Do you want to have a shower or anything?' she said.

'I do actually. I scrubbed the café from top to bottom this afternoon. That's why I texted and said I'd be a bit late,' Jilly replied. 'Deb's really excited to take over. The place is like new. Better than when I took it over.'

'How's she going to manage being a full-time manager and

balancing it with her uni stuff?'

Jilly shrugged. 'She's keen. She wants the money. I'll jump in the shower. Won't be long. Be a love and pour me a wine.'

'I'll wait out on the balcony. I love the view,' Scarlet said.

By the time Jilly had a quick shower and changed into loose, long pants and a T-shirt, Scarlet was settled on the veranda. She had some dip, sliced vegetables, and a glass of chilled Chardonnay with ice cubes on the table.

Jilly grinned and pointed to the vegetables. 'I suppose that makes up the additional food groups and gives us a bit of a healthy meal. I got a vegetarian pizza anyway. I hope that's okay.'

'Yeah, I hate all that spicy meat,' Scarlet said. 'I didn't like to say anything when you said you had pizza. But that is just how I like it.'

Jilly sat down and looked out across the streets between her unit and the beach; the ocean at Bronte was just visible. The downside of the unit was being on the main road, and the constant traffic noise was always in the background day and night.

'Good day?' she asked, picking up her glass. 'And cheers.'

'Cheers,' Scarlet said, reaching over to clink glasses. 'I did, actually. It's not a bad job and it pays well. The best part is when all the books are shelved, and I help man the information desk; I can actually do some uni reading between enquiries. How about you?'

'I let Deb take over the machine all day while I scrubbed.' Jilly lifted her hands. 'I don't think I'll ever get the smell of bleach out. I think I'll get into a different profession when I settle in the north.'

Scarlet put a shaking hand to her face. 'Oh God, Jilly.'

'What's wrong?'

'When I packed up, I went into Cat's ensuite. It still smelled of bleach, and then I couldn't stop thinking about Esther. I don't know that I want to stay in Sydney either.' Her voice hitched with a sob.

'Calm down, Scart. I'm sure the police will get him soon.'

'I hope so. I do like your unit. It's away from the seedy part of the city. If Cat does come back and she agrees, I'd like to take it.'

'That sounds good. But if you don't, I've got a few other options, so don't feel pressured.'

Scarlet frowned. 'Okay, look, I've got something I need to run by you. I hope it's okay. I've said yes but said it has to be okay with you before it's one hundred percent confirmed.'

'What's up?'

'Well, Gavin rang me today.'

'And?'

'Well, when I told Gavin that you and I were going out to visit Cat next weekend, he asked if he and Rod could tag along too. Rod rang me pretty much straight after and said that he would like to come. What do you think about that?'

Jilly frowned. 'I suppose they're good friends of Cat's. I met Rod at Cat's twenty-first. What I think doesn't really matter.'

'Are you sure? It was our road trip.'

'No, it was your road trip, and I agreed to come.'

'I think she'd be happy if we all turned up. What do you think?'

Jilly always cut to the chase; she couldn't see the point of any other way. 'Okay, I think Gavin is a bit of a dickhead, but he's been friends with Cat a lot longer than I have.'

Scarlet shook her head. 'He's not a dickhead. He's always been that way, and I know him well.'

'What way?' Jilly took a sip of her wine.

'Well, it's nothing to do with being a dickhead. It's more about his lack of self-esteem. Most of us in our group come from pretty well-off families. Some of us just fell into environmental science, and it just happened that most of us come from the land. Gav grew up in a low socio-economic suburb, but he's passionate about the environment, and that was the path he always wanted to take. He started off on a scholarship, and I think he just has to prove to himself all the time to feel that he belongs. So, he can be a bit mouthy. And he's really clever.'

'He drinks too much,' Jilly said. 'I've noticed when I've been at the pub with you, he's always the first one to get pissed.'

'Yeah, he does do that. So, is it okay with you?'

'Yeah, I'll survive; I'll just tell him to can it if he carries on.'

'The best part and I didn't tell you so it didn't sway you, is that Rod's offered to take us out in his Land Cruiser, which will be really good because apparently, the last 60 ks is a dirt road. I was talking to Laura, Cat's mum, yesterday. I forgot to tell you last night.'

'You crashed early.'

'Yeah, it was good to sleep well.'

'You have been busy. So, how's Cat?'

'She said she's still going well. Getting better every day. The main reason I rang up was just to make sure that we had no problem finding somewhere to stay. And guess what? If you go on Facebook and search for their property, they've actually got a campground called *Riverbeds*, not far from the main house. They've got cabins and powered sites, and Laura said that she'll get some cabins ready for us. I haven't called back to ask about the guys staying because I wanted to run it past you first.'

'You'd better give her a call now.'

'Thanks, it'll be good because Rod said he and Gavin would share the driving too and we won't have to drive.'

'That's a plus,' Jilly said. 'So, when are we going?'

'They agreed on next Saturday morning if that suits you. Five a.m.?'

'Gah, I'd better go shop for clothes. What does one wear on a cattle station?'

Scarlet laughed. 'Just your usual clothes and a pair of boots.'

Chapter 36

Ceann Mara Station - the second Saturday in October.

Logan woke at dawn and lay there, looking at the fan spinning lazily on his ceiling. He built the house in an A-frame style, with a kitchen, small bathroom, and living area on the ground level. His bedroom was half a dozen stairs up in a loft sort of arrangement. It got quite hot up there, so he'd got into the habit of putting his fan on every night when he went to sleep. He was still getting used to the heat on the Darling; it was very different from the humid heat in Queensland. This was a dry heat that really settled into your bones.

The last week had been like a dream; ever since he'd found the courage to kiss Cat after their picnic at the river, Logan's world had shifted. He tried to talk logically to himself, but it didn't work. He found it too hard to stay on his side of the river, and he was sure that Tom and Laura were noticing his more frequent visits.

He and Cat had spent part of every day of the past week cleaning out the top floor of the shed.

'As soon as I finish this work at *Toorale*, I'll come and give you a hand,' Tom said after Cat had described the boxes to him. 'And you've resisted opening them?' he asked, scratching his head.

'Do you want us to wait until you're with us?' she asked.

'No, go ahead. I've got too much work on.'

'Logan is a really good influence, Dad. He's got me organised. We've cleared a space, and we've moved the boxes to an area where we can work. There's a lot of garbage there—and dust and cobwebs—but we're holding high hopes for what might be in the sealed crates.' Cat grinned at Logan as she spoke, and his heart did that funny little flip.

They acted like neighbourly friends when they were at the house, but as soon as Logan rowed them up the river and they reached the store every afternoon, they had ended up in each other's arms on the wharf before they got to work.

It was new and exciting, but frustrating, but Logan knew it was way too soon to take their relationship to the next step. There was no rush, and they were getting to know more about each other every day as they worked and chatted.

##

Logan could see how excited Cat was when they finally climbed the newly-secured ladder to the top floor on Saturday after a week of hard work getting the space swept out and organised. Her smile was constant, her cheeks were flushed, and she didn't stop talking all the way from the wharf until she unlocked the door of the stone building.

'A little bit excited, are we?' he asked, leaning over and catching her lips in a brief kiss once they were inside.

'You are very observant, sir. Must be the detective in you.' She kissed him back and chuckled. 'Yes, I can't wait to see what's in there.'

'I hope you're not too disappointed.'

Today was the day they were going to start opening the

boxes.

'I know they're important,' Cat said as she stopped on the bottom rung of the ladder. 'They wouldn't be so securely sealed if it was just old clothes or household stuff.'

Logan climbed up behind her, and when he stepped over the top of the ladder, she was already crouched beside the box they'd pulled out the day before. A set of about twenty boxes had been date stamped, the ink faded but still legible, with boxes dated from 1890 through to 1910. They had both agreed that they were likely to be account records from the store.

A smaller box with an oval carving on the top had piqued Cat's interest when she had found it behind three larger boxes stacked in a corner late yesterday afternoon. The sun was low in the sky as she sat there holding it reverently, her clothes covered in dust and cobwebs in her hair. 'This looks interesting. It's different.'

'Do you want to open it now?' Logan asked. 'Or take it home?'

'No, I can be patient. It's been here a long time, and it belongs here. I'll look tomorrow. It's too late today.'

Now, Logan gently prised the hinged lid open with a flat screwdriver. He didn't want to damage it because, like Cat, he thought it may hold something personal.

'It's almost as though it was hidden there in the corner, don't you think?'

'Could be a jewellery box? Something valuable inside?' he suggested as the lid gradually loosened. Before the lid was open, he handed it to Cat who was sitting beside him staring at the small box. She took it, lifted the lid and gasped as she looked into it.

'Oh, Logan, we were right. It looks like letters, look! Look at the writing. It's old-fashioned. Oh my God, I think it's a letter to Catriona from her mother. Look.' She held out the letter and the paper shook in her hand 'It's dated 1869, and says New York. I wonder why she was in New York when Thomas and Caitríona emigrated from Ireland?'

'Can you read it?' he asked.

Her hands were shaking as she held the fine paper of the letter she had picked up. She nodded.

'I can.' Her face was alight, and her eyes were dancing, and Logan couldn't take his eyes off her lips as she began to read.

26 Albany Rd, New York, 26th September, 1869

My dearest daughter, Caitríona,

It is with the heaviest of hearts that I write to impart to you the sad news of the passing of my beloved husband and your father, James Lowe.

Your father departed this life just after nine o'clock on the first day of the month. It has taken me time to write to you as I have been seeking new lodgings as I could not afford to stay where we were living before your father's passing. Your three brothers have all left the city to seek work many miles away, and I am now residing in a lodging house close by to your Aunt Moira so I have some comfort and company when desired.

I have work as a housemaid at one of the hotels, and am comfortable enough, so please do not worry.

In your Da's last days, he was quiet, but when he did speak, he spoke with affection of each of our seven children, even our little Finn, whom we did not have for long, but particularly of his darling daughter, who he missed greatly. Your regular missives gave him great pleasure over the years when I read them aloud; however, as I am sure you would know, there was one letter that I did not share with him. It was always safely stored in the base of my sewing bag.

To that end, and now aware of my own mortality, I have decided to send back to you the letters that you have written to me over the past years since your move to the colony of New South Wales.

Your loving mother

Aisling Lowe.

Logan's throat clogged with emotion as Cat lifted her head. Tears spilled from her eyes leaving dust-smeared tracks on her cheeks. She took a deep gulping breath and tried to speak and then shook her head as she composed herself. He reached over and took her hand.

'That's pretty wonderful. I guess it's the Caitríona you were named for.'

'It is. This is so real to me. I can see her holding this and reading it because her photo is on the wall of Dad's study. There is so much in this one letter. Her parents' names, the fact that she had six siblings and that her mother wrote the letter from New York.'

'There is. You must show me the photo.'

'I will. I wonder what's in that letter her mother was talking about? These must be all the letters she wrote to her mother from here.'

'Do you want to read them now?'

Cat shook her head. 'No. I'll take this box home. I think Dad should be there when we read them for the first time.'

'You're a thoughtful person, Cat.'

'Logan, I just cannot believe what we've found. Who knows what we're going to find in the rest of the boxes?'

Chapter 37

Sydney to Ceann Mara - the second Saturday in October.

Jilly handed her bag to Rod with a smile. 'Thanks so much for offering to drive us out there, Rod. It sure makes it easy for Scart and me.'

'My pleasure, Jilly. It's good to see you again. It's been a while. I think we met at Cat's twenty-first at Coogee Hotel, didn't we?'

'I think so. You were the pirate?'

'Yes, and you were Cleopatra from memory?'

'I was. It was a good night.'

'I've been sick in the gut ever since the police called me.' Rod hoisted Jilly's suitcase into the back. 'I feel bad because I noticed she hadn't been around campus, and I emailed her to talk about working on our thesis topics together, but she never replied. I got too caught up at work, and I didn't give it much thought. If I'd known what was going on, I would've done something about it.'

'What did they ask you?' Jilly asked curiously. 'Do you think they were making any progress?'

'Just what I remembered about the night. All I remembered was Cat arriving after us, having a quick chat and then going to sit in a booth to wait for someone. Gav and I had had a fair bit to drink by then.'

'That was me. I still feel really bad that we didn't get there,' Jilly said. 'So, they didn't say anything else?'

'No, they were interested to hear that she was dancing with one of the new guys on campus, and then I didn't see her after that. She left early.'

Scart walked around the side of the four-wheel drive with Gavin. 'Yeah, he rang me looking for her. I don't know how he got my number.'

'Rohan did?' Rod frowned.

'I thought his name was Royden. That's what I told the police.'

'No, it's Rohan Greentree.'

'Are you sure he's a student? I haven't come across him,' Scart said.

'Yes, he transferred from Canberra to do his honours here. He's across two faculties: agriculture and environmental science. Pretty smart dude. His thesis is on the population dynamics of feral cats.'

'Sounds riveting,' Jilly said. 'But seriously, the police need his correct name.'

'I gave it to them and his mobile. I'm sure they've talked to him by now.'

Gavin lifted Scarlet's backpack into the back of the four-wheel drive, and Rod grinned at Jilly. 'Scart knows how to travel light.'

Jilly pulled a face at him. 'You'll keep.' Rod was a good-looking guy but not her type. She wasn't into academics.

'Come on, guys, let's not stand around gasbagging. Let's hit the road,' Rod said, heading for the driver's side. He held open the back passenger door for Jilly.

'Nice manners. You're forgiven for the suitcase shot.'

Jilly sat in the back with Scarlet and closed her eyes, trying to doze, as Rod and Gavin chatted in the front. She was exhausted from her big week at the cafe and also from a few sleepless nights, as she'd worried that she'd been too impulsive with her decision to move on.

But she had thought about it last night and this morning, and she knew it was time to go. It was up to Louis now to move his business forward by hiring the right manager. She didn't know how long Deb would stay because she was focused on a uni career first, but the money would certainly help her out for a few months.

She drifted off but was jerked awake when the car stopped at a set of traffic lights.

'We'll go out there, catch up with her, make sure she's all right, and try to talk her into coming back to Sydney with us.' Scarlet was leaning forward, talking to the guys.

'Talk her into coming back?' Gavin said. 'Why? Isn't she coming back?'

Scarlet shrugged. 'I'm not sure what Cat's doing.'

'I think she'd be a bit thrown by what happened.' Rod nodded.

'As any woman would be.'

'I can't speak as a guy,' Rod said, 'but I imagine that sort of assault must be the worst thing a girl could go through.'

'What sort of assault?' Gavin screwed up his face.

He was totally full of himself, as usual, not thinking of anyone else. Jilly rolled her eyes.

'The worst sort,' she said from the back.

'Oh,' Gavin said. 'I didn't know.'

What la la land was he living in? Jilly hadn't changed her opinion of him, no matter what Scarlet said.

'Have any of you been out this way before?' Rod asked as he slowed when a car pulled out in front of his vehicle.

'Only when you took me out to your station at the end of first year,' Gavin said.

'I haven't been to Cat's or really out west at all.' Scarlet glanced across at Jilly. 'What about you?'

'No.' Jilly looked at the road signs and realised that they were on the outskirts of Sydney; she must have dozed for a while. 'I went up to the Blue Mountains on an excursion when I was a kid, but I spent most of my childhood in Queensland, and I haven't had a good look around New South Wales.'

'And now, you traitor, you're leaving us and going back to Queensland,' Scarlet chimed in.

'How come?' Gavin asked. 'You're really leaving Sydney?' His tone sounded as though it was a stupid move, and Jilly felt her temper grow. She really didn't like him. He needed to grow up.

She kept her voice easy. 'Yep, when I come home, I'm packing up and leaving. Scarlet and Cat might be moving into my apartment.'

Rod whistled. 'I noticed it was a flash apartment block. I thought it might've been yours. Do you think Cat will come back to Sydney?'

'Why wouldn't she?' Scarlet glared at him.

'You said you were going to talk her into coming back,' Rod justified. 'I wondered if she was going to drop out,'

'She's already done a lot of work towards her thesis. Once she recovers physically, she'll be back,' Scarlet said.

'Are you doing an honours year too, Gavin?' Jilly asked.

He nodded, and Rod chimed in, 'We all are.'

'Is that usual?' Jilly asked. 'I don't know a lot about uni. Never went there.'

'Well, about one in ten students go onto an honours degree, so we skewed the stats in our cohort,' Rod said. 'But I think we all just settled in really well, and we did well, and we enjoyed what we were doing. And these days, the better qualifications you have, the more chance you've got of getting a good job. Wasn't like that in the old days, I don't think.'

'Speaking of which, did Harry approve *your* proposal, Rod?' Scarlet asked.

There was something in Scarlet's tone that Jilly didn't understand.

'He did.' Rod's voice was smug. 'What about yours?'

'I'm through,' Scarlet said.

'What about Cat's?' Rod asked.

'I thought you'd be the first to know. I thought you were working together,' Gavin chipped in.

'No.' Rod's voice was clipped. 'What about you, Gavin? Have you been approved?'

'Yes, Harry was "delighted" with mine. That was the word he used in my interview.'

'Old fag,' Rod muttered before he looked sideways at Gavin. 'You were partnering up with Esther, weren't you?'

Gavin was quiet for a few seconds and turned his head to look out the window. 'Yeah.'

Jilly frowned. There was a subtext here she wasn't getting. She'd ask Scarlet about it later. All she hoped was that this strange discussion didn't happen when they were with Cat. It wasn't the reason they were going to see her.

With a shrug, she rolled her hoodie into a ball and put it

beneath her head.

The politics of university theses wasn't her worry.

A while later, the car slowed. Jilly opened her eyes and stretched. They were surrounded by bush and the occasional cleared paddock full of brown cows. Her stomach grumbled.

'Where are we?'

'Almost to Bathurst,' Scarlet said. 'You've had a good sleep.'

'It's getting close to break time,' Gavin said, pointing ahead. 'There's a pub at Lucknow. I looked at Google Maps. Do you want to stop for a drink?'

Jilly nodded. 'You mean a coffee, I hope.'

'I know that pub. It's an all-nighter. For the miners,' Rod said. 'It's a bit early to stop for a beer.'

'I could go one,' Gavin said. 'We were up at sparrow's fart.'

'Maccas will do me for coffee.' Jilly said. Her gut feeling had been right; this was not going to be a good trip. It wasn't even eight o'clock yet, and *he* was talking beer.

'I thought you'd be a coffee snob. *Maccas*?' Gavin chuckled.

Scarlet, ever the peacemaker, intervened. 'Maybe we can find a pub that's got coffee, and Gavin can have his beer.'

'Surely you can go a morning without having a beer,' Jilly snapped.

'*Surely I can go a morning without having a beer*,' Gavin parroted her, and Jilly decided she *really* didn't like him. This was going to be a long trip.

'The less we stop, the quicker we'll get out there,' Rod said. 'It's a long way, too long to be breaking it by stopping at every pub we pass.'

'Now that's not a bad idea,' Gavin said. 'I did that once with some mates the last year we were in high school. We drove down from Newcastle to have a look at Sydney Uni. We stopped at every pub on the way home. I still remember the last one was the Gunyah pub at Belmont. God, we were pissed.'

'And who was driving?' Jilly said.

'You're a ball of fun, Jilly,' Gavin said. 'Have you always been stuck-up?'

'Some of us can't be fun all the time,' she retorted.

'Come on, you pair,' Scarlet intervened. 'Stop squabbling. Gavin is only trying to wind you up, Jilly. Weren't you, Gavin?'

'Yeah, sorry, Jilly, I was being a jerk. I don't mean to be, comes naturally. I was just pushing your buttons.'

Jilly stared out the window, angry that she let Gavin get the better of her. She'd be as sweet as pie to him now. If he wanted a beer in every bloody town they went through, she'd simply smile and go for a walk.

Comes naturally was right. He was a jerk.

She dug into her bag and blue-toothed her earbuds to her phone. She'd finish listening to her time travel audiobook.

They made a small town called Molong before they stopped, and Jilly smiled at Gavin as they headed to the counter of a small coffee shop. 'My shout,' she said sweetly.

'You don't have to, Jilly. I probably owe you one for being a jerk.'

'No, my shout. First time. We can take it in turns. What does everyone want?' Once they placed their coffee orders and Rod and Gavin had decided they needed a sausage roll for morning tea, Jilly waited at the counter with Scarlet while the guys grabbed a table outside.

The tension between her and Gavin had settled a lot, and

she made a point of trying to have a reasonable conversation with him. 'So, you grew up in Newcastle, did you, Gavin?'

'Some of my childhood. We travelled around a bit. My dad was a labourer.' He lifted his chin. 'I come from a blue-collar family with a working-class background, not like the rest of these rich kids I go to uni with.'

Hmm. Scarlet had nailed it, she thought as she looked around. 'Haven't seen any evidence of that.'

'They're all dressed like grunges to try to fit into the uni crowd, but I know what they're like. I've been out to Rod's place. He lives in this massive ten-bedroom mansion out at Pooncarie, don't you, Rod?'

'If you can call a draughty old house that's freezing cold in winter and stinking hot in summer a mansion, I guess I do.'

'You love it, man, come on.'

'I do,' Rod said. 'Not a bad place to live.'

'What about Cat?' Gavin asked. 'What's her place like?'

Scarlet shrugged. 'I've never been out there, and she's never talked much about it.'

'I haven't either, but it's a well-known station,' Rod said. 'An original homestead, and they're fifth or sixth-generation settlers. *Ceann Mara* has a lot of historical significance. I wouldn't be surprised if it was heritage listed.'

'When I was talking to Laura, Cat's mum, she was telling us about the campground that they've started out there. That's where we're all staying. We don't have to stay in the house.'

Rod raised eyebrows. 'In a campground? In a tent?'

'No, you camping snob, it's cabins,' Gavin said. 'Cat was telling me about it once, what her mum was doing out there. It'd be good to check it out. Might be a place to come for a holiday after uni finishes.'

'You've all got a busy year ahead, I hear?' Jilly looked at Gavin.

'You didn't want to go to uni?' Gavin asked.

Jilly shook her head. 'Couldn't see the point. There's nothing I really wanted to study. I've done all right, and I've been a free agent. I've lived in Melbourne and Sydney, had a few months in Tassie, and a month working in New Zealand. I wasn't stuck in the one place, and I supported myself.'

Everyone was quiet after that. Jilly felt as though she didn't quite live up to their expectations. Maybe she was being oversensitive.

They stopped for lunch at a pub in Nyngan a bit after one.

'You want me to take over, Rod?' Gavin asked as they headed back to the car after a quick lunch. She'd been surprised to see him drinking coffee.

'That'd be good. I'll have a kip. Thanks, mate.'

Jilly wondered what sort of driver Gavin was, whether he was slack in that like he was in everything else.

There was still a long way to go.

##

Bourke to Ceann Mara.

By the time they reached Bourke, Jilly was well and truly sick of being in the car. She'd sat in the front a couple of times as they rotated between seats at each stop. She and Rod had been in the back together for a while between Nyngan and Bourke. Gavin wasn't a bad driver, and Jilly managed to relax enough to snooze off.

They left Bourke after a quick toilet stop,

'Laura asked me to ring when we got to the last town. We've been in and out of service,' Scarlet said.

'That'll be Louth,' Rod said. 'There's phone service there. Some mates and I drove the Darling River Run for Schoolies' week and camped along the river. There's a good pub there, Gavin.'

Gavin took one hand off the wheel and gave him the finger. Jilly couldn't help her smile.

Chapter 38

Ceann Mara Station - late Saturday afternoon.

Cat came back from the store absolutely bursting with excitement; the trip back to the homestead in the punt seemed to take ages. She'd felt like jumping out and running home. She couldn't wait to tell Dad what was in the box she held tightly on her lap the whole way home.

Logan took the box as she climbed out of the punt and then passed it to her carefully before they walked up the bank to the shed.

'The ute's not there. Looks like Dad's not back,' she said. 'Damn, I can't wait to show him. Would you like to wait until he gets home? We could have a cuppa or a drink.'

'I'd better get across the river before it gets dark,' he said. 'We might need to build a bridge.'

Cat smiled and took his hand. 'We will. Logan, I don't know how to thank you for helping me. I think we've found an absolute goldmine there today. I can't wait to read all of those letters with Dad.'

'It's pretty special. And so are you,' he said quietly. With a quick glance towards the homestead, he put his arms around her, and she was thoroughly kissed. 'My pleasure,' he said when he finally lifted his head. 'I'll see you tomorrow. I'm guessing you want to go back to the store?'

'Try and keep me away!' Cat stood at the top of the bank as Logan rowed across the river. Once he reached the other side, he climbed out and secured the punt to a tree before turning and lifting his hand in a wave.

'See you!' he called out.

She blew back a kiss. 'Watch out for snakes.'

He headed up the bank and waved again before disappearing into the bush.

Cat missed his company already. The last week, she'd loved spending time with him. She clutched the box to her chest. 'I think I'm getting back to normal,' she said to herself as she made her way to the house.

She walked up the back steps, took her boots off, left them in the laundry, and smiled as she placed the box on a shelf near the door. The aroma of baking cakes and fresh-baked bread met her as she headed to the kitchen.

'Mum, where's Dad?' she asked.

'He had to go up to *Moana* station, so I'm guessing Rick needed a hand with his sheep.'

'How long is he going to be?'

'I'd say he won't be home until about six-thirty or so. He hasn't been gone that long.'

Cat looked around the kitchen, and her eyes widened. Two large apple pies were cooling on a wire rack, another lemon cake sat with a bowl of icing next to it, and a bowl of shredded cabbage sat next to fresh-picked tomatoes and lettuce. 'Are we expecting visitors?' she asked.

'I just felt like cooking this afternoon,' Mum said, turning away.

'You felt like shredding coleslaw? There's enough there for an army. Logan's gone home.'

'Coleslaw won't go off, just in case we did happen to get visitors.' Mum looked at her intently. 'You're feeling back to normal now, aren't you? Would you be up to visitors, Cat?'

'Why? Are the girls coming home?'

'No,' Mum said. 'I was just wondering. How are you feeling today? Your face is very flushed. You and Logan seem to be getting on well.'

'He's lovely. I'm absolutely on top of the world, and I'm not going to tell you why until Dad gets home. I want to tell you both together.'

Mum's mouth opened, and her eyes widened. 'What are you going to tell us? Is it to do with Logan?'

Cat burst out laughing. 'Sort of, but not in the way you think. I've only known the man for a few weeks.'

'I only knew your father two days before—'

Cat put her hand up and chuckled. 'Too much information, Mum.'

Her mother smiled, wiped her hands on the towel, and walked over to hug Cat. 'It's so good to see you so happy, love.' She pulled back and sniffed. 'Hmm. Is that men's cologne I can smell?'

Cat flushed and stepped back. 'Could be.'

Mum nodded, her eyes crinkling as she smiled. 'Good. I really like Logan.'

'Logan is a great guy, but I'm super happy because of what we found today.'

'Oh, tell me.'

'When Dad gets home. I'm going to go up and have a

shower. I'm covered in dust and cobwebs.' She headed for the hall and hesitated in the doorway when Mum started speaking.

'Now that you're back in a good head space, is it too early to ask what you've decided about going back to uni?'

Cat hesitated. 'No, I think I'm staying here. It'd take something major to get me back there. And what I've got to show Dad makes me want to stay even more.'

'You've got me intrigued.'

Cat surveyed the array of food on the kitchen bench. 'You've got me intrigued too, Mum.'

As she started down the hallway, Mum's mobile rang, and she grabbed it. 'I'll just take this outside,' she said.

Cat knew her mother well; she was up to something. Shaking her head she headed upstairs for a soak in the bath.

As she stripped off while the water was running, she looked objectively at the pink scars on her arms, and for the first time since she'd fled Sydney, she had no reaction. The marks would disappear in time. Her monthlies had arrived a couple of weeks ago, and that had dispelled another of the fears she'd held. She'd asked Dad to take her to Broken Hill last week, and she'd seen Dr Morris and had a couple of STD tests to ease her mind.

She smiled as she eased herself into the hot water. She put her head back and closed her eyes as her thoughts turned to Logan. She really hoped he didn't move back to Queensland.

An hour later, Cat climbed out of the warm water, rested, relaxed, and feeling on top of the world. It was a shame it was just the three of them for dinner tonight. She was disappointed she couldn't talk Logan into staying, but she understood his concern about rowing across the river in the dark. She'd have no hesitation in doing it, but, like she'd told him, he was a new chum.

As she walked downstairs, a clean pair of cargo pants and a long-sleeved T-shirt, her hair washed and dried, and her fingernails scrubbed clean of dirt, a vehicle came up the road and parked at the front of the house. She wondered why Dad hadn't parked in the shed; he was earlier than Mum had expected.

She walked down the front hall, but there was no sign of her parents. She frowned as she spotted a Toyota Land Cruiser parked in the circular drive. As she stood at the front screen door, her heart jolted as doors opened, and out spilled Scarlet and Jilly, and then Gavin and Rod came around from the other side of the car.

'Oh, my God,' she said, opening the screen door and running down the steps. 'You guys, what on earth are you doing here? How did you get here?'

'We drove,' Rod said. 'What does it look like, Miss Cat?'

'But what are you doing here?' Cat was in a state of disbelief, and she suddenly understood why Mum had been preparing such a feast for dinner. 'My mother knew you were coming, didn't she?' she said suspiciously.

'She did. I hope it's okay. She said it would be good to have a surprise for you.'

'Well, it certainly is a surprise,' she said.

Her mother walked onto the front porch. She'd obviously showered and had a good dress and lipstick on. 'Oh, you have visitors, Cat,' she said innocently.

'Yes, Mum, just as well we have plenty of food for dinner, isn't it?' She turned to her friends. 'Oh, my goodness, what a day it's been! I cannot believe you guys are here at *Ceann Mara.*' She hurried over to Scarlet and held her arms out.

Scarlet hugged her back and sniffed. 'Good to see you

looking so well, Cat.'

Jilly was next, and then Rod held his arms open, and she went over for a big hug. They'd been great mates for the last three years, and Cat hadn't realised how much she'd missed her friends. She was a little bit more reserved with Gavin, but he held his arms open, and she returned his hug with a smile.

'So, are you staying here? I guess you are,' she said.

Mum nodded. 'That's where I was this afternoon when you and Logan were up in the store. I was making up the beds and putting some towels in the bathroom down in the campground. These guys get to stay in the cabins now.' She turned to Scarlet. 'I didn't think to ask you on the phone, Scarlet. You girls can share twin rooms, or I can put you in four separate cabins?'

They all looked at each other, and Scarlet said, 'Happy to share. What about you, Jilly?'

'Yeah, not a problem at all. Twin beds are fine.'

Gavin looked at Rod, and Rod looked at Gavin. They both grinned. 'Would it be okay if we had separate rooms?' Rod said. 'I've shared with Gavin before on a couple of field trips, and he snores like a champion.'

'Only when I've had a few beers.' Gavin laughed.

'That's every night, isn't it?' Jilly said smartly, but she was smiling.

'Okay, Cat, can I leave it to you? I'll go back to the kitchen and get some dinner going. Dad just called; he's just leaving *Moana* now, so he'll be about forty-five minutes and then we'll come to the campground and have a barbeque. I filled the camp kitchen fridge with beer and wine. I wasn't sure what you guys would want.'

'That's very kind of you, Mrs O' Byrne,' Rod said politely. 'We bought some beer and some wine in Louth while Scarlet called you.'

'Please call me Laura,' she said. 'Mrs O'Byrne makes me feel very old. That was my mother-in-law. You didn't need to bring anything. It's just lovely that Cat's got some friends here to visit.'

Cat pointed up the road. 'Turn around and follow me in the car, Rod. I'll walk to the campground. You probably noticed that you passed some buildings on the right on your way in. Not far back.'

'Yes, we did notice, and we thought that might've been it, but we wanted to come to the house first and just check it was okay and see you too, sweets,' Scarlet said. 'Make sure that *you* were okay with us staying.' Scarlet took Cat's arm. 'I'll walk with you.'

'I'll walk too,' Jilly said. 'I have a numb bum from being in the car all day.'

'Of course, I'm fine with you staying. I'm absolutely excited to see you all. How long are you here?'

'Probably about three days, then I'm going home to Lismore as soon as we get back to Sydney, and this lady here is moving to Queensland.'

Cat stared at Jilly. 'You're what? What about the coffee shop?'

'My last day was yesterday,' Jilly said. 'I'm heading off to the tropics. And you and Scarlet are going to come up and visit me when you get a chance.'

'Oh no, Jilly, the *Crazy Goat* won't be the same without you.'

'Deb's in charge now; you'll have good coffee.'

'Yeah, but we'll miss you.'

'So, when are you coming back to Sydney, Cat? Jilly has

offered us her unit.'

A ripple of shock went through Cat for a while. Scarlet was talking as though everything was normal, and she would be back there next year doing her honours.

'Yeah, we need to talk about that,' Rod said, 'whether you're coming back or not.'

'I haven't made up my mind yet,' Cat said. 'Come on, girls, let's start walking. We'll have a chat over a drink.'

Cat was happy to see them, but she knew that she would have preferred to have the night with her parents—and Logan—showing Mum and Dad what they'd found.

Chapter 39

Ceann Mara Station - Saturday night.

Cat went to bed that night feeling quite strange as if she wasn't in her own skin; the meeting of her station life and her uni life had unsettled her. It had nothing to do with the assault, but having her friends here at the station was strange.

It had been an okay night with lots of laughter, apart from when Gavin almost fell in the fire pit from having too much to drink and Jilly giving him an absolute mouthful.

They managed to avoid the topic of Sydney, honours, and university. Rod had been really interested in the station, and he and Dad had spoken for a long time about various initiatives that Dad had started and that Rod's father had implemented down at Pooncarie.

'I think I've met your dad at some sheep meetings,' Tom said halfway through the night. 'Tall fella with a bit of a balding head.'

'That's my dad, Barnsey, they call him.'

'Yep, that's the guy that I met,' Tom replied.

'Cat, how about you and I sit down and have a talk tomorrow about theses? Have you spoken to Harry yet?' Rod asked as they started to call it a night.

Cat didn't feel like talking about it. To be honest, she'd found the night a bit boring. She would rather have spent the night with Mum and Dad—and, of course, Logan—and not had to talk about Sydney. That had confirmed for her that her heart was telling her the right thing.

Gavin and Rod helped Dad put the fire out, and the girls washed up in the camp kitchen before they headed into the cabins. Cat climbed into the back of Mum and Dad's twin cab for the short drive to the house.

'You have good friends, love,' Mum said. 'They obviously care about you.'

'They're not a bad bunch. Gavin's a bit immature,' Cat said.

'He'll grow up when he gets out in the world,' Dad said. 'Look at Logan. From what he told me, he was a bit of a larrikin when he was growing up.'

'So he said.' Cat yawned. She was looking forward to going to bed but was disappointed she and Logan wouldn't be going to the store tomorrow. She wondered if he'd enjoy the company of her friends and then decided he probably wouldn't. She'd call him in the morning and suggest she might go over and visit him after she'd shown the guys around the station tomorrow.

'Are you tired, Dad?' she asked, remembering the box on the shelf in the laundry.

'I'm buggered, love. I'm getting too old for all that lifting. Why?'

'I wanted to show you something, but it can wait until the morning if you're tired,' she said.

'I'm leaving early tomorrow. At daybreak. I'm going back

to *Moana*,' Dad said.

'And I've got a quilting morning at Nancy's place,' Mum added. 'I hope you don't mind us leaving you with your friends. I'll be home until late morning, though. I can do morning tea for you.'

'No, that's fine. We'll get the bikes and the quad runners out, and I'll show them around the place, down at the billabong and the airstrip and everything.'

'Oh damn.' Mum put her hand to her mouth. 'It totally slipped my mind with everything that happened today.'

'What did, Mum?'

Her mother glanced at Dad. 'Tom, do you think you'll be home by lunchtime tomorrow?'

'Could be if you needed me. What's up love?'

'When I was cooking today, the phone rang, and it was that detective from Sydney. They're flying out tomorrow afternoon to interview Cat. Do you feel okay with that, with your friends here?'

'Yes.' Cat shrugged. 'They can entertain themselves. I think talking to the detectives is more important than socialising.'

Mum shooed Cat upstairs after they went inside. 'You go up to bed. I'm not even going to make a cuppa. All that cooking today has worn me out.'

After she kissed Mum and Dad goodnight, Cat went upstairs and crawled into bed. Her tiredness fled as she lay there feeling uneasy. She wished Logan was with her to hold her and reassure her that everything would be all right.

She reached over to the bedside table and sent him a text. **You awake?**

The reply dinged almost instantly. **You okay? X**

She smiled at the kiss.

Yes. The police are flying in tomorrow. Can you come over? X

What time?

Before lunch.

Maybe we could go to the store in the morning?

Too complicated. I'll ring you now.

Logan picked up straight away.

'Hi, I didn't wake you up, did I?'

'No, I was lying in bed, thinking about you, actually,' he said.

Cat smiled. 'That's nice to hear.'

'What's complicated?'

'Well, it's been a big afternoon. Four of my uni friends turned up. Mum knew they were coming and didn't tell me.'

'How do you feel about that?' he asked.

'I was okay, but I found the night a bit boring. I would've rather spent it with you,'

'That's nice to hear. What did your dad say about the letter?'

'Would you believe I didn't get a chance to tell him, with them turning up and Mum and Dad being sociable and putting on a barbeque down in the camp kitchen tonight? It was a late night, and then when we got back, Dad said he was tired and he has to go to work at daybreak tomorrow, so I didn't end up telling him.'

'That's a shame; you were so looking forward to sharing it.'

'I was, but it's got complicated now with the police flying in tomorrow and having my friends here. I don't know how I feel about that. Will you come over in the morning, Logan? I need you.'

'Of course I will. What time?'

'Give us time to have breakfast together, and then I said I'd take them out on the property. Show them around a bit. Maybe if you just came over for a cuppa about nine.'

'I'll be there whenever you want, Cat. I'm here for you. Just remember that, won't you?'

'Thank you, Logan.' She felt like saying 'love you', but it was way too soon to for that.

'Sweet dreams, Cat. I hope you sleep well. I miss you.' he said.

'I miss you too,' she whispered. 'Night, Logan.'

Cat rolled over and thumped her pillow. She felt much happier after talking to Logan and knowing he would be here in the morning, but her thoughts were in turmoil.

Maybe it was because they were pressuring her to make a decision about whether she was going back or not. She'd been quite adamant with herself that she wasn't, but seeing her friends from Sydney and hearing them talk about their thesis proposals made her wonder if her decision to stay was a copout.

Then again, the letter she'd read to Logan this afternoon had fired her enthusiasm into staying here and working with Dad, but was that the right decision?

Maybe an honours degree *was* the way she should go.

Then again, maybe not. She'd go for a walk in the morning if she woke early and gave it some thought. If she walked along the river, she could meet Logan.

Why was she so attracted to him? Why did she feel empty every time he got in *Ding-a-Ling* and went back across the river?

Because he's a good man, because he helped me, because he's interested in the station, because he teared up when I read the letter to him, because he gets on with Mum and Dad, and because he is hot.

The perfect man.

Cat smiled and rolled over to go to sleep, Logan's face firmly in her thoughts.

Chapter 40
Ceann Mara Station - Sunday.

Last night, after talking to her friends about uni, Cat had felt guilty that she hadn't checked her email, so when she got out of bed early on Sunday morning, she forced herself to get her laptop out of the car, and check her emails. She quickly scrolled through her inbox with over forty unread emails. Several from Scarlet that she expected to see, a few from student administration with paperwork about her honours year, and four from Harry McMinn, her supervisor.

She swallowed and clicked on the first one from Harry. It proposed a meeting time for them, the Monday after she had arrived home. She pulled a face when she read his second email; he expressed his disappointment that she hadn't confirmed their meeting.

The third email expressed more concern and frustration at not hearing from her.

The fourth email was longer, and Cat widened her eyes when she read it.

Dear Catriona

I would be very grateful if you contact me at the first

opportunity. As I am sure you are aware—or perhaps I am assuming too much—the composition of our honour's cohort has tragically changed for next year. I was hoping to speak to you face-to-face about the situation, but I have no other avenue but to advise you by email.

I need to speak with you as a matter of urgency. With the tragic loss of Esther from our program and the investigation—and the possible exclusion of Rod Barnes due to suspected plagiarism, I need to make contact with you as soon as possible. Please keep that totally confidential.

If it is difficult for you to meet with me, could you please answer the following questions by replying to this email as soon as possible?

Cat read through the questions twice, her brow wrinkling with confusion as she tried to understand what Harry was asking. She closed her laptop, got dressed and walked to the campground.

Rod was sitting outside the camp kitchen, and the smell of brewed coffee drifted over to her; Scarlet, Jilly, and Gavin were nowhere to be seen.

'Where's the others?' she asked.

'Still sleeping off your dad's red wine,' he said.

Good, that would give her the opportunity to talk to Rod in private.

'Want to go for a walk? I'll show you the rest of the campsites Mum's set up along the river.'

'Yeah, sure,' he said. 'Good campground. Even a coffee machine.' Rod threw the dregs of his coffee into the fire pit. 'Good meal your mum put on too.'

'I should have known she was up to something. I was out all day yesterday.'

'You really didn't know we were coming. It wasn't fake surprise?'

'No, I didn't. Should I have?'

'Where did you go yesterday?'

'Oh, just around the station. I was doing some work in the store near the old woolshed.'

'The girls said you had a bit of a meltdown, and that's why you left Sydney so suddenly,' Rod said.

'I'm sure you heard what happened. Scarlet told me last night you and Gavin knew why I left. I know the police talked to you both too. You don't have to pretend to save my feelings, Rod.'

'Sorry, Cat. I just didn't want to upset you. Are you okay now? Will you come back to Sydney?'

'I'm fine,' she said, pulling her hair over her neck. 'Took me a while to settle in at home, but it's good to be here.' She pointed to the levee bank. 'We'll go this way; it's another way to the river. I want to talk to you about something.'

'Our thesis topics?' he asked.

'Sort of. I had an email from Harry.' Cat led Rod to the track that joined the levee bank, and they walked in silence for a while as she wondered how to broach the subject.

'What does Harry want to know?' Rod finally asked.

'Have you had your meeting with him?'

'I did.'

'And?'

'And what?' Rod looked cagey, and Cat's concern grew.

'Did he accept your proposal?' she asked.

'He did. Said it was one of the best he'd seen, and he's looking forward to working with me. Why? Did he knock yours back? Is that why he emailed you?'

'We still haven't discussed mine,' she said.

'But do you think you'll come back to Sydney?' he persisted.

Cat shrugged. 'I'll let you know when I decide.'

Why was he lying to her?

They walked along the road and turned off at the campground Mum had named *Quoll*. Rod kept going down the bank and stood at the edge of the river.

'Your mum's done a great job. It'd be nice to swim here.'

'That's one of the deepest holes,' she called down to him. 'That's why there's no track down to there. A little bit further along, there's a track down to a good swimming hole with our old rope swing. I wouldn't advise getting in at the moment if you're thinking about a swim because there are a lot of snags after the river flooded in March.'

'Come down, I can see some carp,' Rod called up to her.

Cat was unsure of what to do; she felt sorry for him. He would be mortified about the investigation and was obviously pretending everything was normal. She let it go, but she'd answer Harry's questions as best she could later this afternoon.

She walked down the slope to the water. Rod walked along to where she was; the rope swing had finally come adrift from the tree, and he reached down and picked it up, idly running it through his fingers.

'So, there's a good chance you will come back to Sydney, I think, from the way you're talking. I know how you feel about not letting Scarlet down with the flat, and I know that you really would like to finish your thesis,' Rod said.

Cat stared at him. He was being so damn persistent. 'You seem like you know more about how I feel at the moment than I do, but you'll be the first person I'll let know.'

'Come over here. Look at the carp.' He ignored her shrewish reply.

'I've seen enough carp to last me a lifetime.'

'Come on, humour me. Let's see if we can catch any.'

Cat rolled her eyes and followed Rod closer to the water. 'You won't catch any with that piece of rope,' she said.

'You'd be surprised what I can do, Miss Cat.' Rod turned round and stared at her, and a shiver ran down her back as he stretched the rope between his hands. She'd had enough.

'I'm going back up now. The others will be awake.'

'So, tell me first. Why did you want to talk about our project? What did Harry say?'

'Nothing.'

Rod reached out and grabbed her arm roughly. 'Sit down, Cat, and I'll tell you a story.'

The first glimmer of suspicion lodged in her chest, and she shook her head as Rod's fingers pressed into her skin. With one hand, he pushed her sleeve up her arm.

'Nice scars, Cat.'

She stared at him, feeling as though she was going to be sick. Fear crawled down her spine.

She knew.

Struggling to keep her voice even, she forced a smile. 'They'll fade. I don't want to sit down. I'm going back to the campground.'

'Sit down, Cat.' Rod dragged her arm down hard until she was sitting at the edge of the water.

'What the hell are you doing, Rod?'

'You've got no idea, have you, Cat?'

'No idea about what, Rod? What are you doing?'

'I want to know what you remember, Cat?'

'Remember?'

'About that night.'

Her mouth dried, and she tried to humour him as he let go of her arm and sat beside her. 'Nothing.'

'What did you tell the police?'

'Nothing, because I couldn't remember anything.'

'I think you're lying.'

'Let go of me.'

'Or what?

'I'll scream. I'm going back to the campground, and we'll forget about this.' Cat pushed herself to her feet quickly and ran along the edge of the river. Scrambling up the bank, she got away from the water. Rod was close behind her, breathing heavily.

'You can't get away from me, Cat. You were lucky once. Not this time.'

Before he reached her, Cat tripped, throwing her forearm over her eyes as she toppled head-first onto the ground. Her chin hit a small rock as she landed. Rod threw himself on top of her and pinned her down. Blood filled her mouth as her teeth went through her bottom lip, and panic flooded through her.

Rod's weight pressed onto her back, and a sharp stone dug into her stomach, pressing hard between her ribs. His breath was hot on her cheek as he leaned close to her. 'No one's going to hear you, Cat. I'm so pleased you brought me all the way down here. When I tell your parents that seeing all of us from Sydney brought your depression crashing back and that you jumped in the river and I couldn't stop you, they will be so upset. In this deep part, you obviously got snagged in the timber and drowned. I jumped in and tried to save you, but you didn't come up, and I couldn't find you. I was distraught when I got back to the campground, but it was too late for anyone to save you.'

'Don't be so fucking ridiculous, Rod.' She tried to push back against him, but he was too heavy for her.

'It's not ridiculous, Cat. It has to be done,' Rod said, his voice chillingly calm.

His weight on her back was pushing her into the rock under her stomach, and she could feel dampness on her shirt.

More blood. Anger surged through her, and she gave one final heave, but he was too big for her to shift.

'Why?' she whispered, feeling absolutely helpless.

'Shame I have to drown you, Cat. We could have had some more fun, but I guess the others will come wandering down to the river soon. I've had lots of practice the other way.'

'What other way? What do you mean?'

'Cutting other girls. That was for fun. I got rid of Esther because her thesis topic was too close to mine. And then that night in your apartment, it would have been your turn if Scarlet hadn't come home when she did. I got out before she came to your room; that was close. I couldn't let you tell Harry it was your work. He'll believe it was you who cheated now, and I'll tell him I was covering up for you.'

Cat's vision blurred with tears. 'You killed Esther, and you were going to kill me.'

'Finally showing some intelligence, Cat. You're not real smart. It was easy to spike your drink and take your key.'

'But how?'

'I followed you to the ladies, and we went out the back way. I drove you home.'

'But Scarlet was there.'

'No, she wasn't. I went up first and used your key to get in. There was no one there.'

'You can't hurt me here. Mum and Dad know that I would

never do anything like that.'

'It's a shame you don't remember the night. We had such fun. Such a shame you can't be here for us to have another go. You and Esther were in my way, but I didn't have time to play with her. I did a pretty pattern on the back of your legs, but I'm sure I'll find plenty of girls in Sydney.'

'Let me go. I won't tell anyone. Just let me go home.'

He ignored her. 'And then I heard what a mess you were in, you poor darling. Scarlet told me you didn't get out of bed for three weeks. That bloody bitch came home and stopped our fun. She was lucky I left when she got home that night. I didn't know if she had someone with her or not. I couldn't take the risk,' he said almost to himself. 'You were my first failure, Cat, but I can fix that now.'

'Stop it. Just stop it. I know you're teasing me.'

Rod stood up, and for a moment, the release of pressure on her back was a sweet relief.

Cat screamed as pain shot from her scalp down to her neck when Rod pulled her up by her hair. She stood in front of him, her back against his chest as he held her arms in a crushing grip.

'Help me!' she screamed at the top of her voice. 'Somebody help me!'

'Oh, Cat, you're wasting your breath. Good try, though. You'll need all of your breath when I hold your head under.' Rod kicked the back of her knees, and she rolled down the bank and fell into the river. Her head went under the cool water, and her face hit the mud, her mouth filling with silt.

She kept her eyes and mouth closed, holding her breath, determined not to give in. She kicked out with her legs, feeling satisfaction for a moment as she connected with something soft, but Rod quickly regained control, his hand in her hair, pushing her face back into the silt.

Her vision started to fade, and her last thought was that Logan would never know she loved him. Before she lost consciousness, she heard a sharp crack, and as Rod let go of her, everything went black.

Chapter 41
Ceann Mara Station – Sunday.

Mum was crying as Cat tried to wake up. She had to help Mum; something had upset her.

Was Dad all right? Or was it the secret in the letter? She drifted back to sleep again, and when she woke up the next time, Mum had stopped crying.

Her head was hurting, and her mouth was stinging.

Her body stiffened as she returned to the present. Shock held her in its grip as she remembered what Rod had done. Someone was holding her hands tightly, and her eyes flew open as she tried to pull away.

'Cat, it's all right, sweetheart. It's me, Logan. You're safe now.' Logan's face was near hers, and his breath was warm on her cheek. 'It's okay. You're safe; he can't hurt you.' Logan held her hand as he stood up straight. 'Laura, she's awake.'

'Logan, I need to tell you now. I didn't tell you I loved you. I thought it was too late.'

Logan bent down again and pressed a gentle kiss on her forehead. 'I'm very pleased to hear that, Cat.' He stepped back but kept hold of her hand as Mum rushed through the door.

'Oh, sweetheart.' Tears rolled down Mum's face as she

stood beside the bed. 'Oh, Cat, I'm so sorry; it's all my fault. If they hadn't come, it wouldn't have happened. I should have asked you.'

'It's all right, Mum. I would have said they could come. I had no idea that Rod—where is he?' Her voice rose as her eyes widened, and she looked around the room.

'It's all right, sweetheart, he's locked in the cellar.'

'He won't hurt Dad's wine, will he?' she said.

'I don't care if he smashes every bottle. He's secure down there.'

Logan leaned over. 'He's not capable of doing anything, Cat. I shot him.'

'I heard the crack just before I passed out. I was in the water, wasn't I?'

'Yes, you were.'

'How did I get out?'

'Do you need to know this now?' Logan asked.

She nodded. Her scalp was stinging, and she winced.

'I was walking along the other side of the river on the way to the punt, and I heard you scream and then yell for help. I looked over and could see he had hold of you. As I watched, he pushed you into the water and held your head under.'

'And you had your gun with you because of snakes, didn't you?'

'I did, luckily. I'm a good shot. I got him in the shoulder, and he let go of you. I threw my gun and dived in, and swam across the river, terrified I was too late. I pulled you out.'

'And you gave me CPR, didn't you? I can remember that. And then I was dreaming about the secret, and I heard Mum crying.'

'Don't worry about your Dad's wine. That bastard is lying

on the floor, his shoulder bandaged and his wrists and ankles tied together. He's not bleeding much, and the ambulance is coming.'

'How long have I been out to it?' she asked.

'Too long,' Mum said. 'The doctor is on his way, flying in from Bourke.'

'I don't need a doctor, Mum.'

'Oh yes, you do, sweetheart. I think you need a sedative to calm you down.'

'No, I don't. I don't need anything like that. What about the police?' she asked. 'They've got to come from Louth.'

Mum shook her head. 'No, Dad's on his way home. He's only a few minutes out. He rang Detective Nichols. He had his number in his phone, and they were only about twenty minutes away. They'll be landing on our airstrip soon. It's going to be busy.' Mum put her hands over her face. 'Oh, Cat, I can't believe it. We nearly lost you.'

'It's okay, Mum, I'm here. I got a terrible fright, but there was one good outcome. We know who killed Esther.'

'What?' Logan stared at her, and Mum dropped her hands.

'We didn't know what was happening. We didn't know why Rod was trying to hurt you.'

'He told me everything. It was him in my apartment that night, and he said he's done it to other girls—for fun, for God's sake—and he said Esther and I were because he had to.'

'Jesus,' Logan whispered.

Mum's face went white.

'Where are the others?' Cat said. 'Scarlet, Jilly, and Gavin. Are they still at the campground? Do they know what happened?'

'They were shocked, like we were, but Logan took the keys of the Land Cruiser so they couldn't go anywhere just in case. I stayed with you while he sorted that . . . that person out, and then went up to see the others. I'm relieved that I hadn't left home when he carried you up from the river.'

'There's no "just in case", Mum. They're fine. They'll be upset.'

'Yes, Jilly and Scarlet were crying when I left them a little while ago. But I told them you're all right.'

'Please go and get them and bring them to the house. And Gavin. Make sure they're safe in case he gets out.'

'He's tied up and locked in securely, Cat,' Mum said.

'Please go and get my friends.'

'Okay, I'll take my car. Logan, stay with her.'

'I'm not leaving her side, Laura. Ever.'

Mum left with a last look at Cat, and then Cat squeezed Logan's hand.

'Do you mean that?' she whispered.

'I do. I love you, Cat.'

She smiled, but it hurt. 'I'm not going back to Sydney.'

'And I'm not going back to Queensland,' he replied. 'Now tell me exactly what he said to you.'

Cat related everything Rod had said, and Logan shook his head.

'The bastard, I'm sorry I didn't shoot him lower.'

'No, Logan, don't be like that,' Cat said, her voice shaking. 'He'll get what he deserves.'

'Are you up to talking to the detectives?' Logan asked.

The sound of a vehicle pulling up came through the window, and Cat realised she was in one of the downstairs guest rooms. Three car doors slammed, and Mum hurried back into the room.

'I told the girls to put the kettle on.'

'Are they okay?'

'Yes. I said you'll see them in a while.

'I will, and I'm up to getting out of bed, too. I'm all right; I'm only sore in my mouth, stomach, and neck.'

'What's wrong with your stomach?' Mum said.

'When he pushed me over, I landed on a rock, and I think it's cut my skin. I need to get out of bed.'

Logan leaned over and brushed his lips against her forehead. 'Humour me, Cat, stay in bed until the doctor arrives. I won't leave your side, I promise. Ever.'

Epilogue
Ceann Mara Station - Christmas Eve.

Caitríona Mary O'Byrne, soon to become Caitríona Mary Wainwright of *Guntana Station*, held out her left hand so her sisters could take turns admiring her amethyst and diamond engagement ring.

'Well, you're a dark horse, Cat,' Roisin said. 'We had no idea that you'd met someone until that awful day when Mum called to tell us all what happened. Mum and Dad haven't stopped singing your praises yet, Logan. But it's lovely to finally meet you.'

Logan and Cat smiled as her four sisters gathered around them. Roisin and Erin had arrived within half an hour of each other that morning and had both been anxious to meet Logan and see the engagement ring that Cat was sporting.

Shea and Bridget had been home for two weeks, and both had fallen instantly in love with their brother-in-law-to-be.

'Too late, girls, get your eyes off him,' Cat had teased.

'It's okay, Cat, we'll love Logan like a brother. Like we love Jack,' Shea said.

Erin grinned, and her husband, Jack, nodded at Logan. 'They're a good bunch, mate. He held out his hand. 'Welcome to the family.'

Logan shook it and grinned, slightly overwhelmed by the arrival of the whole family.

Dad was in his element, hugging each of his daughters, coming back to Cat frequently to make sure she was all right, as he had done for the past three months, and thumping Logan on the back each time he walked past.

'So, my second daughter is about to get married,' he said to Jack. 'You're going to have a brother-in-law. And I'm going to have another son-in-law.'

Mum had been cooking for a week, and Cat, Shea and Bridget spent a lot of time in the kitchen helping her.

Cat hadn't been this happy for as long as she could remember. The trauma of the past five months had taken its toll, and she had agreed to see a counsellor in Broken Hill. Every time Dad flew her down, Logan insisted on coming.

After a few sessions, she was feeling much better. Her injuries had healed, and her hair, which had been pulled out of her scalp above the back of her neck, had started to grow back.

The scars from the night in the apartment in Sydney had faded to thin silver lines, and she could look at them now without getting upset.

Rod Barnes had been refused bail, and he was currently in Silverwater Prison awaiting the start of his trial.

Logan assured her that with the evidence of what happened and his testimony, there was no chance of him getting off.

'No matter how good a defence lawyer he has, I witnessed what he did to you. And now that we know what he told you he'd done and is in custody, there will be DNA evidence.'

But it was Christmas Eve, a happier time, and everyone was home. Cat and Mum had been Christmas shopping in

Broken Hill last week after her last appointment with the counsellor. The huge Christmas tree that filled a corner of the living room had dozens of presents beneath it.

Dad and Logan had gone to the library together while Mum and Cat shopped. Logan was as enamoured with their family history research as Cat and Dad were, and Mum constantly rolled her eyes.

Dad and Cat had sat together and read Caitríona's letters to her mother over the period of a week. Cat cried, and she even saw Dad wipe away tears at one stage. In the letter that Caitríona had written her mother when James was twelve, she confessed that she had believed that Sean had fallen in love with her. But she soon had had her doubts.

Mam, I was taken in by a man who was merely after what I could give him. I thought Sean and I were friends, but I no longer believe that to be so true. I have been fortunate that I have had a fine husband for the rest of my life, and Thomas has provided a wonderful home for us on the Darling, and Samuel, with his store and the building of the paddle steamers, has also supplemented our income. We have a fine life. I will go to my grave without telling Thomas that James is not his child. I hope our dear Lord will forgive me.

Even though they now knew that James was not Thomas's son, the family mysteries had deepened. They still didn't know why Thomas and Samuel had come to New South Wales and what had become of Sean. They assumed that Caitríona's parents had gone to America because of the potato famine, but Dad was determined to find the truth.

'Well, Dad,' Cat said, 'I'm going to be living across the river, so I'll be over here often helping you.'

'Just the two of us again, Tom,' Mum said.

Cat had decided that an honours degree was not for her, and she and Mum had returned to Sydney to pack up the apartment and see Scarlet.

Scarlet had found another flatmate and had moved into Jilly's apartment. Cat had been surprised to hear that she and Gavin were seeing each other.

Gavin had called and explained that Rohan, who she had danced with at the bar that fateful night, had moved back to Canberra soon after and, as they now knew, had been totally innocent. It was another mystery solved.

Last she'd heard, Jilly was driving trucks at a mine west of Mackay.

Christmas Eve dinner was served in the formal dining room. Four roasts—including the inevitable goat—sat on the sideboard, surrounded by baked vegetables, a steaming pot of green peas and several gravies. Dad stood with the carving knife, ready to carve the roast beef.

Mum shook her head as they all squeezed around the table. 'If it wasn't for your family history, we could all be in that lovely big study of yours, Tom O' Byrne,' she said with a smile, knowing how much the family history meant to Dad. The girls had all giggled when Dad put the knife down on the sideboard, swept Mum over his arm, and kissed her soundly.

'You love me as I am, Laura O'Byrne,' Dad said in his dreadful Irish accent.

Cat looked up at Logan; his eyes were wide as he chuckled.

'You look overwhelmed. Welcome to the O'Byrne family, my love.'

Logan leaned over and kissed her in front of the whole family. 'There's only one thing I'm worried about,' he said.

Cat frowned. 'What's that?

'Do I have to learn that atrocious Irish accent?'

'I'll love you however you speak, Logan Wainwright,' she said.

The sound of a spoon clinking on a wine glass silenced the noise of her sisters all trying to talk over each other. Cat smiled. It was lovely to have her family home.

Roisin stood at the side of the table and grinned at Cat. 'Well, Cat, as you always have done since you were a baby, you've stolen my thunder, but sweetheart, I can think of better ways you could have done it. First up, I'm speaking for the four of us when I say how much we love our fiery red-headed sister. And my sisters and I would all like to welcome you to our family, Logan.'

Glasses were raised with shouts of 'Welcome, Logan!'

'Thank you, Roisin.' Cat smiled at her big sister. 'What do you mean stealing your thunder?'

Roisin walked over and stood between Mum and Dad at the end of the table. She put one hand on each of their shoulders. 'Well, if it's all right with Mum and Dad, I'm coming home,' she said.

Mum's mouth dropped open. 'Coming home? To stay?'

Roisin nodded.

'But what about your job with that famous law firm?' Dad asked.

'I don't like it. I'm sick of divorce settlements, celebrity litigation cases and dealing with city people. I've got a new job.' Her smile was wide as she looked down at Dad. 'Cat is passionate about the family history, but Dad, I know you're just as concerned with the health of the Darling.' She lifted her hands and placed them on her chest. 'Meet Roisin O'Byrne, dear family, the new Murray Darling Basin Authority lawyer.'

Home again on *Ceann Mara* station, Roisín O'Byrne, a lawyer committed to protecting the environment, finds herself embroiled in a battle to protect the threatened Darling River that her family have called home for almost two centuries. But her dedication pits her against formidable adversaries within the government body entrusted with safeguarding water resources, including her enigmatic boss, Seth Brodie.

As her family continue in their quest to uncover the history of the settlement of *Ceann Mara*, and the hidden life of one of the first settlers, Samuel O'Byrne, Roisín delves deeper into the murky waters of corporate interests and governmental corruption.

When an unexpected twist complicates her pursuit of environmental protection—her undeniable attraction to Seth Brodie, a man whose ideals clash with her own yet whose magnetism is undeniable— Roisin has to make a choice.

Will she risk everything, including her happiness, to expose the truth and save the Darling River?

Book 2

Daughters of The Darling

Roisín's story is the next book in the series, *Over the River*
It is available in print at Annie's store
https://annieseatonstore.ecwid.com/
And eBook on all sites
https://books2read.com/u/3nMeL9

Acknowledgements

The Darling River is one of the most beautiful areas in outback New South Wales. In the spring of 2023, Ian and I travelled the Darling River Run from Brewarrina to Menindee exploring this beautiful landscape in our caravan.

We stayed at *Trilby Station* where the inspiration for this story was born. Originally, I was going to write a story about a family in inland Queensland, but the idea of the Darling River stories came from Ian who suggested the series name Daughters of the Darling. He is a great research assistant!

I would like to thank to Liz Murray for the information in the historical museum at the campground on the station. This is where I learned the information about the goat farming and the establishment of *Trilby Station,* and Liz's campground on which my fictional *Ceann Mara* Station was based.

We stopped at various campgrounds from Brewarrina to Menindee, and discovered the beauty of the Darling River. We sat by the river at sunrise and sunset, and absorbed the aromas, the beauty of the trees, and the sound of the birds. It is truly a magical place and if you get the opportunity to travel out there, make sure that you do. There are many beautiful landscapes in Australia and the Darling River Run is up there with them.

From Across the Sea is the first book of the *Daughters of The Darling* series, and I'm looking forward to researching the rest of the series when we travel out to the Darling River Run again later this year, as I write *Across the River*, which is Book 2, Roisin's story.

I'm sure you're all wondering what Thomas and Samuel's secret was and why they travelled from Ireland to New South Wales with Caitríona. Tom and the present-day Caitríona Wainwright will continue their research.

I've been supported by many people in the writing of this book, and I would like to acknowledge them here.

To the many friends I have made in the writing world over the past fourteen years who constantly support me on my journey; I often say I have found my "tribe" and I value the daily contact with like-minded people all over the world. Again, a special mention and thank you goes to my dear friend, critique partner and editor, Susanne Bellamy, and to my wonderful proof reader, Roby Aiken.

To my loyal readers, who look forward to the release of the next book, and who contact me by mail and on social media to tell me they enjoy my stories.

A special mention here to my dear readers, Jill Drowley and Miriam Robinson (who send me beautiful homemade cards each Christmas) Sandy Lewis, Valda Stanford, and my loyal New Zealand reader, Marie Keane. Also, Raelene Brand, Rachel Crossley, Fran Hardwidge, Vicky McCudden, and the lovely May from Thangool. There are many, many more—too many to name—and I value each one of you. If I had known when I began writing that I would gain such a loyal reader base, I wouldn't have believed it! Without readers, there would be no need for stories!

It would be impossible to write without support in your personal life:

To Ian, the love of my life and my partner in research as we travel this magnificent country seeking stories each winter. I could not do this without you. My driver, my chef, my bringer of wine, my fisherman, and my husband of almost fifty years.

To our children and their partners, and our grandchildren: thank you for your love and support.

Again, my love and appreciation go to my wonderful aunt, Maureen Smith, who not only supports me but supports so many Australian writers by reading, loving and sharing their stories. Aunty Maureen can no longer read due to failing eyesight, but enjoys listening to my books, thanks to the Vision Society.

And to you, the reader: thank you for choosing this book. I hope when you read, that you love it and talk about it, and that maybe you will want to visit this wonderful part of Australia. I hope you enjoyed the story of the two Caitríonas.

I would love to hear from you.
Drop me a line at **annie@annieseation.net**
Reviews on Goodreads are always welcome and much appreciated!
eBook links:
https://www.annieseaton.net/books.html

Print Store:
All books are available in print at Annie's store and on Amazon in paperback*https://annieseatonstore.ecwid.com/*

Awards

2023: Winner of the long contemporary RUBY award for *Larapinta*

2023: finalist in the Australian Romance Readers Awards for *Kakadu Dawn,* the sixth and final book in the Porter Sisters series,

2018 and 2020: finalist for the NZ KORU Award

2017: Winner Best Established Author of the Year 2017 AUSROM

2017: Winner ...Author of the Year 2014 AUSROM Best Established Author, Ausrom Readers' Choice

2016, 2017, 2018, 2019: Longlisted for the Sisters in Crime Davitt Awards

2016: Finalist in Book of the Year, Long Romance, RWA Ruby Awards for *Kakadu Sunset*

2015: Winner ...Best Established Author of the Year AUSROM